Landed Gentry

Kamau Mahakoe

Copyright © 2016 Kamau Mahakoe

All rights reserved. No part of this publication may be reproduced, stored in a retrieval system or transmitted in any form or by any means, electronic, mechanical, photocopying, recording or otherwise, without the written permission of the author.

ISBN-10: 1519720491
ISBN-13: 978-1519720498

DEDICATION

To the race of life. To the champions, the pacesetters, the losers, the wagers, the non-starters. To the uneven field. Most importantly, to the horses – the thoroughbreds, the rogues, the bad doers, the studs, the dams and the sires. To the breathtaking gallop down the homestretch! To the wind that might make all the difference.

ACKNOWLEDGMENTS

I am deeply indebted to conversations, particularly those overheard in taxis.

Books by Kamau Mahakoe:

- Barefooted and Clean: Thoughts and Inspiration
- I Love All My Wives
- Yellow and Me
- Prayer to the Motivator (finalist in the 2015 Burt Award for Caribbean Literature)
- I Choose My Men the Same Way I Choose My Jewellery
- The Student's Master Plan: Hardcore Rules For A Lifetime of Success
- There's Something You Should Know About Leroy
- Spotty Dopey
- The Fighter in the Family
- Good Morning, Mr. Daye!
- Landed Gentry
- Please Clear the Way and Let Me Pass

Chapter One

Who doesn't love a horse? Big beautiful being.
When the horse finally says to man, look at all that I have done for you; what have you done for me? Man will not be able to answer.
These were Dezzie's thoughts, gazing at this majestic creature. He was at his usual spot, sitting on the ground beside the horse, risking a solid kick from the back hoof at any minute. But Impetus had never kicked him, though she so easily could. And he had given her ample reason to give him one good kick, with all the pestering he did before each race, for the year he had known her.
"Suh, how tings look for dis race coming up?" he asked the horse. "Yuh feel like yuh gonna win or what?"
The horse whinnied, turned her head with the enormous black eyes and looked at Dezzie as if she understood, as if she wanted to say, get lost, you bum!
"Look here, wid all di money I been betting on you, yuh must can win one o' di time dem! Know what, I jus gwine stop bet my money pon yuh, dat's all."
The horse turned again, as if to say, see if I care.
"When I win di Lot-a-Luck, I done wid horse racing!" Dezzie

hissed. Impetus neighed in her usual self-absorbed, arrogant way. Impetus, the horse with a chip on her shoulder. Why did his brother have to be jockey to the grumpiest horse in the world? Everybody said this horse had spunk. This horse was a winner. Daughter of one of the greatest sires, sister and half-sister to many a champion thoroughbred. Her grand dam, a derby winner. Royalty in her blood. Then, why the hell didn't she win? Or at least place?

But there was something about her that made Dezzie not want to give up on the proud filly. She was just being stubborn. An equine trait that could not be helped. She just wasn't ready yet. She would come into her stride soon, just watch. Even though she was now a pain in the fanny. Meantime, he was glad he had the Lot-a-Luck to fall back on.

"Tell yuh what? I gone," he said, standing and dusting the dirt and hay from his pants, giving the horse a goodbye pat. The filly turned her head away, the way you do when you don't give a damn about a man who says he's leaving. Some coins had fallen from Dezzie's pockets as he stood. He picked up eight one-dollar coins. There were some twenty-cent and twenty-five cent coins scattered in the dirt. He hissed his teeth. "Cho. Mek dem stay. Dem wi grow."

His task now was to get home and raid his woman's purse so he could purchase his Lot-a-Luck ticket for today.

The room was dark. It was by force of habit that Dezzie maneuvered the first few paces because his eyes were in broad-daylight mode. But the smell of the substance was so strong, so overpowering, that he knew without a doubt that it was hidden somewhere in the room. Somewhere. His hound dog nostrils trained on the particular scent, he sniffed the air trying to locate the exact place. He could hear the shower running and he knew, from instinct as well as from the clock, that Precious was just now taking her bath before going off to work at the arcade Downtown. Now was the time to make his move and he could not afford to let this opportunity pass. A gentle breeze drifted in, flirted with the lace curtains and picked up the scent, carried it over to Dezzie's nose. He almost barked.

There was no point searching in the regular places, he figured. This whole scenario had played out so many times and he had been caught, and the hiding places switched and shuffled, that he was sure that Precious had hidden it somewhere remote, somewhere inconspicuous, somewhere unsuspecting. On a flash of inspiration, he drew open her panty drawers with the utmost stealth, gingerly used his fingers to separate the cotton undies that could barely hold up Precious' assets, not to the mention the thongs that got lost between the mountains of her derriere. He came up on a few pairs of queen-sized bras, some slips and a pack of birth control pills. No money. No money! Where in heaven's name was the money? He could surely smell it, as sure as day. The peculiar smell, of ink mixed with sweat mixed with hope mixed with worry mixed with germs. Only money had that sweet revolting smell. Money and bitter almonds. And in this room, on this day, the smell was strong, and it was certainly not being emitted from his pocket.

"Where the hell that blasted woman hide her purse?" Dezzie mumbled to himself. He was becoming annoyed. It wasn't in any of the other drawers, either. He opened two jars that were on the dresser, his fingers trembling with the lids, knowing that at any minute now, the flow of water in the shower would be turned off, and Precious would emerge from the bathroom, draped in her big green towel that she wasn't afraid to swat him with. She had tried to swat him on more than one occasion, and it wasn't pretty. The jars contained pomade that Precious often used to slather into her hair, to persuade it into whichever style was fashionable that week; that was, of course, when she didn't have in her hair extension. "Blasted woman. Always hiding things!" he muttered under his breath. "Better careful she don't hide herself one of these days."

The smell though. It was nerve wracking, nauseating if only because he could not locate the source. The only thing that could kill the horrific smell of money was to trade it in for merchandise, or to use it to purchase Lot-a-Luck tickets. Which was his aim at this particular moment. He needed to find that money and buy that ticket before the daily draw. "Woman always hiding things. Cho!"

The shower stopped. Jehovah Jireh! He raised the mattress and dislodged a scandal bag that had been wedged underneath it. His hopes soared. This was it, Lawd! The crumpled sheets trailed on the floor as he examined the contents of the small bag. Papers. Blasted papers. What was it with women and all these damn papers? He stuffed the bag back under the mattress. He stood calmly for a moment, as if to muster some super human powers of concentration and zone in on the location. "Think, Dezzie bwoy. Think, bwoy."

Then it dawned on him. Maybe it was in her handbag, after all. Shit. He marched over to the brown imitation Versadi bag, which had been in clear view on the bed all along, and drew open the zipper. He took out the purse. His fingers were trembling so much that he could barely hold the purse steady. Beads of sweat had formed on his forehead. He didn't have time to swipe them away. Precious was surely finishing up and was drying off or shaving or some of those other things that women felt they needed to do. Either way, he was sure she would soon burst in and collar him. She was that kinda woman. Then, slowly, the tip of a fifty dollar bill began to emerge, the beautiful pale green edge, then three one hundred dollar bills, and, when he looked, behold! Nine one thousand dollar bills! He was breathing hard. The stench, the overpowering guttural stench that hit the back of his throat and made a lump rise there and refuse to move. There were two credit cards and three debit cards, but he had no use for those. Not now, anyway. What he needed was live ready cash. He grabbed one hundred and fifty dollars and daintily eased back the zipper, straight up to the point where it met the fabric of the bag, and tiptoed out of the room.

There was some shuffling in the passageway. He tucked the money into his front left pocket and started a very unnatural whistle, eased into the living room and bumped into his mother, who was on her way out while searching for her keys in her bag.

The whole operation was not very smooth. But as far as Dezzie was concerned, all had ended well. He had secured the money and Precious was none the wiser. She wouldn't miss that pocket change that he had just taken off her. She could easily replace that in sales today at the arcade, though it was a weekday. Precious was a "money woman". That's what he always called her, especially when he compared the condition of his pockets to what he supposed her purse looked like at the end of an average day, especially a weekend day, knowing that the things she haggled were "cash crops", another proud term he had assigned to her merchandise. He himself was a businessman of sorts. A taxi driver. Well, he drove someone else's car, but still.

"Good. Yuh still here. Thought yuh gone long time. Or is come back yuh come back to raid the fridge?" Bam gave her son her signature head-to-toe scan, her eyes very suspicious, then went back to digging into the chaos of fandangles that she called a handbag. "Seen my set of keys? Can never find the blasted things. Good thing Precious still here can lock up after. Come, Dezzie, give me a ride to work. Ah late again." She turned her face towards the bathroom and cooed, "Precious, ah not here!"

"Shh. Make one woman have to be suh loud?" asked Dezzie, making her eye him even more. "Come, man. Don't you just say yuh late?"

Dezzie closed the door behind them. He was starting to regret not having taken more money. Maybe Precious was still in the bathroom. Maybe one or two of the thousand dollar bills. He hadn't gotten to count them but it seemed like a hefty pile. Hefty enough. Maybe, after taking out the Lot-a-Luck money, and maybe buying a cold stout, he could even treat himself to a haircut. He badly needed a trim. Precious herself had said so, last night, when she tried to ruffle his hair as they romped a little before bed. He already knew where the money was. It wasn't as if he would have to waste time searching for it. He could just go back in and fetch some more and no one would get hurt. Precious often spent hours in the bathroom. There was no telling what she was up to in there, what with all the bottles and jars and tubes and packets that tumbled out of the medicine cabinet each time you went to get a razor, plus what she had stacked around the face basin, plus a few in a box on the floor. She could still be in there, for all he knew. He was sure he had time. What a stupid man he was, to have taken just that little bit of money. He could kick himself. It wasn't as if he didn't give Precious money. He gave her money when he had it. Weren't wife and husband supposed to share, split things down the seam? They were common law wife and husband, but so what?

"Yuh coming or yuh coming?" asked Bam. She was already standing on the pathway, having given up on finding the keys this morning. She had her handbag clutched under her arm.

"Miss, any old clothes for the less fortunate?" Bam thought she recognized the voice. It belonged to a Rastaman who had been making his way down the pathway with two heavily laden bags, one balanced precariously across his back and the other in his hand, so heavy it was almost being dragged at times. He had stopped right at the gate and had put the bags down so he could rest. He exhaled deeply and formed akimbo.

"What this?" asked Bam, very curiously, so that now it was Dezzie who was again urging her to go; a game they had been taking turns in for the last ten minutes.

"Collecting old clothes, old shoes, anything you have that you don't want. We set up a little organization where we collect the things and then give them out to those in need," the man explained. He was using the opportunity to rest, and was holding on to the gate and dabbing his forehead with a handkerchief."

"Hmm," said Bam, which meant that she was contemplating going back inside to see what she had that could be useful.

Dezzie knew her, which was why he tugged at her arm and mumbled, "Bam, not you late for work or something?"

"I might have a few things," Bam was saying. "Had some the other day but throw them out. Hey, aint you one of the rubbish men who travel on the truck?"

The man said that this was so. "Yeah, man. Ras Negus. I come by every Tuesday on the truck."

"Yes. I see you sometimes when it's my day off. I should have some stuff, come to think of it. Tell you what, I'll put them up for you. Might not see me next Tuesday, though. Working that day."

"Yes. Put them up for him, Bam," Dezzie was anxious and he could swear he heard Precious moving about in the room. It was only a matter of time now before she came out and collared him over her money. He walked off, hoping that Bam would follow suit.

"And I'll tell you what," said the man. "Here. This is my number. Just call me when yuh ready. I'll come pick up what you have. Ras Negus. That's my name. This is a land line." He handed her a piece of paper that he had torn from a grey pocket book and scribbled on with a pencil. Bam stuffed the paper into her bag.

"Alright now, Lady?" her son was pushing his luck this morning. He knew she wasn't the type to put up with his shenanigans. Outa-order-ness! Yes, he was a grown man but respect was still due. That's why she didn't bother to ask him to take her most mornings, and found her own way to work. She couldn't bother with the foolishness. And he better not get her on her wrong side this morning. As a matter of fact, she was going to take her own sweet time to waltz down the pathway, late or no late, just to prove that she was her own woman and could talk to whomever she pleased for as long as she pleased. She waited and allowed Ras Negus to hoist his bag unto his back, adjust it till he was satisfied with the position, then get a firm grip on the other bag and waddle off. She allowed him to pass in front of her, wobbling down the pathway, as she waltzed daintily behind him, all the while eying her son who already had the front passenger door opened for her and was shaking his head slowly, all the while muttering, "This woman. This woman."

Bam planted herself down in the seat with a self-contented flourish. "Remember, take yuh time, Mistah. Ah late but ah in no hurry fi meet my maker dis mawning. Ah don't see any coffin that I like yet. We still have time."

This was her pet peeve as it regarded driving with Dezzie.

One of her pet peeves. Dezzie did not drive. He flew. He only wore seatbelts when he saw the police coming or when his fellow taxi comrades hinted to him, through flashing lights, that the police were in the area, and even then, he only wore them until he figured the coast was clear. Seatbelts, to him, represented a surrender to the establishment, a symbol of conformity; and conformity meant you were a lickle bwoy and not a big man. Bam, on the other hand, made sure to buckle up as soon as she got in but then, she was left to wonder if she had committed herself to being trapped in a burning car when Dezzie flung them into a head-on collision with the back of a J.U.T.C. bus; which clearly hadn't happened yet but was surely on the books to happen, what with his recklessness and disregard for traffic codes. And since he had decided to spite her and since she was well aware of this, him being spiteful like his God-forsaken father, she was expecting a very bumpy ride, indeed.

Precious was vigorously rubbing herself as she left the bathroom, so that at moments the towel pulled away from her and revealed her naked flesh and her rolling dimples of cellulite. It was a thing she did no matter who else was in the house. "Bad habit. Bad habit," Bam had said of her daughter-in-law. "Ghetto people ways. No brought-up-cy." Not that Precious cared much what Bam said. She made her way into the bedroom that she shared with Dezzie and immediately knew that something was up. She sheet was not as she had just left it. The mattress had moved and no longer fit snugly over the base. The fitted sheet was disheveled. And, most importantly, her handbag had been violated. She was sure he had tried to replace it exactly as he had found it. Yes. And she was also sure he would have tried to carry the zip all the way back up to the end of the bag, which is why she had left it one inch from the end, so she could know. And she was sure he would think that she wouldn't miss one hundred and fifty dollars of her hard-earned money. But higglers know when they have been robbed, even if it's ten cents. They know, alright.

"Damn scoundrel!" she muttered. She pulled back the curtains and peeped through the window, to see if he was still in the vicinity. "Must be gone to buy Lot-a-Luck."

Precious sat on the bed so that the middle of the mattress sank in and moaned like a woman in the agony of her first birth. The first one that always took the longest and ached the most. She took a bottle of lotion from the dresser and braced her right leg on top of her left so she could lotion it, smooth out the stubborn lumps that reminded her of her promise to cut back on beef patties from Shugberry's. Too much lard in the crust. She was aware of this. Her girlfriend, Desrine, worked there. And all of a sudden, she burst out laughing. "'Ol' scoundrel!" she shook her head.

Maybe she wouldn't mind so much, him taking her money all the time, if she saw where her money was going, or if he tried to help her out in other ways. Like now, for instance. She was headed Downtown to sell at her stall in the arcade. She had an old jalopy that was at the sick bay more days each year than it was in active duty. The mechanics at the garage made a merciless killing off of her. So most times, she ended up having to take the bus. One would have expected that her man of eleven years, for whom she had borne two children, would have offered her a ride. Yes, Downtown was a good way away. Yes, she knew that the car didn't belong to him and that most of the proceeds from the taxi work went straight back to the owner. But still for all. She had invested so much into their relationship, financially, emotionally; physically even. It was her belly bottom that had the scar where the surgeons had ripped her open to take out his children. Dezzie's children. Hers too, of course, but that was beyond the point. And things like these grieved her. They grieved her, when she was in a public bus with her head resting on one bag and two other bags tucked on the ground between her legs and the seat in front. She was contemplating the rough day ahead. Thursday at the arcade. It wasn't Saturday or even Friday but, Thursday was still a rough day, most times. Titanium nerves, cutthroat attitudes, razor sharp instincts. She had them all, of course, or she wouldn't have survived twelve years of it, flying out every month to Panama or Venezuela, in the early days when money was running and things were going good, breezing through customs with her five or six suitcases, she herself dressed to the teeth in one of the killer outfits that she had bought cheap cheap. Other people's Sunday-best used to be her yard clothes, most times. She knew the ropes so well. Hell, she could make some ropes of her own right about now, from scratch. And yet here she was, on a public bus, couldn't even stretch out her feet properly, as the bus came to a halt at every stop. Every single stop! More and more people filed in, taking with them heir different stench, tones, perplexed faces, gossip, worries, throwing each against the other in a crude conglomerate that ebbed and flowed with the sound of the engine.

She blamed Dezzie. Well, not for everything, of course. But every time she had tried to sit him down so they could talk about their future, he had become so cagey and abstract that she always ended up getting mad and saying, "Know what? Figget it. Figget it, Desmond Grant. Guh 'bout yuh business!" and he would come over, try to tickle her and tell her little bits of nonsense in her ears, about him winning the Lot-a-Luck and what he would buy and where they would go and who would have to kiss their ass, big time. It sounded good; except for the "when" part. "When?"

"Soon. It bound to happen. Must and bound and compound! Have to have to have to win it one day!" Which meant, he sure did hope so.

The journey from the bus terminal Downtown to the Pearnel Charles Arcade on Church Street was another thing. She might see some of the fellows whom she knew. They would help her of course, for a smalls. Or she could always say, "Later, man. Mi just come out. Later, when things start run."

Sometimes, she had to wait a good ten minutes before she saw anyone. She knew everyone, of course, all the regulars, but not all could be trusted to help. Not all were people whom she wanted to be in their debt. "Don't want to owe anybody any obligation," Precious would always say. "These People? These people? No, sah! Prefer drag my bag them. Must reach one day one day."

The ride from Greater Portmore in St. Catherine to Downtown, Kingston would have taken her half hour, even in the jalopy. But it was a good forty-five minutes by bus at this time of day, winding through the schemes and stopping every five minutes as passengers alighted and embarked, lugging behind them their sordid cares as well as their plans, their dreams, as the many schemes whizzed by through the open windows. A hundred thousand dreams in the throes of slumber, some just awakening as men in loose shirts and cement-stained pants poured mortar into the guts of blocks from scaffolds. All this could be seen from the bus. For Precious, it was her own dream being erected before her eyes, with the difference of a room or two, but more or less her dream. What she had been working for, what she had been encouraging Dezzie to put aside some money for: a house of their own, instead of cotching with Bam and the indignities that were part and parcel of that. It had occurred to her that everything they owned, every tangible thing they had actually achieved, had been through her prompting, and mainly through her doing.

"Is woman build this world," her mother had said, long ago. "All these house yuh see here, is woman build them, woman sit down and plan them, woman dream 'bout them. Man is nothing without woman beside him. His hands build it yes, but woman make it build."

Precious shook her head. It was true. Had it been up to Dezzie alone, they probably wouldn't even have the dresser or the fan or the television or even the bed. Even the very bed. She wouldn't go as far as to say that he lacked ambition. No, he was very ambitious, in the sense that he was always talking about better days to come when he would own the world and they that dwelled therein. He had fantasies, put it that way. But those lived in the air. He lacked the practical sense of putting things in place and supporting her in her efforts. He was a lazy man. He did the minimum amount of work required to earn just enough to feed the worms in his children's bellies, and keep her, Precious, holding on, deferring. His contributions were as irregular and unreliable as his text messages, which she kept scrolling her cell phone for every few minutes, even now as the bus cruised through the dormitory areas and made to cross the bridge into Kingston, she checked on impulse to see if she had missed a call or text. She hadn't. Not from him, at least. Perhaps she had deleted his, in her casual junking of those unwanted, if not unwarranted, requests from her suitors, the ones who watched her as she rolled by and wished with all their might that she was theirs. She wished that Dezzie would appreciate, or at least acknowledge, her loyalty as something other than what was naturally due to him.

Bam adjusted herself and held on to the handbag in her lap, kept her eyes on the road since she was certain that her son was taking no such precaution. There was some amount of prestige in being there in the front seat, never mind the fact that Dezzie didn't outright own the car, or her trepidation with his sadistic dilly-dallying. Still, she was being chauffeur-driven to work, to all intents and purposes. Most mothers at Shem's Hardware couldn't say that. It could be argued that Bam had it made, somewhat. Her son operated a taxi. He was a businessman, of sorts, lived life on his own schedule and had very flexible working hours, provided he met his daily quota. At random hours, she could call on him if she needed little errands run. Sure, he would fuss, but he rarely said no. And he did squeeze a little money into her hands most month ends, nothing near what he would have had to pay for rent, electricity and water if he and his family had been living on his own and not under her roof. But it was something and it showed that he was aware of his manly duties.

They had negotiated the roundabout at Naggo Head, having survived the stop light at what residents called 85 Stop and the wicked stretch of road in between, along which Dezzie had shown no mercy. But just as they cleared the roundabout, the white Toyota Corolla spluttered to a sudden stop. It had not been unprovoked because, as his mother rightly pointed out, "Ah warn yuh, Dezzie! Ah warn yuh bout the speed! Why yuh can't take time? Look now, what yuh mek happen!"

It came as a shock to Dezzie because the fifteen year old car was not known to suddenly collapse. Bad as things were, he was

Landed Gentry

usually given at least a few hours' worth of squeaks, mutters, and clinks, good enough notice so he could sort things out and avoid the embarrassment of a breakdown in the middle of Naggo Head, with his mother fuming in the passenger seat. The car was in the way of buses, which honked and raved and whose drivers and conductors issued words that were not the least bit kind. Dezzie knew the car was old. It was one of four such jalopies owned by a policeman whom Dezzie knew only as Ping-Wing, and used to ply the Greater Portmore to Portmore Mall route. Ping-Wing had told him that the car was "almost new" when he had approached him regarding being a driver. Then, it had been demoted to a "brand new second hand" that had been given a make-over by a top-notch mechanic called Scatter-Shot. In spite of all the revamping and reworking, the Corolla sputtered and coughed like end-stage emphysema and oftentimes just barely made it into the garage before collapsing. But Dezzie knew the regular creaks from the take-me-to-the-doctor-quick squeaks. Four cars, and the four of them didn't make one, as far as Dezzie was concerned, because he had heard the other men complaining about the cars that they had been given to drive as well. But Ping Wing's personal car was a Honda SUV, which Dezzie drooled over each time he saw it, which was every evening when he went to hand in the day's earnings and give an account of the jalopy.

This time, Dezzie was not sure what was up because he had not been given the usual warnings. Betsy usually gave him some kind of sign. Plus, he had wanted to pull into the gas station to buy his Lot-a-Luck ticket. To make matters worse, his mother was throwing darts at him through her eyes. He wished he could explain to her that when he won the Lot-a-Luck, all her troubles would be over. First of all, he would buy her a car and send her to take driving lessons. Second of all, she wouldn't even have to work anyway, so no more fuss about being late unless she wanted to catch a store at the Mall to go deck out her wardrobe. Third, he wouldn't be driving Ping Wing's old hang-pon-nail hand-me-down piece-a-shit that he called a car, since he would have a brand new Mercedes Benz and a Lexus parked in the driveway, to choose from. He stepped from the driver's side and slammed the door, opened the bonnet and peered in. Nothing looked amiss, not for Betsy, at least. There was always a miscellany of wires and alien gadgets next to the motor, placed there by Scatter-Shot in moments of urgency to delay some inevitable mishap or camouflage some defect, and then forgotten. That was normal for Betsy. Two other taximen who had seen his plight stopped their cars down the street and walked over to ask what was wrong. It was Ruddy and another fellow whom Dezzie recognized as one of those who would park at the taxi stand but didn't know by name. This was typical behavior among them, even those who quarreled everyday and stole each other's passengers. They looked out for each other in times of crises because abduction of taximen was on the rise.

"Overheating?' asked Ruddy.

"Muffler?" asked the other. They both joined Dezzie in peering into the muddle of wires and metal. The matter was inconclusive, even given all their combined years of expertise with automobiles. Dezzie hissed his teeth. He glanced through the windshield at Bam, who was getting ready to blow but trying hard to maintain her womanly composure.

"Just the morning for this to happen!" Dezzie hissed. "Don't even buy my ticket yet. Is what number The Man play this morning?"

"Don't draw yet. Still have time, Man. I just buy mine cross the road. Had a nice dream last night. Chineyman. Number 47."

"True?" asked Dezzie, fiddling with the wires. "Is which number they have for bruck-down-piece-a-ol-junk?"

The other two chuckled. "Just miss it by a inch yesterday," said one. "Run, go do yuh thing. We'll look at the car fi yuh till yuh come back."

Dezzie needed no further persuasion. He darted across the road without saying a word to his mother, and joined the line that led up to the Lot-a-Luck window beside the gas station. As usual, there was a colourful, boisterous queue and he was in for a good wait. But he had a mellow feeling about this one. He had dreamed about a green lizard. Number 12. Couldn't lose. But then, Ruddy had said Chineyman would play. He had momentary doubts but he placed twenty dollars on green lizard, number 12, and collected his ticket for the Easy-Win, and placed some money on the big one, the Lot-a-Luck. He crossed the road and walked back over to the car.

"Where Bam?" he asked. His mother was not in the front seat, nor was she leaning against the door and tapping her finger on the top of the car, the way she always did when anger had driven her outdoors and she was deciding whether to bang his head against the windshield or tie him to the fender and lash him with his own belt. "Where Bam gone?"

"She say she can't bother wait. She walk down to her work place," said Ruddy.

Dezzie hissed. He liked to at least appear as if he wasn't terrified of his mother, though everyone knew she had him under heavy manners. "Blasted woman!" he muttered. He shielded his eyes with his left hand as gazed fixedly down the road. Bam was nowhere in sight. She didn't work very far from Naggo Head, anyway. Just a stone's through down the road. He was sure she had already signed in. Still, he didn't like when she was mad at him. He didn't like that at age fifty-eight, she had to hold down a nine-to-five at the hardware as security staff, though she had one of the lighter jobs and there was a real security guard at the gate. Dezzie chuckled to himself. Bam couldn't stand when he told her that she wasn't a real security guard. Who the hell was she going to stop, if somebody really wanted to steal anything? She couldn't collar anybody! She would more than likely start preaching to them and inviting them to church.

"Look like you need a push, man. We can push it into the gas station and you wait for Scatter Shot in there. Call him and let him know." Ruddy and the other man positioned themselves while Dezzie took the driver's seat and did his best to negotiate a u-turn into the gas station. A helluva job at Naggo Head in morning traffic! He fancied they looked like quite the spectacle.

Dezzie was peeved the whole day. He spent much of the

morning at home eating corned beef sandwiches and drinking beer, and cursing the day he ever agreed to drive the piece-a-rattle-rattle-dead-an-wake-scrap-metal-ol-patchwork. Leave it Scatter-Shot to stem the tide again with some sort of contraption that would last two weeks, at most. By two thirty, he had done just that and Dezzie had the car once more to go pick up his children from the Primary school. It was part of his daily routine; the proudest part. He liked to show off with his children. He had their photos dangling from one of the air fresheners over his windscreen, plus some more on the windscreen itself. He never missed an opportunity to brag to passengers about the two children that he had gotten. There was no photo of Precious because, as everyone knew, that would cramp his style and wouldn't sit all that well with the high school girls that he liked to put lyrics to.

"I need cartridge paper for projects," said his daughter, as soon as she entered the back seat. "Cartridge paper, markers and cello tape."

"Can't tell yuh father afternoon, then?"

"Afternoon, Daddy. I need them by this evening cause project must give in by Friday."

"What?!" Dezzie asked, alarmed, as if he had just been informed of the latest case of police brutality. "But where teacher expect me to get money to buy all these things, by this evening? What, teacher think I have money tree growing out back, where I just go and pick money as I want? But what these teachers really take parents for?"

"Cartridge paper, Daddy. Not all that much."

"Well, buy it outta yuh lunch money then, if it not that much." He fumbled through the compartment in which he kept loose change, mainly coins and a few fifty dollar bills. "I sure you guys have crayons throw down bout the place. Look for them when yuh go home. To hell with markers. Crayons colour just as well, and you two always throwing them all over the place." He turned to look at his son. "And what your teacher say, Sir? What your teacher want this time?"

"Nothing, Daddy."

"Hmph. Better be nothing."

Dezzie slept in for three hours while the children did their homework. Well, they told him that they were doing their homework and he took their word for it. He didn't know his children to be liars. He was biding his time waiting for the rush hour to get into full swing. He wasn't like those fool-fool drivers who cruised the route right through the day like idiots, picking up one or two passengers, sometimes none for the entire stretch, burning gas and wasting strength, and ruining their knees and elbows. He liked to think that he played smart, not hard. He milked the few peek hours at morning and evening, maybe two hours during the day when he had to be on the road anyway to pick up the children and buy the afternoon numbers. The rest of the day was spent sleeping or loafing at home, or doing some random thing. He didn't for one minute see himself as being lazy. He was a shrewd businessman who capitalized on the convenience of rush hours, flashing from point to point to make the best of the deluge at the most opportune time, cramming even five passengers into the back seat, if they were willing to small up themselves. Not everyone was willing to be a good sport. Some complained but he would gladly ask them to find another cab. Cooperation was the name of the game. Everyone wanted to get home and there was no room for selfishness. If he wanted to have just one passenger sprawled at the back of his taxi, he would have offered himself as a chauffeur to the Member of Parliament, his good friend, of sorts, who hired him for charter from time to time.

By eight o'clock, he decided he had had enough of the road. Others were still combing the streets but Dezzie knew when to call it quits. He was no night owl. There were gunmen going around holding up taxi drivers, robbing them, sometimes even abducting them. Dezzie could fight if push came to shove but he wasn't going to put himself in the way of these thugs. He had made a decent amount, never mind having been taken out of commission earlier. He had rallied back and made several full trips in the evening. The deflation came when he had to turn out his pockets and hand over most of the earnings to Ping-Wing, who had the intuition of calculating exactly how much he was due, given the various peak flows of each day. Ping Wing snapped a photo of the fuel gauge with his cell phone every morning so he knew how much gas was in the tank, and another one at night, to see how much gas had been used. An indignity, if there ever was one. By the time he had paid the lady at the tuck shop where he had taken two lunches on credit the day before – one for himself and one for Shelly, the fifth former with the gap between her teeth – and paid two other people whom he had borrowed money from, he slouched home with a few shillings in his pocket.

At least, there was a warm dinner and a woman to watch him eat it. A round, thick-set, hardworking woman, who liked to cook and watch him eat.

"So, yuh pick my pockets this morning, Missa Dezzie."

"Me?"

"Yes, you!"

"Don't mix me up, woman. Must be somebody else. I don't pick people pocket. Shame on yuh, Babes."

She sighed. Shook her head. Thief and liar, never walk far from each other. "Least yuh could do was ask for the money, Dezzie. I woulda give yuh."

"Ah said is not me, woman." His head was down, slurping the red peas soup. Then he looked up, peevishly. "Nearly win today. Just miss it by this much." He formed his thumb and forefinger to make a pinch in the air. "This much. I tell yuh, Babes. One day, one day. Gonna win that Lot-a-Luck and buy yuh everything yuh want. Gonna buy yuh a house up in Cherry Gardens or Beverly Hills or one of them rich place. Maybe Norbrook. Yes, Norbrook. A big three storey house with swimming pool and balcony and garage space for three cars. I broke down in the middle of Naggo Head this morning. Splat in the middle of Naggo Head. When I buy my brand new car, it will never break down. Watch and see. Just watch."

She chuckled and watched him as he slurped his soup.

Chapter Two

Bam had turned her closet upside down and had also gathered all the odds and ends that had been cluttering the drawers of her closet, all into one hefty garbage bag. She had even found some old church hats that she had bought on the advice of her friend years ago and had worn once, because she was just not a hat person, though she liked seeing them on others, especially at Easter time. She had implored Precious to sort through the children's belongings and to see what they had outgrown, as well as herself and Dezzie. They were a family who never threw things out, as a rule, and so there were items there from the children's baby days and from before Precious was pregnant and started gaining all that weight, which she never lost. They had some shoes from when the children were tiny tots, and since Bam had given firm instructions that she wanted no more grandbabies, she was sure those cute little boots would no longer be needed. So that by the time Ras Negus resurfaced, there were three bags waiting for him and Bam was sure he wouldn't be able to manage.

"Looks like you'll have to make two trips, Ras," she advised. "No sense breaking yuh back over hand-me-downs."

"Two trips? No, sistren," Ras Negus grinned. His lean dimpled cheeks heightened in wide mockery of such a thought. "I-

Man carry this kinda load all the time. Remember I tell you, is something we do on a regular basis. We go all around Portmore, and other areas, too." Ras Negus tested the weight of the three bags, one by one, as if making a mental estimate to determine whether or not the task was feasible. He seemed satisfied that it was. "Carry more than this all the while, Miss B. Give thanks, and blessings to you."

"At least, let me ask Dezzie to give you a lift, if even just to the bus stop," suggested Bam.

"No-I. No-I, my sistren. Give thanks. More time." He wore a full khaki suit of bush jacket and pants, the jacket bedecked with buttons and badges bearing the Ethiopian flag, another with the lion of Judah, another with a picture of His Imperial Majesty, Emperor Haile Selassie 1. His woolen tam was knitted in the colours of the Ethiopian flag, of red, gold and green. He wore brown leather sandals with thick straps across the instep and heavy soles for "trodding", a term he preferred to mere "walking". Trodding, seemed more purposeful and dignified, like one had somewhere important to go and a specific way in which to get there.

"Well, alright, then. Walk good," said Bam. Dezzie had been in the living room and had cowered at the mention of the words "ask Dezzie to give you a lift". His mother was always offering his services without first consulting him, knowing very well that he was a working man and needed his rest. She was very kind with his energy! Well, he was glad that had been deferred. He watched through the window as Ras Negus hoisted two of the bags across his back and wedged the lightest firmly under the grip of his right arm, grown strong from nine years of hoisting bags of rubbish into the trap of the garbage truck.

No amount of poverty could cause Dezzie to take a job on the rubbish truck. It was one of those jobs he would never do, and he said it often enough just so the universe could hear, in case it had any such plans for him in future. Garbage collector, labourer, street cleaner – just weren't his kinds of work. He wasn't cut out for it and that was that. Cleaning up other people's rubbish? He could barely stand touching his own. Some people were just born for it, it seemed, and some people weren't. He was just one of the ones who weren't.

Ras Negus mounted the steps of the bus and lodged his bags behind the driver's seat. Luckily, it was a driver who knew him and there was no need for debate. Another driver may have refused him entry into the bus, on account of his luggage. This one knew him and they actually chatted and laughed for a minute or two after the bus drove off. The bus would take him to the heart of Downtown and then he would take another bus to Slipe Road, near Torrington Bridge, and then he would walk the few paces to Mulgrave Lane, just across from Jones Town. This was where he lived, with his woman and five children. It was a tenement yard where no less than twenty people could be counted at any given time. Four families shared the tenement, along with their friends who seemed to be constant fixtures, their enemies who seemed to always know where to find them for a confrontation, which was often, their dogs which, theoretically, were there for protection and deterrence but which scattered frantically as everyone else did when the gunmen or the police or the soldiers came. Which was every other day or so.

It was a life one adapted to. It was not a life one got up and walked away from. There were always ties, of blood, water, sweat, tears or urine. The stale blood of relatives whom one felt some sort of allegiance to, though unreasonable, stale blood smearing the sheets of brothers and cousins in the morgue beside the hospital, twenty years old, if so much. The stale copper-coloured urine that splattered the walls along the side of the road, a late-night piss while fumbling home from the dancehall. The stale water that oozed stagnant from the gullies that connected the underbelly of Kingston. The stale sweat dried on to the armpits and collars of blue shirts, of working men who dragged themselves home just in time to gobble down some bread, shuffle their women over to the corner and go to sleep. The stale tears of toddlers with bang bellies clutching the skirts of their big sisters, whose own stale tears streamed down their faces in two very distinct lines that marked the end of innocence. It was always one of those five things in this place. Blood, water, sweat, tears or urine. Very rarely did it rain.

The bags fell to the wooden floor with a thud. Naph-T rose with a start. She had been resting. Her two smallest children lay asleep beside her on the bed.

"Hush. Bags heavy," said Ras Negus.

She sat up in bed so that her legs hung off the edge and her bare feet rested on the wooden planks that made the floor. Her knitting needles and wool lay in a cardboard box at the side of the bed. "Must have dozed off while putting them to sleep," she said, almost apologetically. "Was washing earlier, and made some lunch. Yuh look tired, though, Ras." She glanced over at the toddlers, King and Lion, fast asleep in the corner, each boy wearing only a pair of briefs. Beads of sweat were on their forehead in spite of the fan. Naph-T reached over, absently, as out of habit and without much alarm, and picked two biting ants from King's legs. She used the back of her hand to smooth the hair on Lion's forehead, and wipe the sweat away. "Open the door now, since yuh come. Kinda hot in here. Yuh hungry?"

"A little hungry, yes. But later. Come, help me sort these out so we can take them up to the clinic."

"Yes, my King-Man." She rose and walked over to the bags, opened each and emptied them onto the floor, kneeling to get a better look. "Lots of children's clothes. Good thing, tomorrow is antenatal clinic. The women will grab these up."

Ras Negus chuckled. "Good timing, then." He stretched out in a wicker chair and removed his tam, a thing he only did at home and only when there was no company. With the tam gone, his locks tumbled across his back and over his shoulders, draping his bare chest. He had removed his bush jacket also, and his sandals, so that now he only wore the pair of khaki pants and he wiggled his outstretched toes as if exercising them. The garbage men were on strike today, a fairly common practice. It was good because it gave him some time to run some errands and catch up on some stuff that had been lagging. He hoped to do some gardening later, in the little field beside the tenement, where he grew some callaloo, tomatoes and a few other vegetables, some ganja shrubs hidden among the lot, which the police had been turning a blind eye to, he was sure.

The clothes were clearly second-hand but none was tattered. There were no buttons or zippers missing, no tears or sagging hems. People could be fussy, even those collecting alms. There had been times when items had been flatly refused. "We poor but we not desperate!" had been the wounded voices, hinging on pride and the refusal to be treated with contempt. So Naph-T had been very careful about what she sent up to the clinic. Even the old men, many of whom were drunks who were scooped from the gutters and often ate from the bins at the restaurants, even they, had been known to refuse certain articles of clothing, on the grounds that they were unworthy. They, the clothes.

"These are nice," said Naph-T. "A little faded, but nice." It was only a momentary thought, but she did picture Lion or King in the cute little shorts sets, handpicked by Precious in the shopping districts of Panama, and there were a few dresses that the two younger girls, Princess or Queen, could wear. But there were others who needed these clothes much more than they did. In fact, Naph-T made most of the children's clothes, from scratch, and she always felt that love was woven into them this way, that the children could feel her care each time the cloth brushed against their skin. Not that there was anything wrong with ready-made clothes. Her children had some store-bought clothes, too. Nothing wrong in supporting someone else's industry, someone else's talent. Naph-T repacked the bags and tied each at the top with a stretch of wool. She labeled them according to the groups that she figured would benefit most from each. The seniors who came to stock up on the pharmaceuticals that kept their silver cord from detaching and floating off into the ether – just barely kept it from detaching. They were old and toxic, which made them sometimes wonder what was the use of a golden age, if so decrepit and cumbersome. The old women would love the hats.

They were from the era when hats were all the rave. The old men would try the pants and realize, to their dismay, how much they had shrunk, how much the family's jewels had depreciated. The hems of the pants would gather in bundles at their ankles and this would be very perplexing to them. Very perplexing, and sad, to men who used to tower. The pregnant women at the antenatal clinic, heavily laden with the guilt of not being able to provide all the things they wanted to provide – not only what they needed to provide, but what they wanted to – for which woman didn't want to swaddle her newborn in luxury? It was a guilt that weighed heavily on their consciences, that and the deathly fear of their bodies being ripped open by a pumpkin-sized head, as their mothers had warned with much foreboding, "Yuh batty gwine hot yuh! Just wait, man!" And since the proof lay only in the eating, they had eaten. They now carried the burden of proof.

Naph-T carried a guilt of her own, though Ras Negus had done his best to quash it each time she raised the issue. It had been almost eight years since she had gone out to work, since she was pregnant with Princess. The last job she had held was at a fast food outlet. She worked around the back, preparing the meals that, as the marketing department would have it, simulated the homecooked experience to a T. There was some truth to it. It was not the regular fast food of burgers or patties or French fries, but authentic Jamaican meals that made every effort to stay true to form. The only thing was, Naph-T was vegetarian and the daily slicing and gutting and seasoning of meat was beginning to make her puke. She wondered how she had ended up here, in this place of meat-eaters feeding meat-eaters, watching the blood ooze from carcasses and coagulate in the pots, the stifling heat that rose from the kitchen and hovered over their heads all day, of spices burnt beyond recognition, justified only by the gleeful faces of the patrons as they leaned anxiously against the counter and checked their tickets to see if they had somehow missed the calling of their number. Nothing sweet like meat. Nothing. This was the general consensus. Give up what? To please who? Meat haffi kill mi!

Naph-T could not make sense of why she was there, except that of all the fourteen places she had tried that week when she had been job-hunting, they had been the only ones to offer her work. Finally, when she could no longer stomach the smell of the kitchen, she asked to be moved to ancillary, where she wiped the floors three times daily and cleaned the bathroom every hour. She much preferred that. But then, she started growing her locks and her boss became edgy. And then, she became pregnant with her third child, and the smell from the kitchen triggered her morning sickness; it was enough to make her retch every time she walked past the corridor, so that she spent most of the time in the bathroom, not cleaning it, but prostrate over the public toilet bowl. So she was fired. And Ras Negus never allowed her to look for work since.

"Better for you to stay here, look after the children," he had said. "Don't want nobody bossing round my queen, and talking down to her. Don't want to have to go to jail."

"But all yuh make is from the rubbish truck, and the little weed now and then. That can't do."

"It will do," he had assured her. "Never yuh mind. It will do."

She shared some steamed callaloo, boiled yam and breadfruit into a plate and he ate voraciously, along with some unsweetened fenugreek tea. He glanced over at his sons sleeping, chuckled to himself because one had his feet thrown across the other. The two boys slept with him and Naph-T while the three girls slept in the other room, a tiny room, where only the bed and a small dresser could fit. It wasn't the best of arrangements, but the boys were still toddlers. Still, Ras Negus was acutely aware that some progress needed to be made in terms of living space. His family was expanding. He couldn't very well expect that the boys would sleep with them forever, and there was no space in the girls' room. Maybe, he could talk his landlady into letting him add another room round back, or something. It might even boil down to finding somewhere else to live. Ras Negus had been born in this tenement. His mother still lived in one of the rooms across the compound, and his brother and his family lived in another. He had lived in other places across the city but always found his way back here, on Mulgrave Lane.

He would check in on Miss Inez after he ate, see if she needed him to balm her feet and wrists. The arthritis had plagued his mother for donkey years, rendered her bedridden many times but the balm seemed to help somewhat. Then, he would walk down to the Primary school and pick up the girls, since he had some time on his hands today. It would surprise them.

The boys stirred. One woke, sat up and rubbed his eyes. The other, like a shadow, did the same. In the daze, they saw their father stretched out on the wicker chair and their mother ironing shirts by the doorway, where it was cool.

"Come," said Ras Negus. He held out his hand. They scrambled from the bed and climbed up into his lap. "Bathe from morning, Fire?" he referred to both his sons as "Fire". They both nodded. "How many toes?" He let them both stretch out their toes. King counted his toes and got ten. Lion did the same. Their father confirmed their brilliance. "But how many fingers, though?" he asked. The children chuckled. They loved this game.

By evening, the deafening din of daytime Slipe Road had been exchanged for a more purposeful chaos, not of vehicles bustling hither and thither, but the steady honking of horns with one direction in mind: home. Most were heading out of town, away from Downtown and up and out into the suburbs and beyond. Only those who had to stay, stayed. Who could leave, left quickly. As quickly as possible. The migrant workers and their bosses leased the town for daily use, from the real proprietors, the dons who were just now awakening to survey their lands, see if everything had been left in order. They were nocturnal in habit but they were kept abreast by minions who made daily raids to collect their dues from the store owners and market women, the arcade higglers and even the handcart boys. Everyone paid, in one way or another, in cash, kind or blood. Ras Negus knew some of these dons by name. Some he watched grew from underlings with their soiled nappies dragging behind them and dried excrement caked between their legs, drinking water from the communal standpipe in the tenement, or in some other tenement scattered across the garrisons, grew into young boys with white-scawled mouths, shifty eyes and light fingers, grew into men eager for a fight, eager to prove they could outdraw and outlive. He did not fear them but he did not cross their path without good reason, and there was hardly good enough reason. A man of forty-six had learnt the ways of avoiding this set. There were ways to live among them and still keep his soul intact. Still, he fretted for his woman and his children, that they would walk into the path of a hungry bullet and be ravaged to smithereens, and added to the list of innocents slain in the crossfire between the law and the lawless.

He was in the garden, plucking weeds from among the shrubs of callaloo, and picking worms and eggs from the underside of the callaloo leaves. The three girls were doing their homework, outside, using the glow from the streetlights. They were content, knowing he was close by. He felt a similar satisfaction with the world, in spite of where their world was, the satisfaction of knowing that his daughters were old enough to help each other with homework. They had passed the worse, as it was said of children when they came to the point where they could help themselves with certain things. They could help their mother as well, help with the washing and cleaning up, even the cooking at times, depending. Ras Negus did not have it all planned out as to what he wanted his children to become, per se, but what he did want was that they live clean, honest lives. No matter how lowly the profession, with integrity it was something indeed, in this world. The girls were doing well at school. Empress was thirteen and was in first form at High school. Princess was seven and Queen was nine. King had just turned three and would start Basic school, come September. Lion was one month short of completing his first year on Earth. Ras Negus wasn't sure if his loins had further plans for himself and Naph-T. He was open to having more children, certainly. That they were born in poverty was not a hindrance to him and should not be a hindrance to them, long as they were rich in spirit, as he always said. But he did harbor hopes of opening a restaurant one day, a vegetarian restaurant, where he would grow the produce and Naph-T would cook, and they both would help serve. And maybe the girls could help out after school. He had dreams. He had nothing much by way of education, but as far as he was concerned, he had listened keenly and had absorbed life's lessons. He had words of counsel for both his sons and his daughters, which he would drop along the way at the right time, like seeds into well proportioned pockets of soil, with the hope that each would sprout and grow to fruition, and none would be wasted.

The girls had closed the books and had walked over into the garden, where he had taken to watering the tomatoes. The streetlight softened the edges of their locks, which bounded their chocolate faces like coils of wool. Princess picked a plummy tomato and sank her teeth into it, nodded her head to confirm its deliciousness, picked another and held it in her other hand in anticipation. Ras Negus smiled. "Empress, pick some tomatoes and take for Miss Inez," he said. "And take some callaloo, too, and some onions. Tomorrow morning I go steam some callaloo for her before I go to work."

The next morning, a bright sunny day, the men back at work with nothing much to show for the strike – not yet, at least. Two men travelled in the front of the truck while three men took various positions at the back, in the area between the trap and the head. In this secret no-man's land, there was enough space to stash anything that had been retrieved from the garbage heap and deemed valuable, such as bed springs, chests of drawers, old iron frames, fans that could be repaired, an endless variety of knickknacks, as well as bags of old clothes that were given to the men to distribute among the hordes of unfortunates that were known to frequent the Riverton landfill in Kingston. Of course, these things were never given at once, but at least one or two were always there after they had completed their rounds. The men could not believe the things that some people thought of as junk. It blew their minds to bear witness to some of the things that were cast off for the dump. Many a treasure was rescued from the bags and barrels, the maggots and gunk shaken off and the item given a good scrub, restored to almost new. Sheer laziness and negligence, and a lack of compassion for those who had nothing, had led these residents to throw out such valuables. Wickedness, was all some of the men could say, as they shook their heads and sighed. Of course, most of the garbage was indeed, garbage. Looked like it and smelled like it, if not worse. The thick leather gloves they wore seemed not enough to protect them from the stench and acridity of some of this refuse. For nine years, Ras Negus had dipped his head into the pits of garbage bins to hoist out bags that dripped slime and reeked of putrefaction, a combination of dozens of smells that had conspired for days, sometimes two weeks, trampled hundreds of maggots under his water boots as he trod back and forth from the heaps to the trap. Some got away, swollen and squirming, looking for dirt to complete their next stage of metamorphosis. The maggots cared not for these men – whether they went on strike or not, a maggot's life went on.

    The garbage men typically went on strike for a day or two, for better pay and more comprehensive health coverage. They were easily consoled by men in white shirts with manicured fingers who never ever came within ten feet of a rubbish bin, not even the ones in their own kitchen. These men worked in air conditioned offices and were employed in labour of the kind that didn't require leather gloves or water boots, in fact only required a pen and a small leather notepad with words engraved in archaic golden font, at times, if that much. But their tongues were of such persuasion that the garbage men always heeded to the negotiations, which weren't negotiations at all but sweet, empty promises. Besides, the garbage men had something that the men in white didn't: a conscience. They had become familiar with the housewives who complained about the garbage piling up beside their kitchen door, where the dogs and cats ripped them to shreds searching for scraps of meat. They were hovering in limbo, between the "no dumping" signs put up by the Municipal workers, and the stench of uncollected garbage in their backyards. Those who worked out faced the predicament of never being there when the truck arrived, and not being able to leave out their garbage without getting a tongue-wagging from old ladies who lived at the end of the pathways, or worse. The garbage men had a conscience, whereas the Municipal workers seemed not to. Besides, these were the very housewives who placed hundred dollar bills into the neat little brown envelopes that the garbage men left in the letter boxes at Christmas time.

A labourer called Barefoot was doing his rounds collecting empty drinks bottles from the wall along the bar, as well as from the garbage heaps. He sold these empty bottles to make a little extra money. The garbage men hailed him; he hailed them back. The truck honked several times so the residents could know that they should take out their bags and boxes, twigs and branches, heaps of mown grass and everything deemed cumbersome or detrimental to efficient residential living. One by one, they filed down the pathways bearing the excrement of Greater Portmore. Each was absorbed in his or her own thoughts, with one focus: get this trash away from me. Take it someplace else; anywhere but here. They stood as far as they could away from the truck and shrieked scornfully when the garbage men tried to help them with the bags, for fear that the horrid gloves would come into contact with their dainty hands.

Ras Negus lifted a huge bag from the pile and immediately a centipede darted out and scrambled up the leg of Barefoot, who had stooped searching for bottles.

"Forty legs!" shouted Ras Negus. "Grab him!"

On instinct, Barefoot clutched the side of his pants several places in rapid succession, until he felt a small squirming mass. He held on to it and squeezed with all his might, until he was sure there could be no chance of life. Then he let go and shook the leg of his pants, and the creature fell to the ground in a brown, gelatinous mass.

Chapter Three

The day she found out that black men loved dolls, Liling had actually started the morning believing herself to be ugly. She had been convinced that, if not ugly, she was at least not normal, and that was sometimes all it took to feel ugly. Not normal, by Jamaican standards, anyway. In her grandmother's country, perhaps, young men may have swum the great Yangtze just to peep at her face, as Waipo Mingzhu said they had done for her, when she was a flower.

Liling had stared into the mirror at her petite, paper-thin frame. No belly no butt hardly any breasts to speak of. She had a moon face, pale yellow-white skin that was flawless. Her eyes had the much-mentioned Oriental slant. Too much mentioned. Why did other people think she couldn't see as well as they did, with their big oval eyes? She saw everything, thank you very much, with those jet black eyes to match her hair. She had twirled somewhat by way of motivation, flopped her skirt back and forth around her hips and knees, and had then collapsed upon the bed, disheartened. She had left out for work, pouting as the Hiace van pulled on to Orange Street in front of the family's wholesale, pouting as her brother and father wrestled to open and hoist the heavy metal security frame at the front of the store, pouting as her two sisters alighted and walked towards the back storage room. They too were paper-thin and not normal, by the standard of the place, and ugly. But by the end of the day, Liling, the white jasmine, seventeen years old, had changed her mind.

It had been summer. The girls were on break from school and were helping out in the shop. As usual, Chang's Wholesale and Haberdashery was chaos and everyone was demanding to be served at once. They were always in a hurry; but how? They were mainly women, buying hair extensions and accessories. They were boisterous and apparently unaware of it. Or, aware of it, and proud. They seized the packs of exotic hair with a triumph reminiscent of the glory days of empires, when knighted horsemen rescued precious loot from the hands of the enemy. They were lascivious in their dress and demeanor, flirtatious in their language. They leaned where common decency would have dictated others to stand. They dragged their flip-flops and waltzed bandy-legged from one end of the counter to another, trying to get the attention of the attendants, who were like them in every way except that they were on either sides of the glass divide. But they would more than likely ride the same bus home later, or prance down the same narrow lanes of the shanties. Some left an air of frowziness and nonchalance trailing behind them, unkempt save for the extensions which they had come to secure. It was easy to imagine them having slept in the same drag they were now wearing. While others were dressed to the teeth, overdone. From one extreme to the next.

These women wore batty-rider shorts and mesh merinos with tube-tops or bras underneath. They were built like champions, thigh muscles ready for the chase, whether as predator or prey; pick your choice. Bosoms firm, scanning for interested eyes and pockets. The younger ones stood on lean stilts like gazelles on the Kingston savannah. The older, more weary ones, breasts sagged, not from the tug of little suckling mouths, but from the burden of many unweaned men with big jawbones and ravenous appetites. Tittymen. Breastmen; they called themselves with pride. The women had silky lacefront wigs of all colours sewn in, tied in, plaited in, or just perched defiantly upon the original base of a vastly different texture. They were shameless. They told of their plans, asked questions of each other what would look better or best, which colour hair would go with which outfit, and such the like. Important things that required much ironing out so the right decision be made in time and flops avoided. They barely took notice of the Chinese girls assisting behind the counter and directed most questions to the local girls who were the regular attendants.

Fenfang, the fragrance of flowers, nineteen. Biyu, the precious gemstone, twenty-two. The girls did not like being in the shop, but they had no choice. This was patriotic duty 101. For two months during the Summer, on weekdays, their parents felt it was imperative that they learn the family's trade, at least by observation. Downtown Kingston was a scary place for anyone, most of all three Chinese girls who understand Jamaican patois well enough but who sometimes pretended not to, and cowered at the raw lingua bouncing in and out and around the store. They could barely be seen behind the counter, the tallest being five foot one inch in shoes. Nymphs among giants. The attendants always wanted to play in the sisters' hair, always spoke and asked the same irritating questions about their hair, always tried to touch it for some reason. Someone had even commented once that they looked like dolls.

So to the matter of dolls. Black men loved dolls, it seemed. And not black dolls, by the way. They loved dolls with long straight black hair, and porcelain skin.

The man eased into the shop but his face was turned to the streets, and he slid something into the band of his waist, just glancing quickly enough to make sure the shop was empty. Everything about him was quick and easy. Fluent in the language of the street. The chaos of the morning had abated because it was Wednesday, and the stores closed half day Downtown. In fact, Liling had been the only one behind the counter, the others having lunch round back before locking up. She ducked at first, thinking the man to be a robber who was making to demand money. This had happened three times before, not to her but to the assistants, and they had all been cautioned. This type was hardly ever a paying customer. But when he walked towards the counter, he was smiling and his posture wasn't threatening. He spoke in the vernacular of the place, and Liling pretended not to understand. But then he said, "Pretty lickle Chiney girl. Whappen, Miss Chin?" and Liling blushed.

He walked over, glancing back twice as if to check if he was being followed. But smoothly, with grace. A dip in every second step. Cadence. If you called him a thug, he would consider it a compliment. You could call him dawg, nigga, gangsta, ghetto youth, ragamuffin, struggler, hustler – he would promptly answer. In fact, it would please him tremendously, and some kind of bond would be formed, a barrage of hand greetings, fists pumped, a salute with one hand over the heart, a bow. Call him murdera, killa, shotta, mafia, and you could have your way with him. He was yours. Long as you didn't call him informa. It was something he was always, but particularly in this moment, avoiding.

Up this far, they could not have heard the muffled shots or got wind of the killing just yet so this was a good hide-out till the commotion died down, further down near the waterfront, at the harbour's edge. He had made his way up Orange Street without much notice and those who did see him and did know, were only too happy for what he had done, or too scared to say they weren't.

Small talk. The kind she had been vigorously warned against. A lean in. A young thug smile, not too much teeth to give away anything, just enough to reel her in. Whispered tones to show how smooth he was, in spite of where he was, what he was wearing, the smoldering cigarette in his hand. He could get her to pull the latch and come out to talk. He could. Just watch. He did.

"Yuh look like a lickle baby-dolly. How you one pretty suh?"

She pretended not to understand, and asked if he wanted something from the shop, maybe something she could show him.

"Want something? I want you!"

He used his hand to flip the horse tail that she had done up in a yellow ribbon. "Long pretty hair, man! Skin smooth and pretty. Nice Chiney girl."

At no point did she resist, but she glanced back several times because she was sure she heard footsteps round the back. Lunch over so soon? So soon? Her father, would have a fit. Her brother, had he still been here, would whip himself into one of his frenzies that would last for days, and would need some kind of over-the-counter medication to sedate him. Do not. Do not. Do not. Do. Do. Do. Learn the difference. You are a dolphin in a sea of sharks. You are a foreigner outnumbered in a land of locals. You are a chopstick among forks. How else can I put it to you, little sister? All this would be said in his loudest Mandarin, the language of home. To him, his voice never seemed to be loud enough, mandarin being a light language spoken for centuries by soft tongues, nodding heads, smiles and bows. He sometimes wondered if he should say it the way a Jamaican brother would have said to his baby sisters: you are a cockroach among fowls, and have no business in any arguments or conversations between fowls. Hear dat? Learn dat!

So why would she pull the latch at the impromptu bidding of a fowl? A sensible girl, just graduated eleventh grade and now looking forward to her first year of sixth form at a very upstanding school. A smart girl. A girl with a future almost guaranteed in this country, looking as she looked.

He needed pics. He just had to have some pics of her. She was just too pretty. Most beautiful Chinese woman, she must surely be. She smiled. He took pics with his cell phone. Saved them. Showed them to her. She giggled. She was nervous. The way a school girl is nervous when in the middle of doing things her big brother had warned her not to. A rebellious nervousness. Spiteful defiance. Intrigued.

"What's your name, Miss Chin?"

"Liling."

"Naw, man. Chinno. Chino yuh name," he laughed. She giggled, slightly covered her mouth. Reflex.

He scrolled down to examine the pics. Nice. "Wouldn' mind getting some more wid yuh in yuh uniform. Eh? Me name Mongrel."

Definitely shuffles from the backroom, and a din from the streets. Somebody shot? Down the waterfront? People were talking all kinds of things. The noise was sudden and uproarious and snatched Liling from the stupor of the moment, in time for her to close the latch before Mr. Chang bolted out and demanded that the shutters be lowered and padlocked as soon as possible. They would probably leave through the back. She turned again to find that the store was empty. The young man had disappeared. But she remembered him, would not forget that rugged face, the tall lean body and his sure smile, lips stained by cigarette smoke.

What had she done? He had her pics in his phone! Well, she was fully dressed. Nothing much he could do with a fully dressed pic. She could always explain to her brother, or whomever, I was not aware. You know how these ghetto guys are. Very presumptuous. Obnoxious. Can't handle the word 'no'. They snap your picture anyway. But then, she was smiling ever so coyly, looking straight on. So aware of being captured. Compliant.

And that evening, Liling stared confidently into the mirror, this way and that; every which way, for an hour. Pancakes for dinner, she chuckled. Everything flat, as it should be. Big butts get in the way. She was sure you couldn't sleep well on them. Must be hell for the back. Those poor women with those heavy butts. Hindrances. She let down her hair, which fell way past her shoulders. She brushed and combed it. She showed her teeth – something she rarely did – always opting for a plastic smile with thin lips that stretched from cheek to cheek, only with no teeth visible. But now, why not?

"Li is happy." Waipo Mingzhu was eating noodles and fried pork cutlings, with her chopsticks as she had done since a child in Shanghai Province, in the motherland. She had no teeth now, but she was managing. One does as one can with what one has left. She was eighty-seven. She could eat pork with gums if she felt like it. This was nobody's business. The Chinese will eat anything, she had heard people say, in jest as well as in offense. Taken equally in jest and offense, depending. The Chinese make everything, and they will also eat everything. Everything is made in China, and eaten in China. Waipo loved her people, more so than she loved any other people. She reasoned that this was as it should be, for all peoples.

"Li is happy. Come, Li." Liling was her favourite, the youngest grandchild, the runt of the litter. Liling was not usually happy in the Summer, when she had to spend many days Downtown in the noise and the heat, packing and tagging and labeling this and that, even among her beloved sisters. "Come, Li."

Liling rose from her place around the table, where her dinner had hardly been touched, and stood behind her waipo very closely. She put both hands on the old woman's head, as she often did. Her parents looked up from their meal, smiling, her mother concerned about the unfinished meal, her father beckoning her to leave grandma be and eat up. Jingjing, her only brother and first child for her parents, always in business mode even at dinnertime, tried to sustain his father's attention regarding matters at the Lot-a-Luck office, which the family owned.

What does Li want with her old uniform? It's Summer. Take a picture, Waipo. How? Press this button here. Take another one.

Jingjing preferred to go by the name of Michael, in his regular day-to-day dealings with people outside of the home. When in Rome, etc. People insisted on calling him Missa Chin no matter how many times he pronounced his name or indicated to his name on paper. He dreaded to think what they would do with the name "Jingjing". They would have a field day with it, no doubt. Michael, they could work with. It saved him a great deal of trouble. It was bad enough coexisting in a country in which he never really felt at home, never really at ease. But where would he, except home? His real home, among half a billion men who at least looked like him. They all look the same, it had been said of his people. Well, what better place to feel at ease, than among people who all looked exactly like you? The least sexually desired male on the planet, was the magazine's take on it. This had been just last week. News just in. Asian women are seen in the west as exotic, sexy princesses and are fetishized. The Asian man, not so. This had sunken into him. It was not nice. The tiniest man. The most soft-spoken man. The least threatening male on the planet? And his woman, the world's fetish?

His father had said, "Make sure to marry an Asian woman. Not a headache in sight. Don't get a Jamaican wife. Caribbean men have to learn to submit to their cantankerous wives."

Yet, Jingjing knew for a fact that his father, the docile Bingwen, bright and cultivated one, had kept several women during the course of his marriage, and all of them black.

So what now? Jingjing, the golden mirror, was unmarried. He wasn't ready for a wife, whether or not she came with headaches. This displeased Bingwen greatly. His own wife, Huian, obliging and peaceful, the kind quiet one, had lived up to her name. she had brought much peace to his soul. Not a headache in sight. A man, in his thirties, should be getting ready for grandchildren. The house should be full of happy noise, and the voice of grandparents telling them to hush. The family should be busy selecting dozens of names, from the millions of options. So many names. So many things to become. So many things to live up to. These things were important.

Bingwen felt that for too long, the noises in the house had been the shrieks and giggles from teenage girls, his own daughters; bedroom doors slamming, more hushed giggles. He wasn't sure what to make of these sounds. They were new to him. he wanted the old familiar sounds of water splashing in the basin, screams when soap got into the eyes. Hold still, baby. Little feet running across the living room floor, slippery with mud. The sound of crying, a thud, someone slipped in the mud, maybe knocked a forehead that would need ice. A milk tooth loosened but it would grow back. The sound of things falling, breaking. Oops. It's ok. Things fall from time to time. Just be careful. Those sounds.

Too scared to figure out what to do with teenage daughters in this harsh world, he could hide in the task of raising grandchildren, he figured. If his son would only give him some.

Bingwen had settled in to read the papers after dinner and yes, there were giggles coming from the bedrooms upstairs. He sighed. He wouldn't worry so much if there were as many boys who looked like them and shared their culture, shared their values, shared something. The pickings were few. He worried.

"Oh lord, did he really send that?"
"Yikes!"
"My goodness! Look at the size of that thing!"
"Li! Feng! What are you doing with my phone?!"
Giggles.
"You girls! I swear, I need my own room. Sharing a room with two little twerps!"
"Biyu, your boyfriend is photogenic!"
"Oh yes, Biyu! Veeery!"
"Twerps!"

Huian, the wife who came with no headaches, had had the house properly feng-shuied by a professional so that the qi, the energy, would flow throughout and maintain harmony and goodwill in the home. Well, as professional as a Feng Shui practitioner could be on a Caribbean island. She suspected things may be a bit watered down but she would take what she could get. One does not turn one's back on a three thousand year old practice simply because one is away from home, in the West where there is almost no life force. It still mattered – in fact, probably mattered now more than ever, that the life forces be aligned, through the orientation of structures – the five elements: wood, metal, fire, earth and water. What a thing was made of, mattered. Where a thing was placed in the house, in relation to other things, mattered.

The bed in the commanding position, never with feet facing the door or window. This was hard to achieve, but vital. No mirrors in the bathroom or in front of the bed. Toilet seat cover always down, bathroom door always closed. Fountain flowing in a central space. Water is wealth. And many other points. She had written them down, and kept checking. It sometimes became a bit tedious, all these rules, some conflicting. And with her son constantly saying, utter rubbish! Utter rubbish! Quackery!

"Shorter?!"
"Above my knees."
"Really?!"
"Thanks what he said!"
Giggles.

What does Li want with Waipo's old sewing machine? And the scissors? Li, come here.
"It's nothing, Waipo. Nothing."
Giggles.

Mingzhu, bright pear. Her husband, Fa, setting off. They had indeed set off, from all of one whole world away. Why? Who remembers, why? But wasn't it to mother they had come, for her porcelain, her much guarded art of silk-making, her ancient treasures? Why now must mother's children be leaving? And so far? Where did you say the place was, Fa? Remind me of the name. Do they speak our tongue?
You are my wife. You must come with me, whether or not. Besides, we have family already there, who sailed before us on boats. Now we take the aeroplane. See, things are better already. We will be fine.
She still had the tendency to cover her mouth and lower her eyes when she giggled, something she had passed down to her daughters, and theirs. Her back was hunched now from the tendency to bow slightly, in respect. Fa, too. His hunch more pronounced. Her most peculiar trait, the object of her granddaughters' fascination: her feet. Tiny feet that were bound

as a girl, a practice almost entirely abandoned now but in her day, the only way to ensure beautiful feet for a young girl who would be promptly wedded. Lotus feet. Much prized, tiny feet in a woman. Much outrage, for those who did not understand. At four years old, and for years after, her feet were periodically soaked and bound with bandages, her toes broken one by one, she the eldest daughter, a privilege set aside. It would force her knees to bend slightly, her hips to acquire the dainty, erotic sway much appreciated by men. Yet, she married a man not much richer than her father.

"Feet binding! Not for us modern girls," her granddaughters would say. They massaged her feet, respectfully. They could not understood such a tradition. It was not for them. They would think it, but would never say, it was barbaric. Those words were not uttered in the presence of Waipo Mingzhu.

Three smooth porcelain dolls, a foot tall; a set of china with a splendid blue and white willow pattern. A wedding gift of her parents to her and Fa. These were her only remaining relics of home. Fa had his little red book, still. Still. The sleeping giant, someone had said, in the glory days of the Chairman, yes, as a girl, she had heard it said, China is the sleeping giant. Do not wake her.

Who had said it? One of those big-boned white men, who loved to say all kinds of things. Fa would know. Fa would know who said it.

Fa? Fa? are you sleeping?

Chapter Four

Shelly had a gap between her two front teeth but that wasn't the only thing that Dezzie used to identify her. Even standing at the bus stop amidst dozens of other school girls in their uniforms, he could pick her out because of her hips. Classic hips, even at seventeen. He would normally honk his horn whenever he approached a bus stop, so people could know he was a route taxi, since he had no identifying red plate. But as he was only interested in picking up Shelly right now, there was no need for any silly honking. All he had to do was drive past her and maintain eye contact, a flick of the head indicating that she should walk away from the pack and meet him further up. Which she did. She always did. Today, he intended to take her around the Back Road, if she was up to it. He hoped that all the boxed lunches that he had been buying her, and all the free rides and compliments, would now work in his favour and make her up to it today. Three weeks of ground work were enough. Payback time.

She slumped into the passenger seat. "Sexy-body girl," teased Dezzie. "How you one suh sexy? Leave some for other people, nuh. Healthy-body, Shelly."

The girl glared at him then stared off haughtily through the window. Her hips were so wide and her uniform so short that when she sat, her skirt rode up four inches above her knees. She didn't carry a school bag, just a folder which she held firmly across her bosom. She did not look her age. She was one of those young girls whom people referred to as "big inna body", meaning that she was tall and statuesque and could pass for a grown woman with very little effort. This was the kind of school girl that Dezzie went for. There were other taxi drivers whom he knew of, who didn't care much about appearances, but he did. It had to feel right to him, even if it wasn't right. It was easier for him to convince himself that he wasn't a dog.

"Gimme a little touch, nuh," said Dezzie, using his left hand to caress her leg while his right hand maintained the steering wheel. She shoved his hand away. "But wait! Can't touch yuh again?" he asked, pretending to be vexed.

"Have a bone to pick with yuh, Mr. Dezzie!"

"Bone? With me? What I do now?"

"How yuh mean to tell everybody that I let yuh kiss me?"

"Me? Who me tell that? Me?"

"Yes, you! Who else?"

"No, sah. Not me."

"Then who else, then?"

"Yuh know people love chat. Let them talk all them want." He hissed his teeth. "Anyway, my girl, today is our day." He stroked her chin, using his finger to gently pry open her pouted mouth. The gap in her teeth was making him dizzy.

"Move yuh hand! Don't know where yuh finger coming from," she fumed, pushing his hand away again. "What yuh mean, today is our day?"

"I was thinking we could go round Back Road, yuh nuh. Do our thing. Don't yuh think is full time?"

"Take me round Back Road, then tell everybody? Me, Dezzie? I look like fool to yuh?"

"How yuh drop it suh, girl? Who I going to tell? Yuh going to give mi piece or not? Cho!"

By this time, he had passed the roundabout at Bayside and had made the left turn that would take him onto the Back Road, the notorious stretch of road that offered motel services during the day, a few legitimate eateries to tone it down, and at night, skimpily clad ladies decked the sidewalks plying their wares.

"Where yuh taking me, Dezzie?"

"I was thinking we could get a room, yuh know. Full time now we crank it up a notch."

"Look here, Dezzie. I not giving yuh nothing. Yuh too chatterbox!"

Dezzie hissed his teeth and stopped the car. "Then, why yuh take mi food, and mi free ride them?"

She clutched her folder and stared off, pouting. "Look, just turn back and leave me and the bus stop, and don't stop yuh taxi for me again."

"Look here, little girl, don't take big man things if yuh don't plan to let off something! Damn waste of time!" He too sat staring ahead, thinking of all the boxed lunches he had bought, and all the times he had driven past perfectly good passengers who had their fares, just to pick up Shelly. "Hear what I say, little girl? Stop take big man things! Think is everybody easygoing like me?" He wagged his finger at her. "Have a good mind slap yuh a box cross yuh damn face."

He turned the car with a fury and sped back to Bayside, slowed down just enough so that she could get out without being run over, and then sped down the road towards Greater Portmore. The only thing that could calm him now was the feel of a Lot-a-Luck ticket in his hand, the smooth edge of a promise made, a promise that would be timely kept and not deferred on the whims of an overgrown schoolgirl. A temptress unaware of her power; or all too aware? He turned into the Greater Portmore Shopping Centre and pulled up in front of the Lot-luck outlet. He was still pissed, and horny. He was in no mood to join any line, so he stepped all the way up to the counter and demanded service.

"Listen here, Dezzie. Sure yuh see one dozen other people in the line before yuh!" shouted Cherry, the attendant. They knew each other by heart, the Lot-a-Luck people, those who bought and those who sold, and those who hung around haplessly wishing they could buy. They all had seen each other at some point, had shared dreams and tried to correlate numbers and, after the numbers weren't played, they had all joined in cursing The Man; the faceless, nameless, heartless Man. Most were regulars who stopped by every day, sometimes two or three times a day, depending on the hunch or the cash flow. The weather was of no consequence. Few other matters, if any, seemed to take priority. They were a faithful, loyal, boisterous lot with no patience to go around, like cigarette smokers stepping into a bar; never could wait, needed service right away, regardless. Dezzie banged on the counter, quite to the chagrin of the other patrons, not to mention Cherry, who had an attitude all of her own.

"Want me to just don't bother serve yuh, then?"

He hissed his teeth and stood at the back of the line. Stupid girl, taking his boxed lunches, as if she didn't know what he wanted from day one. Why the hell would he be buying her boxed lunches, and giving her free rides? Did he look like some kinda good Samaritan or something? And the line was moving slow, on top of it. The day was off to a bad start. He grabbed the ticket from Cherry and stormed off.

"Don't slam my door!" he shouted at a passenger. "Think is steel it make out of?" The woman frowned at him. "Sorry, Sar," was all she could say.

"Lady, yuh didn't know yuh had a five hundred dollar bill? Why yuh didn't tell me before ah pass the gas station, so ah could get it changed? But why these people always come in here with five hundred dollars and thousand dollar bills? Where ah must get change from? I is bank or something? But what they take taximan for?"

He was seriously pissed. The lady who had slammed the door on her way in was very careful not to repeat the offense on her way out. She gently closed the door, too gently, in fact, so that it swung open when Dezzie rounded a corner, and he had to use his expert skill to close it while continuing to drive. These passengers, bwoy!

"Here," said a man from behind Dezzie, handing the driver

his fare. Dezzie ignored him. "Ah said here!"

"Look here, man," said Dezzie. "Yuh have to wait till the convenient time to give the driver yuh fare. Don't yuh see ah trying to concentrate to negotiate the road?" He knew very well that he was in the habit of collecting fares wherever and whenever, priding himself on being skilled beyond words. He could collect fares, drive and talk on his cell phone all at once, while circling the roundabout at breakneck speed, on a rainy day. Piece-a cake! But that blasted Shelly had taken the wind out of him. He pulled into the taxi stand at the Portmore Mall and got out to take a breath, all while shouting out, "Greater Portmore! Greater Portmore! Any two an' ready!"

The guys were in a riotous commotion regarding their exploits with the police, who were said to be on the prowl today. There were days when the police played it low, and days when they stepped it up, depending on a number of factors. Only a few of the drivers were registered taxi operators with red plates on their cars. They wouldn't have it any other way. What fun was it to be registered and compliant? No car chases. No conspiratorial blinking of headlights to each other to signify the approach or retreat of the cops. No opportunity to make up cock-and-bull stories when pulled over for questioning. No heartrending stories of injustice at the pound when your car was held for two weeks, with charges added every day, plus wrecker fee, plus this fee and that fee, plus God knows what. A red plate life must be a dull life, indeed. White plate was where the action was.

"Six days! Six days they have the blasted car!" Beres was saying, his hands in the air revealing the papers, as proof of his most recent plight. "Six damn days. Twenty thousand, plus wrecker fee!"

The others felt his pain. They had all been through it. A rite of passage into manhood. Mostly they bribed the police but there were times when they threw themselves headlong into the bureaucracy and let themselves be carried by the torrents, just for the sake of experience, something to compare notes with the fellows.

"What The Man play today?" asked Conda, not meaning to interrupt but, business was business.

"Fifteen," said Joe. "Teenager."

"Fifteen? Teenager?" shouted Dezzie. He had bought twenty-three. Kiss-and-tell. "Fifteen? Rahtid! If I did know!" He should have figured that he should have bought fifteen, for all that Shelly had put him through this morning. What on earth had he been thinking, to buy twenty-three? Who cared if he told a couple of the guys about kissing Shelly? They all told each other that kinda stuff. "Is the big one I really want to catch, though. How much it reach now?" Dezzie asked.

"One-fifty million!" someone said. And someone else confirmed. Dezzie needed no confirmation. He knew it was in that region, and climbing. He wanted it to climb climb climb till it reached five hundred million. Six hundred million. He knew he would win.

"Mine that!" he declared, which of course, everyone challenged, since they all knew it was theirs. "When I win that, I park this piece-a ol' car same day! Just park it what's-it-not and walk weh!"

"Talk bout!" shouted Beres, doing his special handshake with Dezzie, which led to everybody doing their special handshake, and groping their crotch. Instinct. "When I win that, first thing, going buy a boat and me and twenty girls just going cruise over to Lime Cay for two weeks."

"Girls?" scoffed Dezzie. "All they going do is eat out yuh money!"

"So what? That's what girls for, man!"

"Make sure they let off, first!" warned Dezzie. But he was still in his high Lot-a-Luck mood.

"No girl can't done out my money when I win," said Joe. "Was reading 'bout this basketballer yesterday. Five years ago the man worth three hundred million dollars! U.S. dollars! Now, he bankrupt! Bankrupt! Not a dime. Owe everybody. Hiding from people. Government on him case. Couldn't happen to me, no sah!"

"Fool that!" shouted Dezzie. "Damn blasted idiot! First thing, you have to invest in real estate. House and car. Yuh have to use yuh head."

"Don't see how a man can have three hundred million U.S. dollars and then flat broke, no matter how many years past." lamented Joe. "Couldn't happen to me, no sah!"

"Me, neither," said Dezzie. He was running the numbers through his mind and the list of things he would do with the money, when he won the big one. He didn't realize that the other guys had made a mad dash for their cars and had sped off. They had called to him but he had been in a daze. He came round as the police pulled into the taxi stand, and he drove off in the nick of time. Luckily, the rookies had not planned for a chase today, or his goose would have been stuffed, baked and served with hot sauce. Yes, they were rookies. He knew them by heart. The rookies were sent out in the low period, just to scout out a smalls. The real vets took charge in the peak hours when dollars were flowing and something substantial could be made, with the right threats and wagging of fingers. They knew whom to target. They knew those taximen who were on the payroll of their fellow lawmen, whom to stop and whom to let off with a poke and a promise, just for show. Dezzie felt he had most of them in his pocket but there were a few, like Corporal Haynes and his batch, whom nobody played around with.

Dezzie had calmed down, to the point where he even allowed a passenger to buy apples from the vendors at the stop light, a thing he rarely did because the passengers were so fussy and always wanted to inspect each and every apple, which they didn't have time for since it was a stoplight, but they didn't seem to care. But today he stopped. He was so focused on winning the Lot-a-Luck. He was willing to bribe whoever it was that was in charge of dreams, to make him dream the right number. He would give the man a sizable portion of the money, whoever that man was, after he had cashed in the ticket.

He took his children home and slept for a few hours, while they did homework. At four o'clock, he got a call from the

Member of Parliament, Mr. Dacres, who wanted Dezzie to pick up his girlfriend later in the night and take her to a party, in Norbrook. That was the kind of charter that Dezzie liked. Nice, easy money. Why Mr. Dacres was in the habit of chartering Dezzie's jalopy was a mystery to him, a mystery which he didn't look into much. Maybe the man just loved how he drove. Or maybe not. No-one felt safe with Dezzie round the wheel. He didn't know why the man kept chartering him, why he would want his girlfriend to arrive in Norbrook in a beaten down old Corolla when he had his expensive car and chauffeur. Maybe his wife was using the car. But then, his wife had her own car. Dezzie didn't look into it. He was being paid good money. He left it at that.

Mr. Dacres lived with his wife in Hellshire. But he wasn't going to the party with his wife. His girlfriend, Cassandra, lived in Caribbean Estates in a house that Mr. Dacres paid the rent for. She was kept. Dezzie didn't care. It wasn't his business. Cassandra was gorgeous and he could understand perfectly why Mr. Dacres would fall for her. Dezzie knew the schemes through and through so getting to Caribbean Estates wasn't a problem. The real issue was getting into the gated community, the security guards being such a hassle. It took them a full ten minutes of calls back and forth, before he got clearance to proceed.

Cassandra wore a red velvet mini dress, the likes of which Dezzie had never seen before, not even on tv. He was sure her heels were ten inches high, and she was already tall to begin with. Her perfume filled the car as soon as she eased into the back seat, making a mockery of his air freshener and making him want to unhinge the thing and toss it. The perfume smelled expensive, the kind that would stay where you put it and not fade with the first gust of wind, like the cheap scents that Precious was always dabbing onto her temples and wrists. Cassandra carried a small clutch. Who knew what women had hidden in those clutches. Precious had bags, not clutches. If she had a clutch, it would make life much simpler for him when he needed to go for money.

Cassandra was at ease, in spite of the raggedy upholstery of the back seat, and the old grease-smudged tyre in the trunk that stank to high heaven. She seemed to be making the best of the situation, by blocking it out. Maybe she was pretending that she wasn't there, that Bossman had finally bought her that Honda he had promised and so she could finally use the drivers license he had lined up for her. Dezzie kept glancing at her, wondering if she had on any underwear. It was a preliminary thing he always wondered about women. All women. The women who came into his taxi. The women who came to pick up their children at the Primary school. The women pushing trolleys in the supermarket. The women leaning against the wall in the Lot-a-Luck line, waiting to pool their lot in with the other hopefuls for a chance at fortune. Some he could tell outright, some he couldn't be sure, and these kinds of things seriously perplexed him. It could keep him up at night, if he wasn't careful. He occasionally peeked through the rear window to see if she would make the mistake of parting her legs, so he could confirm once and for all. She never did. He checked her hips to see if there was an imprint of a panty line beneath the dress, but the velvet was not thin enough to put his mind at ease. Still, he stood no chance with a girl like Cassandra, a light-skinned girl with flowing Indian hair. A Black man definitely had to have money to get that kind of girl. They were impressed by nothing else, it seemed.

"Where's the Bossman?" Dezzie asked. It may have been the second time he was speaking to her. Cassandra looked up from the reverie she had been engaged in with her cell phone in her lap and glanced at him, as if just becoming aware of his existence.

"You said something?" she asked.

"The Bossman. Him gone up already?"

"You mean Tony? Gone up where?" She seemed confused and annoyed.

"Up to Norbrook. Where I'm taking you."

"Oh. No. He'll get there later." She immediately returned her full attention to the cell phone, a mischievous smile slowly sweeping across her face as she resumed her texting, absorbed in a private world that Dezzie was not privy to.

He wished with all his might that he could read the texts that were being transferred between Cassandra and whomever else it was at the receiving end of them. Maybe it was Bossman, buttering her up for tonight. Dezzie grinned. Yup. It would sure be nice to read those texts. Better yet, that he could open her mind and read her thoughts like a first grade grammar book, till he knew them by heart. And even much better, that he could reach back and pry her legs open and probe about the matter of the panties. His nose was telling him she was wearing none. His nose was very rarely wrong about these things. He could sniff, in spite of the expensive perfume, the delicious earthy scent of her exposed pussy, which was at that very moment stirring a raw and rabid desire in him, a desire that was all the more maddening because it was too late to even think about Shelly and too early to even think about Precious, yet futile to even think about Cassandra. These things made it extremely difficult for a man to hold the steering wheel properly, driving at night over a bridge that spanned a lagoon, as they headed towards the dazzling lights of Kingston.

The only time Dezzie dared say anything further to Cassandra was when they came to the stop light at Three Miles and two street boys rushed over to wipe the windshield of his car. He allowed them to do so, thinking it would make a good impression on Cassandra that he was a man who encouraged industry in the young.

"I love to see these boys find something to do," he said, as if talking to himself but with enough accentuation that she could surely hear. "Better than just roaming the streets begging."

"Worthless. All of them," Cassandra scoffed, her indignation all the more convincing in the fact that she looked up from her texting to make the point. "Just look at that nasty water that he is smearing across your windshield! Did anyone ask them to do it? Disgusting. Why did you let them start in the first place? They need to go find decent work, and leave people's car alone. Sickening."

"They trying to earn a little something," said Dezzie. He

didn't want her to take it as if he was arguing with her, or even disagreeing with her, for that matter, but that he was trying to be objective about the matter. A man with an open mind, considering the plight of the unfortunate youngsters. She glared at him and at the boys in a panoramic condescension that made Dezzie wish he hadn't opened his mouth, wish he hadn't even stopped at the stop light. He glanced into the bucket that the two boys shared, into which they repeatedly dipped the sponge that they used to wipe across the windshield. The water did look a little dirty, especially now that he thought about it, and the street lights were conspiring with the glare of the night, so that the water swashed in the bucket with the heaviness of countless dips, of malicious reuse. Dezzie said nothing further, and after a final pout as the lights changed and the car drifted away from their presence, Casssandra retreated into her world of scrolls and refreshes, of shares and pokes, of likes and dislikes regulated by her roving eyes and the spontaneous flick of her right index finger.

The rich had parties any day of the week, it seemed. Or perhaps Dezzie had misheard, or had misinterpreted. Perhaps just a small late-night gathering of friends on someone's patio, for drinks, and to chat a little while their mistresses leaned against banisters and enjoyed the lights of Kingston down below. So what if it was neither Friday nor Saturday? So what if no wives were present, not even that of the host? The house was tucked away in the upper extremity of Norbrook. Dezzie had been to this particular house several times. Well, more precisely, he had driven to this particular gate and his passengers had alighted and had disappeared behind the bougainvillea and the terraces, into dimly lit patios. Dezzie himself had never had opportunity to venture beyond the gate, but he had reason enough to believe that an entire world was hidden therein, a world of screens and clinks and buzzers and concealed cameras, and vicious dogs that were kenneled but could be let loose at a moment's notice. And children who were tucked away in the left wing of the mansion, by nannies who had long descended into the slums to feed their own progeny on the scraps that they had stolen. And glasses that always yearned to be refilled with something fermented. Always. The rich were thirsty and water would never do. Water, so weak, and their tastes so cultured.

Cassandra opened the back door on her own, stepped out and whispered – whispered – a "thank you" so flimsy that she almost never said it, and he almost never heard it. Maybe, he had imagined it, after all. She slammed the door shut and glided down the walkway, after being buzzed through by the security guard who grinned sheepishly at her and assured her, "the dogs not out now, Miss. Not when there's company. Go right in. You are expected."

And when he could no longer see her, Dezzie realized that he would never know whether or not she had been wearing panties. He hated when this happened, and it happened often enough. He almost had a fit driving back down through Norbrook and into the city streets, cross the bridge and back into Portmore. Why did women do these things to men? Even more, why did men do these things to themselves? Or maybe it wasn't all men who subjected themselves to this torture. Maybe it was just Desmond Grant, who felt his sanity depended upon knowing these things. No, it wasn't just him. When he was at the taxi stand with the boys, and their conversations reached the fever pitch of derision, they each confessed to bouts of perversion that made themselves feel right at home with each other.

He slapped his woman's ass, as a kind of compensation for his lack of luck earlier that day. He kneaded her buttocks in his hands as if he was testing the quality of soil on his acres of land, feeling the texture of it and seeing positive signs that it was fertile. At least, he didn't have to take this woman to Back Road, and he knew exactly whether or not she was wearing underwear. She wasn't. Precious never wore underwear to bed. He slapped her ass. He parted her buttocks so he could see the flesh of her insides, and he could sniff her pussy.

"What a mood you in, though," teased Precious, pretending to push away his hand. "After yuh just waltzing in at this hour, coming to slap mi up!"

"Yuh is my woman. I can slap yuh backside when ah ready!"

"Where yuh been, though, Dezzie? Couldn't even call me or nothing!"

"I went to drop the Bossman girl up at Norbrook again."

"Yuh mean Dacres? When he become your bossman? Just because he charter yuh every now and then?" She hissed her teeth. "Bet yuh start to put lyrics to the man girlfriend. I know yuh, enuh Dezzie!"

"Me? Me, Precious?" he slipped his fingers between her legs, closing his eyes as he felt the warmth and moisture of her inner lips. "You know of me to put lyrics to anybody but you?"

She hissed her teeth again. "Bet yuh wish yuh had a brown skin girl like that, eh?"

"Who, me? Brown skin girl? No, sah. Not my type."

She rolled over and glared at him. "Suh, yuh wouldn't deal with her , then? That's what yuh saying, Dezzie?"

"No, sah. You know I love them jet black, just like you, Precious. The jet black one them, when yuh part them legs and the deep pink colour just hit yuh!" He parted her legs, and this time she let him do so freely. "Pretty pink, bwoy! Blouse and skirt! Pink with all that black round it."

"With your sweet mouth self," she pouted, playfully, adjusting her body so that he had full reign. "Think yuh sweet mouth going make me forget all my money that yuh been thiefing?"

"Cho. When I hit the big one, I going give yuh back all that money and more. I going buy the world for my woman. Yuh know that, Precious. Me and yuh coming from far far. First thing I going do, two ah we going cut ten like big shot on the North Coast. Poppy show!" They both burst out laughing.

"Promise is a comfort to a fool," said Precious, spreading her pink flesh apart so he could go deeper.

Chapter Five

It was not the first time that she had seen a dead man sprawled in the middle of the road. This one had some of his marrow oozing from the back of his head. It was not the first time that he was young. This one could not have been more than twenty-two. It was not the first time that she knew who he was, and had spoken to him just the day before. She was not shocked but still appalled. Recurrence could lessen the shock but no amount of times could make it less appalling. Every pixel of this scene had been here before, had carried this hue. The stalls knew. The shrieking faces knew. Even the asphalt knew. Death in this town was nothing new, whether at the hands of the law or the lawless.

Precious could feel the vibes as soon as the bus had pulled into the terminus Downtown. When you spent your days in a town such as Kingston, you trained yourself to feel the vibes, to duck even before the warning shot, since it may very well not come. For some reason, the driver had decided to use the almost defunct bus terminal close to the Coronation market, rather than let off at North Parade. The vibes had been strong. Death had soiled the air. The people had gathered around and Precious sensed the commotion before she actually stepped from the bus and saw it. Shetland's body had not yet been covered. He had been shot just moments earlier, though the sound of the shot itself had been somewhat indiscernible. He wore a white merino and blue jeans pants, and his hair had been done up into very neat corn rows, for which he had sat between the legs of his woman eating boiled green bananas and mackerel while she plaited, just that morning. The corn rows were shattered by the lone hole that had made quite a mess of the back of his head, one bullet being all that was required. He wore a gold earring in one ear, a wash-over chain that coiled around his neck with a pendant of a cross. A checkered navy blue handkerchief stuck out from his back pocket. A foot of his sneakers lay within three feet of him, the other fully laced and ready to walk on, but to where? No one knew for sure where young men like that went, after they were murdered. Some speculated that the fiery furnace was the only possible venue, they having been so blatantly rude. Some, more optimistic, suggested that a fervent prayer within the final split second of life may have wrestled the soul from damnation, thanks to the powers of the Great Negotiator, who was apt in those matters. Pray? But he didn't even know the bullet was coming. Took him absolutely by surprise, this one, this time. Young men never expect to die, no matter how many of their friends have died. Death is something the young will never fathom, particularly their own. No; he could not have prayed. There was therefore nothing to negotiate. But the fliers announcing his passing, and the obituaries that would be read in his honour, and the murals that would be painted along the walls in Denham Town, where Shetland lived, would without doubt, without doubt, proclaim him to be in Gloryland, among his cronies.

No one knew for sure whether the shot had been random or intentional. But by the sound of things, the voices emerging from the crowd that had started to throng the street, the police were at fault. Impromptu placards had already been hoisted, and justice was being demanded. The people alighting from the bus had to hop and swerve daintily to avoid stepping over the body. Someone called for a white sheet to cover it up. A white sheet! A white sheet! Don't you know, a white sheet must always be kept handy? Or even a ganzie, then. Put something over him, nuh! A ganzie, even if it's not white.

"Is what happen? Is weh him do?" Precious sought to procure answers from people who themselves didn't know but who were all too keen to speculate. On instinct, she tried to scan her own mind for clues, anything that he had done or said in the last day or two, or even longer, that could tie anything together and make sense of the senseless mass of blood on the pavement. She came up blank.

"Him nuh do nothing! Damn dog them kill the youth!"

"Them seh him have gun. Him neva have nuh gun! Ol' parasite them kill the innocent man!"

"Is jus a lickle weed the man guh buy! Him nuh do nobody nothing! Them plant gun pon him! Ol' wicked them!"

A police vehicle sped around the corner of the street and stopped beside the body. Two policemen alighted, heavily armed and scanning the environs, for the most part keeping a back-to-back posture. Another vehicle pulled up and two other men walked out, they too carefully scanning, but with less vigilance, since they had to hoist the body onto the gurney and place it into the van, amid the chaos.

"Alright. Break it up. Break it up," the lawmen were saying, their arms cradling their weapons, their eyes hidden behind shades, their hearts shielded by heavy vests.

"Murderer!" shouted one man, dashing back into the crowd. "Ol' murderer! Kill the youth over lickle weed?"

The policemen made as if to fire a warning shot, and the people scattered. He didn't bother. Perhaps, he hadn't intended to. Maybe he knew the threat would have been enough, the memory of other times when he had followed through in answer to them calling his bluff, sufficient to quell the riot in them, for now.

Luckily for Precious, she didn't have much by way of luggage; just two small travelling bags with clothes and some pairs of shoes. She warded off the loadermen who tried to pry her bags from her arm in offer of help. She did it instinctively, without malice, so used to them and not at all immune to the services they offered, when she felt she needed it. But they would have been somewhat of a hindrance on this morning, when she wanted a load to carry to console the survivor guilt that Shetland's death had plunged her into. She made her way quickly up Princess Street and on to North Parade, crossing over into Church Street and entering the arcade, where all was as she had left it the night before. Not that they hadn't heard or didn't care. No. They heard too loudly, too often, and cared too much for too long without reprieve, to let it ruin their day today. News did spread fast and one death had its power, but it could not dent their resolve. They knew better than to let it.

It was Saturday, the day when even the street mongrels had ample work. The higglers, handcartmen, peddlars, conartists of every variety thronged the streets and the corridors, lined the pavilions in front of stores, leaned against light posts and urged all who whizzed by to stop. Stop. Hear them out. Look at what they had to offer. Touch it. Try it on. Buy something. Anything. They scrutinized every face for susceptibility, and zeroed in like hawks without mercy. All they needed you to do was stop. Or if you didn't, they were more than willing to trail behind you for a few paces. A bit of mobile negotiation had sealed many a deal, with people eager to be rid of the nuisance.

Almost everyone else had already arrived and had mounted their wares in the arcade, from as early as four o'clock that morning. They had swept in front of their stalls and sprinkled water to wash away the bad spirits that had been set there by their neighbours and competitors. They had searched the crevices and corners of the stalls for even the faintest hint of white powder or the vaguest scent of oil, with a murmur of, "Get thee behind me, Satan," to play it safe, even if nothing was found to be out of whack. And, if anything suspicious had surfaced, a rendition of, "The blood is against yuh. The blood!" would do to delay the blow, till the matter could be properly rectified. All this was in keeping with the tradition and Precious had honed in on these rituals as part of learning the ropes. There were many who professed that they did not believe, but they did it anyway, just in case, since those who did believe had a certain power that came with just that. It was rudimentary knowledge that a higgler should sprinkle water in front of his or her stall, first thing in the morning. Wash away and rebuke the bad vibes, unset anything that had been set, cancel all that needed to be cancelled.

The soup vendors and lunch stall operators had already started to wash their pots and pans and to get the charcoal ready for the day's endeavor. These were huge cast iron "Dutch pots", forged out of scrap metal and indispensible to the trade, complete with heavy metal covers to seal in the goodness, and huge metal spoons to match. The cooks swore by these, and the customers attested to it. Things tasted better when cooked in a Dutch pot, especially over a wood fire. No one demanded, no one seemed to care, that these chefs procure food handlers permits. All that seemed to be required was a familiar scent whiffing across the arcade, even if the faces weren't all that familiar – they would be anyway, in time – it was absolutely crucial that the smell and the taste be recognizable. And so what, if one or two of them made it to the nightly news, accused of selling dogmeat patties and horse head soup. They were in the minority. It was well worth the risk, it seemed. These lunches were served on spot, along the sidewalks, the backdrop being the bustle and commotion of Downtown, Kingston, the stench of the gutters and overflowing garbage bins, overpowered by the subtle dance of thyme, scallion, scotch bonnet peppers, onions and curry powder. Indispensable. The delicate strangling the horrid. Amid the honking of bus horns, the fluctuating pitches of vigorous barter, the screech of car wheels as someone almost got hit, the guttural rein of expletives from the one who almost got hit, most likely a Kingstonian who fancied himself swifter than a four-wheeler and had just realized, reluctantly, that he was not.

The higglers were mostly done setting up, by this time. It was a tireless act of ingenuity, a daily remounting of hope against the odds. It was meticulous and painstaking and, one would think, very out of character. There were dapper pairs of blue, black or brown pants and men's coloured shorts hanging from parallel cords strung across the breadth of the booths; dress shirts, polo shirts, t-shirts and merinos, caps and belts and shoes for every outing you could fancy. Always in style; the "in-thing". "Ah dis a lick right now; ah dis a wear," they would assure their customers, "If yuh naw sport one ah dis yuh naw seh nutting!", meaning, buy one if you intend to get with the program.

Some specialized in men's wear or ladies' wear, or children's apparel, while some dabbled in every category, even branching into bags and gift items. Hardcore or nix-knacks. Whatever could be sold, was sold. Whatever was asked for, was available on the next trip. These higglers adhered to strict codes of supply and demand, of what was fashionable and could go fast. They were mainly sole proprietors who flew out to handpick the stock themselves, on one of the "small islands" if they didn't have a United States visa, or in Miami or New York if they did. Some had relatives who combed the sidewalks of Jamaica Avenue, in just the right season for particular bargains, and packed barrels upon barrels to be cleared at the wharf, or smuggled via customs on all manner of pretences. The vendors fancied themselves fashion savvy, conscious that their own proletariat tastes modeled that of their customers. They did not have the interest or the stupidity to delve into matters of eccentricity or uniqueness. Their stock was dictated by one thing only: the demand of the masses. Needless to say, this resulted in a monotony that could have been nauseating, had the masses not been so coordinated and conformant. But as it was, they didn't mind at all.

A vendor herself and well versed in routines and protocol, Precious had nonetheless been getting sluggish. It was not just her obesity. It was her spirit. She waddled and took her own sweet time to mount the displays, a ritual which in years gone by she had accomplished with much purpose and efficiency. Several times, the items of clothing slid from the hangers and had to be remounted, with a hiss and a threat, and sometimes she couldn't bother and just let them remain where they had fallen. It was

Dezzie that concerned her. Her future with Dezzie. Was there even one? Where were they headed? Where was her money going? He considered himself a working man and he was versed in arguments towards this end, so that she always gave in and agreed that, yes, he was in fact a working man, but always when she was alone she started to question the matter afresh. A working man, yes, but where was the money to show? He was always broke, always borrowing, always raiding her purse. There was always an excuse as to why he came up short, why she had to foot the bills, why she had to pay the school fees, why she had to carry him through to this month end, and the one after that, and the next. Always another excuse, another valid reason that justified the indefinite extension of her purse, though her gut cried foul and her higgler instinct wanted to scream, hell no! And then, the love. And then, the wounded face as he complained that his woman had hurt his pride, to even insinuate that he wasn't trying as hard as he could. Don't hit a man when he's down, was the permanent defense, which always left her just short of signing an affidavit of support.

Poochie-Lou, Brenda and Sweetie had long set up their stalls and were already in chill mode, eying Precious as she slugged from task to task. Actually, they were waiting on her to finish so they could get to the pressing matter of Rick's fate. Rick, of course, being their most recent tv crush, who had married into wealth and was a shameless gold-digger, but that didn't matter because he was so cute, as in, he had a sweet goatee and a six pack and he worked out! And he was really in love with Maria but she was poor and clingy and he couldn't be bothered with her because Laura could buy him the fancy suits and let him drive around in her Ferrari and go on trips to the French Riviera, wherever that was, but who cared, because he was so cute!

"Precious, yuh catch 'Santa Cruz' last night?" They were eager to delve into the daily suss.

"Hmm?" asked Precious, preoccupied. "What?"

"What yuh think going happen to Rick?"

"Oh. Couldn't bother watch it. Tired last night. Go straight to sleep."

The others sucked their teeth. "Is ol' woman yuh turning ol' woman, Precious? Eight o'clock a-night and yuh gone to bed! Poppy-show! Kiss mi neckback!"

"Is what yuh get, body-come-down? When since yuh too tired to watch 'Santa Cruz'?" This was followed by a ceremonial sucking of teeth, complete with cut-eyes, a vexed combo. They didn't mean anything by it. All this was routine, whenever they annoyed each other. And Precious had been annoying them lately.

"Send fifty dollar credit to mah phone, Precious. I pay yuh back later," said Poochie-Lou, while still keeping up the conversation with the other two and puffing at an emaciated ganja spliff. Precious hissed. Poochie-Lou always wanted her to send credit to her cell phone. Poochie-Lou spent hours talking on her phone, and always needed people to send her credit, which she felt no obligation to return. After all, what was phone credit among friends, who had each other's backs day in day out in the wicked arcades of Kingston, a creed reminiscent of the kind of loyalty rampant in the Brazilian favellas and the Mafia-infested streets of Sicily? What was phone credit, among women in a cutthroat male kingdom of threats and extortion? Poochie-Lou was known in these parts to be very versed at reading the digits from the back of call credit cards, freshly scraped and held in the palms of unsuspecting folks, and dialing them into her own phone faster than the person could type in the number onto their phone, thereby stealing their credit. She never owned up to it, but there was enough anecdotal evidence to have branded her. She was very much feared on account of this.

"Precious, yuh sending me the credit or not?" demanded Poochie-Lou. She had brought her son with her today, a twelve year old boy who missed more days of school than he actually attended, in any given term. He had a knack for his mother's line of work and, since his father was not around and hadn't been around for some time, the boy felt himself obligated to assume the role of part-time provider in the extended household, to which his mother did not object. Besides, he had very cunning ways of pulling people in for a sale. Never mind that he often got into fights with whomever. Poochie-Lou would rebuke him for it but it was a half-hearted reprimand; the kind of two-faced smirk that parents often wear when their child fights back, or even if he lands the first blow: annoyed at his defiance but relieved that he wasn't a wimp.

"Why yuh always begging credit? Yuh hustle just like me. Why yuh never have money to buy yuh own credit?" asked Precious, sourly. The others glared at her. It was not a typical response, albeit justified.

Brenda was sipping on some fevergrass tea that she had bought from the man out front, and munching on saltfish fritters. She was sitting on the edge of her stall, her bare legs swinging back and forth like a toddler in a pram. Her blonde lacefront wig had been sewn in so that the irritated scalp underneath could be discerned with minimal scrutiny, the skin of her face and neck bleached to a chrome in contrast with her melanated lips, ears and arms. She was multi-tasking, sipping tea while maintaining a brisk conversation with the other two and a bitter condescension of Precious, while scanning her produce and mentally checking if she had made the correct mark-ups, while all the time keeping an eye out for customers. The mark-ups weren't fixed, mind you. There was standard starting prices but really, every customer had their own price, depending on the assessment done as it regarded the capacity of their pockets, an assessment that was as accurate as it was immediate, and the prices adjusted accordingly. It was not just enough to break even. Profits had to be maximized. She knew who would squeal from a pinch and who would barely flinch from a punch. It all lay in that critical initial assessment. She wore a pair of Jet-Set sneakers, without any lace or socks; the in-thing.

Brenda was known as the warboat of this clan of four, the "skettel" decked in everything false – from hair to nails to eyelashes to her concept of reality. Always more likely to be a "matey" than a "wifey", not that she minded or saw anything disparaging in being "the other woman" to a string of beer-bellied middle-aged men with receding hairlines, who owned or managed businesses Downtown and sought her companionship after work. She referred to them as her "boops" or "sugar-daddies". She listened to them keenly and used any lapse in the conversation to tell them about her five children, for whom she was hustling so hard to send to school and keep a roof over their heads. Brenda was boisterous and uncouth, even when the situation didn't call for it. The situation usually didn't call for it, as in now, when she wanted Precious to weigh in on the gravity of Rick's fate.

"So, yuh think him gonna dump Laura and go back to Maria? Maria too boring, though. Can't stand girl who boring! Too deady-deady!"

Precious shrugged, absently hanging a blouse that had fallen.

"Laura is my girl! Not deady-deady at all!" shrieked Poochie-Lou. "Check har last week when she and Rick deh pon the boat! Chat 'bout!" she clapped her hands and slapped Brenda's lap, so that the fevergrass tea nearly spilled. Brenda hissed her teeth and pulled away the hand with the tea, then burst out laughing, too.

Sweetie, always the most subdued of the lot, sensing that Precious was not her regular self, decided to delve into more sober matters. "Ah can still get my partner draw next weekend, eh, Precious?"

"Hmm," Precious nodded, her mind far away. She was the banker for one of the tunteens that were operated among the vendors in the arcade. This particular one had started in February and had nine members. Precious, being banker, was entitled to first and last draw. The others, mainly women this time around but almost all the vendors were in one form of partner or another at different times, each got their draw at specified times agreed upon at the beginning. This partner would end in July and each draw was forty thousand dollars. Precious had barely been able to give Brenda her draw last week, and she had two hands in the partner. She had scraped and banded her belly just to come up with the money, relying on the others to throw their hand. She dared not tell them she kept dipping into the funds to lend money to Dezzie, who always needed something to offset some loan or bill or crisis or other. She regretted the day he had found out about the tunteen. She usually kept this sort of thing from him, but he had been nosy and had eavesdropped on her, splicing this and that the way he always did in matters pertaining to money. And then he discovered that she was the banker, and it was downhill from there. And these were not the type of women whom Precious wanted to get into entanglements with regarding money. The women themselves carried knives in their handbags or on their persons, the way other women carried feminine wipes and tampons. And if that failed, their men were never very far away, and carried knives of their own – or worse.

"Yeah, man. Friday. Friday," said Precious. She sat down and sulked.

Sweetie retreated into her own reverie as to the fate of the draw that she would get. It was already planned out. "It done already," the women would always laugh, regarding their draw, or any other income, from stall sales to spousal support to child support for their children to side earnings, courtesy of the sugar daddies, even the Lot-a-Luck that they were each sure to win. "It done already. Don't even get it yet and it done already."

Sweetie had paid down on a two-door refrigerator with water dispenser and stainless steel finish. One hundred and twenty-three thousand dollars. Brand new, state of the art. "But that could buy heaven and get back change!" her mother had said. Sweetie had hissed. The old woman didn't understand modern-day life. The refrigerator was huge and was sure to cramp the space in the small kitchen, but they could always keep it in the living room. In fact, that was the plan. Keep it in the living room, where Danny could see it when he passed through to look for the boys, so he could see that she wasn't suffering without him and that her house could look stoosh, ghetto or no ghetto. Come Friday, she would run over to Big Dee's and pay off the balance on the fridge. Or, better yet, she could pay twenty on the fridge and pay down on one of the thirty-inch flat-screen television sets, and finish off with the fridge in three weeks when she got her other partner draw, from Debbie, who sold sandals over by the far corner of the arcade. They would probably deliver the fridge the same day, or maybe Saturday, just in time for Danny. Maybe they would be unloading the television set just as Danny turned the corner, with his two long hands and deadbeat self! Her mind was racing, weighing the possibilities. She did not for a minute consider that Precious may not have the money. Precious was always on time with the payments, unlike some of the other bankers, who stalled and gave cock and bull stories and, worse yet, ran off with the entire pool of funds. Precious was known to be reliable and upfront.

By around eight o'clock that morning, the arcade was teeming with shoppers browsing and negotiating, their handbags clutched under their armpits, and the space between the stalls narrowed so that squeezing past the hindquarters of the customers became a matter of life and death, attempted only if absolutely necessary. Most of the customers had recently arrived into town and had not heard about shooting earlier. Those who knew about it had not forgotten, but had tucked it to the side to make room for life. This they had to do; had done for years.

The four higglers withdrew more and more into the focus of their enterprise, each aware of the others, of course, but only having time to converse if someone couldn't make change or if someone needed an eye to be cast on her stall while she ran to the bathroom. Many times, Precious went an entire day without using the bathroom, so engrossed she was in getting the merchandise off her hands. Then, she wouldn't remember until she was in the bus heading home or, when her car was working, when she was on the toll road with nowhere to stop for a pee. Using the communal bathroom at the arcade had been a peeve for her at first, but now it was not so much of a biggy. It was something she came to accept as a crippage of where she worked and the sort of people she had in her sphere. She carried her own toilet paper to keep from having to pay ten dollars for four squares. She spread some on the seat and still hoisted herself well out of harm's way, always conscious of being as expedient as possible so as to get back to her stall.

The loose change from the sales she kept in her pockets. Occasionally, she would go through and remove the larger notes, fold them and tuck them into her bosom. Once in a while, things would get so hectic that she didn't have hands to sell. At other times, there was a trickle of customers, some of whom would not part with their cash unless the vendors resorted to the kind of strategy that was just short of groveling. All kinds of days. But there were rules regardless. And one rule was, remove the larger notes and tuck them safely away. Another rule, trust no one – not even the four women whose stalls were juxtaposed to yours, who cut their ten and blabbered about soap operas and silly dance moves, and encouraged you to watch your back cause they'd heard some things, and assured you that they had yours, and asked you if you'd heard things. Never, never admit to having heard anything, even the talk that Shetland had been set up by Stephanie's man, Lloyd – Stephanie, the resident hairdresser who would give perms and washes and braids on spot, at half the salon price, since she had obtained the products free of cost, from her man, who routinely stole them. He, in turn, collected protection money from the vendors, on behalf of Mongrel, the area don. All this was known to everyone, and was spoken of by no one, except in the strictest confidence and in the lowest tones.

Bam had heard the news about the Downtown shooting, after she returned from her lunch break that day. It had been, of course, an internet frenzy and eyewitnesses had even posted gruesome photos of Shetland's body, from varying angles for good measure, before the police had descended and closed off the scene. There was the usual outcry and demand for justice, the buzzword which not even the masses seemed to know what it meant, and the perpetrators certainly didn't care what it meant; but both sides cast the word back and forth in the riveting dandy shandy of the nightly news. Bam had immediately thought of Precious and, by natural extension, Dezzie, whom she could not reach by phone all afternoon. So she had called Precious and found out that her daughter-in-law was, for the time being, safe.

"Watch out for later. I hear they planning a demonstration," Bam had cautioned. "Maybe even a roadblock. Travel by Half-Way-Tree side when yuh coming home, if anything, just to play it safe."

Precious would do no such thing; both she and Bam knew. A demonstration Downtown was not a thing to avoid, not if you sold in the arcade and not if you knew the young man whose death was at the heart of it, and not if you knew most if not all of the people who would most likely be holding up the placards and pieces of cardboard, and screaming at the top of their lungs. One did not sell Downtown if one was of the sort who instinctively avoided danger, even if one never went out of the way to seek out danger.

"'Member, yuh have a man and two pickney. Try come home safe," Bam had said, before pressing the red button on her cell phone and returning it discretely to her handbag. She was not allowed to make out calls during the day. Not that she would have gotten into direct trouble, but the practice was frowned upon. A security guard, especially, had to give the least suspicion of being distracted. She knew she wasn't a real security guard. Her son always joked about it but she internalized it as a serious infraction, on her own part. A private joke on the part of her employer? She hoped not. They treated her with enough sagacity. True, there was another security guard posted at the front gate, who subjected the customers to another round of checks. Bam was never sure whose checks were the more crucial – his or hers. She sat by the door of the hardware store and looked through the bags to make sure that the items listed on the receipt were the very ones being carried out – a task which was not only tedious but proved somewhat of a redundancy, seeing as the checking counter was a mere ten feet away, with no aisle between there and the door and hence only a minute possibility for theft from there on out. Most times, Bam only pretended to do a thorough check. She mainly did a cursory scan of the interior of the bags, stamped the receipts and made a mark at the bottom with a red marker, smiled and wished the customers a pleasant day. They were, overwhelmingly, decent citizens who didn't mind paying for what they left with. Once in a while, the metal detector would beep or the scanner would indicate that something was amiss. The customer would be stopped, kindly of course, since it was usually a false alarm, and then Bam would apologize, on behalf of the store, and curse the malfunctioning contraption.

There were thieves, to be sure, maybe one or two each day; some days none for a stretch, some days too many at once. Like at Christmas time. But the average day found her sitting behind the desk, in the endless drone of searching bags and stamping receipts, the roguish hope that the alarm would at least go off, to temper her boredom, but it hardly ever did. Tedium. Well, so it seemed to Bam, in the monotony of stamping, pretending to check, stamping, wishing them a blessed day. Sometimes, she did wish that a thief would turn up, just to create a ripple in the lake of mundanity. When they did turn up, and the loot snatched from their bags or bodies, Bam and the manager would both put on self-righteous smirks and, for the moment, pretend that they had never taken anything that did not belong to them, in their entire lives. The manager would summon the police, who also would arrive in an official flourish of self-righteous smirks, and Bam would feel vindicated that her post was not redundant and her forty hours were good for something.

During her lunch break, she could stretch her legs and go around the back where the warehouse was. It was not the ideal place in which to eat, with the sawdust and cement, the air heavy with the smell of paint, grease and lacquer, the bare floor crunchy with the fragments of wood chips and broken ceramic tiles. But it was the superb spot to sit and watch the young men packing and lifting, their clothes stained with all manner of fluids, natural and unnatural, their beards, moustaches and gloves covered with thinset and cement dust. They were feisty and unruly, maintaining the slimmest protocol to keep from being fired. They laughed at each other's expense, pretended to be offended, rallied back with offenses of their own; but they could take it. They wore hard hats and back braces, gloves and rubber boots, prerequisites of the trade. They stepped with tired gaits and complained each time they were given a task, but Bam swore that she could see the imprint of their muscles just under their khaki shirts, the bulge in their thighs and arms that laboring men almost always had. Her admiration of them was private. They were of the type that would have pursued the matter to the fullest extent, had they the slightest hint of her obsession. But to them, she was the kind-hearted but vaguely grumpy middle-aged lady who wore the uniform of a security officer but who could not chase after a mongrel dog that snatched a chicken drumstick from her boxed lunch. Bam watched them, yearned for them even, laughed at their burly jokes and even teased them when she was in the mood; but it never went beyond that.

These young men were decidedly strong. They spent the day lifting, bending, holding, hammering, maneuvering the forklift through the narrow lanes of the warehouse, that were stacked twenty feet high with lumber, cement, tiles, blocks and miscellany. They thrived on the work, though you would never guess by their complaints. All throughout the municipality, there were dream houses being erected at fever-pitch, two-storey mansions the likes of which could once only be found in the posh communities of Kingston and St. Andrew, perhaps the North Coast too, but now the working class were at their heels and the hardware stores that plopped like mushrooms after rain, were the prime facilitators of this. The customers would line up with their receipts and wait for the men to source the desired goods, check them for faults and pack them into delivery vans or cars. Quite often, the items on display were out-of-stock and could not be sourced in the warehouse, a truth which was discovered only after the men had performed a vigorous and grump-infested search. The expletives would follow, under their breaths, and the customers would rage and march off back to the front showroom, to lodge their complaints.

"Put the damn thing-dem on display and know they not 'round here! But why they bother have all these damn computers, though? Don't they check to see if the stuff available before the cash them?"

But a well-stocked display case was sometimes more alluring than a well-stocked warehouse. The customer could always be consoled by promises, once his money was already in the system. The hardware stores did their best to keep up with the frenzied pace of housing construction throughout the schemes. It was only this very schematic layout of the Portmore communities that put any kind of cap and girth on the housing expansions. The rising cost of materials and delivery seemed somehow not to be a hindrance. Not yet, at least.

This afternoon, the young men were debating the situation of the Downtown shooting, each claiming to have some kind of inside information on the matter or, at least, clearer insight than the rest. They could vaguely imagine themselves in his place, since there had been many shootings in Portmore in recent times, but their cognitive dissonance afforded them the role of third person narrators as they bore witness to an event that happened miles away. Each claimed to know why, who and how, from the safe distance of the gated hardware premises.

"Big riot start! Suh mi sister seh!" declared one.

"Pure shot a-go buss tonight! Hear mi seh? Pure shot!" predicted another. "When Mongrel and his man-dem ready tonight, watch out! Babylon better run! Hear mi?"

It made Bam cringe and she hoped that Precious would for once follow her advice and go to Half Way Tree, though it was the longer way home and the traffic congestion would take a chunk out of her time and her nerves.

The commotion could be heard all the way from Parade. People thronged the sides of orange Street and Princess Street, but most were gathered by terminal, where the shooting had taken place. Five patrol cars were parked along the side of the old arcade, and countless police officers were posted at various points. The people were demanding justice.

"Damn Babylon Boops!" some were shouting. "These police not for the people at all! Babylon Boops dem!"

They had lit a fire from old car tires and debris, but this had been quickly put out by the Fire Department and now it only smoldered. The smoke, however, was still enough of a bother for the people to feel pleased. They wanted justice. They had sheets of cardboard to this effect, and their hoarse voices too echoed this sentiment. It was a generic proletariat sentiment, and Precious suspected that most of the people gathered had no clue what had happened, or why. They were bandwaggonists, who thrived on being so compliant with the shouts of the rabble-rousers that they were almost faceless and nameless. By nightfall, curfews would be declared in their respective garrisons and they would have a helluva time getting in or getting back out. For the moment, though, the sweet thrill of being a part of a monster that was, if not terrifying, at least huge. Into this seething mass she threw herself, carried by the tide of their shouts and their upward pounding fists, their bland demands that would never be met, not only for the reason that they were bland but because so too were the consciences of the powers that be. The people's amnesia of the demonstrations that had been mounted before, the impotence of the efforts, spurred them on and gave them fresh hope, regardless. At least two television vans were on scene and countless press reporters covering the proceedings. They would dash through the side roads of the city to avoid the traffic, towards their headquarters, in time to make the seven o'clock news, where the Superintendent of Police would emphatically belch into the microphone,

"Let me state categorically that this young man was not shot by the police. He is a known criminal who was killed, either by his cronies or by gang fire. We are urging anyone who witnessed this incident or anyone who has information that could lead to the arrest of the perpetrators, to come forward."

Chapter Six

The garbagemen had mixed feelings about the way people looked at them, frowned at them, despised them. Most times, it gave them a feeling of inferiority. It made them feel untouchable, in the crudest sense: not "untouchable", as in, so high as to be out of reach of the common man; but "untouchable", as in, so low that no one in their right mind would want to touch, let alone cohabit with. Yet, these men – and they were always men – had families and homes that were kept clean for them, children who pined after them, women who sat at windows watching with their chins propped up on their palms, hoping the dinner wouldn't get too cold before the man of the house arrived. They were human beings.

These men did not want their children to grow up to be like them. Their job was something worthy that needed to be done and they, by the wickedest decree of fate, had woke up one day and found themselves doing it. It was not information they willingly gave out to people who didn't absolutely need to know. The stench of the trade was something not easily washed off, not even with loofah and carbolic soap, which couldn't penetrate to the spirit, where it was most needed. The stench stayed with them, mainly in their heads, clinging to the hairs inside their nostrils, even while they locked limbs with their women at night and compensated with a gentle touch and a firm grip on her pleasure. Compensated, because a garbageman feels like no man, sometimes.

But there were other times, and other feelings. Sometimes, they felt like kings who could withstand any plague, any pestilence that threatened their kingdom. When all around them people were dropping like flies and drooping like withered pansies, laid up in bed and scouting for all manner of remedies, the garbagemen surveyed the scene from the lofty rails of their trucks and they felt vindicated. They hardly ever got sick. They were hardy and resilient, shrugging off colds and fevers with the same indifference that they shook off the giant maggots that crawled onto their waterboots and up the legs of their trousers. Shook them off, and crushed them without a flinch.

The residents who carried bags and boxes to the truck placed them well away and dared not hand them directly to the men, lest they come into direct contact with the filthy gloves. No amount of disinfectant could reprieve the contamination, they were certain. Where and when did these men eat? Where and when did they use the loo? Did they even eat and use the loo, was the question, which most did not even bother to ask. They assumed, these men either didn't have such needs, or took care of those needs in ways that were suspect and taboo.

Ras Negus was perched on the rails in the middle area of the truck. It was Monday so they were doing the rounds in Sector Two East, not that this was a strict routine but it was likely that, on a Monday, this was where the truck would be. Force of habit and instinct made him hold tightly to the frame and he would not have fallen even with a sudden jolt of the truck, but his mind was temporarily removed from where his body was. In the short lapse between pickups, as the truck turned the corner before stopping again, he was thinking about Naph-T and the fact that she was pregnant again. She had gone to the clinic and they had confirmed that she was two months along. He was happy and he was worried. He was proud and he felt a bit embarrassed. Nowhere in his mind was there space for the notion that a child of his loins could ever be an accident or a mistake or a burden or a hindrance. Such thoughts he rebuked in others and did not entertain in himself. Yet, he had hoped that by now he would have been in a better position to provide for his family, so that his woman could feel more confident and less apprehensive as she rubbed her belly and felt, or imagined, a sweet fluttering of arms and legs.

The truck pulled into 53 Place and reversed down the stretch past four walkways running both left and right of the Place. The piles of rubbish had completely covered the "no dumping" signs at almost every post, a blatant disregard of the Municipal order and, too, a response that said they had no choice, kicking the ball back into the field of the Local Government office. If you want no dumping, then let there be fixed pickup days and no delays. The residents could not be expected to comply without the cooperation of the Solid Waste office. "Two wrongs don't make one right," the people were told. "Well, two rights would do us just fine!" they responded.

The truck came to a halt and the five rubbishmen descended on cue, heading in various directions to grab the bags and boxes and throw them into the chute, after which they would be channeled into a compacting area to make room for new loads. The bins were emptied and replaced, to be retrieved by the residents who had placed them along the banks of the road. As formidable as the truck was, there were items that could not be processed. The residents failed to understand this. They threw out everything that was no longer of use to them, regardless of size or component, regardless of warning labels that cautioned against random disposal. They took it for granted that whatever was worthy of use in their abode would be worthy of the truck. Still, the acceptance or refusal of any item was at the discretion of the rubbishmen and they took something of a pride in this. Many times they left things exactly where they had found them, to the chagrin of the residents. It was an empowering feeling, to be able to reject something, in this line of work. It was not often, but often enough.

Two huge black garbage bags stood on the bridge at Forty-six way like sentinels. Clearly, someone had left them to be picked up. The fact that there was a small basin with laundry detergent and bleach sitting next to the bags was seen as a mere coincidence and Ras Negus did not for once consider the fact that these bags may not have been filled with refuse, but with dirty clothes headed for the laundromat. In his habit of grabbing and tossing anything in a rubbish bag, and in his absent-mindedness regarding the news of the expansion of his family, he hoisted the bags into the chute and immediately sent them into the compactor, before it even registered in his ears that someone was shouting to him.

"No! No!" the woman screamed. "Is not rubbish! Is clothes! Is not rubbish!"

"Who? What?" said one of the men, confused.

"The bag-them! The bag-them that the Ras just take up! Is not rubbish! Is clothes!"

And just then, the taxi pulled into the Place, the taxi that would have taken her to the laundromat.

"Idiot! Don't yuh did see the soap and the bleach? Who put out garbage with soap and bleach?" the woman cursed. "Open the truck back. I want my clothes!"

One man rushed to stop the chute.

"What? What she seh?" asked another, holding a bag from which something putrid was leaking onto the asphalt, making the woman cringe even more.

"My expensive clothes-them! Who the hell tell yuh to pick up my bag with my expensive clothes-them? I want back my clothes!"

"Lady, them-clothes deh can't get back. They already press in with everything else. Gone into the compactor already. Lest yuh want to come to the dump and sort through for them."

"But kiss mi blasted neck! But what this man telling me, that I can't get back my expensive clothes, and I didn't ask yuh to take them up? Two bag full of clothes, some brand new! What yuh telling me, though? Why would I put out garbage bags with soap and bleach?"

"Lady, if yuh want to come to the dump, come to the dump," said the driver. "Today is rubbish day. People put out bags. We collect bags, put them in the chute. Everybody know that's how it guh. Your bad luck today, lady. Is a innocent mistake. Can't blame rubbishman to take up rubbish bag."

"My bad luck? My bad luck? Guh show yuh bad luck!" she charged at the men and the taxi driver intercepted, holding her at bay.

"Is not our fault, Lady. Just misunderstanding," said Ras Negus, trying to quell her and feeling guilty nonetheless, even though it was indeed a misunderstanding. That someone could mistake something valuable for something useless; it could happen. Happened every day. The clothes had been packed in garbage bags, for one. Had they been in laundry hampers, that would have been different. As to the soap and bleach, there was nothing that people wouldn't throw away. Ras Negus had ceased to be surprised at the perfectly good things that were tossed away. It was just one of those things.

"Open the damn truck and let me look for my clothes!"

"Lady, it don't work like that. Everything compressed. We can't open it from here. If yuh want, yuh can come to the dump."

The woman sat on the concrete bridge and started to cry. The taxi driver tried to comfort her. "Know how many pairs of name-brand pants?" she asked no one in particular. "Eh? Buy them just the other day when I went off the island. Just the other day. My husband gonna kill me. All him work shirt-them, him blazers, and my going-out dresses, and the children's dress clothes. Good thing is not a weekend. All-them school uniforms and my work suits would be gone!" She held her forehead. The truck engine started again. "Suh, yuh really gonna drive away wid my clothes-them?"

"Lady, nothing we can do," they sighed. She shook her head. The truck drove off. They had had to leave a whole stream of garbage along two pathways and they would surely have to return some other day, hopefully tomorrow, but then that would mean that the pickup in some other area would be hindered. Still, better that than overload the truck till it broke down, because then no one could say when it would be repaired.

Ras Negus resumed his post and this time he had a clear head, sobered by the loss that would be somebody else's gain, but still a loss to that particular woman. As soon as the trucks emptied their bellies of the putrid loot, the human scavengers would descend and pick from the rubble what was their subsistence. Maybe, he should have promised the lady that he would keep an eye out for the bags, which he had intended to do but he didn't like making promises that he wasn't sure he could deliver on. Even so, he wasn't sure if she would still want the clothes; that kinda lady, he figured, would sooner call it a loss than try to retrieve something that had entered the Riverton Dump.

"Guess yuh don't bother want the charter, eh, Miss Carol?" asked Dezzie. He was edgy because now it would look bad that he was still going to ask that she pay him. "Ah could drop yuh over to Riverton if yuh want. Wi can just lay wait them and trail the truck and see what we can salvage." He was trying to work it so that the trip was not in vain and something would come of his time and gas.

"Me? Trail rubbish truck to Riverton? But what I look like?" she asked, with the severest offense in her eyes. She hissed her teeth. "How much for the one-way to come here?" she asked, knowing him well enough to guess that he was fishing for payment.

"Miss Carol, man. Ah won't kill yuh, under the circumstances. You is my customer for years. Just give mi back the gas money and we cool." He chuckled.

"How much?" she asked, peeved.

"Two hundred and we cool," he said. "Should be three hundred, still, but as it's you, Miss Carol. Ah know yuh always look out for my taxi."

He collected the money and drove off. The woman went into her yard and closed the grille behind her, then came back out because her neighbours were calling, wanting the lowdown on what the commotion had been about.

Dezzie pulled into the shopping centre. He had the money that he had just gotten from Carol, and he had seven hundred dollars that he had rescued from a compartment in the refrigerator. Precious had taken to hiding money in the kitchen, thinking that his ravenous quest for food would somehow defer the smell of the money. No such luck. The smell of the money in the fridge had been so strong that it had hit him as soon as he had opened the fridge door and, though the bulb had blown, Dezzie had zeroed in on the location before anyone could say, "who that?" This smell was awful in a regal way, not like stale sweat or rotten meat or milk that had passed its expiry date. It was the way a lion would smell, or a dragon would smell; awful and powerful, bearable because of the power, so addictive that it urged you to enter the cage and dance with death. The money had been wrapped in foil paper and tied in a transparent plastic bag, and wedged between the carrots and the cucumbers.

Dezzie knew exactly which numbers he would buy today, for the Easy-Win as well as for the big one. Bam had awoken last night, screaming and holding her ears. In fact, she had fallen from the bed in her mayhem. It was soon discovered that something was crawling inside her ear canal, a matter which she didn't handle with much composure, not with his consoling and certainly not with his cursing. He did both, as usual.

"Pour some candle wax into the ear," Precious had suggested. She figured it would hurt somewhat but then, perhaps it was time Bam felt some pain for all the emotional trauma she had caused her daughter-in-law over the years. As soon as Precious had determined that the matter was not life-threatening, the house was not on fire and no one had broken in, she had resolved to go back to sleep by any means and satisfied herself that Dezzie would take care of the matter. It was, after all, his mother who had the bug in her ear. Precious knew that her own mother would never subject her to that level of drama. Bam was stomping her feet and tapping the side of her head, hoping the bug would fall out. From Bam's own account, the insect seemed to have taken the taps as encouragement to burrow deeper. She was terrified of creepy-crawlies, never mind that she was a country girl from the hills of St. Ann, who spent the days chasing croaking lizards up into mango trees. That was then. Now, some six-legged critter was burrowing into her ear, probably nibbling at her eardrum for all she knew, and her son was standing there shouting at her, and her daughter-in-law had gone back to bed. That was what a body got for pushing children into the world.

After much turmoil, the bug had decided to come out the way it had gone in, making it on its own halfway and then scooped out by Dezzie with a cotton swab for the remainder of the journey, its legs and antennae covered in wax and its large eyes beaming with adventure.

"Peenie-wally," muttered Dezzie, referring to the firefly on the swab. Then, it hit him. Peenie-wally. Number fifty-eight. The man would certainly play number fifty-eight today! These sorts of things did not happen just so. For Dezzie and so many like him, life depended on the grace of God, the luck of the draw and the guts of the gamble. Dreams, visions, incidents, anything that happened out of the blue, had meaning firmly established in the system of numerology. They, of course, didn't call it that. They instinctively knew it to be so and they had seen proof of it, time and time again. The fact that they had also seen proof to the contrary was not enough to dissuade them against breaking their necks to catch the tickets before the drawing, and stopping random people along their way to find out what The Man had played that day. There were three minor plays during the day that they could catch, but always they reserved their biggest bet and their most lucid visions for the big one, the Lot-a-Luck. This was the one that had the ability to propel anyone who won it out of poverty for good. For good good good, never looking back. They stopped whatever they were doing or saying and cocked their ears especially keenly when this drawing was being announced, and hung in suspended animation until all the numbers were called. Then, they railed in misery about how they had just missed it by this number or that, or how they had followed the foolish advice of friends or family and had picked this number or that, when the dream had clearly specified the other. And they could kick themselves in the head for not having followed their minds. Yet, they thanked the grace of the Almighty that there was such a thing in this life as another chance.

Dezzie felt the surety of the win coursing through him. He had never felt so sure in all his years of buying tickets, even placing bets at Caymanas Park, where his brother, Seymour, worked as a jockey and often gave him little tips straight from the lips of the prime stallions themselves. Not even then had he felt as certain as he did, that today would be the day and this ticket would be the ticket.

He walked past the supermarket, where Otis was seated on the ground outside the door, with his outstretched hand bearing the sign, "I'm blind and hungry. Please and thanks," and his raspy voice reiterating this.

Dezzie waited his turn in the line, patiently, which was enough to make Cherry regard him with suspicion. When he did get up to the counter, he spoke with the calm confidence of an English gentleman placing his bet on a thoroughbred that everyone knew could not lose. He knew peenie-wally was fifty-eight. He bought that number for all the other three plays. The big one needed seven digits. Dezzie reasoned that he should start with fifty-eight, out of respect for the hardly little firefly. He added six for the number of legs, two for the number of wings, one for the cotton swab and ended with number fourteen, for candle wax. He had worked it out in his head before leaving home and he had even written it on paper, which he handed to Cherry.

"Put this on the big one," he announced. "Tell Mr. Man this is the last he will be hearing from me – except when I come back to collect my millions."

Cherry shook her head, rolled her eyes to the sky, put his money in the till and handed him his ticket. It would suit Dezzie better to break into the bank one starry night and load all his pockets with cash, than to sit around waiting to win the big one. He didn't even win as many of the little ones to justify all the cash he had exchanged for the chances. But she couldn't tell him that. Her boss had decided to do a spot check on the outlet. He was in the background, busying himself with particulars of the operation, making sure that all was as it should be. On mornings like these, none of the shenanigans of other times came into play, not from the vendors and certainly not from Cherry, who was as meek as a calf munching alfalfa on a warm summer day.

"Hey, Missa Chin! Make sure get my big bundle ready fuh me, hear?"

Michael Chang glanced up and peered through the glass window, which was tinted and only had two small openings near the bottom and the middle. He could make out the face and saw that it was that of a man, but he didn't recognize the face or the voice, and Michael Chang made no effort to do so. He knew that the words had been directed at him. "Missa Chin" was what he and almost everyone who looked like him were called. It was a generic name branded on all men of Chinese descent, their female counterparts being, of course, "Miss Chin". No one had bothered to find out his real name and it didn't seem that it would have mattered, either way. What did they know about him or understood about him, and what did he know or understand about them? They had only assumptions about each other, assumptions which were so embedded in the psyche of each that none was willing to concede. They coexisted in a world where none seemed to be able to fathom the other, except that each possessed something that the other desperately needed: one, the chance to cast their luck asunder and reel it back in big time; the other, the chance to collect the pool of these castings without interference, and return a trifling by way of token. Being told to get a bundle of money ready for an unfamiliar face at the other end of the glass window, in the mind of Michael Chang, constituted interference, enough to make him place his fingers cautiously over the handle of the licensed firearm in his waist.

"Ah coming to pick it up tomorrow, hear?" shouted Dezzie. Cherry tried to shoo him off by calling the next customer. "Hey, Cherry, tell yuh bossman to line up my things. Coming for it tomorrow, soon as the numbers call!" He was becoming so boisterous that it was almost out of character, even for Dezzie.

Michael Chang did not take his eyes from the glass divider until the man outside had removed himself from view, and even then, the Manager waited a good while before leaving. He made sure to secure the documents he had come to collect, and clutched them closely to him. It was uncommon for customers to address him directly. It was not uncommon for them to make reference to him, however, as if he wasn't there, or as if he was a statue that represented something only vaguely familiar to them; familiar in that it was generally agreed upon as being alien. Michael Chang did not concern himself too much with what the customers thought of him. He enjoyed the sweet soft feel of the bills in his hand, the gentle slide of the tickets as they were propelled through the slots. He loved how the numbers balanced themselves out at the bottom of the sheets. That was his job and with that alone did he concern himself, in this place.

Dezzie pocketed the tickets. He was in good spirits. As soon as he entered the taxi, he glanced over at the passenger seat and found that a cellular phone was wedged between the seat and the gearstick. This was a common find. Cellular phones were always falling out of bags and pockets, sometimes even out of hands. Many people traveled with two cellular phones, from different providers, and the distraction with one was often so great that they lost track of the other. Most times, he would discover the phones when he heard the strange electronic jingle that he knew was not coming from his phone, though he changed the ringtone often enough. This one was a name-brand smart phone with all the amenities. It was locked, but he knew enough about phones to see that this one had set back the owner several thousand dollars. Forty thousand, at least, he figured. It was well cared for and in great condition. No scrapes from keys or coins. Not an iota of dust on the keypad. He could easily sell this one for fifteen, maybe even twenty or thirty thousand, to the right buyer. It was how he made a little extra money at times, when Precious was playing stingy.

Whenever he found phones, he kept them. He could sell them at a good price, depending on the condition, or give them to school girls as gifts that could provide crucial leverage for negotiations, or he could give them to Precious or to one of his relatives. Today, he was actually in the mood to return the phone, which was what many taximen routinely did, as long as they didn't have to go too far out of their way. He tried to remember who had been the last few passengers to sit in the front passenger's seat. It hadn't been anyone whom he knew personally, or even a regular customer. Since he only allowed females in the front passenger seat, he did recall that he had picked up some hot chicks since that morning. It couldn't have been Carol's phone. She always sat in the back seat, even if she was the only passenger in the taxi. Some people were like that. He supposed it gave them the sense of being chauffeur-driven, a kind of aristocratic delusion, as opposed to the common front seat. Or maybe they dreaded head-on collisions that would maim them for life and disfigure their facial features, since the front passenger almost always came in for a banging. But this was only one line of thought. There were others who put premium value on the front seat and liked to think that they had the "front appearance" to justify their frantic dash for it. There had been a few chicks who had had front appearance that very morning. Indeed.

Dezzie waited anxiously for the phone to ring. Maybe he could line up a date with her in exchange for his kindness in returning the phone. She may not have realized yet that the phone was missing, but she would. Dezzie sped through two red lights, for no other reason than to test his driving skills. Three passengers had entered the car by then and they were complaining about his recklessness. He overtook a long line of traffic on the road leading into Naggo Head, squeezing back into the lane just as he screeched through the roundabout. He saved himself exactly three seconds by driving through the shopping centre at Port Henderson and dilly-dallying across the gravel road, just to avoid the traffic that had built up, only to find that he was still stuck because an accident was up ahead. The passengers were swearing and threatening, and Dezzie was trying to explain to them that they didn't understand the art of driving. In driving, judgment was the key. One thing he had was judgment. The passengers begged to differ.

"Judgment my backfoot? Judgment, and run through two stop light, like yuh neva see the policeman at the corner?" asked an elderly man from the backseat behind Dezzie.

"Policeman?" sneered Dezzie. He sucked his teeth scornfully. "Policeman? Cho. That's my brethren. Him cool, man. Sometimes yuh have to take chance to beat the traffic."

"Take chance with yuh own life, when yuh alone in here!" argued an overweight woman.

Had Dezzie never been sure of winning the Lot-a-Luck that day, and had he not been saving his energy for the celebrations that would follow, he would have answered her properly. But he only glanced back at her and shook his head. These people did not understand the innate need for speed that flowed through the body of a red-blooded male. Dezzie had read stories of big-shot young fellows who raced their fast cars down Old Hope Road, the stretch of road from Papine to Liguanea, continuing on to Half Way Tree, in the middle of the night when the scaredy-cats were asleep. Now, that sort of thing was just up his alley. Dover, even better. He had always wanted to go race at Dover raceway, in St. Ann. Portmore didn't have the type or length of tracks that could quench his thirst for speed. Portmore couldn't hold him; which was another reason why he needed to win theLot-a-Luck, buy himself a fast car so he could race down Old Hope Road with the rich guys. He saw another taxi up ahead, heading towards a bus stop that was full of people. Dezzie sped up and overtook a line of traffic, again branching off into the shopping centre, to no avail.

"Leave me right here, driver! Right here, before yuh kill me!"
Dezzie refused to stop.

"Don't yuh see the accident up top? All the vehicles coming

down blinking their lights, don't yuh see?" asked the old man. "Is another one yuh want to cause? Why yuh brucking yuh neck and yuh can only pick up one other passenger?"

It was true, after all, but it was just in his blood. The rush of driving, the thrill of beating another taximan to a bus stop full of passengers – even if you could only take one more. Sometimes, though, he could squeeze them in if they were pliable, if they weren't too fluffy or had too many bags, if they didn't have any children with them. He could ask them to small up themselves and get four or five onto the back seat, easy. Especially if the coast was clear. The diversion had taken him closer to the scene of the traffic accident and Dezzie saw that an SUV had run into the back of a route bus.

"But how him manage that, though?" Dezzie asked himself. He, like every driver, fancied himself an expert, and cursed every other motorist. The road was their world and they each liked to think that they had mastered it. Chasing each other along the route and trying to outsmart each other by stealing passengers was their recreation. "Damn fool! But how him manage that? Really and truly!" He hissed his teeth and pitied the simplicity of the idiot who hadn't seen that he should not have made such a turn. The SUV was clearly at fault. He shook his head. Blasted idiot!

The woman seized the opportunity to exit the taxi, though she hadn't reached her stop. She handed Dezzie a one thousand dollar bill. Again, the poverty-stricken Dezzie would have used the situation to cast some expletives into the ether, asking if he was a bank or something, and why was it that people didn't come into his taxi with change, or at least tell him early on so he could stop by the gas station and make change. However, since the sign of the peenie-wally in his mother's ears was as unmistakable as day, and since he would surely be giving back this old broken down jalopy as soon as his winnings were declared, he decided to bide his time and bite his tongue, till such time. He mustered up some change and handed it to the woman, who wobbled off to catch another, safer, cab.

Dezzie collected the rest of the fares while driving towards Bridgeport, just to make sure no one else had any stunts up their sleeves. Someone asked for a turnoff into the scheme at Bridgeport and, just as he was about to turn, Dezzie glimpsed Shelly standing at the bus stop, with her big hips wrestling with the tight uniform. He drove past the turnoff and the passenger started to raise an alarm. "Right here, Driver. Right here." Dezzie didn't hear. He wanted to drive right by Shelly so he could cut his eyes at her and speed past. He slowed down just so she could see him cutting his eyes at her. She returned the insult. They each acknowledged the other's indignation and their own superiority. Then, he sucked his teeth and sped off. The old man cursed all the way to the Portmore Mall, and swore never to take Dezzie's taxi again.

Silly girl telling him about she wanted to hold her head up. He wasn't trying to stop anybody from holding their head up. When did a little sex ever stop anybody from doing that? He wondered if she knew that, had she been born in one of those countries over yonder, she would have probably been married with five children by now. But then, he looked at the dashboard and saw the picture of his own sweet daughter, and cringed.

The loadermen flocked to the car as soon as he pulled in, eager to be the ones who would get to load each new car. These men were very touchy and passengers often had problems with their method of loading the taxis and buses. They would hold on to the arms of the passengers, offering help with the bags, help which the passengers felt quite uncalled for. These men were very unnecessary, as far as most were concerned. They were a nuisance, to boot. It wasn't like Downtown or Spanish Town, where there were people who sometimes had come from afar and weren't sure which bus or taxi to board. This was Portmore, where just about everyone knew where he or she was going and needed no help in securing a robot taxi. Still, most drivers complied with the service offered by the loadermen, who rumor had it, earned anywhere upwards from two thousand dollars each day, just for shoving people into vehicles that they had fully intended to go into anyway. As soon as he parked, a loaderman approached and started loading his taxi, asking for a smalls in the process. Dezzie assured him that he would get a little something later on, which triggered some amount of vexation both ways.

He was so happy he would soon be done with this tedious living. No more altercations with yellow-belly cowards, who wanted him to creep like a snail while everybody else was racing like mad to get all the passengers. No more negotiations with unreasonable loadermen, who seemed to want a dime out of every dollar that he hustled. Follow them and he would be flat broke, if he went with their plan. No more feeling so stressed that he had to resort to talking to himself while he drove, so that passengers thought he was talking to them. Then they would take to answering him and offering advice that he didn't ask for, let alone want. He knew other taximen who had no qualms with telling passengers every detail of their lives, when sorrows weighed them down and they felt like talking, particularly the older ones whom the retribution of life had seen fit to bite in the ass and they wanted a chance to explain their sorry side of the story. He, Dezzie, didn't mind discussing politics or the random topical issue but he was particular about whom he spoke to. Some passengers gave him the creeps and some just didn't give him the vibes. And a taximan had to know how to read the vibes. It could be a matter of life and death. But even that would be a thing of the past. After tomorrow, only good vibes. No more hoity-toity school girls who dressed like women and carried you to the brink of your sanity, then left you high and dry and accused you of all manner of evil, like all men didn't brag about the girls they had been with. It wasn't just him. Why was Shelly behaving like such a ninny? How long did she think she was going to keep that overripe fruit from dropping splat? Why not let him pick it, than any other guy? So glad tomorrow he would be rich, then he could get any girl he very well wanted. Girls – plural – as a matter of fact; plus his rightful woman. And he was gonna make sure to drive by with his girls in his posh car so Shelly could see what a fool she'd been.

He could not explain it. He could not explain why he was so

sure. It was a hunch, a winner's hunch. More than a hunch, in fact. Seymour had told him about such hunches. Seymour was a jockey and he sometimes told Dezzie of days when certain men would just show up out of the blue with their life's savings and a great big hunch. Nothing but that. And they would leave fully loaded. Never underestimate a hunch. Why would a peenie-wally have crawled into his mother's ear, other than to hint him on the numbers? What reason would an insect have to do that? Damn, he hadn't seen a peenie-wally since he a was a boy in St. Ann. He didn't even know that peenie-wallies were in Portmore, much more that they crawled into people's ears. It was surely a sign. An unmistakable sign.

He had placed some money on some of the small ones as well. At midday, on his way back to Portmore, he turned into the gas station on the pretense of needing change, and used the opportunity to run over to the Lot-a-Luck outlet to check on the drawings. After five minutes of being parked in the blazing sun in an overcrowded car, the people started to complain, but their complaints were to each other because Dezzie was nowhere to be found. Plus, he had already collected the fares. One woman came out and wrote down the license plate number.

"I going to report the wretch!" she promised, with a finality that indicated she meant business. "Long time I keep telling myself to report him. All the while he do this kinda foolishness!"

The others said they would mark his face when he returned, and never take his taxi again. "Is true. I always hear people talk about this taxi driver. Never knew it was him same one."

So there was that to come back to. But Dezzie didn't mind much because he had found out, to his delight, that The Man had played number fifty-eight, for two of the three small ones that he had bought. He had amassed four thousand dollars. He was on a roll and this was only a hint of bigger things to come, he was certain. He would stop by and buy some fried chicken for Precious and the children later when he was coming off the road, and some jerked pork for Bam. It was her favourite. And he would treat himself to some tonic wine. Long time he hadn't had some.

So he completely blocked out the noise and curse words, and Dezzie wondered if they even knew who they were talking to. By the time he unloaded the last passenger in Greater Portmore, he decided he had had enough for the afternoon and would take a break till later on in the evening. It was during this time that the mystery phone rang. He had almost forgotten about it, in the excitement about the winnings.

Yes. The voice did sound like it belonged to a hot girl with front appearance. He pictured her in something skimpy and flimsy and easy to pull off. He imagined that she wore a long blonde wig and that she knew how to apply her makeup so no flaws could be visible. He had carried a girl like that this morning. She had been very curvy with a champion body. This girl on the phone sounded very grateful; that was always a good sign. A big plus. She was eager to arrange a meeting so she could retrieve her phone. Eagerness in a woman. Another good sign. Dezzie told her where to meet him. She knew the place. She sounded young and her voice was slightly seductive and he had his hopes up. His loins had started to tingle and he used his left hand absently to massage the bulge. He wanted to caution her to come alone, the way the villains did in the movies when something major would go down if the cops got involved. All deals off. But he didn't tell her and he was sorry he hadn't. She turned up with her boyfriend, a muscular guy who looked like he rented a room at the gym and only went home to blend up high protein shakes, to take back to the gym. The girl was much older than she had sounded; pretty, yes, but a bit too seasoned for his liking. Still, he sensed it was too late for him to back out. He had already divulged enough information about himself and as soon as they saw him, they came over to claim the phone.

"Easy come, easy go," said Dezzie. "Win some, lose some. But I'm on an everlasting winning streak today!"

He could not resist the temptation to drive by the shopping centre in Greater Portmore and gloat to Cherry about the start of his great fortune. She ignored him at first but then her ears perked up.

"Four thousand?" she asked. "But Dezzie, yuh is one lucky brute, man!"

"Better believe it!" boasted Dezzie.

"Pity it couldn't be me. I would give anything for that four thousand dollars right now."

"Eh? What? Things not running right for yuh?"

"Bailiff probably at my door right now, trying to kick it off!" Cherry exclaimed. "They supposed to come back for the bed from last week. I owe them four thousand dollars more."

"Four thousand, yuh seh?"

"What a coincidence, eh?" Cherry sighed. "Come in like is God send yuh, Dezzie. I would do anything if yuh could give me the money to pay the bailiff. I would run guh pay it right now, on my lunch break."

"Anything, yuh seh?"

"Yuh know how me and yuh move, Dez-Dez," she said softly, batting her false eyelashes.

Dezzie got home after ten that night and he was starved.

"Is not you call today and seh yuh was coming home with chicken?" asked Precious.

"And pork?" asked Bam.

They hadn't prepared any dinner because he had promised.

"Something come up with the car. 'Ol jalopy. Yuh know how that car misbehave when it ready, Precious!" said Dezzie.

"Well, at least call and let me know to cook something, then," was all she said. She rose to go make some sandwiches for the children, who had caught wind of the promise of fried chicken and had been salivating all evening.

Dezzie went straight to sleep. He was hungry but he was too tired to eat. Besides, he still had Cherry on his mind. She knew all the moves, bwoy. Precious knew her stuff too, but one girl couldn't be expected to satisfy him, what with the voracious appetite he had. Yes, Cherry knew what she was doing, even if she insisted he put the money on the dresser first. He had had his eyes on her for a mighty long time, and his luck had reeled her in today. He had found his way easily to her house in the evening, from the directions she had given. He had given her the money and they had gone through the rituals of seduction, the play of barter.

As was her habit whenever she felt something was amiss, Precious had waited until Dezzie was fast asleep and she had taken it upon herself to search through his pockets. As expected, things had turned up. A three-pack set of condoms, with one missing. And, in spite of that, semen on his underpants. The cell phone number of some girl named Alicia. The address of some girl named Cherry. Fifty dollars in paper and thirty dollars in coins, a Lot-a-Luck ticket with the number 5862114. Women and gambling, that's where his money went. Women and gambling, every day of his life. It had certainly not been the first time that she had found such items in his pants pockets. Confronting him never amounted to anything. Dezzie would take God off the cross, as her mother would say. He was barefaced and dry-eyed. He would look you in the face and swear blind that he had done something, or had not done something, whichever he needed to be true at the time, even when he was caught red-handed.

She thought of calling the woman whose number was written on the paper, and going to the house of the other one, first thing tomorrow. She had done both time and time again. Calling women, warning them to leave her man, knocking on gates with a hefty piece of rock in her hand, and meaning to use it if push came to shove. Sometimes she did, sometimes words were enough. A few times, her clothes were ripped from her body and she, having inflicted some serious damage herself, just missed being carted away by the police. More often than not, the women didn't know her, didn't know of her, couldn't care less about her, and couldn't see her reason for the harassment. A young woman even laughed her to scorn one time. And when she thought of it, Precious couldn't fathom why she would fuss over Dezzie. It wasn't as if he was a prime catch. He was more of a hindrance, a noose she had tied around her own neck with the strings of love. It made her question even the goodwill of that thing they called Love, which seemed to get underfoot like a frisky kitten when you were trying to get somewhere, and Love only wanted to play. She was so frustrated with him, she felt like waking him up and getting into a fight. A physical fight, fist to fist. It had happened before, and she knew she could take him. She was ready for it. Dezzie couldn't fight. He would run off his mouth but if he saw that you were serious, he would be the first to back down. But she thought about her children, their innocence and their right to a peaceful sleep. She crushed all three slips of paper in her hand, flung the condoms onto his head as he slept, and walked into the kitchen. He flinched, wiped his sleeping hand across his face, rolled over and continued with his dream. Without pausing, Precious tossed the papers into the garbage bag that they kept hanging from the lower cupboard.

Just as Ras Negus had worked out in his head, the rubbish truck had to return to Sector Two East the following day, which meant that the garbage collection in Three East would be pushed back, and so on. It was a perfect wonder where people generated so much garbage that a perfectly hardy rubbish truck had to make two trips in one sector. Yet, these were the very ones who complained about being poor. How, in the name of all that was rational, could poor people find so much to throw away, so often, and with such indifference? Bags and barrels of junk. Well, one man's junk, as they said. Ras Negus knew of many men who would give their right eye in exchange for some of what these people called junk. In fact, he witnessed every single day the frenzied rush as the trucks entered the landfill and unloaded. Sometimes, he couldn't explain how they kept from being run over by the trucks. And it wasn't just the men. Scavengers of all ages, and sizes, male and female, grown and tender, destitute and not all that bad, but still not well. They would never admit to being well, for fear of being immediately disqualified from their trade. It went without saying; they were not well.

Ras Negus was in his favourite position, leaning against the rail, taking in the cool breeze and getting ready to hop from the truck as it braced to make another stop beside a hefty pile of garbage. The stench was overpowering. The dogs had rummaged through the pile, ripped the bags and boxes apart and scattered the contents all over the pavement. At some point during the week, a resident or two had tried to sweep up the mess and rebag them, but the futility of this endeavour was evident in the way the dogs returned every night on their savage prowl. The residents had relented. They could hear the dogs all during the night. they imagined the carnage they would face in the morning. They hissed their teeth. They rolled over and pulled the sheets over their heads, and went back to bed.

The maggots, of course, were crawling about because it was early morning. Their time of day for emerging from the filth that they had grown fat on for days, from which they had filled their guts from perpetual feasting, and now they crawled forth in the coolness to see if the coast was clear. As the sun came out with more intensity, they would scamper as best a maggot could, seeking solace in the soil, where they would incubate for some time and emerge as flies. For now, they wiggled their way through holes, rolled down the sides of bags and boxes, in pursuit of dirt. That, or being trampled underfoot.

Ras Negus wondered if he would see the lady whom they had encountered the day before. He saw a woman lugging two bags down the pathway and he thought that it was her. He had hoped not to see her so soon, because he still felt a bit guilty about the whole affair. He knew she didn't want the clothes anymore, and he knew the clothes had been ravenously distributed among the scavengers, but still he wished things hadn't happened the way they had. At least, she would learn her lesson and stop putting good clothes into garbage bags, or to be more vigilant about them if she did. He braced himself for some cut-eyes and a sneer that would last the full length to the heap and back. He made up his mind to offer his help to her, as he would have normally, had there been no mishap between them. But as it turned out, it was not Miss Carol. It was the lady who had donated the bags of clothes that he had taken to the orphans and the elderly.

"Miss Bam. Miss Bam. How yuh doing?" asked Ras Negus,

helping her with the bags and trying his best not to let the despicable gloves brush against her hands. "Good while nuh see. Good little while."

Bam dropped the bags at her feet and allowed him to carry them the rest of the way. "Whoa!" she said, in relief. "Don't know how you guys manage!" she repeated, as she continued back down the walkway.

"Part-a the job, Sistren. Part-a the job," said Ras Negus. He liked appreciation in whatever form. It was rare that men like him were appreciated. Even at Christmas time when they snuck their little empty envelopes into the letter boxes, only a few of the residents bothered to put a hundred dollars or two to show their gratitude. It was, by and large, a thankless job. He picked up two other bags along with the two that Bam had carried, because his arms were feeling extra strong on the tonic of her compliment. As he hoisted all the bags into the truck, a blob of paper fell out of one and he stepped on it. In fact, he stepped on it three more times going back and forth, carrying several other bags. On impulse, just before the truck drove off, he noticed the paper and took it up, unraveled it and found that it was not one piece but three separate small pieces of paper. One had a woman's name and telephone number. The other had a woman's name and address. The third was a Lot-a-Luck ticket, purchased the day before. Ras Negus did not find it any more curious than other things he had picked up over the years, most of which he had discarded anyway, and these would have met with a similar fate had not a tiny voice in his inner ear urged him to hold on to the ticket. But why? What good was it to hang on to a crumpled Lot-a-Luck ticket? He was sure it was just a useless set of digits, like countless tickets that had been crumpled and tossed away, some ripped in exasperation as someone's hopes were once again thrown up against reality. Ras Negus himself never gambled. He never found that he had money to spare for that kind of enterprise. Gambling was for the rich, since it unanimously favoured them, it seemed. The poor man had very little luck with gambling. The scales were tipped very much away from him. Ras

Negus was not even sure he believed in luck. He tossed the other two pieces of paper into the back of the truck. Still, something told him to fold the ticket neatly and place it into his billfold, in his back pocket, where he quickly forgot about it and continued with his work.

The ride back into Kingston triggered him back into his reverie, thinking about Naph-T and the baby she was making. He knew she had endured much inconvenience, living in that tenement yard, so caged up at times, depending on how things were running, afraid to leave the door ajar unless he was at home. Those little things. And she had never complained, not within hearing shot of him. He felt he loved her even more for having taken a chance on him, with so little prospect for change, though he was full to the brim of ambition. And he meant her well. The other men riding in the back of the truck were locked in reveries of their own, though occasionally someone broke the silence with boisterous laughter at some irrelevant thing or another. It was hard to laugh in stench, even if they were used to it. And it was hard not to notice the squeamish faces of pedestrians who scurried away from the truck once it was possible to do so, or those of the motorists and passengers who held their breaths and prayed that the light would change in time before they collapsed from breathing in the pungent air that emanated from the truck and trailed it. The men would pretend not to care. The people seemed to be of the conviction that these men could not have sisters and brothers and mothers and children, and wives and girlfriends and sweethearts, and babies on the way.

A heavy smoke had descended over the South-Eastern side of Portmore and was drifting sluggishly towards the West and North, towards Spanish Town and the Hellshire Hills. This smoke was from the Riverton City landfill, which was where the truck was headed, a fact which conspired against them this morning and made their exit seem all the more villainous. The fire at the landfill had made the news last night again, in fact, had made the news four nights in a row. The authorities were adamant that they had done all that could have been done, and that they were not to be blamed. The residents argued that the authorities had been negligent. What everyone agreed on, however, was that the smoke was a menace and needed to be muffled and, if possible, prevented in future. At present, it showed signs of worsening and, as the truck pulled into the gate of the landfill, it was evident that the conditions had deteriorated. The scavengers wore wet handkerchiefs tied over their nostrils and mouths, even as they scampered to what goodies the trucks had dragged in from all over Kingston, Portmore and beyond. The garbage men, having their reputation of resilience to uphold, walked unfazed around the landfill. They added their voices to the suggestions as to the cause and the cure of this recurring problem.

Back in his clean clothes and heading home, Ras Negus stopped in Cross Roads market and bought a jelly coconut. Again, he encountered the Lot-a-Luck ticket as he pulled a hundred dollars from the billfold.

"What time they draw the Lot-a-Luck, anyway?" he asked the jellyman, absently.

"Lot-a-Luck? Hmm. Not till Saturday again, I think," the jellyman said. "Day after tomorrow."

The jellyman selected a jelly that was to his liking, tapped it with the machete to confirm whether it was soft or hard. He knew Ras Negus wanted one that wasn't too soft but not too hard, either. He wanted something pliable that he could scoop out with the side of the husk that was chopped just for this purpose. Nothing he had to wrestle with too hard. The jellyman chopped the top of the husk and left a hole. The jelly was full to the brim and some of the sweet water trickled in libation to the ground, revealing the soft delicious meat inside. He knew better than to offer the Ras a straw. He was no tourist. Men like Ras Negus took great pride in turning a jelly coconut to his head and draining it instantly. He could easily have gulped down one or two more straight. Easily.

"What? Yuh buy some numbers?" asked the jellyman.

"No, Sah. Not I!" exclaimed the Ras. He chuckled. "Numbers? That is for people who have time and money. No, I-yah!"

He wiped his mouth with the back of his hand and left the market, heading down Slipe Road towards his home.

———

Chapter Seven

It was Saturday, the day of the Lot-a-Luck draw. Nine o'clock in the morning. Dezzie calculated that he had about eight hours of poverty left, the draw being scheduled for six o'clock that evening. Eight hours of poverty left, after thirty-odd years of full immersion in it, wasn't so bad but there was the immediate matter at hand; the matter of the growling in his stomach, a testament to his hunger. Since he had left out early to avoid an argument with Precious, who had been particularly annoying for the past couple days, and since Bam was in the country visiting relatives, Dezzie had made himself some cocoa tea and a corned beef sandwich with what he could rustle up from the kitchen. That had been at six thirty and then he had snuck out when he heard Precious stirring in the bedroom, to spare himself the altercation. There had been no opportunity to take a smalls from her purse because she was right there on the bed, and she didn't sleep soundly at all. She would wake if a pin dropped in the hall, because she lived in terror that gunmen or duppies, or lizards or spiders, would creep up on her in her sleep, so at least one of her eyes was always half open. Plus, she had not hidden anything in the fridge for some time and he had not sniffed any new hiding places yet, though he was always on the alert. Now, his belly was threatening to take his business to the public domain by way of growls and rumbles, if it was not expediently appeased. His stomach did not care if he would be filthy rich by evening. Fact of the matter was he was filthy poor right now.

Dezzie was in the supermarket, standing in the snack aisle, scanning the field of possibilities and making mental calculations. Every now and then, he braced back and stroked his chin, and scratched his head. A precursory dip into his pockets five minutes prior had alerted him to the distressing fact that he had but sixty dollars to his name, a good amount of that being in one-dollar coins that made an embarrassing jingle when he walked. He was in a way postponing the trip to the cashier, who would frown and painstakingly count out the coins one by one, with contempt. He knew that moment would come because he was determined to get something to eat, but right now he needed to decide on what he could afford. A soft spiced bun and a slice of cheese would have been great, with a cold beer to wash it down, but that was flatly out of the question. Sixty dollars couldn't even buy the bun, much more. A box of six jelly donuts was well out of his reach, at the moment. In fact, his present reality was that he would have to forget about anything to drink, and content himself with a pack of sandwich biscuits or banana chips, or one single donut. He stood in the aisle for ten minutes, contemplating.

Then he remembered hearing someone – it could have been Beres or Ruddy – say that anything that is eaten in the store would not constitute theft, since it had not been removed from the store. Dezzie may have argued with the fellow at the time, during one of their heated debates about topical issues such as this, that he would indeed be walking out with the item, it being in his belly, but the general consensus had been that, no, it was not theft if it was eaten in the store, so long as you weren't caught eating it in the store (this latter clause having been added after due reflection). And it did make sense, now that he thought about it. The fact that the scanner would not dare beep if you passed with the food already in your belly was logic enough to prove that no infraction had occurred. The only thing was the fact that there were several security cameras strategically placed, with view of almost every nook of every aisle. Dezzie had often wondered if managers even bothered to view the footage of security tapes, or if the tapes even recorded anything to begin with. Who really had so much time and money to waste? Could have been a great big hoax to try to pull one over on the common man. But how could one be sure? Still, eating a few items in the store constituted a much better prospect to him at this time than making a legitimate purchase with his measly sixty dollars, and calling down embarrassment upon himself in front of the cashier.

He decided he would have something to eat in the supermarket. He was, after all, a regular customer, and this was a huge store. They certainly wouldn't miss a few items. He was sure they had gained tremendous profit from his purchases over the years. Come to think of it, this was one of the most expensive supermarkets in the Portmore area, with exorbitant mark-ups, compared to prices in other stores. He had often heard people complain and he himself had had a few bones to pick with management, now that he reflected. Perhaps, it was his calling at this time to level the balance on behalf of his fellow shoppers, so that justice could prevail. He grew more brazen and, the more he convinced himself of the righteousness of his misdemeanor, the more he drifted from the snack aisle and ventured into the forbidden territory of delicacies, which were once thought too expensive for his taste buds but he would try them now, since it was on the house. He decided to upgrade to a tin of pink salmon and a pack of savoury crackers. He flicked the can of salmon open and dived into the delicious meat without draining the water, at the same time munching down two or three crackers in one mouthful. He stuffed the empty cracker bag into the empty tin of salmon and replaced it on the shelf, using the back of his hand to wipe his mouth. Saturday morning was not a busy time for supermarket shopping. Most people were at home doing chores or at Coronation Market Downtown, or were still too hung over in bed from a Friday night at the club. They wouldn't throng the pavilions of the plaza till late afternoon. The aisles were, for the most part, empty and thus, very conducive to what Dezzie was presently up to.

Now, he was thirsty. There were dozens of different brands to choose from. A round of Red Stripe beer would have been ideal to kick off the celebratory mood for later, but he had no bottle opener on him and his teeth weren't in the best condition to unhinge the cap, so he opted for a quart of orange juice and turned it to his head, standing in front of the freezer so the door could hide him somewhat. Dezzie could not believe how easy it was, and to think of all those times he had been hungry and had languished around the steering wheel of his jalopy, when he could have just come into the supermarket and helped himself to some lunch. Within no time, he emptied the box and replaced it on the shelf in the freezer, wiped his mouth as usual, looked twice over his shoulders, and marched down the aisle like a newly crowned king. The only thing he felt for now was a pack of red flame grapes, not because he was hungry – which he wasn't – but because he had always wanted to know what they tasted like. Dozens of times over the years, he had picked up the packs of grapes, their vibrant purple bulbs tantalizing his eyes, and he had scrutinized the prices, and tossed them back down on the display rack. The same applied for imported apples, peaches, plums and strawberries. Dezzie didn't know what they tasted like. They certainly did not emit the strong, heady flavours that the local fruits gave off from a mile away, and so Dezzie had always comforted himself that they might just taste as bland as they smelled. But now, with the presentation of this new opportunity, he would satisfy his curiosity, once and for all.

The produce section was a bit more open and a few shoppers were strolling past, some lingering to fondle the papayas and mangoes and check for firmness, some swooning at the price of the imported apples and plums. Dezzie picked up a pack of red flame grapes but decided he wouldn't eat it there. The area was too open and the security guard, though hovering by the front of the store, could easily see down by the produce section. Dezzie went back into one of the less trafficked aisles, gobbled the grapes four at a time, and tossed the empty packet onto the shelf. The security guard was chatting with the lady who gave out tickets and kept the bags of customers while they shopped. Fully satiated and bored by the ease of his conquest, he departed the store.

The line in front of the Lot-a-Luck outpost was long as usual, today especially being Saturday and this evening being the big draw. For once, Dezzie didn't feel inclined to join the line. He was content that he had already purchased the winning ticket. He had searched for it in his pocket earlier and realized that he had changed pants. He knew it was still in the pocket of his old jeans pants because Precious had threatened to stop washing his clothes. She wasn't serious but still, he figured she would spite him for a week or two. So he made a mental note to be sure to get home by five, so he could have his ticket in hand for the drawing. He pitied the simplicity of the persons in the line, knowing that the winning numbers had already been chosen and that he had them.

Today was to be spent with the guys, shooting birds up in the Hellshire hills. They had agreed to meet at ten o'clock, right there at the plaza. Three of the guys would be coming from Dunbeholden side and the other would be coming from Waterford side. The five men had been bird shooting a couple times before and it had become a sort of monthly ritual. They were all taximen and Saturday was generally the busiest day for hustling the streets, but none of them seemed deterred by this. One Saturday a month for a few hours wouldn't kill anyone and besides, being up in the hills gave them a good vantage point to peer down at the young women bathing at Hellshire beach down below, or making fun of the pot-bellied sugar daddies who catered to their every whim, running behind them with beach towels and slippers.

It was Beres who had come up with the idea, having heard a passenger make mention of it, of how he had seen a bunch of big shots go up into the Hellshire bushes with guns and emerge with guns and bagfuls of birds. Dezzie hadn't believed it at first. What kinda bird could be up in Hellshire dry bush? He was sure there was nothing up in that parched scrub to look at, let alone shoot at. But then he had asked around and word on the street said it could very well be so. Till one Saturday he witnessed for himself some men doing just that. He had heard the shots and thought of raising an alarm, and then he put two and two together and realized what was happening. They at first had no idea what kinds of birds, if any, lived in the Hellshire hills and whether or not they were edible. The fact that this entire stretch of land was a part of an even more expansive game reserve was of no consequence to them. The fact that it was not even hunting season to begin with was of even less significance. None of them knew or cared about hunting licenses or quotas or regulations. Shooting the birds was more a nostalgic experience than one of procuring meat. It conjured up images of their much younger selves running through woodland areas, each in their respective parish of birth, with their sling shots and stones aimed at pecharies and baldpates, pulling back with strong lean arms and letting go to the sound of whoosh, as the birds descended. Then, the frantic chase to find the place and claim the title. The men had no guns, just as the boys had no guns. They were in it for the glory and the fresh break from sitting hunched over a steering wheel begging passengers to enter their taxis, and for the erotic thrill of watching bikini-clad girls on the beach below.

Dezzie suspected that the men would be late, for no other reason than that, to them, being early was just as cheap as being a wimp. No Jamaican man who had even a trace of street swag would allow himself to be early for anything. Punctuality was within the domain of middle-aged women scurrying off to attend to church matters and children who were ushered off to Sunday school, pouting as they went. No one else seemed to see the necessity of it. So naturally when the men had said ten o'clock, they had truly meant eleven or twelve and they all knew that's what they had meant. Dezzie thought about cruising the route for a little while but he was acutely aware of the fact that there was no gasoline in the car. He had not taken the car to Ping Wing last night because he had blown all the money he had earned yesterday, entertaining his comrades in the bar and sweet-talking the barmaid, till by the time he realized it, there were not even enough funds left to buy a little twups of gas. Ping Wing would have filled the tank, but he also would have demanded his money, which Dezzie didn't have. Six of one, half dozen of the other. Ping Wing was a policeman and as a general rule, Dezzie didn't like pushing his luck with people who carried guns. So now he had his car in the parking lot of the plaza and he couldn't rove. He probably just had enough gas left to take him to the gas station. Luckily, they had decided that they would all bunch up in Ruddy's station wagon for the trip to Hellshire, and pool together for the gas. Since everyone knew how cheap Dezzie was, no one really expected that he would have anything to put towards the gas.

He walked past the Lot-a-Luck post several times and winked at Cherry, who was making a ritual out of ignoring him. He walked by the ice cream parlour and eyed the different flavours of ice cream, imagining how each would taste, and creating various combinations in his mind, from memory as well as from scratch. He peered in so long that his face was almost flattened on to the glass of the store front and the customers started to speculate about his intentions. Dezzie realized that his hunger was returning. Breakfasting in the supermarket had been easy but he wondered if he should chance it again so soon. A little boy was approaching each patron in the ice cream parlour, holding out a sheet of white paper to them and pointing at something for them to read. After a while, some of the patrons took money from their pockets or wallets and handed it to the boy. Some even patted him on the head. The boy smiled and thanked them for the money, then moved on to the next person. Dezzie wondered what the little rascal could be up to. As soon as the boy exited the store, Dezzie stopped him.

"Yow, Youth-man! Over here!" He signaled for the boy to come over to him.

"Yes, Sar?" asked the boy. He was about twelve or thirteen, on the slender side and a bit bashful.

"What's that there yuh got?"

"Oh. A walkathon form, Sar, to support my church. Want to sponsor me, Sar? Twenty dollars for each mile."

"What yuh mean, twenty dollars for each mile?"

"Don't know, Sar. That's what they say."

"Who say?"

"Sar, see it here on the form. Twenty dollars for each mile. We going to walk next week, to raise money to build the new church. See, other people pay them money and sign, and tick how many miles." He showed Dezzie where several people had already contributed towards the walkathon.

"Walkathon, my backfoot! Build what kinda church? Is Pastor want the money for himself, to go sport wid young girls and drink rum!" Dezzie hissed his teeth. "And have people pickney walking round begging people them hard-earned money! Give me this!" He snatched the paper from the boy, checking to make sure no one was looking.

"But, sar! Is them give me at the church. I have to carry it back in, with the money!"

"How much money we talking 'bout?"

"Three hindred and sixty dollars, Sar." The boy was on the verge of tears, his eyes fixed on his feet.

"Tell yuh what," said Dezzie, lowering his voice and mustering all his sweetness. "Give me the money. I will go up to the church and take up the matter with Pastor. Where yuh live, bwoy?"

"Seven West, Sar."

"Awright, then. Give me the money and go on back home. I will go up to the church and sort this out."

The boy frowned, made to dip into his pocket, then seemed to reconsider. "Give me back the paper and I will carry it back to them," he said, becoming more courageous.

"Bwoy, but is what yuh think, that I going run off with the money? Is pastor want to run off with the money, not me! But what a piece-a liberty! Look here, go on home before I take off mah belt and lace yuh skin!"

The boy scampered away, leaving Dezzie with the walkathon form in his hand. Twice he glanced back over his shoulder but he kept running. Dezzie smirked. He studied the form and scratched his head. There were several rows for names and spaces to tick the amount being donated. Money for miles! Only a pastor, he said to himself, shaking his head. But as he walked through the plaza, it began to dawn on him that this was an easy way to hustle up some gas money and make a few rounds before the fellas came. If Pastor could do it without blinking and got away with it, well, so could Desmond Grant. He knew he had to be selective because time was a factor. He had to avoid the pensioners, the prim-and-proper, and anyone who stared at an item too long, which meant they couldn't afford it. He had no intention of approaching any man. His victims would be, decidedly, female. He entered a store and walked meekly over to a lady. She neither looked well-off nor poor. He figured she would therefore have neither reason to chastise him nor give him cock-and-bull stories.

"Good morning, Miss. My church is having a walkathon to raise money," he said, in his most eloquent English. "I'm asking if yuh would please donate. Is a worthy cause."

"A walkathon? To where?" asked the lady.

Dezzie had to check back on the form to find out where they would be walking. He also had to make quick check-backs to remember the name of his church.

"Oh, I attend this church! Oh, yes. The walkathon. Never see yuh there, though. Yuh just start?"

"No, man. I start long time. Just that I late sometimes, so I tend to sit round the back."

"I can't go, though. My arthritis." She dug into her purse and took out one hundred dollars, and handed it to him. "Walk five miles for me, my brother. And may The Good Lord richly bless yuh."

Knowing his rich blessings had already been sealed and sanctified, Dezzie thanked the woman. "Yes, Sister. I will remember yuh while ah walking. Blessed name."

So this was the day of finding out just how easy it was to

make money, just when he wouldn't be needing it, and all this time he had thought that he had these kinda things under his belt. Only went to show that you learned every day. Stealing from Precious wasn't really stealing, as far as he reasoned. She was his woman and his baby mother and what was hers was his. And besides, he knew Precious didn't mind him taking a few dollars, much as she raised hell. He knew she loved him. The fact that she kept hiding the money, and kept changing the hiding paces when they were discovered, was no hint to him that, maybe, just maybe, she had other plans for it.

Dezzie made sure not to approach any males, since from his experience, a male could very likely be in the middle of a scam of his own, and there was no being sure exactly what type of scam, or the complexities involved. He had had to help a brother out of many a tight spot, due in no small way to his quick thinking and the dexterity of his own tongue. It was just the way things were and he didn't want to interfere with another brother's game. Things were as they were, men ran games, all kinds of games, on all kinds of people but mainly, on women. He made sure to approach only the softest looking women, preferably those with children, since those were less likely to rave at him for fear of setting a bad example for the little ones. Not to say that these women were pushovers. Oh, no. He knew better than to succumb to that fallacy. But fact of the matter was, some were easier than others, and he had honed the eye for them, and that expertise had earned him two hundred and eighty dollars within the hour. He folded the form and decided to keep it in the compartment below the dashboard, as a lucky charm. He barely coerced Betsy into the gas station, bought some gas and made two trips to the Portmore Mall and back, before returning to the plaza in Greater Portmore, where the fellas were already in Ruddy's car, waiting.

They were in heated discussion about something. Beres had a flask of rum that he was passing round, and the men sipped it, undiluted. They had all been established rumheads since their teen years. Today, all five men needed a special boost of liquor because one from among their peers had been snatched. While they drove out of Greater Portmore and turned right on to the Hellshire Road, Dezzie was made to understand that a taximan by the name of Butler had been abducted the night before. His car had been found in the wee hours of morning, deserted along the Dyke Road. Dezzie had seen him leaning against his taxi at the Portmore Mall last evening. He had been wearing a yellow ganzie and a pair of blue jeans pants, and a yellow cap, and white sneakers. All the other men confirmed this. They were a group of men who fussed and raised hell all the time but there was camaraderie among them and they looked out for each other. At least one from among them was bound to know what the other was wearing, just in case, and they tried to tell each other where they were headed off to, particularly if they had been chartered by a suspicious-looking fella, and especially late at night. It was an unspoken rule among them never to pick up more than two men at any one spot, and never to do turn-offs in certain areas. Even certain women came under scrutiny, as they were sometimes in league with the villains. The men wondered what could have become of their colleague, and they speculated among themselves as to the reason, and whether he was dead or alive. They did not wish bad on their friend, but this had not been the first or second time and things normally didn't fare well, under the circumstances. And the more time passed, the less hope one could muster.

Last year, two Portmore taximen were abducted, in separate incidences, and none of the two lived to tell the tale. They both were found riddled with gunshot wounds, one to his face, which the men determined as proof that he may have been involved in hanky panky with undesirables and pissed off someone in the inner circle, because this was their official way of handling such affront. A shot to the face, a clear giveaway. Unmistakable, the men had agreed. Another had missed it by the skin of his teeth, as three gunmen had boarded his taxi and, as soon as he had caught the rake, he pulled his door, jumped out and blazed through the scheme for all he was worth, while residents screamed. The men had chased him for a few paces, then drove off in his very taxi.

Now, they wondered if Butler's body would be found and, where the bullets would be located. Still, they hoped for his safe return. His cell phone had rung without answer all night, and no one who knew him could account for his whereabouts.

"Wonder if is woman yard him gone, though?" said Joe.

"Woman yard, and leave him car on Dyke Road wid the door open?" challenged Conda. "Naw, Man. If it was woman yard, him woulda did drive to the woman yard, or park down the road if is not fi him rightful woman. Me nuh think so."

"Wonder if is robbery, or if is some drugs or thing him get mix up wid?" suggested Beres, who was driving.

They were all acutely aware that none among them was an angel. Yes, there was a hierarchy as it regarded the levels of skullduggery but no slate was anywhere near clean. Drugs, guns and money, of course, being the main vices but a man could lose his life for something as simple as a bitter comment to the wrong passenger, or a wink at the wrong man's woman, or an unpaid bribe promised to the wrong policeman. A man could lose his life for the simplest thing and what most people didn't understand was that this taximan work was a dangerous work! This was what the taximen knew to be true. They looked out for each other the way soldiers look out for other soldiers in a war zone, having secret messages passed through codes, a hand signal that meant one thing to a pedestrian or passenger or even a policeman, but meant something completely different to another taximan. It was a system they had worked out, sometimes subconsciously and extemporaneously, among themselves in moments such as this, when it was just them who understood the dangers and the complexities of their trade.

"If wi don't see him by later, yuh know that's it," said Beres, his voice dipping, though they were driving past the stretch of road where the soft shoulder was almost fluently merged with the beach and the rolling waves of the blue Caribbean rushed up as if they meant by all means to force their way into the vehicle and pull the occupants out. The smell of raw fish and fried fish, the ones still alive below the waves and the ones simmering in coconut oil in the series of gazebo-style restaurants along Hellshire Beach. "Yeah, man. Don't bother look for him if him don't come in by tonight."

The men agreed, silently. They unanimously feared the worst. It was a damper on their mood but they still intended to enjoy the hunt. In any event, Butler's death wasn't confirmed. He could still be out there, maybe even enjoying himself. Who knew? People had returned after all manner of false alarms, especially men. Laying low for a year or two to evade the law or avoid a spouse, or shirk some kind of responsibility or other, was by no means out of the question. Then they would return, "dragging them dead selves", as people would say, begging forgiveness or just barefacedly picking up where they had left off, without apology or remorse.

The area where they would shoot the birds was in the hilly region about a mile up from the beach. Hardly anyone went there. These lands extended all the way Westwards to Clarendon, as part of the vast Portland Bight protected area, if you were inclined to venture that far. The terrain was sparse semi-desert scrub like the rest of Hellshire hills, almost nothing edible in terms of vegetation and just about the same for animal life. A mongoose or two fled past. If you wanted to spot a crocodile, you would have to go a little further inland, and on to flatter, wetter lands, just behind the Greater Portmore scheme. There was nothing much to be seen in these highlands, save for the view of the beach, which of course was spectacular. The seabirds flew over on their way to dive for fish, or some of them, on their way back to the nesting grounds. It was the fly-over that the men were interested in. They were accustomed to shooting the pecharies, baldpates, barble doves and pigeons, in bygone days, and of course, they were all too familiar with swatting Portmore's national bird, the pestilential mosquito. But as to these pelicans and other water birds, the men were not even sure if they were edible. Of course, neither of the five men had any guns like the big shot bird hunters would have had. They brought along homemade slingshots that they had put together from memory of boyhood days, when these catapults made of twigs and elastic bands were all the rave. Every boy who was a true boy owned one.

"Wonder if it going rain, though?" said Joe. He was a fairly cautious man who was often the voice of reason among this rowdy lot, though he was of course outnumbered. It was, for example, only he who would had bothered to question the legality of the activity they were presently engaged in, a concern which was quickly quelled by a shrug of, "Who bizniz wid dat, anyway?"

"No, sah. Our rain come from the South. The South sky blue blue," said Ruddy, reassuringly.

They brought down two pelicans among them, one unknown bird and four John crows. The John crows, of course, having feasted on carrion, were undesirable as food. Truth be told, there were not much game birds in these parts. The pelicans were regal, much larger than they looked hovering on the air. One had a fish in its bill. All of the birds lay huddled in anguish, after they had been rounded up.

"Fool-fool bird dem-ya!" fussed Beres. He considered the two hours wasted.

"If is bird meat yuh did want, why yuh never go buy piece-a fried chicken?" sneered Ruddy. "I come for the thrill of the kill!" He burst out laughing, grabbing his crotch the way Jamaican men sometimes do when a joke sunk in deeper than expected. "So what? Poor man can't kill for the thrill of it, like everybody else?" This too, was a sweetness that coursed through him, mixing with the rum and melting away the worries regarding Butler, at least for the moment.

A light drizzle started, to everyone's chagrin. They left the birds piled one atop the other, the blood streaming down their sides, some of them not bleeding at all but their bodies pulsating and their necks cocked to an awkward tilt. The hot blood had a smell of its own. Dezzie remembered the smell. It was peculiar and very strong, triggering days when he had watched the ramgoats strung up in the big yard in Moneague, head down and forearms reaching for the ground, an everlasting cut from head to belly bottom, and all the innards scraped out, and the body left draining. It was that smell, which the rain was trying to wash away and which, if it didn't, the rangers would pick up the scent of and discover the illegal massacre in a protected area – for there were legal ones – but these had been granted no permit and had followed no protocol. But they had made their getaway. No time would be served and no fines paid. And the birds would return to the arid Hellshire soil, a Taino offering.

"Listen when ah tell yuh, my number go play this evening!" announced Dezzie.

"Your number go play every Saturday, and every Wednesday, too!" the men jeered, in unison.

"Awright, then. Just watch and see."

"Just make sure put aside my little much, when yuh win, then," said Beres.

"And mine," said each of the others.

"But of course," said Dezzie. "All-a we brethren from long time. I couldn't leave out my brethren them. First thing, as I get my millions, is a big party!"

The men roared with laughter, though they knew it would not come true, but still, it wouldn't hurt to imagine the music and the revelry, each of them sitting by a pool sipping something cool, with a pretty girl perched on each leg, maybe one behind massaging his shoulder and moving her waistline to the beat. It didn't hurt a body to take a flight of fancy, knowing they were still firmly hooked to dry land by the coil of their car keys. They all had bought tickets, as they always did, and they all hoped for the best. But when they realized that Dezzie was blowing this thing all out of proportion, and making outlandish plans, each man gradually withdrew and looked silently out of the window at something that was of little interest to him, but far more interesting that Dezzie's nonsense. Those on the right gazed at the sea, now bluish-grey with the upheaval of the afternoon rain, a rare enough thing in Portmore. Those on the left stared at the dense mangrove and wondered if, at that very moment, a crocodile would emerge and start crossing the road.

Dezzie slept for a couple hours, in spite of the noise that his children were making in the living room. The salty sea air and the heat of the day had made him drunk, and the sudden rain may have given him the sniffles. He lay across the bed, spread-eagled, since Precious was still downtown at the arcade and Bam wouldn't be home for a little while, either. He had given the children full run of the kitchen, hoping that Desrine would have felt the female instinct to fix her father a little something to eat, which she hadn't. He could however, tell by the bangs and clings and the whispers and the hushed damage control going on, that Precious would not be happy when she came home. The rain had made the heat more intense, it seemed, rather than cooling the place down. Perhaps, it had not been enough to dissipate all the heat that had accumulated for months in rocks and trunks and the immense concrete jungle that the schemes had become. The few drops had only tickled the heat to a smirk, and had not been enough for a chuckle, much more a laugh. The place was still vexed.

Butler had made the five o'clock news headlines and there would be a follow-up at seven. But before that, the Lot-a-Luck draw at six, which Dezzie had already tuned in to and which the children had already gathered to witness because their father had jumped from the bed when the alarm sounded. They had to bear through three other drawings of the small ones, as Dezzie called them, and when the announcer started going through the numbers for the big one, it was then that Dezzie remembered that he hadn't looked for the ticket. So he made a frantic dash for his pants in the dirty clothes hamper. He found the pants but could not find the ticket, and the announcer was calling out the numbers so he stopped searching for the ticket and shouted at Desrine to jot down all the numbers being called, which she had already decided to do. And with each number that was called, he confirmed that it was his number. And when all six had been called, and repeated, and repeated, he was as shocked as he was sure. The children started screaming, and Dezzie began a more thorough, and more nerve-wracking, search.

He wondered if he was asleep but then, the children seemed real enough, the house seemed real enough. The lady on the tv was imploring anyone with the winning number, if anyone, to come in and claim their money. A whopping five hundred and twenty-six million dollars!

"Five hundred and twenty-six? Million? Know what that can buy?" screamed Dezzie. But then, if he was dreaming, surely someone would wake him up because that kind of commotion could not be contained within dreams. It was a known fact. Anything beyond a certain decibel always filtered out of the dream and someone was sure to be annoyed and wake the dreamer. No one was waking him. He was not dreaming. And the children were helping him to look for the ticket. He was not dreaming. Bam was pulling the gate and then the door. He was not dreaming.

"Grandma! Grandma! Yuh see the ticket?" the children were shouting at once, and Dezzie ran out into the living room and was asking the same thing.

"What ticket?" asked Bam.

"The ticket! The ticket!"

"Dezzie, yuh turn damn fool or what? Which ticket?"

But when she had been told the full story, she too was frantic. "Maybe Precious put it up for safe keeping," was all she could muster. She sat down on the couch, trembling. Goose bumps covered her arms. Five hundred and twenty-six million. "Yuh sure, Dezzie? All the numbers? Yuh double-check?"

"Double-check, triple-check, quadruple-check!" shouted Dezzie. "Ah pick the numbers from the night with the peenie-wally. Ah know it must did win! Is like ah just know it!"

"Then, where yuh put the ticket, then?"

"Woman, if ah did know, ah would ask yuh?"

"Awright, then, make we calm down little bit. Maybe Precious put it up."

They still searched everywhere. Precious came in, exhausted. She didn't know what Dezzie was harassing her about. She didn't know what any of them was harassing her about.

"Where the blasted ticket, Woman?"

"Which ticket? But what wrong with this man, eh?"

"Precious, the ticket was in my pocket, Wednesday. Ah take off my pants and now the ticket not in the pocket. Five hundred and twenty-six million!"

"Five hundred and who?"

Precious jumped up and ran into the room, emptied the laundry hamper and searched like she had never searched for anything in her entire life.

Chapter Eight

They were allowed to splash. The two boys sat with their backs leaning against the curved metal frame of the tub, the soapy water up to their chests, their knees bent to accommodate the fact they had been growing fast. Their father was pouring fresh water over their heads to rinse away the shampoo, at the same time instructing them to rub behind their ears. He patted their backs alternately, as the clean water flowed from their locks and onto their shoulders, and down their backs.

"Awright, now. Up." They stood, on cue. "Roll back." Each boy held firmly on to the tip of his genitals and pulled back on the foreskin. "All the way back, Lion. Gently. Don't drag it. Gently, man. Doan tear it."

Ras Negus dipped the bucket once again into the drum of water that he had been using for their bath. He poured the cool water over their entire bodies as they stood. They shivered, stepping out of the bath pan and onto the rocky area at the back of the tenement, where their father had bathed them ever since they could sit up on their own. He gave them each a soft cotton towel to dry their bodies with.

"Flash! Flash, Fire!" Ras Negus burst out laughing.

They knew what to do. The boys bent over and flashed the remaining water from their locks. Even so, when they stood again, a few isolated drops streamed down their faces. They put their slippers on and walked across the yard towards the door of their quarters, walked past the stand pipe where their mother and older sister were catching water to prepare the evening meal. They lay down on the bed, outstretched, one beside the other. Ras Negus poured a few drops of coconut oil into his palm from a glass bottle, then one drop of myrrh oil from a cobalt blue vial onto that. He had gotten the myrrh oil from an elder at the Ethiopian Orthodox church. He rubbed the oleiferous mixture together in his palms and proceeded to massage both boys at once, beginning with their faces and smoothing his way down to the tips of their toes. The room was pleasantly sultry with the fragrance of myrrh. Supple thighs rubbed and patted, their leanness reflecting the gauntness of ration. Now, it would be time for reading, which today was Queen's turn to read to her siblings. Then, it would be dinner, and then bed, for the youngsters.

A neighbor walked by as Ras Negus was going into the yard. She had her slip pulled up above her breasts, which themselves sagged, not from the gentle suckling of famished little lips, but the tugging of hard-grown lust, late night and, subsequently, late mornings, too late for redemption. Her chest was white where she had wrestled with the powder puff and sanctified herself with baby powder. It was a common practice in these places, unsightly and unseemly, illogical. She waltzed by and cut her eyes in contempt, not because anyone had done her anything wrong or owed her any unpaid obligations, but simply because she had been raised to mistrust anyone whom she didn't understand, and she didn't understand this Rastaman and his strange ways.

"Evening, Sistren," said Ras Negus. She didn't hail him back, and he shook his head. He had long resigned himself not to grovel, but not to be condescend, either, towards people who either despised or detested him. It seemed he had a double take on being the scourge of the tenement, being a garbage collector and a Rastaman. Yet – and this no one could argue with – he was the one who was always sweeping the yard, sweeping the very street outside the yard, scouring the communal bathroom when everyone else bathed or flushed and stepped away. He was the only one who had taken the time and put in the effort to make the yard livable, by planting flowers and herbs in places where no one expected they would grow, even among rocks. He set drums to collect rain water just to avoid arguments about using water from the stand pipe for gardening, though it was general knowledge that no one from the tenement paid any water bill – or electric bill, for that matter, since the utility companies were scared stiff of the residents of these innercity communities. They dug out the meters and ran illegal connections along the ground and through the trees, to everyone's detriment. The woman was visiting one of the tenants who lived at the far end of the compound. She was only one of his regular female visitors.

Naph-T eyed the woman as she slowly passed. Her gait was slumped and everything about her was frowsy and uninspired. She knocked four times at the door of the man whom she was visiting. Getting no response, she started to bang louder, hurling expletives at the door. She picked up a rock and threatened to break the door down, but then she relented, tossed the rock aside, and left. Ten minutes later, the man stuck his head out, then he emerged and looked around, then the other woman whom he was with stuck her head out, and sneakily left the tenement.

It was cornmeal porridge for dinner. The children loved when the porridge was thick and had cooled to the point that a rich film had formed at the surface, which they liked to skim away with their spoons. Empress fed King while she ate her own porridge. Ras Negus fed Lion. He was dipping the tiny metal spoon to scoop up a batch of delicious yellow goodness, when he heard the familiar jingle playing next door and his ears perked up.

It was familiar and at the same time alien. Familiar in that he heard it every so often, he could not tell precisely how often, but often enough, and whoever was tuning in to it always had it on full blast, as if not wanting to miss a beat. But alien because he had never really listened or cared to know what it was all about. It had always been background noise, irritating noise, which he couldn't wait to end. This time though, because he remembered that he had placed the ticket on the dresser and Naph-T had said that she wanted to hear the draw, just for fun, to see how close they had come, whoever it was that had purchased the ticket. Naph-T was resting on the bed, nauseous. She didn't have morning sickness, like other pregnant women, but evening sickness, if there was ever such a thing. So most evenings after she had prepared the dinner, she lay down for a while. Ras Negus didn't want to wake her. He asked his oldest child, Empress, to reach for the ticket.

"Hold it by the light at the door. Check to see the numbers they are calling," he said.

Empress looked at the numbers. "Can you hear them good? Step out into the yard a little."

She could hear them. They had called all the numbers. She said it casually. She didn't quite understand. Nor did her father.

"All the numbers? Hmm," he said. "Lucky fella, and yet not so lucky. Him probably win four thousand dollars. Maybe five or so." Ras Negus smiled. "Imagine that. Losing a winning ticket. Five thousand dollars could buy a whole heap, if yuh spend it right."

"Yuh going to claim it, Daddy?" asked Princess.

"Claim it? No-I, mi dawta. I neva buy it, I can't claim it."

He had no idea who the ticket could belong to. He didn't even know how one went about claiming such a ticket. Four thousand dollars could do him well, yes, if it was even so much, but he could not claim winnings that were not rightfully his. He knew it had fallen from one of the garbage bags, but there was just no way of telling which, or who had brought it out. They pretty much all looked the same, and had been all huddled together. If the person remembered what number it was, he or she would be a miserable one this evening.

Ras Negus promptly forgot about the draw and took to collecting the empty bowls, scraping away the remainder of porridge from the gourds, which they called calabash. He washed the gourds from a huge bowl near the stand pipe, then rinsed from another bowl of fresh water, using his hand to rub the interior of the calabash, flashing them and then stacking them so they could dry in the open air. Later, he would take them indoors and cover them with a kitchen towel.

By this time, Naph-T was stirring inside, getting the children ready for bed. By eight o'clock, Ras Negus sat alone in the kitchen garden, at the back of the yard, burning a spliff and meditating. He was barefooted, which was how he often went about the yard. He sat here alone most evenings. It had its own peace, though just beyond the fence, the cars zipped up and down Slipe Road and the tenants vied for sovereignty of the airways. At any minute, there could be a raid and several police officers could descend from all directions, frisk him before he could stand properly, demand a handful of ganja as unsolicited hush-money. A stray dog could enter from under the fence and start up a barrage of barking for no apparent reason, and his canine cronies from neighbouring lanes, needing no further persuasion, would follow suit and keep up the howling well into the night. All of these sometimes happened, could happen just now as he took the next puff and inhaled deeply. He could exhale for the last time. He had seen it happen, and not far from here, and more than once. There was still a strange quietness in this garden and he found it consoling.

From the street light, Ras Negus could make out two tiny figures in the yard. They were certainly human but much too small to be dwarves, if that made sense. He looked closer. Yes, it made sense. They were not dwarves. They were babies. Twin boys. Two years old. What were they doing out? They belonged to Cutty, the man whose woman had almost beat down his door earlier. The twins did not belong to her, either. Their own mother had died, in a drive-by shooting, about a year ago. Where was Cutty? Ras Negus rose to see if he could find the man in the yard. The twins were bent over and stood one behind the other, dry-humping each other. They were giggling and imitating sexual sounds that they must have heard while watching their father on one of his many trysts in the room where they were supposed to be asleep. What other explanation was there? And now it was night. The twins had no shirts on; just their disposable diapers, which hung and bulged with accumulated waste, by the look and smell of things. Ras Negus was growing more and more infuriated. He started shouting Cutty's name, louder and louder and still no response. His own mother, Miss Inez, came out to see what the matter was. They walked over to Cutty's door, each holding one of the boys. Nobody answered the door.

"Must be gone to dance," said Miss Inez. "Hear the music, how it loud? Coming from clear over Jones Town. Must be there him gone. Almost sure of it."

"But look, the twins out here by themselves!" exclaimed Ras Negus. "Look like nobody change their nappy from mawning. Poor thing-them, probably don't even eat!" He asked his mother to keep the boys and to give them some food.

Ras Negus marched through the gate of the tenement. He didn't even stop to tell Naph-T that he was leaving out, so upset he was. He didn't even put on his shoes or even his tam. He never ever went on the road without his tam. He marched down the maze of lanes with makeshift walls of galvanized zinc eight feet high, with their narrow winding walkways to limit the mobility of any policeman in hot pursuit while the outlaw grazed the fence and was long gone. He came upon a clearing and then crossed the main road, and a bridge, all the way till he came to the area where the dance session was being held. Men lined the entrance, nursing liquor in bottles of various sizes and colours, and potency. All seemed intoxicated, or on the verge of. They were mainly young men, some teenagers. A few older men were making asses of themselves by challenging the younger ones to a dance-off, with outdated skanks that were relics of a smoother, classier time. A bike pulled up and a woman, who had been gripping the rider around his waist and hoisting her behind unnaturally in the air for emphasis, hopped off and revealed her scant attire, to the glory of the throng. Another group of men swarmed the jukebox. They had their lighters burning and hoisted in the air, the other hand stretched upward in solidarity of, it seemed, unanimous agreement that the song being played was the bomb.

Ras Negus kept parting his way through, asking everyone he

knew if they had seen Cutty. These people weren't strangers. He may not have known every name or even every face but, as a group, he knew them. He had been through here in more sober hours, distributing clothes, visiting the destitute and the infirm. No one there saw him as a threat, per se, though he did seem out of place, he was frantically looking for someone. That someone, he discovered, had been in a corner of the compound, grinding a very fat woman whom he had leaned up against a light post. He held a bottle of beer in one hand, nonchalance in the other. Perhaps, too, he was a little high. It took some amount of persuasion to unlock the couple, so tight they had been. For a moment, Cutty did not have any idea which twins the man was talking about, and what this knotty head fellow wanted with him, anyway. Then, when he came round, he assured Ras Negus that the boys were very sensible and knew how to take care of themselves.

"Think is fool-them?" he said, ready to give an anecdote or two of something very sensible that the twins had done. Ras Negus almost cuffed him. He clutched the man by the collar and hauled him back to Mulgrave Lane, Cutty stammering and threatening and issuing rounds of expletives. He asked to stop so he could pee, and when the Ras didn't budge, the man peed on himself.

"Look here, know how much I nearly win tonight?" he asked himself. "Mercy! Whoa!" He burst out laughing. "Ah miss it by three numbers. Some lucky fucker probably win five hundred and odd mil! Damn lucky fucker!" He hissed his teeth.

"What? What yuh seh?' asked Ras Negus. He stopped just outside the gate of the tenement. "What yuh jus seh?"

"What?" asked Cutty. He had lost his train of thought, what with all the harassment this knotty head man was giving him. "What seh what?"

"What yuh nearly win, the Lot-a-Luck?"

"Yes, to raas!" shouted Cutty. "Three of the number I get. Some damn lucky piss-tail bwoy win five hundred and twenty-odd million, to raas!"

"That's how much it play? The Lot-a-Luck?"

"Yuh deaf or what, sah? Miss it by three damn number!"

Ras Negus was quiet. He led Cutty towards his room, took the key from him and opened the door. "Look, the boys will stay with Miss Inez till tomorrow. Get some sleep, man, and clean up yuhself!" He almost pushed the man into the room and locked the door.

He heard a thud behind the door, which could only be Cutty tumbling to the floor. That was where he would sleep off the liquor till morning, Ras Negus figured. Those boys needed a mother. They didn't need random women popping in all hours of the day and night, boxing food out of their mouth and not giving a hoot about their welfare. They needed a father who wouldn't lock them out of their own house, while he rub-a-dubbed women against light posts, high off his own delinquency. It may not be long before the boys became wards of the state or, worse yet, living on the streets. One of the twins already had a gash across his forehead where he had tried to climb the fence and had fallen, perhaps a month ago. Seven stitches, and many questions from the nurse. The boys had no one looking after them. And what could he do? He had five children of his own, another on the way, a woman and a mother to think about, plus himself. There was just so much he could do for people, just so much.

He told Naph-T all that was on his mind, when they lay in bed that night, the two small boys tucked to the corner. There was so much that had transpired. She, for one, could not get over the Lot-a-Luck winnings, the absurdity of it all. The amazement. So much money and a ticket with no owner. And they having the ticket. What would they do? She knew her man. She knew he would not claim what was not his. But then, whose was it? He had found it, right? Finders keepers, right? Everyone agreed on that, once there was no owner. And what if it was destiny – their destiny – that the lost ticket had found its way to them and to no one else? And now, when she was pregnant? Could that be chance? They never gambled. They never bought any of those tickets, whether big or little. Why would the ticket have found its way to them, of all people? Maybe it was a sign, from the Almighty One, deliverance, a gift, a second chance. It did not have to be a bad thing. What would they do with the ticket?

Then, there was the issue of the twins. They couldn't stay like that. It wasn't safe. What were the adults in tenement legally bound to do? The Minister – one of them, the relevant one, whoever it is – had said that any adult who knew of or even suspected that a child was being abused or endangered in any way, had a moral and legal responsibility to report the matter, or they both could face the penalty. And these weren't strange boys. These were boys born in the very yard, from a mother who had grown up in the very yard, just about. Her life snuffed out, and now theirs on the verge. What was to be done?

"Tell yuh what, Sistren," said Ras Negus finally. "Let us not do anything, yet. Let us just watch and see what happen, see if anybody come forward. Just see if anybody seh anything. Then, we will know what to do."

Naph-T agreed, but neither of them could sleep.

What does a body do with five hundred and twenty-six million dollars?!

Maybe, it was just as well if no one claimed it. The anecdotal accounts of so many who had hit it big, only to relapse into poverty a year or two later. These were legendary. And always, the ones telling the joke would affix their postscript: could never happen to me. I would surely know what to do with that quality money. Put it to good use. Buy this, buy that. Make sure of this, make sure of that. So certain they were of how to most economically utilize that which they would never have. The thrift, the frugality, all the more pious because it would never be put to the test. The movie stars, singers, athletes who had blown outrageous fortunes in an equally outrageous blink of an eyelash. If they, who were accustomed to the highfalutin life, could blow it, then what to say of those nouveau-riche Lot-a-Luck winners? It would be like gobbling down an entire bottle of champagne on innards that have only been accustomed to beer. It would be like inhaling one huge whiff of eucalyptus oil, for the very first time. It was sure to go to the head.

The following morning was Sunday. Naph-T had prepared breakfast of steamed callaloo and boiled dumplings, green bananas and sweet potato. She had made a pot of soursop leaf tea, sweetened with honey. Ras Negus had two cups, one in each hand. He kept pouring the tea from one cup into the other so it could cool for the smaller children to sip. He held one hand much higher than the other and as he poured, the steam escaped from the tea and carried the fragrance of soursop across the room.

"That cool enough now, Ras," said Naph-T softly to him. "You go and drink your tea now, before it get cold."

He allowed a little bit of tea to drip on to his inner wrist, as a test, and then he poured equal amounts into each cup and handed it to the boys. Everyone ate breakfast in silence, which was not strange in this household during mealtime but now the silence felt even eerier. Outside, Miss Inez was chastising Cutty about the incident the night before, which by the way, he had no recollection of and was flatly refuting, though he had awoken to find that the twins were not in the house. Miss Inez was threatening to call the Child Welfare Department. Cutty took the boys and marched them off into his room, admonishing them to be careful of bad-minded people. Ras Negus shook his head and talked himself out of marching round to the backyard and setting matters straight. He had, to some extent, outgrown the boyish instinct of railing to decapitate anyone who dissed his mother. To some extent. It was a natural instinct, but still boyish, and still a dangerous attitude to have. There was a time when that sort of thing would not have gone unchallenged. He had matured to the point where he could calmly deflect the insult and pity the perpetrator. And Miss Inez could handle Cutty, long as he kept his tirade on a level, and as words only. But if he ever so much as cast a speck of dirt in the direction of Miss Inez, Cutty would certainly meet his Waterloo.

There were the typical Sunday morning sounds. The very old and the very young were getting ready for church, to the tune of religious songs which had usurped the airways, as planned. This switch was facilitated every Sunday, the coup d'etat to accommodate the moral crossover in the minds of the tenants. Radios that just hours before had blared a succession of Dancehall hits with lyrics promoting a lifestyle of guns, drugs, sex, bling and swag, now issued a steady, soothing flow of Gospel songs – old favourites and new releases – proclaiming the faith of the fathers, the evidence of things that the youth had never seen. The youth, the ones in between, contributed but a measly number to the church-bound. They were mainly still asleep, some having just coiled up still in their club outfits, make-up still on, lacefront wigs still intact. They too appreciated the Gospel songs, even if they couldn't completely relate; they instinctively believed that such songs were in order on a day like this. Sunday morning had a different feel to it. It had a drowsiness and yet a peculiar sprite, a happy, sunshiny sprite. The dinners would be started early on this day. The meats would have been sliced and marinated from the night before, the red peas soaked and the fish thawed, scaled and salted, and put out to dry for frying. The soursop juice or carrot juice or fruit punch would already be in the fridge, ready for orders. Those who hadn't had a decent bath, fully naked, all week, for whatever reason, would make sure to have a proper scrub on this day. Even the best of the yard clothes were reserved for this day. Enemies, warboats, instigators, sell-outs, snitches were all warned not to let the tenants have to unleash their tongues, on this most sacred of days.

    By late morning, Ras Negus decided to walk up Slipe Road and head for the market, to stretch his legs as well as to get some fruits for the family. There would be less people in the market on Sunday, of course. Jellyman worked seven days a week, so he would be there, certainly. Ras Negus walked down Mulgrave Lane. Just outside his tenement, some ladies were gathered across the lane, stooped in front of their own gate, a little girl wedged between the legs of her aunt, having her hair plaited into tight, neat cornrows that tugged at her scalp and made her cringe. In only a few years, these taut cornrows would surrender to the flaccid, chemically processed version. It was almost a given.

The family kept a bar that opened onto that very street. It was closed presently but by two or three o'clock the men would start drifting in and would remain there till some bad hours of night. The little girl, Fantasia, had a different streak from everyone else who lived in that yard, it seemed. She was a child whom Ras Negus always observed, especially on Sunday mornings when she would kneel, her dress tucked under her to protect her knees, and she would polish and shine the red-ochred floors of the bar with a coconut brush. The beautiful fragrance of the floor polish always seemed out of place, pleasantly so. She would water the crotons and hibiscuses that grew along the roadside. By evening, the floors would be splattered with footprints of heavy-set men who cared not where they stepped or on what they trampled. They would pee, vomit and spit on the crotons and hibiscuses, and in the corner of the yard against the wall that bore the sign "Don't piss here", and on themselves and on whomever was near. Their drunken stupor would have them uproot the flowers as they fell asleep in the patch, or as they dragged some uncouth harlot down into the bushes, among the discarded condoms and slime of their fornication. They would harass the jukebox without mercy, shout after any female that happened to walk by the road, which could be a church sister on her way home from fellowship, at which point they would receive a mighty declaration of the ten commandments, plus tax.

What does one do, think and say, when one lives in a rathole and is not a rat? Fantasia, for instance, still within the clutches of innocence, a girl of nine, perhaps, trying to keep something clean that could by no means be kept clean. Boys smoking ganja and telling high tales of their exploits with women – women – and their escapades with the police. Always, always, they managed to escape - until they got caught. Then, they were forced to speak of each other, and paint murals along the full stretch of the walls, in honor of young lives snuffed out before a real chance had been given. A real chance. These boys, who drank and smoked from before they started to wear long pants, from before they started to smell themselves, as the grown-ups called it. They knew where the guns were hidden. They had been sent to hide them. They knew the short cuts and the hide-outs and the side streets and the safest corner to crash under at night. They knew in which direction to point you if you needed weed or crack or booze or pussy, if you would give them a smalls. But they had long abandoned the road that led to school.

These boys were wayward. They lazed by the Kingston Harbour and dived in for coins that the people tossed in, for fun. Their preoccupation was the Almighty dollar, not necessarily how to make it or even how to keep it; just how to get it fast. They lingered by stoplights and the entrances to supermarkets, their arms outstretched, their lips employed in the sorriest of stories, after which they would retreat with the coins or the crumbs and be satiated for a while. They would hop from their perch on the walls with lightning speed the minute a patrol car turned the corner; always dodging one of three officials of authority – the police, the teacher, the social worker. The young girls would walk around in their slips and brassieres, which showed all too clearly the disparity between the colour of their faces and that of their bodies. They cared not to hide the evidence of their bleaching, blatantly sporting the white creams on their faces and necks, to the extent that they could afford, to bleach away, they hoped, the curse of being born in this place. An atonement to the gods of reason, who proved all the more unreasonable. They shrouded their faces from the glare of the sun which, they had been warned, would not only undo the results of their labour, but worsen it in time. And so, the young men walked past with handkerchiefs tied under their chins, in the fashion of certain movie stars from the silver screen era.

Ras Negus passed by the group and hailed them. The mother lifted her eyes slightly, though she knew his voice, and this morning she was in the mood to hail back. This wasn't always so, but he had learnt to ride with the tide, to accept their howdy-dos and to live without them when they were rationed. These people were as sometimish as the rain, as fickle as the clouds. Their goodwill, or lack thereof, fluctuated like the Stock Exchange, depending on the price of bread, the number of pangs in their bellies and which political party was ruling at the time. Someone with whom you had fancied yourself as being on the best of terms just weeks or days or hours prior, would refuse to hail you though nothing had transpired between the two of you since. Nothing that you were aware of, anyway. Perplexing. And it always seemed that the very worst off would be the first to accuse their neighbours of working Obeah on them, and plunging into a malice that the other could not account for. It took some knowing but those, like Ras Negus, who had studied the obstinate ways and wont of these shanty folks, had mastered the art of skipping lightly among them without much ado.

Jellyman was peeling sugarcane and cutting them into smaller strips, to be bagged and sold at one hundred dollars a bag. He specialized in young jelly coconuts and sugarcane but really, he could very well have any random fruit that he had procured from the country. Pineapples, oranges, watermelon, he wasn't partial, once he could get them at a reasonable price so he could resell. The men of his trade were feared because of the long machetes that they wielded. These machetes were razor-sharp and could sweep through the thick green husk of the young coconut, or the hard shell of the mature one, whichever you preferred, or could remove your head from your neck, if you preferred that. Their skill was legendary. They could hold a coconut up to the light, hoist it in one arm and determine, by the weight, shake and sound of a good firm tap with the machete, how much of the sweet water you could get or, whether the meat inside was soft or hard. No one in their right mind messed with a jellyman. Further, no one in their right mind messed with a jellyman's woman.

Ras Negus did very little talking, on that Sunday. He slumped on the edge of the cart and gulped his jelly, not in one go as he was in the habit of doing, but in parts, which aroused the suspicion of the jellyman but he dared not inquire of his customer what the matter was. Men of a few words should not be interfered with if their words got even fewer. Some men lived on the inside, as Jellyman had observed over the years, in this trade where people sought him to quench not only their thirst but their spirit as well, sometimes. Yes. It was a humble job but sometimes he played the role of counselor, and confidante.

Back down Slipe Road with a burlap bag of coconuts, oranges and three small plastic bags of sugarcane, brooding, weighing heavily on the events of the last few days, searching for meaning. Always, it seemed, things boiled down to one of two options – the one which would leave your integrity intact, and the one which wouldn't. And before today, it had never seemed so hard to choose. What he would do, he decided finally, was to return to the scene of the crime – he was thinking in his mind that it was almost like a crime, though he was certain he had done nothing wrong – for somewhere in Greater Portmore, there was someone who was the rightful heir of five hundred and twenty-six million dollars, and might not even know it. And what if he knew it? That would be five hundred and twenty-six times worse, he was sure.

He felt like a villain as the garbage truck pulled into the scheme. He carried the Lot-a-Luck ticket in his pocket, the way one carried contraband, glancing nervously from side to side. He knew he was being foolish to feel this way, but then. He also knew that most men in his position would not have even thought twice about turning in the ticket and claiming the money. Ras Negus was so out of touch with those matters that he wasn't even sure where one would go and whom one would talk to, and how one claimed that much money, and what time frame was given before the ticket would be declared null and void. He had had no reason to know any of those things. Yet, he was sure that everyone else would. He was sure any child in the street could tell him. There were some things, it seemed, that the average man in the street was born knowing. Ras Negus decided that the safest person to ask was Miss Bam, since she was a community woman who was always in the know. If anyone had raised an alarm about the missing ticket, he was sure that word would have spread and in that case, Miss Bam would have certainly caught wind of it.

Ras Negus hopped off the truck when it got to the cul de sac of 53 Place, and told the fellas that he would soon be back. He ran down the walkway where Miss Bam's house was, and he knocked at the gate. It was then that he heard the moaning sounds coming from the garden that had been constructed in the swale, behind him. Just then, Bam came out of the house and was about to open the gate to enter the garden. She carried a glass of juice in her hand, and a bottle of rubbing alcohol.

"Miss Bam, greetings! I was thinking you would be at work, but look like I lucky to catch yuh," he said, but his attention was on the moaning man who was lying outstretched in the garden, and her attention was, too.

"Is mah son," she said, absently, herself dazed. "Fits."

"Oh. Him trouble with fits?"

"Not really. Just since the other day," she muttered. "Whole heapa stress, knock him out and give him fits ever since. Epilepsy, yuh know. Hit him down three times since morning. Ah can't guh to work since. Have to mind him all day."

"Sorry to hear," Ras Negus said. He was genuinely concerned, and mused on how vulnerable the human body was, that stress of a particular kind could wreak such havoc on a normal, hearty young man, and reduce him to this. "Aint that the taxi driver? Your son? Aint it he who drive the taxi, Sistren?"

"Yep," she said. "Can't drive anymore. Five, sometimes six times a day, since Saturday evening, fits hit him."

"Since Saturday?" asked Ras Negus. It was such a sad thing. "And the doctors don't know what caused it?"

Bam hissed her teeth. "What they know? Blasted fool-them. All they talking 'bout is to run test. Had to borrow money to do all type of scan. Scan on top of scan. Nothing. Everything normal normal. No tumor, no bleeding, no swelling, no nothing. Damn doctor say is in his mind. How it must in yuh mind to drop yuhself down six times a day, just suh?" she hissed her teeth again. "Mah daughter-in-law going to carry him to a reader woman, Thursday. This not right, Ras. Supp'n inna supp'n. somebody set him suh. Somebody salt him up."

Dezzie, who was recovering from the latest attack, was still staring off into space. A pillow had been placed under his head to brace him up a bit. He lay stiff and still trembling somewhat, and a little froth streamed from the corner of his mouth. Ras Negus could barely recognize him as the fellow whom he had spoken to just days before.

Bam suddenly pulled Ras Negus aside. "Ras, ah tell yuh supp'n but don't spill a word of it!" And before he could promise that nothing of it would be spilled, she continued, relating to him the events of the past few days, how her son had struck the most outstanding luck, had placed a bet on the peenie wally and had come into a massive fortune, only to realize that the ticket was gone! Nowhere to be found, as if duppy walk in and gone with it! And since that night, her son had been having seizure on top of seizure, refusing to eat, losing weight and talking nonsense, relapsing into bouts of delirium.

"Somebody set duppy pon him. Somebody do it!" Bam declared. She poured some of the alcohol into her palm and wiped it across her own face, then poured some more and massaged her son's arms, neck and face. "Hear what ah tell yuh, Ras? Obeah! Bad-mind, grudgeful people dem. 'Ol wicked red-yeye people dem!"

Ras Negus could not believe, and yet he could believe, the uncanny series of events. He remembered Bam coming out with the two bags, and him taking them from her. And that was roundabout the time when he had seen the papers on the ground, though he had not really picked them up until long after. He was astonished and relieved, and terrified. And so was Bam, when he revealed to her why he had stopped by her gate that morning, and the bizarre string of events that had led them all to that garden – the day all their lives would change, for better or worse.

The epileptic seizure wore off within half an hour, which was typically how long Dezzie slept following each one. He was still exhausted and, of course, could remember nothing of the seizure itself, but since they had been telling him of what happened during one of the fits, what he did, and they had shown him pictures that they had snapped on their cell phones, as proof since he had been reluctant to believe; he figured he was recovering from one. He had stopped asking, whenever he saw flustered faces gathered around him. But now his mother's face seemed different than at other times that he had returned to reality. He snapped out of his absence to find her joyous, and animated. The Rastaman, it seemed, had brought good news of some sort.

Ras Negus took the ticket from his pocket and handed it to Dezzie, who realized immediately what it was and what it meant. But he was too exhausted to scream and too ill-mannered to offer the man a handshake, as a symbol of gratitude. There was no gratitude, in fact.

"Damn thief! Is you have mi ticket all this time!" Dezzie shouted at the man, who stepped back in shock.

"The man return the ticket, and this is how yuh behave?" demanded Bam. "Really, Dezzie? Yuh must be still in a trance! Ah shame ah yuh, true true! Not my pickny yuh. No, sah!"

"I buy that ticket!" shouted Dezzie.

"And yuh lost it, and Ras find it and bring it back. Fair is fair. Ras must get some of it. Fair is fair."

"Get some of what? Is my money! Get some of what?"

"Is awright, Miss Bam. I didn't want any. Just wanted to return it to its rightful owner."

"No, Ras, fair is fair," insisted Bam. "Yuh didn't have to bring it back. Most people wouldn't did bring it back. Fair is fair. If ah have to dead over it, him gonna give yuh some of the money."

"But is awright..."

Bam glared at her son with contempt – the same son whom she had just massaged with alcohol and whose head she had braced with the pillow. It was his ticket, yes, but fair was fair.

Within minutes, Dezzie had jumped into the jalopy and had disappeared down the road, with Betsy making the strangest noises as she went, though Bam cautioned him about the seizures and at the same time was telling him, "Remember yuh ID, Dezzie. They going to want yuh ID and all ah that!"

It was one of those rare moments when Ras Negus felt really

satisfied. He felt light. He felt that he had done the right thing and had chosen the way of his integrity. It really didn't matter to him whether he would be compensated for his honesty, since honesty was its own compensation. He had always considered himself to be a wealthy man, even when he went to bed hungry. He was wealthy in his spirit and in his plans. He was sometimes surprised when he had caught people asking each other, "Which number The Man play today?" so casually, as if asking, what time is it? And these were the people who complained of being poor, and always wanted to know what someone would do for them, to give them a bly – the government, the doctor, the police, the Almighty. They were content to leave their fate to chance, while handing over the little that they did earn, to "The Man", whose returns were so sparse and unreliable. It amazed him sometimes to see the caliber of people who were asking what The Man had played, people who, ordinarily, one would never suspect of being caught up in such rainbow chases, since they acted like they knew better.

Chapter Nine

Ras Negus sat up in bed and used his palm to wipe the sweat from his forehead. He could not sleep. He had not been able to sleep for two nights straight, save for a few brief five-minute lapses when he dreamed that he had been given ten million dollars. He woke up in flushes, only to realize that it was true and it scared the daylight out of him.

At first, he had flatly refused the money. He had gone home and talked it over with Naph-T and, when he told her about the behaviour of the taximan, she had refused it, too. Ras Negus kept reminding himself that he hadn't given anyone any money to put down, and that no one owed him any obligation. But then, Miss Bam had pleaded with him to take the money and, when he really looked at it, he needed it and the money would do himself and his family a lot of good. Much as it was, it was only a pittance compared to what the taximan got, and to think that Dezzie could have gotten nothing at all! Miss Bam had raised hell about her son's stingy, ungodly ways, and had demanded that Ras Negus be given more, but Dezzie wouldn't budge. The whole thing had been a maelstrom and they all were still reeling. It was indeed a stomach-wrenching twist and, if it had been a movie and he had been at the Carib Cinema in Cross Roads, like back in the older days when he was a regular of the kickers and Westerns, he would have been at the edge of his seat with eyes wide open and his hand clenching the knee of the sistren sitting next to him. As fortune would have it, he was inside the real movie and he hadn't been given any script, and the director was saying, "Action! Action!"

Naph-T was sleeping but she was not in a deep sleep. She never slept soundly if she sensed that Ras Negus too was agitated. Every so often she rolled over and faced him, and placed her fingers into his, or rubbed his leg, or encouraged him to get some sleep. But how can a man sleep, when ten million dollars has just been deposited into his bank account? He had resolved not to touch a dime of the money until he was certain it had not all been a hoax. The lady at the bank had instructed Naph-T on how to set up an online link to the bank account and how to check the balance, and Naph-T had gone down to the parish library to use the computer just this afternoon and sure as day, the money was still there! And then, there were all these plans that were darting through Ras Negus' mind, all the things he had been dreaming about and filing away since his boyhood days, and the plans that had solidified into manhood but which he had never been able to carry out, so they had floated in suspended animation just above his head and in front of his eyes, visible but unreachable. And now, apparently, they were very reachable. But he had to formulate a plan. He would not allow a dime of the money to go to waste. He would not squander a penny. Everything would be accounted for. He had expressed this concern to the lady at the bank, and she had advised him that he might want to set up a standing order, so that only a certain amount of money could be released at a certain time, by request. He had determined that that was what he would do, after he had sat down with Naph-T and the two of them had figured things out.

Sometimes, Ras Negus chastised himself that he was making this whole money thing get to his head. If ten million dollars was keeping him up at night, his face streaming in sweat, then what to say of those men whose pockets were laden with dough and whose bank accounts were so heavy that they sagged? And even worse, what about those who were swimming neck deep in blood money, ill-gotten gains, to whom the devil had issued blank checks and easy access to his private vaults? How did they sleep? Did they not stay awake thinking of the interest payments that were accruing and that would, ultimately, be due? Ras Negus had heard, and had lived long enough to see proof, that the devil did not reopen negotiations after a deal had already been sealed.

Maybe, he was just overwhelmed by the novelty of it all. Surely, he knew that countless millionaires existed and had always existed, even on this tiny piece of rock in the Caribbean Sea – yes, even on Jamrock – there were millionaires and billionaires and maybe even bigger players. Who knew? Some of those guys preferred to play in the shade, and the bigger they got, it seemed, the more they dodged the light. Fact of the matter was, there were many rich people about, people vastly richer than ten million dollars – in fact, ten million would be like pocket change to some of them; chicken feed. Some had been born into it and some had earned it and some had stolen it and killed for it and some, like Dezzie, had been of the handful who had haply dreamed it into being. They had found a way to take it in strides it seemed, though there were some infamous ones who had found it impossible to cope and had found a way to make a mess of the situation. There were certain things that had to be taken into consideration. Of course, they had to beef up security. That was a must. And Ras Negus could well imagine that these people had to constantly watch their backs, not just from enemies but from friends as well, for obvious reasons.

Ras Negus got up from the bed and stood in the darkness for a while. He took off the merino that he slept in and stood in his underpants. He could make out the images of his woman and children as they slept, Naph-T tossing as if she sensed that he was no longer beside her, the boys having rolled all the way to the corner and huddled together. He definitely needed new beds. He needed at least two rooms, where the children could have their own quarters and not have to sleep with him and Naph-T. He wanted his family to be comfortable. Ras Negus lit a candle so as not to startle the others with the light from the bulb. He pulled up the wicker chair and took out pencil and paper from one of his daughters' bag. He began to jot down the barrage of thoughts that came to him, too slowly to keep up because they flooded his brain. Never in his life had he been so bombarded by ideas. They were gushing left right and centre, and the more they came the more they came. It seemed that all his dreams had been piling up behind the dam and finally the spew-way had been breached. By the time he was done, he had three pages of notes, some of which were smudged by the cold sweat that had streamed from him. He dabbed his forehead with the merino that he had taken off, folded the notes and placed them in his pants pocket. He lay back down but could not go to sleep.

There were three reasons that made Dezzie decide to stop operating the taxi. He had driven Betsy into Ping Wing's yard and had handed over the key, saying to himself, "Good riddance to bad rubbish!" He had done so with a flourish. Ping Wing had shaken his head and pouted his mouth in Dezzie's direction, mumbling, "Poppy show! But kuh yah to!"

The first reason was that he was now a rich man and would not need to operate a taxi anymore, least of all one that involved a broken down jalopy that could not be trusted to drive five paces without complaint. And that reason would have been enough. But there were two other reasons.

Second, Butler's death had been confirmed. His decapitated body had been found in bushes along the Dyke Road, and he had been castrated. John crows had been hovering about and the stench had also led residents to the spot. His head had been found two miles away, with his genitals stuffed into his mouth, causing people to suspect that Butler may have gotten involved with the wrong man's daughter, or had been on the downlow and playing the field with one too many men. It was a signature type of crime, and it was said that such men did not mess around when time came for retribution. Sad as it was, these speculations gave some morbid kind of comfort to some of the taximen, because they could rationalize the murder as being personal and hence, granting them the illusion of safety. But for others, it came too close to home and they were perturbed.

And the third reason was somewhat an extension of the second. On the Monday morning following Ras Negus' revelation, Dezzie had taken to the road because it was imperative that he tell as many people as possible about his great fortune. He was never one to keep a lid on things, and what was the point, anyway? Everyone was bound to find out. It was ludicrous to even try to keep such a thing a secret, in Portmore of all places, especially he who was beknown to every Jack and Jane for miles about. Why cover a candle under a basket? So, as much as he didn't need to, he had jumped into Betsy and had been cruising, very leisurely, you must understand, stopping from time to time and signaling to such and such a person to pull over on to the soft shoulder, for a quick chat. He also spent a great deal of time parked at the Portmore Mall, just gallivanting with the fellows, who were in equally jubilant spirits on account of the news. He couldn't afford any liquor yet because the funds hadn't landed, but they got drunk off the expectation.

It was on this very day that a man approached Dezzie, while he was leaning against the open door of his taxi and in the middle of a very sweet joke. He thought the man was a passenger and so he was trying to explain that he was on his break and not taking passengers at the time. But the man wanted something else. He was Shelly's father, and he pulled Dezzie to the side and informed him that Shelly was pregnant, with his child.

"Mine? No, sah! Yuh crazy! Not mine at all, Papa, find somebody else!" which threw the man into quite a temper. He was a man in his early fifties, worn for what it was worth, too much hair on his face and not enough on his head. He wore a shirt that had at one time been a dress shirt but had, after the long haul, been demoted to casual wear. But it still looked out of place, since he was not at a wedding – though it seemed he had come to arrange one. Shelly had named Dezzie as the father of the child she was carrying. What a wicked girl, thought Dezzie to himself.

All they had done was kiss. Yes, he had exaggerated a bit and had told the fellas that he had gone further than he really had. But Shelly, of all people, knew he hadn't.

The man was taking no foolish talk. "What, want mi to report yuh, then? That yuh want? Some jail time yuh want?" His voice was gruff and you could see he had a temper that had not been tamed. "Breed mah chile and then saying is not you?"

"Look here, man. Ah neva even touch har pum-pum. Ah swear!" shouted Dezzie.

The man held him by the collar and leaned him up against the car. "Suh, then, who send har all these text message, eh? Eh? Who name Dezzie, eh? Eh?" He flicked the screen of the cell phone in his hand with much finesse, for an old foot, while still pinning Dezzie so he couldn't move, and he scrolled through a million messages that had been sent back and forth between Shelly and Dezzie.

"Look," said Dezzie, trying in vain to break free. "Ah talk to yuh daughter, yes. But I never even touch har! Tell har stop tell lie pon mi!"

"Oh, suh all-a dem slackness yah pon the phone, is not you send it? Eh? Is not you send all ah dis?" He replaced the cell phone in his pocket and landed two right hooks across the side of Dezzie's face. "Look here, you. If she seh is you, then is you! And don't bother try hide. I going find yuh blouse and skirt! Yuh gwine min' yuh pickney!"

And then he had released him. And Dezzie never went back to the Portmore Mall, especially since the others had reported seeing the man hovering around.

Two days later, Dezzie was on the evening news and on the front page of two local newspapers, though his jaw was still swollen and hurting. But what was a swollen jaw to a rich man? And who to tell how far his face and name had gone, with technology being what it is? For all he knew, some man in Katmandu or some woman in Timbuktu may have seen him and had wished to be him. They had done up one of those fancy larger-than-life cheques and a press conference had been held, and many cameras had recorded the moment that Desmond Reuben Grant was handed his cheque for four hundred and sixty-two million dollars. That was what The Man had decided to give him, after taking out whatever there was to be taken out. Dezzie had pouted about the matter but then, it happened to everyone. That was just how it went. The Man needed his taxes, and to cover his overheads, and such the like. Several journalists had interviewed him and had all asked the same stock questions, but he was never tired of explaining how thankful he was, first and foremost, to Father God, who had blessed him and delivered him from tribulation, to his mother, who had fathered him, to his sweetheart, Precious, who was going to help him spend it. And everybody had laughed, and Precious had blushed, and Bam had made sure that everyone knew that she was the mother being spoken about and that that was her Dez-Dez, her baby boy, her pootus.

That the ticket had survived in tiptop shape was a miracle unto itself. Had it appeared to have been tampered with in any way, the deal would have been off. Dezzie had gone to Cherry's post to claim his winnings, naively thinking that he would have been given at least some of the cash on spot, to carry him over. Then, he pretended that he knew all along that he would have to go to the head office in Kingston, that there would be a tiresome interview and that certain documents would have to be presented. Cherry was exceedingly amicable in pointing all this out to him, her voice trained to a sweet melodic pitch. In fact, if he wanted, she could take the day off and accompany him to head office, just to make sure he filled out everything right, but Dezzie had declined, to her dismay. At head office, after a lengthy explanation in which certain things had to be repeated with much tedium, Dezzie had decided that he would opt for the lump sum payment, as opposed to the annuity, which Precious had expressed would have been better. Dezzie's logic was, tomorrow was guaranteed to no one. He didn't want The Man to hang on to his winnings any longer than the time it took to sign the cheque. He wouldn't be able to sleep, knowing that for countless years another man would be in charge of his money. He preferred to take his chances with the live ready cash, to invest or spend it as he saw fit, the way an independent man should, never mind that the amount was much reduced with this option. But cash was cash, and a good-sized bird in the hand was worth a huge bird cut up into twenty pieces and rationed out to him every year. He wanted to do with his bird as he pleased. He was a grown man, after all.

For the first time in his life, Dezzie opened a bank account. He had to, evidently, and it felt strange. He had never seen the need to do so before, since his existence had been hand-to-mouth. Moreover, he doubted the goodwill of bankers towards the common man; a proletariat mistrust, from the observed zeal with which their deposits were sought and the encumbrance that they faced when time came to procure a loan, or even to withdraw their very own money back. He had always been one of they who had vowed that, should they ever come into a substantial amount of money – or even if it wasn't all that substantial – they would rather hide it under the mattress or in a corner of the fowl coop than put it in a bank, for the obvious fact that you would have next to nothing to get back should the bank fail, as they had seen on the news and read about in the newspapers countless times. They would have no reprieve and no one to blame for placing their cash in the hands of thieves.

That said, Dezzie soon realized that it was much easier to speculate upon what you would do if you had something, than it was to deal with the reality of having the thing. It very quickly became clear that in no way could he liquidate his fortune and store it under the mattress, or anywhere in his house. Apart from the physical and logistic impossibility of the feat, there stood the danger of robbery. As it were, he was already paranoid about his children being kidnapped, or even his mother or Precious or someone else close to him being abducted, and an outrageous ransom demanded. It was not farfetched. In fact, the very thing had happened before and had gripped the country in a weeklong national frenzy, till the bandits got their way and the victims were released.

He could just imagine what would happen if undesirable elements got wind that his residence was loaded with dough. No. that was absurd. He saw it now that the money had to be banked. He had asked around and had chosen the bank that he felt would be least liable to crumble and take his fortune away from him. He went with the oldest, most stable and most scandal-free bank. He chose Fidelity National Bank and Trust, Portmore branch. He had been issued a debit card and a credit card, though he hadn't asked for either, and he was assured that this was standard procedure. The manager at the bank , Mr. Fitzroy Cummings, had been mighty pleasant and called Dezzie by his first name, ushering him into his office and telling him that such matters were beyond the realm of a simple bank teller or supervisor. This was top management stuff. He had made Dezzie feel like a real VIP, offering him investment advice and promising to hook him up with some real big players who knew the market inside out and could earn him some hefty returns on his money. He gave Dezzie a business card and his private number, and promised to get back to him regarding some private contacts for the businessmen mentioned. This was the big league. He would be swimming with sharks.

Mr. Michael Chang had not recognized Dezzie as the man whose blurred face had issued what he, Mr. Chang, felt to be threats, through the window of the Lot-a-Luck post. He saw Mr. Desmond Grant as just another commoner who had somehow found a way to breach the fortress of the Lot-a-Luck jackpot. He had crossed the moat and had scaled the walls. A few had to be allowed to do this, to keep up pretences. It was a concession that Chang gave with some amount of resentment, a necessary cog in the running of the game, that the spew-way of the dam be left open to avert controversy. Mr. Chang consoled himself that the money would in some way or other find its way back to him, or to those of his clique. In any event, it was amusing to watch as each one, almost every time, dizzy on the novelty of their unearned and unaccustomed wealth, went on a year-long splurge in which they squandered the money left right and centre. He said year-long, being nice. By year end, they were usually flat broke. The shrewder ones made it to two years, tops. And it was a matter of great ridicule among his peers, to observe the rise and imminent fall of the undeserved.

When the man had been brought before him in his office that day, Chang had smiled. A smile for himself and a smile for the man; two different smiles, stroking two different egos – the one crude, vulgar and vulnerable, the other refined, sophisticated and on top of things. Grant had come in with his mother and his woman – the usual crutches for people who needed crutches. The mother had been very verbose. The common-law wife (wasn't it always common-law among this lot, Mr. Chang had sneered as he massaged his solid gold wedding band) had been a little more contained and reticent, albeit excited. In his role as manager at the gaming office, Mr. Chang considered it as part of his duty to inform the winners of their rights and their options, to encourage them to make the best choice, which was the annuity, though he secretly wished that they would opt for the lump sum payment, which would deflect more of the money back over to his company. Also, the lump sum payment would free up more money sooner to be channeled back to him, since all or most of the friends and relatives and leeches and beggars and all who would be given money, whether pocket change or those who hoped to milk him dry, would use a good amount of it to buy more tickets, for a chance to be like Mr. Grant, which most certainly would not be the case, since he had already been selected as the one out of the million.

Michael Chang suspected that the common-law woman would be the voice of reason in this outfit, beseeching the man to be frugal and thrifty, and the mother would be the opposite. It was easy to see, if you knew what to look for, and Michael Chang knew what to look for. He had seen many come and go. He met with the winners only once really, for official purposes, and then maybe another once or twice after that, for showmanship and promotional obligations. He had no intention of forging any further bonds with them because, at his core, he always considered their wealth to be bogus and undeserved. Of course, a generic smile and a firm handshake were extended to all who walked through these doors and had the momentary pleasure of sitting on the luxurious office chairs. It wasn't until the man cornered him with a coonish grin and patted him on the back, that Michael Chang recognized the delusional character, and the voice came back to him.

"Ah did tell yuh, Missa Chin! Ah did tell yuh ah would come claim mi winnings!" Dezzie bawled in raucous spirits, as if talking to an old chum from Primary school, remembering a silly bet they had made.

Michael Chang smiled to indicate that he had gotten the joke and that, yes, it would appear that the joke was on him; but he said nothing. For such a simpleton to come into such fortune, was unnerving. His secretary ushered them out of the room, much to Chang's relief, and gave them further instructions on how to proceed. And that was that. That was that.

As the man and his entourage trumpeted through the lobby, Michael Chang could hear him saying, presumably, to his mother, "Mama, yuh life set right now! The only thing yuh have to worry about when yuh wake up is what colour panty yuh want to put on, and whether yuh feel for cocoa tea or coffee with yuh breakfast. Everything done cook and curry."

When they stood outside the head office, waiting for the taxi that they had hired to take them to and fro, Dezzie was very animated. He was telling Precious that she should sell out her merchandise cheap cheap and close down her stall in the arcade, since she would no longer be needing it, and that she should give away her car to her mother, since he would be buying her a new one.

"Yuh want people to malice me and say I get rich and switch?" asked Precious, tickled at her own joke. "Yuh know how Downtown people stay."

"Who business with them?" asked Dezzie. "Step-up time is step-up time. Who business what grudgeful naygah seh?" He hissed his teeth, but he too was chuckling. "They think yuh want to sell in Bend-down Plaza all the days of yuh life?" This was the term that people used to describe the arcade, as well as people who sold along the streets of Kingston, because some of the merchandise were laid out on canvases on the ground and vendors had to sometimes stoop to view the wares or to make their purchase.

Dezzie had amassed quite a local following in a very short time. There was the homegrown crew of Beres, Conda, Joe and Ruddy, who behaved as if they were his body guards, personal assistants and gofers. A pecking order had quickly evolved among these men. It was understood that Beres was the right-hand man and Ruddy was the left side-kick, and the other two were deputies, and there was little feud about this, except the fact that with any hierarchy, there was always the silent threat of overthrow. They were always with him when Dezzie was cooling out on the ends, at the bar sipping Red Stripe beer and reflecting on old times, as in, last week times. There were random stragglers who sought his company whenever he was available, some asking for handouts and picking up crumbs, waiting patiently for the free round of beers to be ordered, giving jokes for gungo soup, as the old timers would say. The shameless opportunists would be like the bartender, who jacked up Dezzie's tab and overcharged for the liquor, then pocketed the extra or just didn't bother to give the man his change, knowing that he was too drunk to remember or too high on his horse to ask for it. If Dezzie seemed like he was on to things, he never raised a fuss. He would only chuckle and say, "Don't bother rob me, eh nuh!" and pointed a chastising finger at the bartender, who responded primly, "Naw, man! Wouldn't do that to mah long-time brethren from on the corner!"

There was Seymour, Dezzie's brother, whose presence on the Greater Portmore scene had become all the more visible with Dezzie's rise, but the two had never really been close and so he was not seen as an immediate challenge to Beres' position. He would have to work his way up the rank and file like everybody else, brother or no brother. Seymour was short and had the jockey's gait, his twiggy bow legs giving him that peculiar step that he swore the girls loved. This, apparently, made up for the lack of height.

Since Dezzie had had no incidence of epileptic fits after the news of his winnings, he had thrown out the medication and Bam had reconsidered her theory about him being the victim of Obeah. Stress, she figured, had been the culprit, and since Dezzie was now stress-free, all that was behind him. Behind them. A party was held in celebration of the Lot-a-Luck winnings. This party, of course, could not be contained at the residence and it spilled onto the walkway and onto the streets of the Place, where a bounce-about and trampoline had been ordered for the children's amusement, and three jerk chicken drums had been ablaze in a corner, manned by persons who were rumoured to be top quality chefs from the North Coast. The selectors, who mixed the Dancehall medleys that blared throughout the night, were also said to be of high quality caliber, who only played at celebrity sessions and even then, only by appointment and a hefty downpayment. So if anyone had doubted that Dezzie had indeed struck it big, now would be a good time to eat his dust.

His mother was particularly pleased with the turn of events. She had bought a suit Uptown just for the party, a suit which may not have been appropriate for her age and certainly was no complement to her protruding tummy but – there was a but – age was just a number and she also had very nice legs, truth be told. Everyone said that she looked wonderful and that her face showed no signs of crack, and kept asking her if she was really positively sure that she had given birth to four children cause she herself looked like sixteen, which put her in a mellow mood for the whole night, the effect of the liquor being but a brawta. Bam was proud of Dez-Dez, which she had taken to calling him lately, especially as he had been the one of her children least likely to amount to anything, if she were to follow bad-minded people who loved to cast doubt on other people's children.

Dez-Dez had come into the world after a hard pregnancy and a horrific labour. His had been a breech birth and the doctors had had to reach in and turn him and even then, he ultimately had to be delivered by Cesarean Section, which had left her cramped and immobile for weeks. His father had run out on them and Dezzie hadn't seen the man in years.

Bam saw to it that word got around about the trip they were planning to the North Coast. They had selected an all-inclusive resort that was family-oriented. There were nannies who would tend to the children while the grown-ups saw about the business of enjoying themselves. Bam saw to it that everyone understood that this was no chump change that would be required. Dez-Dez intended to go all out to make his family happy. No expense would be spared. All-inclusive meant that every single thing was included, from lodgings to meals to snacks to liquor to pool to beach to everything. She wondered if they knew that. And there would be a kitchenette where they could even prepare their own meals if they wanted, but they were just planning to make use of the all-you-can eat buffet cause, both she and Precious were tired of the cooking and just wanted to unwind and let someone else slave over the fire for a change. They had chartered a taxi to take them down, as Dez-Dez wanted a break from the driving, and to experience being chauffeur-driven. The tables had certainly turned.

The neighbours and friends and complete strangers stared on awestruck, listening to the details, eager for it to get to the part where they could drop a few words to the effect that they had this brilliant idea to do such and such and needed but a little push in the right direction. A financial push, you understand. Or, that though they were not the type to look for handouts, they would appreciate a little help with the bills or the medication or the mortgage or the children's school fees, such and such a child being so bright and doing so well at school, and the father a dead beat.

Dezzie was particularly excited about the trip, even more so than the children. It reminded him of when he was a schoolboy looking forward to the class trip, and the morning would never come, no matter how many times he got up through the night. On the morning of the trip, he was the first to wake up and get ready. The bags had already been packed. The children were readying themselves and Bam, Miss Early Bird, was on the couch waiting, with her shades and hat already on, looking like a real dry-land tourist. Precious was taking her time to apply her make-up and adjust the strings of her summer dress, a lovely light dress that she had bought in Panama years ago but had never worn before. She was feeling a bit shy about her weight and wondering if she should change the dress. The taxi arrived and Dezzie was going from room to room gathering everyone.

"Come nuh, Precious! Time going."

"But why the hurry? Is pantomime wi going? We have to get to the hotel by a certain time?"

"The taximan reach!" shouted Dezzie.

"Coming, Dezzie!" Precious shouted back.

"Stop the coming and come, woman! Time going!"

The trip to Ocho Rios would take them through the rolling green hills of the St. Ann interior, where Bam was born and raised and where Dezzie spent much of his childhood. He sat in the front passenger seat and he soaked in the weirdness of that, while the two women and the two children sat in the back. It was hard to hold back from telling the driver what to do, or to ask him why he was going so slowly, or to chastise him for not taking over a line of traffic before a huge eight wheeler pulled out in front of them, slowing them up big time. But Precious was shooting some mean glances at him, which meant that she wanted him to just relax and enjoy the two hour ride, and not tell the man what to do.

Dezzie leaned back and tried to relax. He was wearing a very dapper custom-made suit that he had ordered from Baz, the tailor. The two women had said that the suit was a bit out of character, not to mention too hot and dressy for where they were headed. But Dezzie had shot back that they were only jealous of his one-in-the-island outfit, and that they should leave him be. If he wanted to be hot, he could very well afford to be hot. But he was really very uncomfortable and by the time they had gotten to the Flat Bridge, he took off the jacket and hoped that no one noticed. They all noticed, and laughed him to scorn.

At the hotel, they received a warm June reception. This meant that the staff was off-guard because it was nowhere near the Winter tourist season, and so they could afford to be gracious to locals. Had it been anywhere from December to April, the family mightn't have received that many smiles. At that time of the year, their fellow locals who were employed in the tourism service industry reserved their enchantment for those who could return the favour by way of tips. And since it had been discovered long ago that local dry-land tourists were averse to tipping, they received nothing but the vilest frowns and cut-eyes from the attendants, chefs, bellboys, maids and nannies. But as it were, only a handful of foreigners could be seen, and so the Grant family was cordially ushered upstairs to their self-contained quarters, complete with all the amenities and a panoramic view of the Caribbean Sea.

Desandre took control of the television remote and Desrine seized the remote for the air condition unit, which she kept adjusting but no one reprimanded her for it. Dezzie plopped down spread-eagled on the queen-sized bed in his quarters and moved his arms and legs up and down, laterally, to show his great comfort. He vowed that these were going to be the best four days of his life. The start of many more best days to come. Precious wanted to christen the pool as soon as she unpacked. Bam wanted to see what the spa had to offer by way of rejuvenation for her weary bones, forgetting that she had declared herself to be permanently sixteen. They all intended to sign up first thing tomorrow for scuba diving and jet skiing and a ride on the glass bottom boat. But of course, the priority of the moment was to seek the famous all-you-can-eat buffet which, rumour had it, was presently in full swing downstairs and a few paces to the left of the main lobby. They had made sure to ask for directions.

It was forgivable, them being nouveau-riche, for them all to have loaded their plates with far more food than each could possibly eat, even Dezzie, who prided himself on never having backed down from a plate of food in his life. The chefs at the resort knew what time of day it was, for sure. If this was lunch, they could only imagine what would have been laid before them at dinner time. The attendants frowned as the family members piled their plates high, causing Dezzie to mumble, "Is not their food, don't know why they frowning. I pay for this shit!"

But they would have him know that their genteel guests who visited from Up North, some of them every year and stayed for months on end, only took from the buffet the most delicate serving of only what they knew they would eat, unlike certain forced-ripe follow-fashion monkeys who were pretending to be tourists and couldn't manage tourist life. But the attendants, since they were forbidden by protocol to vent any such diatribe, just smiled at the family and raised the giant lids so they could better select from the fare.

Precious reminded everyone that they should make sure to save some space for the barbecue, which had pizza and burgers and French fries and popcorn, and ice cream and what-not. They dragged their bloated selves down to the beach afterwards and splashed, too heavy for a full swim, till they each collapsed in a pile of delirious satisfaction on the sand. They remained on the beach for hours, till it was time for dinner, which resulted in another feast in which they gorged themselves, sampling everything. And then, they ordered pasta and grilled snapper and basmati rice from the Italian restaurant, and asked that this be delivered by room service, for when they got hungry later. It so happened that no one ever really got hungry for the rest of the stay, but they did manage to pack away the Italian dinner by morning.

They slept in and missed the morning boat ride, and had to sign up for the afternoon one instead. It was the first glass bottom ride for all of them, but Bam recalled going out in small boats as a child, with the fishermen from Ocho Rios bay, as her father had been a fisherman. Less than half-mile out, Dezzie started to regret the whole thing, especially when the tour operator pointed out that if a shark swam by, they would surely see it through the glass. Dezzie asked if he was joking, right, and he said no, he wasn't, he had seen many sharks that way. And that's when Dezzie got sea sick and started double-checking his life jacket, and couldn't wait to be landed again. But he did enjoy the view of the different types of coral, and watching the fish shoal up for crumbs that the man threw into the water. He wanted to set a good example for his children, though he was scared.

The next day, Dezzie beefed up his courage to the point where he found himself strapped on to a jet ski behind the operator, with Precious and Bam also on jet skis, and the children together on the back of one. They sped through the blue waters and created salty foams that sprayed into their eyes and make them squint. They went all the way past Dunn's River and several other waterfalls along the coast of St. Ann. They passed other resorts, some more private it seemed, and glimpsed middle-aged white women lounging as their rent-a-dreads massaged suntan oil onto their backs. These young men, it was said, were some of the very ones who doubled as chefs and bellboys and maintenance men in other hotels along the coast, capitalizing on their birthright of chocolate skin, firm bodies and substantial endowments. Some hoped to marry one of these women and thereby earn a Green Card or Citizenship in any of these Northern lands, where most of their patrons hailed from. Sometimes, the deal went through. Other times, it ended with the departure of their white lady love. But they were resilient, these men. They were well sought after and had come to place a price on themselves, for better or worse, proving themselves versatile and adaptable. "They don't call it the service industry for nothing," Precious smirked.

These women were not oblivious to the fact that, while they soaked up the sun and frolicked with their young Black gigolos, meanwhile, back in the room, their husbands or boyfriends were up to some hanky panky of their own, flirting with the maids and nannies, offering tips in return for favours, and expecting these favours as part of the package. It seemed, it had all been subconsciously planned, so each spouse was duly fulfilled in his or her fantasies, and returned happy. Or perhaps, they had come solo as lonely single folks in quest of sexual adventure. They may have heard a rumour or two and wanted empirical proof, to the order of personal experience, which was of course the most convincing proof. Perhaps, they had invented rumours of their own, languishing in a steady nine-to-fiver in some backwater Mid-Western town, and had conjured up notions of what a Third Worldian was or ought to be, had saved up every penny they could muster and had picked a rock and landed, with expectations, and foreign currency to boot.

That afternoon, Dezzie found himself in the middle of one such liaison, which had Precious very vexed and darting cut-eyes at him, though she recovered later when he ordered roses to be brought up to her, and dark chocolate, and some red wine. He was on his way to becoming a connoisseur. What happened was, two white women were frolicking along the beach and Dezzie was walking by. He was known to parade the beach in his swim trunk, ever since his mother had made a very stray and innocent comment that his six-pack was gaining on him. He had taken it to heart and since then, he had become unstoppable. He could have easily been mistaken for a lifeguard, the way he patrolled the area. Which was why they mistook him for one, and had stopped him to ask about the yellow flag that had been posted on the beach. He didn't know the reason, either, but then they had gotten into a conversation and one thing led to another, till Dezzie was invited to have a seat on the empty lounge chair beside them, which he did since he was a man of good breed, as his mother had often pointed out to him when he had done things to the contrary. By the time he returned to his family, he had already divulged the information regarding him winning the lottery, and he also had an American accent. A reasonable trade. Precious was fuming and threatening to pack her belongings and take her children and head on out back to Portmore, and he could stay with his mother and his two white bitch-them, to which Dezzie responded that he had only been trying to be friendly with the other nice guests.

"Cho, babes! Yuh know ah just being mah own sweet self. Don't look into things too deep. This is our time. Cho, man. Don't make it look so bad."

It was on the third day that they ran into Mr. Dacres, the Member of Parliament, and his girlfriend, Cassandra. They had just arrived and were in the lobby checking in, and Dezzie had been on his way to the tennis court, where some brave and patient soul was going to teach him how to play lawn tennis. Dezzie had his racket in his hand and a towel around his neck, and he was looking like a professional tennis player in his white shorts and jersey, and headband to match. He was sure he had made a good impression on the unimpressionable Cassandra, and he was very happy about the coincidence. Mr. Dacres invited Dezzie to meet up for drinks later, which they did, all four of them, Precious reluctantly tagging along. The prime interest, of course, was Dezzie's newfound wealth, and Mr. Dacres, a man of experience in such matters, was offering advice on how Dezzie could invest it, or tactfully dispose of it. Same difference. Neither Cassandra nor Precious tried to make conversation with each other, each looking off into the distance, Cassandra notably bored and Precious notably perturbed. Precious did not like to be among company where she had a strong feeling that she didn't belong. Within the hour, even the men had run out of things to say, each acutely aware of the discomfort of his lady, and not wanting to jeopardize his chances for love later. An invitation was extended to Dezzie to come to the M.P.'s home in Hellshire on the following Saturday, where they could talk more casually and at length.

They didn't see each other for the rest of the trip, though Dezzie looked for Cassandra till his eyes hurt. He wished that he could get the chance to see her in a two-piece bikini, her long hair streaming down her back the way the water had trained it, her long stately legs barely touching the sand. He adored her. He dreamed about her that night and many other nights to come. He would be willing to drink her bath water, if she consented to it. He would be willing to spend all his money on her, if she would let him.

Dezzie really went to Hellshire to see Cassandra, though he knew there was a strong chance that Cassandra would not be there, since the M.P. was married and lived with his family. As it turned out, Cassandra was there and Mrs. Dacres was abroad with the children, on Summer holidays, Dezzie assumed. Cassandra seemed to take a bit more interest in him, actually directing questions at him – probing questions that signaled interest – and laughing at several jokes of his that he himself had known to be corny. This would make great fodder for when he next met with the crew, and tell them how Cassandra the beautiful had taken a liking to him.

"What? Dacres' woman?" they would holler in disbelief.

And he would smile and say, "Better believe it!"

"No sah, that's prime property. Can't take Dacres' woman from him!" they would insist.

And he would say, "Oh yeah? Watch Dezzie the Don-Dada at work!"

This boost in confidence extended into several areas of his life, where he now boldly said and did things that he would have shrunk from just weeks before. For instance, he had always wanted to apply for a visa to enter the United States, but he had lacked the confidence to do so, feeling that he would have been turned down. His mother had applied four times and had been turned down each time. She had become disillusioned and perhaps, this had rubbed off on Dezzie. He also knew many other people who had been turned down, after paying the non-refundable fees, gathering all kinds of documents and waiting in line for hours. Dezzie had had no assets, no papers to show anything, neither education-wise nor otherwise. No one would want him in their country, as he was bound to be a burden on their economy. That was what he had told himself, in his wallowing. But now, he had a new bout of confidence and he felt absolutely sure that he would get through. He applied, not only for himself but for his mother and children as well. When they were all turned down, he cried. He actually cried on the grounds of the embassy, in the men's room, trying to figure out where he had messed up. So, Uncle Sam didn't want him poor and he didn't want him rich, either? Uncle Sam just didn't want him, full stop?

Not even his children? He hadn't bothered to ask the lady at the counter why he had been turned down. After he had regained composure, he herded his family off the compound and sulked for the rest of the day.

Ras Negus was still having trouble sleeping. In fact, he was more awake at night than he was during the day. At night, the thoughts flooded his mind like the high tide coming in with a vengeance. He had made several pages of notes. Naph-T took to setting up with him some nights, going over the plans, and she made recommendations too as her own dreams, long muffled, began to unfold and breathe new life. They planned to open a restaurant. It was something they both wanted. They had vowed to tell as few people as possible about the money, at first at least, till they decided exactly what they were going to do and were well on the way to seeing it through. They had only told Miss Inez and Naph-T's parents, and their own children under oath of secrecy, and Ras Negus had told the jellyman.

He confided to Jellyman about the ticket that he had found, and about the fact that he had been granted a certain amount of money as compensation for his kindness, and that he had a business proposition to make. He wanted to go into business with Jellyman, selling bottled coconut water and cane juice, which Jellyman would provide at wholesale price. He beseeched Jellyman to keep a low profile till such time as he would decide to divulge the information to others, at his discretion. Jellyman was enthusiastic about the proposal, and determined at once that he would check out the price of the bottles, caps and labels. He expressed joy and gratitude for being privy to the information, and the opportunity.

Chapter Ten

Some people have the worst luck. The very worst luck. Dezzie never realized how unlucky the people around him had been, till his luck began to chip in. Matter of fact, the two seemed to work in inverse proportion to each other. The better his luck got, the worst their luck got, and the more they came to him to offset their misfortune.

His father, whom Dezzie hadn't seen in donkey years, found his way from Walkers Wood to Greater Portmore on nothing but a sniff and a hunch. He found his sons and estranged wife neither shocked to see him nor elated to see him, but they weren't on the offensive either, which was good. They seemed to have been expecting him. In fact, if he had had the gift of clairaudience he would have heard Bam say just a few days ago, "Bet yuh any money that yuh 'ol wutless father going find yuh, now that yuh rich. Him must hear 'bout the winnings already!" and lo and behold, there he was, seated across from Dezzie in the living room, with the most inventive and touching hard luck story of them all. No one could say he was lacking in originality, though his countenance could have been a bit more convincing.

"Nuh hold nuttin 'gainst him. Is done yuh father already. Give him something, even if him don't deserve it," was the advice that Bam whispered to her son, though in her heart she wished he would have the steadfastness to send the wretch back to country without even as much as bus fare. The nerve of him, coming to seek pension when he deserted them all this time! She had a good mind to tell Dezzie to chase the old fart from the yard. Lucky thing she wasn't the type to carry grudges or to box food out of people's mouths. She offered Reuben some refreshments and extended her warmest hospitality to the man. Dezzie was indifferent towards the whole situation. He had resigned himself long ago to the notion that he had no father, in fact, that his mother was both mother and father and that he needed nothing more by way of parental guidance at this point. When he had needed a father, he had had to make do without one, and now he was alright with that.

Reuben Grant was a countryman at heart and he had returned to St. Ann long ago. He was a farming man, hardworking, but prone to promiscuity and not at all averse to "hiring help" in the sex department, which had led to him becoming separated from his wife in the first place, years ago, and still ran his life now. He seemed to be content to assume that his estranged wife and four children were alive and well, despite his lack of contribution to their well-being. He had no idea that the two older girls had long left to seek their fortunes in the tourism industry on one of the small islands, leaving the boys in the shadow of their mother. Reuben didn't immediately ask for money, or anything for that matter – but they all suspected it was coming, hanging on every unfinished sentence and lurking in every lowering of his head as he averted his eyes. He would be staying by Seymour's house, in Naggo Head, he said. He would be there for a while, if they needed him – or if he needed them, Bam added in her mind, as she smiled and walked him to the bridge at the entrance of the walkway.

There were neighbours who had run into some unbelievable hard luck. Unbelievable. They knew that no one would have ever suspected, they couldn't blame Dezzie for not having suspected, since they had tried their best to hold things together and not be a burden to anyone. But things had reached the point at which they no longer felt they could cope. At first, Dezzie had made the foolish decision to keep a certain amount of cash on hand, at the house, for when these relatives, friends and neighbours approached him with their tales of grief. Though he had established a reputation for being stingy back in the day – that being, last month – he now felt the spirit of humanitarianism taking possession of him and he reasoned that he was somewhat duty-bound to help.

These were the very people whom he had lived amongst for years. They argued and laughed and reveled in their shared misery. He knew when they flushed their toilets. He knew when the wives weren't on speaking terms with the husbands, and when they had reconciled. He knew what they prepared for breakfast, lunch and dinner. He knew when they ate out or ordered pizza. All these things were easy to know. The houses in Greater Portmore allowed for minimal privacy. The residents were tight-knit in their shared predicament. He had caused some of the predicament, having deflowered many of their daughters and initiated many of their sons into a life of rum and recklessness. It was not that Dezzie yearned for any kind of redemption. He didn't think he had done anything wrong. But he did feel obligated to help. But when they realized that money was on hand, and that all that was required to fly the gate was a tilted face and puppy dog eyes and a wounded voice, they turned on the switch. And they had no mercy. They had no discretion. They had no limit. They had no sense of enough.

Shelly's father had returned, somewhat more sober but still insisting that Dezzie was the father. He had found his way to the house and now that he had heard about the winnings, the matter of the wedding became even more imperative. Dezzie swore he hadn't touched Shelly but then, the more the man insisted, the more blur the whole thing became in Dezzie's mind until he himself wasn't quite sure. He had been with so many school girls. Who to tell if he had been with Shelly, too, rather than just kissing her, as he had maintained? Maybe he hadn't lied to the fellas at all. Push come to shove, there was the paternity test but then, he didn't have his former confidence and he didn't want to remove the element of doubt, since that could mean jail time if he didn't play his cards right. And with so much money now involved, the stakes were high.

"Just give them some money and mek them gwaan," said Bam, when Dezzie confided the matter to her, well out of range of Precious. "For a peaceful life, give them some money and mek them gwaan."

"If I give him one time, him coming back another time," said Dezzie, in one of his wise moments. He decided that he would ignore them for the time being, as much as one could ignore a pregnancy.

True to his word, he bought Precious a car. He also bought himself a car and, on the advice of his local fraternity, headed by Beres, he bought three cars that he would put on the road as taxis. Beres, Conda and Ruddy would operate the cars, and report to Dezzie nightly, as he had done with Ping Wing. They in turn handed in their old cars to the rightful owners, with some amount of attitude, it should be mentioned.

It had been a very special day when Dezzie found that he was able to walk right into a car dealership and walk right back out one hour later, the owner of a brand new BMW. The wheels, which he referred to his car from then on as, had set him back a good couple million. Precious had chosen a Lexus because it had been her dream car from ever since. She had always fancied herself around the steering wheel of a Lexus. So they had gone to the Lexus dealer that same day and filled out the paper work. The following day, Dezzie and the fellas had gone to another car mart Uptown and he had selected three brand new Toyota Corollas, though Precious had said that maybe it wasn't such a good idea to put brand new cars on the route as taxis, knowing how treacherous taximen could be with other people's cars. But Dezzie had said he was a man of quality and that everything henceforth would have to be strictly brand new. He may have been born poor but that didn't say. Now that he could afford it, why should he pretend like he didn't love top quality stuff? The fellas, of course, were all in favour of this. They saw that the dividends of the friendship were coming in. They were mighty pleased.

The BMW and the Lexus created quite a stir on Fifty-three Place. It was not a shock, per se. It was expected that a man would step things up now that he had the means. They all would have done it. But it was a thing to see.

"Don't bother mash it up with your reckless driving now, yuh know, Dezzie!" was all they could manage to say without betraying their deep-rooted envy.

It was a powerful car, fully loaded. Dezzie had overestimated his driving skills. He had never in his life been around the wheels of such a powerful car. He could feel the surge run through his arms just from touching the steering wheel. Maybe it was all in his head. No, it was not. The drive from the dealership in Kingston to Portmore was the most nerve-wracking in all his days on the Earth. He was certain that he would lose control of it and that the car would run off the causeway bridge and plunge into the lagoon below. He would die a happy man but he wasn't ready yet. He wanted to live some more life. A man couldn't really say he had lived life if he had been poor. He was scared to touch any button. Then, stupidly, he started watching the rear-view mirror for signs of the police. Maybe they would think that he had stolen the car. He was going to have to make sure to always have his papers on him. He breathed a sigh of relief when he pulled into Fifty-three Place. All who had been on the Place when he arrived cheered as if it was the first time they had seen a live BMW. It made Dezzie feel proud, like a superstar. They gathered round to look at the interior. Some of the boys wanted a chance to sit inside the car, which Dezzie refused at first but then he took pity on them. He allowed them to honk the horn once, and to turn on the stereo for five minutes.

"Awright. But wipe oonuh foot! Mek sure!" he said, shaking his head. He didn't want to see even one single footprint on the carpet, not even one finger print on the white leather seats. The boys daintily inspected the interior of the car, giving out bridled shrieks of ecstasy, and then Dezzie quickly ushered them out, and checked if everything was in order, and sprayed some air freshener to revive the ambiance of the interior.

To his own children, he granted a little more leverage. They talked him into taking them for a joy ride in the evening, they dressed up as if they were going to the national pantomime, because their father had said his children have to look sharp every time. Dezzie himself went inside to "hol' a fresh and slick out", as he phrased it, which meant that he took a long hot shower from the newly installed water heating system, and dressed himself in proper attire. He had become rather suave. They went for ice cream at Devon House, and brought back enough to full a section of the brand new refrigerator. Dezzie pulled up and parked the BMW beside the Lexus. Of course, there was no parking space in front of the houses and so residents had to park on the Place, which was not very secure. The two cars took up most of the available space. This created the potential for strife among the neighbours, some of whom had already claimed those spaces, though really they were up for grabs.

The next day, on his way to the bank, Dezzie ran the BMW off the road near Naggo Head and a haulage company had to be called in to retrieve it, though the car was not physically damaged. The incident made the evening news. He suspected that some people had found it amusing, maybe some of his very friends had snickered, but they never dared do it to his face. He vowed to get over his fear of the powerful car and to stop being intimidated by his own rise. Because that was all it was. Intimidation. Was Desmond Grant, the superstar driver, going to let himself be manipulated by a car – BMW or no BMW? Hell, no!

There were shopping sprees and shopping sprees and shopping sprees. Precious had reluctantly sold out the merchandise in her stall to the other vendors, who had taken the liberty to ask for discounts. She had ended up giving them away, you could say. Those women drove a hard bargain, that being their trade. It was her trade too but Precious had been high on her new life and all the freshness of not having to worry about money. She knew that behind her back they would snicker and sneer, maybe call her a sell-out and a hurry-come-up hoity-toity whatever. She knew these women. She had spent her days among them, year in year out. There was bound to be some jealousy. It wasn't that she was deserting them, either. Precious really would have liked to keep her stall and maintain her independence, but Dezzie had assured her that this was not necessary. She had not put up much resistance because the upward tide of mobility round her had been so great. It swept her away. Her feminine instinct made her more cautious and prudent than Dezzie was. That was not to say, however, that she wasn't as excited as everyone else was, and that she didn't want to splurge as everyone else did.

And the hard luck stories kept flowing in, till Dezzie wondered if he should search for a safe place to hide. He started instructing people to say that he wasn't at home, when he was, or that he was cooling out in the country, when he wasn't. If the fellas saw him in a new gold chain or watch or designer pants or name brand sneakers, they wanted to get a wear off it, or to just let them borrow it till they could make a rounds to impress someone and return, or outright, if they could have it. It wasn't as if he couldn't easily buy another, they reasoned. They borrowed his BMW and didn't return it at the appointed hour. Knowing what he knew, Dezzie well suspected that they had gone to impress some woman into thinking that the car belonged to them, which is what he would have done, so he didn't hold that part of it against them. But the constant sponging and leeching and the outlandish loans that he had to be giving to men who were working, this was starting to get to him.

"If ah follow all ah yuh, I end up in the almshouse!" he shouted at them one night, when they had ordered a round of Johnny Walker without his consent, and instructed the bartender to add it to Dezzie's tab.

And they had all broken out in raucous laughter.

Chapter Eleven

It had been some time since Ras Negus had visited the tabernacle at the Ethiopian Orthodox Church. He was not opposed to the communal aspect of the religion but he much preferred to trod through on his personal journey. There were some who walked better with the group and there were some who walked better alone – with his queen, of course. The formal structure of worship had never appealed to Ras Negus. Still, he had been raised in the Ethiopian Orthodox Church and he did visit from time to time.

On this evening, the church was not in session but he wanted to speak to the elders on a pressing matter. He sought counsel regarding the money and how best he should spend it. Though he and Naph-T had plans of their own that they had been thrashing out on paper and discussing late into the night, Ras Negus wanted to uphold the tradition of seeking guidance from the venerable elders. He himself was forty-six years old, ripe but not ripe enough to pick. He had lived, yes, but there was still much ground to cover. The elders had traveled further and had climbed higher and thus could see beyond the horizon of a man who hadn't yet hit the half century mark.

The elders had lived at a time of much persecution meted

out to the brethren by Babylon, much worse than now. They had lived at a time when the Rastaman and woman were victimized and brutalized for the knotty dreadlocks on their heads. A Rastaman with money was not the same as a bald head man with money. This was understood. Ras Negus knew that many such situations had been brought for counsel. And he had known the elders to be wise, because since his childhood days, he had sat and listened to them in deep reasoning, when he was allowed. Men his age and even older had come to seek consultation on heavy matters. Of course, then, he had been silent. Now, he wished to speak.

    Elder Emmanuel and Elder Jacob, and High Priestess Rahel and Queen Mother Beth, were present. The women were dressed in the Rastafarian tradition, ankle-length cotton skirts and flowing tops, their hair in continental wraps, sandals strapped about their feet. They wore amulets and beads of red, gold and green, cowry shells in their locks, anklets made of various natural elements. The men wore what appeared to be military uniforms made of khaki, the insignia of the Lion of the Tribe of Judah upon their crests, epaulets to complete the order. Their hair completely covered by tams or wraps. One of the men was barefooted. Their beards were long and disheveled. It did not seem to matter in which direction the beard grew, so long as it grew. All held ganja spliffs and were stooped around a smoldering makeshift fireplace under a shed. The evening had an ashy smell to it, a smell of ganja burning and a wood fire lighting the minds of griots.

    Ras Negus expressed that he had come for advice. He made a gesture of bowing slightly and placing his right hand over his heart. He respected their word and would heed it. They were slow to speak. But each in turn did speak. And it was confirmed: land was of utmost importance. Get land, Ras Negus. Above anything else, get land, as much land as they will sell you, as far away from Babylon as you can. Get land and plant things. Yam, coconut, potato, dasheen, callaloo, onion, thyme, cali weed. A little bit of everything. Go high up to the hills where the air is clean and plenty of good rain falls, and grow a little bit of everything in the natural ways of our forefathers. Be upfull and self-sustaining. Money is good. Land is better.

It is good when leadership confirms what you had been thinking to yourself all along.

Ras Negus and Naph-T organized a treat for the children who lived along Mulgrave Lane, in Jones Town and along Slipe Road, and environs. The treat was held on the no-man's land separating Jones Town from the Mulgrave shanty settlement. They had erected two tarpaulins so that each served as tents, with different purposes. The one tent was where the children stood in line to receive lunch, which had been ordered from a catering company on King Street. They received a hot meal and fruit juice, and wrapped sandwiches and snacks to take home for later, and they could help themselves from the fruit baskets that had been placed in the right hand corner of the tent, laden with oranges, ripe bananas and otaheiti apples. In the other tent, there were prepackaged carton boxes which contained an assortment of clothes, toiletries, personal care products and multi-vitamins, specifically for the old-timers, and other packages containing exercise books, stationery, socks and school bags, for the parents with school-aged children.

Naph-T had gone all out to pack the cartons to meet the specific needs of the community members, whom she knew so well because they were the same ones who visited the clinic and the community centre, some begging for alms. There were many indigent and homeless, deserted by the family and left to fend for themselves. It was not in her place, she decided, to judge their situation or to speculate on what manner of retribution was responsible for this, whether or not they had been caught in a karmic reel that they had to endure before their souls could be renewed. It was not her place to ask them what on Earth could they have possibly done to their offspring, why they would have been deserted like this in their old age and left to die a lonely, miserable death. No. All that was in her power to do was to assist, to the level that she was now able, and to quietly attend to her own karma.

And this would be the beginning. They intended to open a soup kitchen on King Street, maybe within a month or so, to provide two daily meals for the indigent and homeless. They would feel out the situation and see how best to avoid exploitation of the soup kitchen, by those able-bodied loafers who were simply opportunistic leeches on the goodwill of others. Ras Negus had very sharp instincts regarding this. He had seen the likes of them at the landfill, foraging for things to sell back Downtown. These were physically sound but morally bankrupt. Ras Negus and Naph-T promised themselves to be on guard for this set.

The realization slowly dawned on them, that they would leave Mulgrave Lane. It was met with some resistance in both their minds. It wasn't so much sentiment, as it was a sense of duty and the desire not be accused of abandoning their roots. There was nothing to be nostalgic about. Save for the homely familiarity which all humans feel for the place in which they have lived many years, there was nothing to be mushy about, really. Mulgrave Lane was not a place that was conducive to the growth of anyone – child or adult. It was a place you stayed in if you had nowhere else to go. It was a place where, if you excelled, it was in spite of being there, never because of being there. If the children of Mulgrave Lane grew to be honest, law-abiding citizens, it was not for want of Mulgrave Lane trying to make the exact opposite out of them. Many times, it boiled down to the luck of the draw, the staunch dedication of parents, and some degree of divine intervention.

Miss Inez would come too, of course. Where else would she be other than with Ras Negus? She was getting way up in age, fiercely independent as she was. She would have more sentiments than he did, having lived there from the days when there had been happier memories, things to really cherish. The days before the politicians segmented Kingston Proper into umpteen garrisons that came to be affiliated with one party or the other, of the two, and the walls of the community were either orange or green, and you could be killed for wearing the wrong colour shirt or being caught on the wrong side of town, even if visiting relatives. Miss Inez had been there donkey years before the guns flooded in and the dons took charge, aided and abetted by the said politicians who had sworn to eradicate them. She could be sentimental about the Ska days, and the pantomime days, and the Grand Market days. Ras Negus could not. He had five children to think about – and another one on the way – to protect from stray bullets, curfews, ratchet Dancehall lyrics, second-hand violence and area leaders who required that they be sent on a platter as homage for the family's protection; homage of the first fruits.

It would not be a clean break – could not. A case in point: Ras Negus had stayed on as a garbage collector for another month and a half, and then he had resigned. It was now near the end of July. He had given no other reason for his resignation but that he would from henceforth be self-employed. He could not deny to himself that he was proud, taking off the smelly old clothes for the last time, knowing that Naph-T would not have the displeasure of washing them – not that she ever complained, but still – then walking away. He felt proud and, of course, scared. Pride and fear often walked together. You always feared losing that which you were proud of, especially if it was newfound and tentative. But the point was, he did not sever ties with his fellow garbage collectors because, that very week of his leaving, there was another strike – they were known for their many strikes – and he had seen fit to join them in the courtyard of the head office, chanting out their grievances and their demands. They were happy to know that he still had their backs, and they spent a great deal of time pumping fists and forging their solidarity. It was his way of saying, without saying, that he was not leaving them but leaving the system.

He was going to try his hand at entrepreneurship, something he had always wanted to do. Now, he was going to see if he was up to it, if he had what was required. He was going to buy some land up in the hills, near a river, with enough space to grow some crops. He was going to set up a restaurant in the city. He and

Naph-T had talked about all this till they could close their eyes and recite it like a memory rhyme.

There would be a separate area just for the compost heap. This was very important. The land would ideally be in rural St. Andrew, not too far from Kingston but, at the same time, far enough away to still be considered country. It would be away from the smog and grime and heat, but close enough to see the city lights at night, from a select vantage point. There would be ample space for the children to run and climb trees, and scrape their legs on the stones in the river, and heal their bruises while soaking up sun on the river bank. The hills were lush and cool and, save for the landslides in certain places, it was fertile land to build and grow food on. They would grow the food for sale and for use in the restaurant. The elders had given Ras Negus the name of a man who had some land in Cavaliers, a little further up from Stony Hill. Ras Negus intended to go see the man but first, he would call and set a date for the meeting. The lands here would be much cheaper than any land in Kingston or lower St. Andrew. In fact, there was no land in the city for farming, on the scale that he wanted, though the plains would have been ideal. Kingston had long been claimed by the industrialists and the men of commerce, the residential developers, the amusement providers and the government planners. The only dirt left was the sparse stretch along the gully banks, where the rain could still trickle in to spare the city dwellers the consequence of flooding. It was never enough drainage in times of torrential downpour, in May or October. In the hills, there would be plenty of dirt, space, and all the drainage a heart could request.

Ras Negus had heard the horror stories surrounding the purchase of land. Many of them had made the news and some very prominent lawyers had been ushered off to jail. It would appear that the amount of money that changed hands in real estate deals was just too much for many lawyers to resist the temptation of swindling, or redirecting till a date more convenient to them. Misappropriation. They had always intended to replace the money; this was the explanation offered when they each had their day in court. Ras Negus did not want to be caught up in any such scandal. He did not want to be the victim but he did not have the slightest clue how to avoid being one. He knew that at some point a lawyer would have to be involved. He would close his eyes and hope for the best, when that bridge came up, which was really all he could do as he had no lawyer as a personal friend, and knew no one who did. The elders did recommend one Mr. Paul Sharpe, an attorney based Downtown, on Duke Street. He was a criminal lawyer but he might know someone in real estate. So this was another person that Ras Negus would have to make an appointment to go see.

Ras Negus was feeling very happy. He felt something gelling inside him. At the same time, he was scared. It was very easy for a man like him to feel overwhelmed, given the fact of how his life had been. He could read and write, but barely. He had never been in business. The only thing he had managed was the collection and distribution of old clothes, and that hadn't required much brain power. It had required a little guts to walk up to perfect strangers and ask for alms, though on behalf of someone else. But still, most people wouldn't have done it. Too much pride. It required a whole lot of muscle and he had that. For sure. But as to whether or not he had any true head for business, any savvy in him at all, was left to be proven. He would test the river one toe at a time, holding on to a tree.

Ras Negus knew that Jellyman already had a keen business head and that was why he had approached the man, a fellow Ras like himself, hopefully with the same principles. He did not know Jellyman more than seeing him in the market and being his patron for years. Seeing a man and living with him were two different things, as country people always said. But his innards were telling him that Jellyman was a safe bet and this was another thing that had to be sharp for a man to succeed in business. He had to have reliable innards. He had to be able to rely on his guts because there were no real profits to be made without real risks – but sensible, calculated risks.

There was much he could learn from Jellyman. Yes, he only

owned a six-by-three foot stall in Cross Roads market, but, so what? It was his business, and he was successful at it. Jellyman had been self-employed at this work for at least fifteen years. It had sent his children through school and kept a roof over their heads, plus he regularly kept other women, in addition to his rightful woman who was the mother of his children. Ras Negus knew this to be a fact, because he had been privy to their exchange when the women came at various times to collect their money. There were special buying days when the trucks would come in from St. Thomas or Portland or St. Mary, and Jellyman would have to be at the Coronation market Downtown from three or four o'clock in the morning. He never failed to be there, rainy season or not, unless he was sick. Ras Negus had known of many big shot businessmen who had run themselves into bankruptcy, even after having had a mighty headstart in terms of capital, and having graduated from the top business schools. So it boiled down to common sense and street sense, and integrity, too. So, yes, Jellyman was a businessman – a small businessman – from whom much could be learnt. Ras Negus was sure to make other associates along the way, as his own business expanded and flourished.

    Another matter that Ras Negus had to think about was the registration of his restaurant, which would not be immediate but it certainly was imminent. He had promised himself that whatever they decided to do with the money, in terms of business, they would do it right. They would go the official way, with forms and licenses and fees and waiting periods when everything seemed stalled and hopeless, and the rigmarole of government bureaucracy. They would endure it all. It meant that they had had to go scrambling to get original documents that they hadn't seen in years. Miss Inez could not find his birth certificate and, though he was a man of forty-odd years, he hadn't seen his birth certificate in many moons bcause he just hadn't had need to ask for it. They eventually found it, after three days of relentless searching, in a series of plastic bags wedged under Miss Inez's mattress. Then, they had to apply for tax registration numbers, and such the like, which really made them feel like they were stepping up in the world. Doing big-people things, at last. They wanted to do the right thing, no matter how long it took, no matter how the government workers slouched and dragged themselves from cubicle to cubicle, no matter how many days they wiped the benches with their behinds for an eternity before their number was called, or stood in line till they felt like they would collapse from exhaustion. It would be worth it in the end. Legitimacy was worth it. Both he and Naph-T, and whomever they employed as chef or waitress or bottle washer or what not, would do the test for the food handler's permit. They had written all this down on paper. Everything was planned out. The ten million dollars was broken down into smaller sums to account for all the purchases and fees and infrastructural improvements that they would have to make. Nothing extravagant was made room for. Jellyman, whose real name was Rufus Wright, would be asked to sign an official document that stated the terms of their business venture, and this would be notarized.

"This is not a little hurry-come-up thing we doing," Ras Negus had said to Naph-T one night, as they sat up in bed planning. "Everything going be official and straight. We going have papers for everything. We taking this to the sky. High high."

Being vegetarian, of course, the restaurant would be a vegetarian restaurant. A few of them had popped up in and around the Corporate Area, but not so many as to cause him to fret about demand. In fact, there was reason to believe that the demand was much greater than the present supply, there having been a surge in health conscious articles in the newspaper and on the radio and television feature segments, showing that more and more people were starting to eat right and to take their health into their own hands. Whenever Ras Negus had visited the vegetarian restaurants that he knew of, though it had not been often, he noticed that the lunch hour traffic was great and even flowed over into two or three o'clock, because sometimes the restaurants just couldn't manage the load. The dishes were expensive, mark you, and that was another matter he hoped to address with the farm, which could allow him to set much cheaper prices for his meals. The prices of the natural juices were something to speak of. Ras Negus did not think this had to be so. It was not necessary to jack up the price of things just because they were at a premium, because the cheaper you made it, the more people would buy, if that was really your original intention and not just the profit margin. Yes, of course, a profit needed to be made, but most of the businesses in the health food industry were making a killing. Most times, he never could afford to order a meal and sit in. He usually just bought a tofu patty or ackee patty or callaloo loaf, or a slice of whole wheat carrot cake, and he would leave the restaurant and eat somewhere on the outside. And even then, this had been once in a blue moon. Only the bourgeoisie, it seemed, could afford to eat regularly at a vegetarian restaurant. He hoped to change all this.

Chapter Twelve

"Orange man! Sweet orange! Hundred dollar a dozen, give yuh the sweet juiciful orange!"

The peddler was balancing two huge boxes on the rim of the bicycle. One box contained oranges, bagged by the dozen with a few loose ones to be given as brawta. The box at the top contained a few dozen ripe bananas and two watermelons, sliced and bagged. His dexterity with the bicycle handle and the way he balanced the boxes with minimal effort showed that he had been doing this for some time. When he stopped to make a sale, or to hail one his regular customers, he spread his legs out on either side of the bicycle so it stood perfectly immobile and so both hands could be free to make the commercial exchange. Peddlers were commonplace in Greater Portmore. They sold everything from fruits, clothes and newspapers, to household items and gadgets.

Precious couldn't remember when last she had been in bed to hear the orange man passing. Now that she no longer sold in the arcade, she had the luxury of lying in bed till well into the morning, even till noon or beyond, if she felt a mind. She had ordered pizza with five toppings, for lunch, and she was listening out for the pizza delivery bike. Dezzie lay asleep beside her.

Everyone was at home. It was the last day of July and tomorrow, August 1, was Emancipation Day. Within five days after that, on August 6, it would be Independence Day. The family would have a mighty lot to celebrate, on top of what the regular folks would have. Emancipation from poverty and independence from work. Bam too was relaxing in the living room with her grandchildren. The fact that she no longer worked out had given her a calmer disposition that made her more tolerant of their noise and their antics. She was finally settling into her grandmotherhood. They were simultaneously watching cartoons, playing video games and arguing with each other about random things, making more commotion than the electronic gadgets combined. Bam went out to collect the two large pizzas, swiped her debit card gingerly as she realized that this was the first time in her life that she was paying for anything by swiping a card. It almost gave her goose bumps. She had always had to pay for things cash, and very grudgingly, and each transaction always reminded her of how much her funds were being depleted. Now, she only had to swipe and there was very little concern as to how one drop from a bucket would matter to the bucket. All that was required of her was that she remember her secret number, her PIN. It sounded so sweet: her PIN! Like she could prick you with it and you couldn't do or say a damn thing. Aligning the right side of the card with the electronic beam of the gadget, took some getting used to. She was always turning the card the wrong way, with much awkward girlish giggling to offset the embarrassment.

"Dez," said Precious, poking the sleeper who always seemed as if he was out cold no matter how long he had been sleeping. "Dez. Pizza come."

She placed the box of pizza on her lap and removed a slice, wrapped it in a napkin and held it, waiting for Dezzie to budge. When he didn't, she started nibbling on the pizza and watching him as he slept. She decided not to wake him, and sat instead watching him sleep coiled in fetal position, in only his underpants. Dezzie had been keeping a low profile for the past few days, having mainly an indoor existence and venturing out mainly at night, if at all. He had been dodging some people. Many people. He had spent the days wandering through the rooms, making sure that the curtains were drawn and the front door was bolted, which was a new thing in this household, since the days were so hot. It was a common thing for Portmore residents to hear roaring thunder and see magnificent flashes of lightning in the distance, in nearby Kingston or Spanish Town or maybe on the hills of St. Andrew, and wonder, "Where is our rain? What have we done why no rain comes our way?"; in that semi-desert inferno in which they had seen fit to set up their abodes. So most times, only the very paranoid would close the doors and windows. Even when there were several fans to each room, which spun non-stop, the heat was tremendous. Some houses had air conditioning units, which Dezzie had ordered and expected to have installed by the following week. But at the Grant's residence, the two exterior doors and all the windows had been left open until well into the night. Until now.

If a call came in on the land line, Bam had to screen it. She would take a message but most times, she didn't bother to hand the paper to Dezzie, who had given strict instructions that he had no more money to give or lend to people claiming to be his friends or relatives, and especially not to perfect strangers. As he remembered the popular saying when he was young and in Primary school, whenever someone asked for a piece of food he was eating, "Who beg naw get, who nuh beg nuh want!" Bam was reopening her theory that someone or ones may have or were in the process of setting duppy on her son. Leave it to wicked people to work Obeah on others. If they couldn't get the money one way they would get it another way, or at least make sure he wouldn't get to enjoy it. All this gave Bam a paranoia all of her own, even gave her reservations about telling everybody of all the things her son had bought or promised, all the things he had planned, how he assured her that his Moms would be taken care of and would be in need of nothing. It grieved her that she could no longer brag, except to a handful of women in her church study group. Her tithe envelope had gotten fatter and of this she was mighty proud, and even the first lady had offered that she come sit up in front row last Sunday, and had extended an invitation to Sunday dinner the following week at their mansion in Hellshire.

In spite of the glory of being the new money in town, of having everyone stare and fuss and want to be in his company, it was quickly becoming clear to Dezzie that he needed to leave this place. He could think of so many things that were wrong with Portmore. Not that anything had changed, but they were so much clearer now that he had the option of leaving. Everybody had said – had been saying from every since he could remember – that Portmore was well on its way to becoming another slum community, in fact, the biggest slum community in Jamaica. It had been planned that way, they had said. They, being, the people who had invested their life's savings into buying one of these quads, had implicated themselves further by taking out loans to expand on the empty lots, and did not wish to see this "ghetto" prediction become a reality. They had a heavy feeling about it and they prayed to the Supreme Being that their premonition was off cue. Still, who could ignore the signs? It was rumoured that the people from the slum areas of Kingston were moving across in droves, taking up residence in the Portmore houses that were being rented out large scale, the original owners seeing fit to escape to Hellshire hills or elsewhere before the pandemonium. Again, it was reiterated, this was in accordance with the original plan. The developers of Greater Kingston would have the rowdy and undesirable elements of the Innercity take leave, so that the capital could breathe and be made presentable. They would undoubtedly be dumped into Portmore, the semi-desert that was prone to flooding and infested with mosquitoes and crocodiles; houses chocked up on former cane lands that were once havens to scorpions, crabs, biting ants and centipedes.

The ghetto people of Kingston were moving in slowly. The Portmore schemes were insidiously being overrun by them, infiltrated by their antics and their disgraceful ways. Though physically separate, the houses were becoming merged and communal like those of the Downtown tenements, expansion filling the spaces between fences. The newcomers, some of whom already knew each other from having met at the dancehall sessions or the clubs, quickly recognized one another and took to criss-crossing into each other's yards, trespassing on roofs as bridges, or shouting across as they were wont, without regard to pitch or content. A cancer was creeping up on the walkway, on the community. It was as if half of the walkway had gone bad, like a gangrenous foot that could not be amputated without making the owner feel less than whole. Yet, many were conscious of the upward creep of death, and swore that it was imminent. There were no curfews here, as yet, but there had been a number of shootings within a short space of time. Just at the end of this very walkway, two months ago, the sound of a table being overturned and feet scattering. The next morning, to learn that a neighbor had been shot, the others having fled leaving the domino table and the dominos scattered across the bloody road. Three men had walked up in the middle of the game, and had opened fire. Always, the residents had consoled themselves with the thought that this had been personal. "Dem come fi him. Dem know exactly who dem looking fah." It had not been random, hence, nothing to worry about, if you stayed away from the ganja pushers and the gun wielders. But still. They would have preferred if this sort of thing stayed out of their peaceful, working class community, if at all possible.

    The community had always had its faults but never anything of this sort, or on this scale. Portmore's latchkey children had always been up to hanky panky, for example. Their parents worked out and they came home from school to empty houses that offered a range of delightful possibilities, with minimal prompting from friends or neighbours or, a step-father maybe. They could stare at internet porn for all the length of time that it would have taken to complete two sets of homework and finish reading their Literature books, plus time to put the chicken to thaw, wash the plates and sit coyly on the sofa as their parents let themselves in, exhausted from their commute. The community had always had problems with its very own Council. The fact that most of the residents were renters who had never seen a copy of the contracts signed, they were not aware of the do's and don'ts as it regarded the expansion and use of dwellings in the scheme. And those who knew did not feel that the rules applied to them, since their good intentions justified the breaches. So there were always letters that had to be distributed, and court action threatened, and structures being demolished for not meeting the construction codes; but these were a select few to serve as examples, compared to the vast amount of noncompliance. But Portmore had found a way to swerve around these minor obstacles. The community forgave itself of the infractions, understanding that some amount of delinquency was acceptable in its adolescence.

But now there were new problems, more immediate and ominous. There were neighbours now who had no qualms with blaring explicit lyrics from their sound systems, so loudly that no one else could concentrate for a few blocks around, except their cronies who shared their sentiments. They quarreled loudly and even fought, at times, in front of their own children and, consequently, in front of yours, unless you closed the doors but even then there were the degrading sounds. Twice, they had chased each other down the pathway, one time with rocks wielding and the other time with knives. The police had been on at least one chase on the Place, but the bike men had dallied through the walkways and gotten away, as the residents held their heads and screamed, "Mercy! Mercy! Portmore going to the dogs!"

Just yesterday, peeping through the window when he heard the commotion, Dezzie had witnessed two women arguing over whose responsibility it was to clean up the mess that the dogs had made of the rubbish. One woman, who had twin boys, had left her garbage outside and the dogs had ripped the bags, scattering the contents, which included soiled diapers, all over the other woman's yard. They both felt that the other should clean up the mess. While they argued and threatened each other, the boys sat in the dirt, feeding each other dirt, and the mother didn't notice.

These kinds of things never used to bother Dezzie so much before, but now they were really getting to him.

"He is getting the colour of the house," Precious said to herself. She chuckled, as she remembered when she was a little girl and had heard the women talking about somebody in the neighbourhood, saying, "Har man have har inside all day long. She getting the colour of the house!" and Precious had taken them at their world, and imagined the woman slowly becoming blue, or green, or whatever colour her house had been. "Hiding from people and catching the colour of the house," she repeated out loud. Dezzie stirred. "Hmm?" he asked.

"Want me to warm up some pizza?" she asked him, stroking his forehead. Without waiting for a response, she rose and took the pizza box into the kitchen and placed three slices in the new microwave. They had given the old one to Seymour.

Dezzie rolled over and, on reflex, scrolled through his phone for missed calls and text messages. He had long disabled his voicemail feature, finding it easier to ignore the written pleas than the spoken ones. He was, however, expecting calls from Ruddy and Beres, who had failed to submit their earnings for the taxis for about a week. Dezzie hadn't seen or heard from them. The car that Conda operated had been seized because it had not been properly insured. In fact, none of the three cars was straight. Dezzie had been meaning to get around to the paperwork but he kept putting it off. Now, he had ticket charges and pound fees to pay, in addition to the regular fees. The whole thing had been a major headache for Dezzie. Not even his links with his police brethren could save him. It was a choice between paying the fees and bribing the police. Six of one, half dozen of the other. The same tricks that he had played on Ping Wing were now being played on him, to an even greater degree, and he didn't find it funny at all. He was seriously thinking of selling the Corollas, and wiping his hands clean of the taxi business, once and for all.

The people whom he had lent money seemed to have misunderstood the terms of the loan. They may have thought that it was indefinite and that they should repay him only if they came into some extra money, which they never would. They never had extra money. He was beginning to suspect that the loans would never be repaid, and he was right. He had not had the foresight even to record the loans, to write down who was borrowing and how much and when they should have come in with the money. He had just figured that, from one brethren to another, or from one human being to another, the promises would be kept. He, of all persons, should have known better.

And now, his immediate neighbor to the left, with whom he had been on fairly good terms, had moved in her cousins who seemed to have hailed from the deepest depths of the Big Yard, meaning, the Innercity tenement, and had brought with them all of the accoutrements of that kind of life. First, Dezzie often awoke to find that the cistern of the washtub out back was very wet, which should not be so that early in the morning. He lay-waited them one night and discovered that these cousins had screwed their water hose to his tap and were stealing his water, channeling it into a drum in their yard. He said nothing to them. One of the cousins was a burly fellow with a rough face and gruff voice. Another one smoked weed all day and was always in a dreamy state, but looked like he would wake up right quick if he were to be challenged. The third cousin had a mouth that dripped obscenities, and beat up on his woman – well, she seemed no older than seventeen – who was the mother of his three year old daughter. They all crammed into the two rooms, and fussed every single day.

Another time, Dezzie found that some bottles that he had left at the side of the house were missing. They were empty malt beverage bottles, about two dozen of them, which he had collected and had placed in a scandal bag. There was a lady who always asked him for them, so she could sell the empty bottles and make a little money. When the lady was passing and Dezzie went to look for the bottles, they were gone. He had a good idea who had taken them.

"We think yuh was going to throw them away," said one of the cousins.

"Oh. So that's how people just take up other people things outta them yard, and don't ask," said Dezzie, trying not to seem so pissed. The cousins returned the bottles. They did not think that they had done anything all that wrong. Maybe a little wrong, but nothing much.

"You don't miss what you don't know," thought Dezzie to himself. "These people have never known the good life. How can they even know when they do something wrong?"

He watched the seventeen year old mother going to the shop on one occasion, her daughter dragging at her frock tail. She stooped and picked something up, presumably a paper money, by her smile. She opened it discretely then folded it again. Just then, a young fellow came by, his eyes fixed on the ground as if searching for something. She realized that he had lost the money. He walked up to her and asked her if she had seen some money. She asked him, how much. He told her. she said she hadn't seen it, and walked off. She passed Dezzie along the walkway and smirked. "Must be want to it go buy more ganja," she muttered. "Or buy some pussy." She stepped into her yard, where her man and his brothers sat smoking – ganja, no doubt.

Having a problem was one thing; knowing he could solve it was another. This was new. A solvable problem. Being uncomfortable was one thing; knowing he could ease his own discomfort was another. All the spending he had done thus far, even including all the unpaid loans and parties and treats, and all the bling and name brand items he had bought for himself and the enormously extended family, had not even put a dent in his net worth. It was time Dezzie faced the fact that this place couldn't hold him. He needed more space, more comfort and more security. He needed a better school for his children to attend, a school that offered the best trained teachers, who would insist that they conduct themselves properly and speak in standard English and be polite. They deserved the type of school where not any and any body could waltz in off the road and have access to them, a place that had modern facilities and the cutting edge technology, and the most refined friends to interact with.

The children at the present school were very boisterous and rough, very much like hooligans, if you asked him. It was time he faced the fact that his children deserved better. Also, it was high time for him to look around for a house, preferably up in the hills above Kingston.

Norbrook immediately came to mind because, truth be told, it was the only real posh community that he had been to, and only at the bequest of the M.P. Surely, the Bossman would be able to give him a link about any house that was up for sale. He was certain he would be able to afford it, maybe two or three of them, one for Bam and another one just to have. How much could one house cost?

He ran into M.P. Dacres at the Emancipation celebrations, held on the grounds in front of the Municipal Office. Mr. Dacres, in the tradition of his forebears, had increased in stature particularly in the region of the tummy and the cheeks. His wife was keeping him well satiated. Dezzie couldn't imagine that it had been Cassandra who was to thank or blame for this, because, as the country people liked to say, Cassandra seemed like the type of woman who lived very far from their kitchen. She seemed like the picky type of eater who was constantly watching her weight and only took dainty nibbles of salad, and would not subject her facial skin to the harassment of a steaming pot. In other words, she was the type of woman who was groomed by her mother to understand that she would require a maid, since her complexion and countenance were commensurate with high living. She was the type of woman whom had to be wined and dined with alarming regularity. A kept woman. A high maintenance woman, who would give the time of day to none less than a sugar daddy.

Today, Mrs. Dacres was in her finest regalia on the arms of her man, and they were joined by the other Portmore dignitaries in the celebration of the freedom of the slaves. Dezzie didn't catch up with the man until well into the evening, when the dignitaries condescended to mingle with the crowd for a little bit, upstairs in the reception hall. He cornered Mr. Dacres and they sat alone, munching saltfish fritters and rundung.

Dezzie told him that he was thinking of buying a house, and asked whether he knew of anywhere for sale in the Norbrook area.

"Norbrook? Your chest is high. Very high," laughed the M.P. "You know you're talking millions, right? Plenty plenty millions. But then, you have what it takes, don't you?" he almost winked at Dezzie and the two kept up a conspiratorial whisper, making Dezzie feel like he was a part of the big league. "What price range yuh thinking?"

Dezzie said that he wasn't sure, but money was no object. He had always liked that saying, that money was no object. He wasn't sure what an object was but, based upon how it was always used, he gathered that a man was in good stead whenever he was able to say that money was no object. And he, Desmond Grant, felt it to be an indubitable fact that he was now in good stead.

"No object, eh? I like that, Dezzie," beamed Mr. Dacres. "My, how things can change in the twinkling of an eye, eh? Just the other day you were running taxi. Guess you not up for charter anymore, eh?" he chuckled.

"No more. No more," agreed Dezzie. "I always said better must come, and now better certainly come."

"You're one lucky brute! I play the numbers every now and then, but that's not where my luck is. The common man bet on numbers; the bigger fellas wage on horses. You ever go by Caymanas and set your money on a horse?"

"My brother is a jockey. I bet on horses all the time. No luck for me, not horses," said Dezzie.

Mr. Dacres frowned. "Hmm. Different men, different luck, I guess. But we talking some hefty payouts, and much much more frequent than the Lot-a-Luck! I can tell you! Those horses, man. Well, if you bet chump change, you get back chump change. But a man like you now, Dez, you can make a killing with the dough that you have at your disposal. You have to make your money work for you. That's what the big guys do." He swirled his glass to circulate the ice in the fruit punch, and loosened the neck tie a bit. This was the worst part of the job, by far. Cooped up for hours at these never-ending ceremonies, official this and official that, meetings with neither resolution nor end in sight, but duty-bound to be a part of it all. How he wished to be among his real friends, sipping some real juice. Scotch. Maybe some bourbon. Something worthy of the ice it was served with. Here he was sipping fruit punch, pretending to be happy. But he was glad he had run into Dezzie. Dacres had in fact been meaning to give the man a call. Dezzie needed expert guidance, with all that new money and still so pedestrian in his ways. He needed a mentor, of sorts, to show him the ropes and tell him where to invest it, where to hide it and, of course, how best to spend it. Yes, some of it had to be spent. Had to be spent. But here was not the place for that kind of talk. They agreed to meet the following day, in Hellshire.

Cassandra was there. Dezzie wondered how it was that Cassandra was at such ease in the home that Mr. Dacres shared with his wife and children. Yes, Dezzie was no spokesperson for monogamy but still, in spite of how many women he had, he would never think of taking them into his home. They either went to their own home, whether they lived with a man or not – a double standard which did not seep through to him at all – or, they rented a room round by the Back Road, or push come to shove, they adjusted the side lever on the passenger seat so that it reclined all the way back, and made a makeshift bed out of that.

Cassandra was not only at ease, this time, she was the most cordial hostess. She wore a sleek mustard summer dress with spaghetti straps. The dress nearly touched her ankle but there was a catch. Two long splits along the sides went all the way up to her sumptuous thighs and cancelled any joke that the length of the dress had been playing. Dezzie spent the evening staring at her thighs, even through the rounds of straight liquor and the cocktails. He wondered if the Bossman could sense his infatuation. Maybe he did and just shrugged it off. More than likely, he was quite used to men losing their minds over Cassandra. She looked, moved and spoke like a goddess. She was one of those girls who had been born on the wrong side of town but who had the looks and attitude that could fix that oversight right quick. She was the kind of daughter that mothers guarded against certain elements, because they were to be preserved for only the most eligible of bachelors. The most eligible. And even if that most worthy of suitors was late in coming, even as they climbed towards their golden knight so he could better see them, no time or word was wasted on serfs.

He could not tell the difference between her breath and her perfume and he had resigned himself to believe that there actually was no difference. There was just an alluring, mesmerizing fragrance and all that fragrance was Cassandra. Maybe, if he had still been a poor man, he would seek to know if she had a sister or cousin or even friend who looked even slightly like her, who might condescend to take a chance on him. But as it were, he felt confident in the position to declare, to himself and to Cassandra by his eyes, that he intended to have her for himself, and he did not care if anyone objected.

"The house must have a swimming pool, theatre room, entertainment area and helpers quarters," said Dezzie, matter-of-factly. "Must must must." He remembered Precious saying that she wanted these things. They had discussed the matter down to the last detail. Precious was fond of watching those home and garden shows where they went into the homes of celebrities and showed just what you were missing, and those travel shows where you saw how people lived in first world countries. Putting it all together, Precious knew what she wanted and she even knew the real names for things. Dezzie, most times he had to describe what he meant, and then someone would tell him the name of it. But he was learning. At first, they had thought to build a house from scratch but then, Precious had said that maybe it would prove too much of a hassle, these contractors being the crooks that they were, and the workmen being no better. Even if you made sure to get a top notch contractor, you could still end up disappointed. Made sense to just find a house that already suited them, even if minor adjustments had to be made.

"I called a few friends this morning, and I think there are a couple houses that might interest you," said Mr. Dacres, handing Dezzie some photographs. "They gave me these. Three houses, all brand new. All in Norbrook. Hard to find a spanking brand new house in the Norbrook area these days. Better catch them quick, if you really serious."

There were at least two dozen photos. Dezzie's eyes widened as he thumbed through each one. It was quality print but he was sure that even the worst camera couldn't have made these houses any less desirable. He may very well have bought all three but one was definitely tugging on his heart strings. It had all the facilities that he had outlined. Precious would certainly not be washing any more clothes, or dusting, or dicing carrots or trimming meat, unless she wanted to. There was a helper's quarters and someone – or ones – would be hired to live in and take care of all that. Of course, one or two gardeners would be needed to tame the lawns and foliage, maybe a different person to tend to the swimming pool. From the looks of things, the developers had put all their know-how into the planning stage, as well as the execution.

This particular house had five bedrooms. Dezzie imagined himself and Precious sharing one. Each child would have one, of course, his mother another. The last one could serve as guest room, or maybe he could bunk out there whenever Precious was brooding. No need in being silly and thinking that she would no longer have need to brood, now that she was rich. Best for a man to have a contingency, in case of emergency. There were enough bathrooms for everyone to attend to the calls of nature in at their own leisure, no line or hassle, a half bathroom and powder room downstairs near the foyer, for guests. The kitchen was fully equipped with stainless steel refrigerator, stove and appliances, and granite counter tops that were accentuated by a backdrop of stained glass tiles, in turquoise and gold. There were marble tiles in the living room and foyer, and Spanish porcelain tiles throughout the remainder of the house, except for the floors of the theatre, which were hard Belizean redwood. A huge elegant portico led the way onto the pool area, which offered a panoramic view of the local golf course, Manor Park and its environs.

"How much this one going for?" asked Dezzie, absently, still admiring the photos. Mr. Dacres leaned forward, to check which one.

"I believe he said one point seven mil," he responded, himself also unruffled.

"One point seven million? Really? But that's not bad!" Dezzie exclaimed. "I can more than afford that. Easy!"

Mr. Dacres chuckled. "You do know that's U.S. dollars, right?"

"U.S. dollars?"

"Of course! You wouldn't think a house in Norbrook would sell for one point seven million Jamaican dollars? Are you nuts?!"

"No. Of course," said Dezzie, trying to keep his composure so that his voice wouldn't tremble. "But....how much is that, in our money?"

"Hmmm....roughly one-thirteen to one. Call it two hundred million Jamaica. Not exactly that but close, with closing fees and such."

"Closing fees?"

"Of course! Remember, you have to go through a lawyer. You never buy a house before? Even the government have to get their cut."

"Well....two hundred mil. I can afford that," muttered Dezzie.

"If you prefer, you could get a townhouse, same place in Norbrook. Forty to fifty million Jamaican. That might suit you better."

"What do you mean, suit me better? So, you think I can't afford the two hundred mil?"

"But why would I think such a thing?" exclaimed Mr. Dacres. "I would be presumptuous. Just giving a friend some good advice, though. And who said you had to buy the house cash. Most people wouldn't even be thinking along those lines. Most people would take out mortgage, anyway."

"I'm not most people, Bossman."

"Of course not! That goes without saying. Most people don't win the Lot-a-Luck, after all."

"Cash. I'm buying cash," said Dezzie.

"Suit yourself, my good man," said Mr. Dacres. "I'm just telling you what most people would do. You just won, how much? Less than five hundred. Two hundred is a lot to spend on a house, cash. Just the same, there are some men who do everything cash. You just might be one of them."

"Better believe it," pouted Dezzie. He was slightly offended.

"Think you're a real big shot, eh?" Mr. Dacres chuckled. He eased back onto the couch and eyed Dezzie with an air of concealed amusement. Then he let out a longer, more guttural laugh and raised his glass, "Cheers, Mr. Big Shot! Mr. Norbrook!"

Cassandra raised her glass, too, and so did Dezzie, though his stomach had tightened and he felt he no longer wanted to be there. He sensed that he was being mocked, though he couldn't figure why. Did the M.P. feel that only educated men like himself should want to buy things cash? There were some men who resented a small man breaking away from the pack and trying to live big. They felt that only they should have a go at it, and that certain things were off-limits to men who had barely scraped through school, men who had been thorns in their teachers' fanny and whose head backs the principal had been glad to see for the last time. Maybe, Mr. Dacres was jealous that Dezzie's wheels was much better than his, by far. That kind of envy was understandable, even if cumbersome. Well, uncomfortable as he was, Dezzie felt that he needed to keep the link with the M.P. till such time, at least, because this was a man who moved among the A-League and had the right contacts. See, in just one day he had found three houses, with pictures and all. And it was also possible that Mr. Dacres had only been teasing him. Men liked to tease each other at times. Maybe he shouldn't be so tender. Wealthy men needed to have thick skins, it seemed.

What he would later find out, after Precious had done some asking around, was that he wouldn't have qualified for a mortgage, anyway. He did not have any points at the housing trust because he had never contributed any payments in his entire working life. Come to think of it, he didn't even have a National Security Number. He would have to get one, at some point, but he had accumulated no points and could not have gotten a mortgage, even if his pride would have made him condescend to getting one.

Dezzie wondered what the Rastaman was doing with his ten million. Probably already bought a whole truck load of ganja seeds. Dezzie was still resentful about having to give the man out of his winnings. It was he who had bought the ticket. It was he who had chosen the lucky numbers. It wasn't his fault that Miss Miserable Precious had seen fit to toss his ticket into the rubbish. How could he be blamed for that? It did not make sense that he had to part with ten million dollars, just like that. He had been furious about it from the get-go and had it not been for his mother who had been pushing the whole thing, all hell would have broken loose. He had eventually let it slide but now that he thought about how much a house in Norbrook was going to set him back, he realized that he could have made good use of that ten mil. Sure he would still have a good amount left back, but that didn't say.

The following day, Dezzie was taken to the Kingston office of the owner of the property that he liked best, the property that he had given the name, Grant Manor. He was surprised to find out that the owner was a woman, Mrs. Shoucair, whose husband had died recently and who was in the process of migrating. Her children were all grown and were thriving in the States, tending to their own lives. Her husband and herself had delved into real estate and owned four properties, three new houses in upper St. Andrew and one, being the family home, in Coopers Hill. Mrs. Shoucair was the Personnel Manager at a prominent bank, and her husband had been some fancy lawyer, according to Mr. Dacres, who was in the know on that sort of thing. Mrs. Shoucair took both men in her Pajero to view the house in Norbrook. She didn't mind taking the time to show him the property. She was just wrapping things up at work anyway, executive stuff before leaving. Still, she was dressed to the teeth in her grey ramie-linen business suit, and the shades confirmed the look she was hoping to achieve, of a real dignitary. She drove very fast, for a woman. Dezzie noticed that she drove barefooted and he had come to realize that many women preferred this. Well, he could just imagine how cumbersome it would be, pressing the brakes in six inch heels. It all made sense.

Within a very short time, they were at the house. Of course, it was much more impressive than the photos, appealing as they had been. You just couldn't experience that type of luxury on paper. Not even a glossy centre spread in a high-end magazine could have done it justice. It was hard to imagine that there were Jamaicans who lived like this. No wonder they rolled up the windows of their air conditioned SUV's as they blazed through the streets of the city, or even faster through the slum communities that almost always lined the way into the upscale areas. The devil's arrangement, a play on the conscience of they who, it seemed, had next to none. Of course, Mrs. Shoucair had verified the claim of this man to be on her property, or she would not have wasted her time in the first place. But when she learnt that he would be paying cash, she had been especially excited and she showed Dezzie the courtesies that she would have shown a legitimate bidder. Because, really, she did see him as somewhat like a bastard child, a claimant by default, though a claimant nonetheless.

She led the tour of the entire house, which was set back against the hillside and had a sprawling lawn out front. It took a full hour and a half to wind their way up, down and across the expansive property, to admire all the features, to pause so Dezzie could ask all the frivolous questions that popped into his head as they went along. He was sure that when he took Precious and Bam, next time he came, they would have questions of their own and he wanted to have a one-up over them, so to speak. He had just about made up his mind that he would buy the house. Precious had fallen in love with just the description that Dezzie had given her based on the photos and she needed very little by way of further prompting. Bam was sold on the idea of moving to a posh neighbourhood. She was sure that any house in Norbrook was a great house that would suit her fine. It didn't much matter. A house in Norbrook was a house in Norbrook. She was sure that the original owner had taste enough and had dedicated much time and money to getting it just perfect. It was a brand new house so that meant no duppies had had a chance to take up residence. No echoes of cantankerous late-night quarrels when husbands dragged themselves home stiff-stoned drunk and reeking of cheap perfume - or, worse, expensive perfume. No reverberating accusations of infidelity or threats of divorce or promises of you-will-pay-for-this-I-will-drag-you-through-the-court-yuh-not-giving-this-damn-house-that-I-invested-half-my-life-into-to-yuh-dutty-whoring-gyal-dem! Nothing of the sort. No old spirits lingered to envy them of their happy life. Everything was fresh and clean and beamed of novelty.

Mrs. Shoucair assured Dezzie that she was still in touch with her husband's many associates who could get the ball a-rolling, if he so desired. It was only a matter of dialing the right numbers, of which her fingers were versed. The paper work would be a breeze, and the family could move in as soon as those preliminary matters were taken care of. In fact, these associates were the ones who were handling the sales of her other properties and the clients had had no issues, so far. Mrs. Shoucair would highly recommend that Dezzie follow suit. Mr. Dacres seconded that notion. Dezzie agreed, as a vote of confidence to his Member of Parliament who, not even his enemies could debate, had fixed the roads and cleaned the drains and eradicated the mosquitoes till next rainy season, as promised. Mr. Dacres was a man of action who maintained a firm grip on his team of Councilors in the respective Divisions. Dezzie called him Bossman, for good reason. No one could take from him his good work in the community.

On Independence Day, August 6, Dezzie was really in the vibes to celebrate and he determined that he would take the whole family to see the Grand Gala, at the National Stadium. He had bought a suit just for the occasion and the ladies, as usual, were kicking up rumpus in the fashion department. Bam was outdoing herself makeup-wise these days, after having hidden under all that drab for so many years. It was getting to where he could hardly recognize his own mother at times, hair extensions and all. More power to the old lady, Dezzie said to himself. They shared in the excitement as the crowd thronged the terraces of the stadium, as the festival songs from way back when and the more recent ones too blared across the airways and gave everybody a good, nostalgic, back-a-yawd vibe.

The military parades and the performances by the many dance groups, all themed to showcase the diverse culture of the island, were spectacular. Normally, Dezzie would have contented himself with watching the Grand Gala live on television, with the pretend consolation that the only real front seat was the one in his living room. But a noble, philanthropic, patriotism had overtaken him and he felt duty-bound to bear through the sometimes unruly crowd and take his place among his fellow men. Perhaps, they might even recognize him as the fella they had seen on the telly, the one who had won the how much millions in the Lot-a-Luck. They might want to come over and pat him on the shoulder, just so they could tell their friends that they had dialogued with him. They might even want an autograph. As fate would have it, none of that happened. No one recognized him, and maybe that was for the best. Who to tell if one or two of them wouldn't have had the gall to approach him directly and ask for a smalls. People could be so brazen, even in public. Better to avoid all that.

It took some skill to move out of Greater Portmore unnoticed. They had decided unanimously, and for very obvious reasons, that it should be unnoticed. For this reason, they moved in the dead of night, almost midnight in fact, when it was said that only dogs and duppies and policemen and prostitutes were still prowling the streets. They chose a Wednesday night because that was one of the more quiet nights. No money to spend on a Wednesday night, not much happening streetwise. Too close to

Monday to let your guard down, too close to Friday to attempt a celebration. A Friday, Saturday or even Sunday night would have proved disastrous.

They only needed one moving van because most of their belongings were to remain at the house, where Precious' mother would now stay. They had told no one of the move. Well, Bam had told a few church sisters but she had sworn them to secrecy, and they in turn had only told a few others and sworn them to secrecy, and so on and so forth. Dezzie's three Corollas were still in the possession of the taximen, his long-time brethren, but he had plans to seize them and eventually cut off all ties. He was going to sell the cars. The men were giving him too much headache when time came to get his money. He wondered if that was how Ping Wing had felt about him. Surely he hadn't been that bad. Surely. He had collected less than a quarter of the money that he had given out as loans. He had done everything short of getting the police involved, a thought which he had not ruled out but one mind was telling him to just turn them loose to time. Karma would bite them in their asses, he consoled himself. The fact was that some of the individuals were intimidating just to look at, plus he knew for a fact that a couple of them well were mixed up in dirt, the kind of which he wanted to put behind him. Best to just move on, he figured.

The family drove ahead in Dezzie's BMW while the moving van followed. Precious' car had already been taken to the house. They moved in October, in the midst of the rainy season but this particular night was dry. At least, in Portmore it was dry. Dezzie cringed as he approached the stop light at Three Miles because he had been setting for the carwash boys, who frequented that spot. He had been rehearsing a speech in his head, which he intended to reel at them the minute he saw them step forward.

"Don't even think about touching this windshield!" he was going to say, very forcibly.

But then he remembered what hour it was and he felt relieved. The carwash boys were already in their beds, most of them coming from the Backto or Seaview Gardens area, or

Riverton. But some were homeless and may not be in any beds. They may that very moment be haunting the streets in other roles, all towards the same end. What mattered to Dezzie was that they were nowhere near his BMW at this time.

By now Dezzie knew the way by heart and he felt proud of where he was headed. He was proud that he had made a step up in life and that he was taking his family out of poverty. The life that he was leaving behind did mean something to him but when he thought about it, he was more open to brand new experiences than wallowing in old ones. Besides, the men whom he had known to be his brethren all these years had proven to be just a set of con artists. Fleeing Greater Portmore also put him out of harm's way from Shelly's father, who seemed intent on becoming his father-in-law, by hook or by crook – or by the book! There was no way the man could trace him to Norbrook – he hoped. His own father had also gotten too close for comfort and Dezzie wasn't used to having the man in his life, much more so lovey-dovey and all up in his beeswax. It gave him an icky feeling and this was another man he hoped wouldn't trail him to Norbrook. Seymour was not too bad. But what he really wanted more than anything was to make a clean break and start a new life, away from the commoners.

Even in the night it was very clear that this was a different part of town. The streets were cleaner and were lined with beautiful flowers. Noticeably, there were a number of dogs lying just outside their open gates. These were dogs that clearly had some pedigree. You could tell by their size, the sheen of their coat and the guttural force of their bark. Dezzie remembered Mr. Dacres telling him that some of these dogs were let out for spite, because the people in these parts didn't want just anyone coming into their neighbourhood. In the first place, they wanted no pedestrians. Being a pedestrian was one of the first signs of being poor, as if you were shackled to poverty at the foot. Of course, the dogs were let back in and the gates closed, in time for the aristocratic pedestrians, the morning joggers and walkers who bounced up and down the hill in their expensive track suits, yoga pants and the latest padded sneakers, and litre bottles of spring water.

As they pulled in a light drizzle started and this exploded into a full downpour within minutes, but they had removed what few items they had brought from the van. The rain lasted for a few hours. It seemed that a system had snuck across the island from the East, catching the weather watchers unawares. Of course, Bam read it as a blessing. "Showers of blessing," were her exact words. "Washing off the old crosses and starting fresh. Amen. Praise be to God!"

It was hard for anyone to disagree that rain meant cleansing.

The interior of the house was painted in warm, earthy colours, a bit too bold for Bam's taste. She felt that interior walls should be white or off-white. She would see to it that her own quarters were repainted. The family settled in and slept deeply, not noticing that the rain had stopped. In the morning, the lawn was still moist and there were intermittent drops from the awnings and eaves all around the house. They surveyed what they could see of the property from the portico, but later after breakfast they strolled together around the compound to see what was what, and where was where.

"Definitely going to need some dogs," said Dezzie. "Can't have a place like this without some big Doberman. Maybe even some pitbulls."

"Pitbulls?" exclaimed Precious. "Don't you hear those things illegal? Where yuh going wid pitbulls? Some Doberman or Alsatian or German Shepherd, fine, but pitbulls overdoing it, Dez."

"The way these thieves moving nowadays, look like only pitbulls they 'fraid of," Dezzie insisted. He was already picturing himself with two or three of the ferocious dogs in tow. It was a well-known fact that nobody messed with pitbulls.

"What we definitely going to need is a pool man," said Bam. "This nice lovely pool going to need somebody to care it. And we need at least two maids. This big big house would tired out any one woman. No sah! One lickle woman cyan clean all a dis! Mussy mad!"

"Hmm," said Dezzie. He was still daydreaming about the pitbulls. To him, it was the ultimate symbol of manhood, to be able to keep bitbulls. He remembered seeing the men walking a team of pitbulls through the scheme, though they weren't supposed to, but it was a beauty to see them tugging at the leashes and threatening the mongrel dogs, who could do nothing more than get out of the way. The pitbulls would rail up and act as if they would rip the other dogs to pieces, just you say the word. Dezzie loved this show of savagery in a guard dog. He felt this was how it should be. He would find out from Mr. Dacres how one went about getting some quality dogs for protection.

Bam said that she already knew two nice young men whom she could get to tend to the pool and the garden, some men whom she used to work with at the hardware. Dezzie nodded. He was game for anything the ladies prescribed, that would make the overall family experience safer and more comfortable. He was not the man to spare costs. Whatever his family needed, would be arranged. Precious would supply the maids, she had said, as she had already spoken to two ladies that she knew from the arcade. Everything was coming together nicely. Before the week was out, Precious would go down to several of the prominent Prep schools and see which one would be most suitable for Desrine and Desandre. It was the middle of the first term, yes, but surely something could be worked out. Even if it meant they had to pay a little extra.

In the warmth of the afternoon, they decided to go for a stroll around the community, for as far as they could go without losing their bearings. The houses here sprawled like castles onto themselves, not chocked up and adjoined like the Portmore houses. Each had adequate yard space, most had a swimming pool and some even had space for a tennis court, based on what they could see. And who to tell what couldn't be seen? Quaint special purpose rooms spawned from the imagination of the Mistress of the house, no doubt, or the ambitious draftsmen to whom the mandate had been given, "Build us something unique, something grand, something inimitable."

This was the remnants of the old Jamaican aristocracy, the local landed gentry, as the British would call them. They tried to have the airs of their European forebears but lacked the authenticity, the Caribbean breeze having diluted it, or rather, seasoned it. They didn't have the knack for pomposity, for some reason, they sniffed about themselves and sensed something was amiss. They were at a loss as to what it could possibly be. Those observing them on this day would be called the Nouveau Riche.

In the evening, the Grants sat on the deck of the swimming pool. Bam served fruit punch to the youngsters and rounds of rum cream for the older heads. They sat chatting and laughing and remembering old times, which were not so old, come to think of it. The mood was similar to that of a wake for a not so dearly departed relative whom everyone had tolerated but no one had really truly loved. His death had been unexpected, as deaths went, and they felt duty-bound to mourn but they expected to make a full recovery.

There was much to learn and not much help by way of tutelage. There was a strong sense that the residents of this community were acutely and immediately aware of any changes that occurred within their environment, like they could sniff it in the wind, or were being kept posted by sentinels. There was an edgy alertness about them, like junkies anticipating a bust at any minute. There was a strong sense that their blinds were drawn just enough to leave room for eyes that scanned the coast for threats. Threats, being, strangers. Particularly, strangers who were unaccompanied and had not been vouched for. Cars slowed as they passed, their windows quickly lowered and then up again in a split-second reconnaissance. The family was being watched. Scrutinized. They had been put on indefinite probation. Being the friendly, down-to-Earth fella that he fancied himself, Dezzie often waved to the neighbours as they made little appearances on their patios or in their gardens, but they never seemed to tarry long enough to return the gesture. He figured he would go over and introduce himself and the others, soon as they got settled in. He decided that the best thing to do was to host a little party, welcoming himself to the high life, so he could get to know the neighbours and they could get to know him. He would of course, slide into the conversation the fact that he was loaded, so that by the end of the evening there would be no doubt as to his authenticity. There definitely would be a little party.

"So soon though?" asked Precious.

"Better sooner than later," said Bam. "At least they will know we are nice people, not some little ghetto trash. I think is a good idea."

"At least, wait a couple weeks. We don't want them to think we are eggs-up, or anything," Precious suggested. "These kinda people funny bad."

Dezzie found that he could not wait more than one solid week after his arrival to make his presence known. He was eager to mingle and to prove that his family was made of good stuff. They may have come from lowly origins in terms of their place of birth, but they were of quality stock. And like it or not, they were here to stay so it was best the Norbrookites learn to deal with it from now. Dezzie personally invited eight persons, telling them to bring the rest of their households, and between Bam and Precious, four other persons had been invited. Mr. Dacres would be there and would take along a few associates.

"Just a little get-together," Dezzie had said, coyly, but he knew in his heart that he hoped for it to be a bash. He would see how it went, and would use the reception to gauge the opinion of the neighbours.

Of course, there was shopping to be done. He was more than willing to leave this in the eager hands of his mother and his woman, who had taken the liberty of making lists to ensure that none would leave the party pouting. The stores in Manor Park were not necessarily grander in terms of size, but they were certainly different from the ones in Portmore, in terms of the quality of merchandise. Clearly, these stores were catering to a different sort of crowd, one of higher social caliber, with refined tastes and deeper pockets. There were imports lining the shelves for miles, it seemed, to satiate the acquired tastes of those who had travelled far and wide, and often, and had brought back their appetite for the unfamiliar. They were on their third or fourth passports, which had accumulated all kinds of exotic stamps in them. It was the first time that Precious had seen bottles of snails or dried octopus fillets or spring chicken. She didn't care about the fancy names; she knew what she saw in the containers. She had heard that somewhere, in some remote and unconscionable corner of the earth, there were people who ate snails, but it had never dawned on her that such expats could be here, within these shores, and that they would have the gall to take such a thing up to the counter. There were products that neither she nor Bam had ever heard of, not even on her travels to buy merchandise. Not to say that all these foreign goods were suspect. There were loads of delicacies that made their way from the shelves to the shopping cart no sooner their eyes had met.

The other women, who pushed their trolleys daintily down the aisles, in doing so indicated three things: One, they had a ridiculous amount of time at their disposal, since they either didn't work out or didn't have to, or held some symbolic post that was as enormously compensated as it was redundant. Two, they could afford all the items that they or their spoilt, fidgety children tossed into the shopping cart and there was no concern as to how much the cash register would declare. Three, they were mainly overweight from easy life, slouchy and impeded in spite of the treadmill and yoga mats in their home gym. These women made little trips down to Manor Park and back up. Some dared not venture further, lest they become obstructed in the congestion to the South. Sometimes, they drove in the other direction through to Liguanea.

The men got away with wearing old clothes and flip-flops, a crime on the level of treason among the rabble. The teenagers zipped down the hill in their parents' deluxe SUV's and emerged in their halter backs and panties; the boys, in their jeans shirts and merinos that revealed their freshly acquired tattoos and heavy gold chains. The couture of the women went from one extreme to the other. Some tapered off the far end of drab. Can't be bothered. Don't have to bother, really, since hubby won't notice one way or the other. My husband of seventeen years, who is fifteen years older than I am, is sleeping with his twenty-three-year old Secretary so, why bother? That kind of thing. Others seemed a bit too well attired for shopping, if you asked Precious. They were slim and trim and well preserved for their ages – which you could seriously tell that they were old – but they were embalmed and glowed for it. These wore miniskirts, huge shades and broad customized rings where their wedding bands used to be. They scraped their heads almost bald and dyed what was left of it blonde. Their calves were toned form daily exercise, and they still had their own good teeth, which were dazzling from care.

But both groups exhibited the infamous rigid upper lip that they had inherited from the British side of their forebears, together with their fixed stares that penetrated the jovial greetings from the Grant clan. It would have been more than enough of a deterrent, had the roles been switched. But as it were, both Bam and Precious were unfazed. They were determined to prove that they could withstand the aloofness and, eventually, merge.

Certain women plan on it. Maybe some were born with it. In any case, it seemed to be a well-kept secret. Precious was browsing through the cosmetics aisle, which had not been barricaded and guarded as she was accustomed to seeing, and she wondered if she was at liberty to dab a little something from the samples of expensive perfumes on her wrist and temple. A smiling rep gave her the go-ahead, both of them avoiding the vernacular which they would otherwise have delved into at break-neck speed, had they been in the arcade Downtown but since we're here. Precious bought three bottles of perfume and two bottles of musky cologne for Dezzie. She rejoined Bam in the liquor aisle, tending to the sacred duty of selecting the wines and spirits for the festivities, and just for regular chilling when they were in the mood. A well-stocked and ever-ready wine rack was a necessity on this side of Nirvana. Not only did it show that you had taste but, that you could back that taste up with the dollars required to procure the goodies.

Precious found that she did not argue with the prices, as had been routine when shopping in Portmore. It was almost a part of the everyday shopping experience in Portmore, complaining about the prices. To show her disdain, she would often change her mind about items on route to another aisle, after brooding on the injustice, and would just shove the thing into a crevice of any old shelf and walk away, with a cut-eye and a cheups. Not that she didn't feel she could get away with that kind of behavior here – but she just didn't want to. It was not called for.

The extravagance in the height of the shopping cart was matched by the extravagance in the pride on the two women's faces, and that matched by the extravagance in the smirk on the face of the cashier. Hurry-come-up poppy-show fool-fool people. Mek it suh obvious seh oonuh nuh used to whole-heapa money! The cashier scrutinized the brand-name everything, from food items to liquor to houseware to the delicate toiletries made from finest cotton and laced with aloe vera gel, and soaps that were so pure that they floated, and lotions that were hypoallergenic. They were items she had always wanted to try but had to console herself with guessing, as she passed them through the scanner on her eight hour tedium at the counter. She had often longed to taste some of the delicacies, and had resigned herself to the introspection that maybe they didn't taste all that good anyway. They were from Foreign and Foreign people had no skill with the skillet, just a whole lot of hoopla over bland commodities that had no Caribbean rhythm. But still. But what she hated most of all was when these kinds of people came in pretending like they had been shopping this way for donkey years, as if it wasn't obvious they hadn't.

Chapter Thirteen

"Let's get this party started!" said Dezzie.

He was talking to his reflection in the bathroom mirror. He was dressed to kill. He had returned fresh from the barber and was sporting a goatee and a very low cut, which made him see himself in a brand new light. The two women of the house had given him the thumbs-up and congratulated him on his vision, though it had been the barber's suggestion and Dezzie had fussed all the way through, sure he would have been disappointed with the outcome. But he liked it. He liked it.

"Sure it not too much?" he had asked. And everyone had said he was dapper and that the look fit him; which made him wonder why he hadn't thought of it all along. But nothing before its time.

Dezzie leaned forward and examined his face. He had many lean mean years left in him, for sure. His cologne was making a helluva noise and the suit that Precious had picked out for him really accentuated his dark skin. Back in the day, he would have been content to dab on some cheap khus-khus cologne, or to borrow some of Precious' scents that may have made him a little too flowery. But no need for that now. He liked the face he was seeing and he liked how his complexion highlighted his white teeth. Chocolate and mint. People had always said that his dark skin went well with his white teeth, especially in the night hours. He looked like a really sophisticated ladies' man. This was the face of a man who could get a party started. But for that, one needed at least a few partiers.

He went downstairs and gangsta-leaned onto the portico, where the music was already blaring but it was Saturday evening. Surely music could blare tonight if it wanted to, even in Norbrook. They had extended invitations to neighbours and to the odd passerby jogging in the mornings. Mr. Dacres had kept his end of the bargain, spreading the word to the bigger heads. This was standard procedure. A party was the thing to do. Everyone agreed.

None of the guests had yet arrived. Bam was already dressed and relaxing by the pool, which so far none of them had even dipped a toe into but that was another story. Dezzie couldn't swim, Bam had no interest in learning at this late stage of the game and was content to watch the ripples in the evening breeze, and Precious had vowed to learn at some elusive point in the future. The children would certainly learn how to swim. Their Prep school was beginning to sort out that matter right quick. Which rich kid didn't know how to swim? Now you tell me!

Someone Dezzie knew from way back when and whom he had run into the other day, was warming up at the controls, promising some oldies but goodies later on when the time was mellow but now some groovy pop to set the stage. Dezzie had been prime chef at the grill just an hour or so before, jerking chicken and pork like a real man-a-yawd, with apron and cap and everything. He was in his element. That element being, riding the waves of the high life like he was born doing it. He had his brand new bike parked just beside the portico - which it didn't have to be. There was room in the garage but, who could see it there? He was no expert biker but man the wind felt good in his face.

Mr. Dacres arrived at around nine-ish, with his left arm

cradling the sink of Cassandra's back and his right arm waving to the folks seated on the portico. In tow were three men who had arrived in a separate car and who had trailed the couple up the driveway. Clearly, they were friends of the Bossman and hence, friends of Dezzy. The host bounced over to greet his guests, and Precious graciously sent for a round of drinks for everyone, to grease the wheels of the machinery that they hoped to operate well into the night. Introductions were made, a wave of raucous laughter from the newcomers, who took their perch and swirled ice delicately in their glasses, smiling contentedly. Whether they meant it or not, they were good at it.

The men were investors, as Mr. Dacres explained to Dezzie during one of the moments when he eased him to the side.

"What you need are some investments, Dezzie, to turn over your money and make it work for you. If a man just keeps spending his money, it will surely finish in no time! You have to invest, man!"

It definitely made sense and Dezzie was told that later on, they would all go for a drive further up into the hills – the menfolk, that is – and start discussions. Dezzie felt a sweetness, separate and apart from that inspired by the liquor; a sweetness of belonging to a class of men whose companionship was not liberally extended to all. But here it was, being extended to him.

"Who else coming to the party?" asked Precious. It was one of the few times she had spoken directly to the M.P. and though she was never one to put on airs, she did muster a certain graciousness that was unfamiliar but becoming. She had waltzed over to where the men were standing, and had offered another round.

"Well, I had rustled up quite a few fellas," Mr. Dacres announced, addressing everyone. "Thought they would have been here by now. The night is still young, nonetheless." He chuckled.

Precious turned her attention to Cassandra, who had been sipping daintily on the same pina colada since she arrived. She sometimes strolled so dangerously close to the pool that Precious wondered if she intended to jump in. Some of these girls can't handle their liquor, Precious thought, remembering her Downtown days when some of the guys would bring their uptown girlfriends to the Dancehall sessions, and after a few sips they would go berserk. But Cassandra didn't seem drunk. Maybe just bored. In spite of the boisterous uprisings from the men's circle every now and again, and the hip tempo of the music, nothing much was happening. None of the other guests had arrived – not the ones that Mr. Dacres had invited, and certainly not any of those that the Grants had invited. No neighbours, no joggers, no nobody. It was as if they had signed and were enforcing a clandestine petition to boycott the festivities. Cassandra, being the only female guest, could not be blamed for aimlessly wandering the grounds, checking her shadow on the ground that it remained true to form, but how could it?

Precious could not help noticing, however, how much Cassandra seemed at home here, how she seemed to complement the environs. Maybe, it was all in her mind. Subconsciously, Precious had come to associate light-skinned girls with places like these. She knew, from Dezzie, just who Cassandra was. Her status as "the M.P.'s other woman" did not seem to diminish her in her own estimation, or in anyone else's. It seemed, if anything, to propel her to a plane of enviable notoriety, as if to say, only a certain caliber of girl could be the M.P.'s other woman. Cassandra certainly carried herself with the grace of a goddess who had descended to mingle, all the while aware that she was doing everyone a favour.

She wore a sleek mustard mini dress with a collar but bare at the back, that had immediately caused Dezzie's mind to stray along the lines of, was she wearing any underwear? He couldn't help it. For the life of him, he could not discern the imprint of strings or mesh or anything that indicated a panty line. He was intrigued. He had avoided Cassandra's eyes, though her countenance seemed to have changed somewhat from the usual irritated indifference towards his existence. Several times he had noticed something on her face and had managed to confirm, in spite of the sultry nightness of things, that it was indeed a smile.

Twice, she had outright laughed, possibly at something he had said. He wasn't sure because he had been too taken aback by the sheer laughter, to know for sure if he had been the cause.

So when Mr. Dacres cruised over to his beloved and asked playfully if she was bored, and suggested that Dezzie give her a tour of the new house till the other guests arrived, Dezzie was flustered. He was almost sure that the politically correct thing was to ask Precious or Bam to do it, but then he had heard Precious say that she didn't like being alone with girls who were stoosh and speaky-spokey and went on as if they were better than other people, and she had been looking in Cassandra's direction with pouted mouth when she said it – the way Jamaicans sometimes pointed disdainfully with their mouths at things they didn't find favourable. He wasn't sure which one Precious would cuss him more for later – taking Cassandra on a one-to-one tour through the sprawling house, or signing Precious up to do it. He figured he was going to be cussed out anyway, so he decided to be cussed out for the more personally enjoyable of the two options – if for no-one else, enjoyable for him.

"Yuh been into many of these houses already, don't?" were his first words as she led her upstairs. He felt stupid for saying it but, she smiled and nodded. "Well, this is my first one!" he declared, again stupidly, only highlighting more his lack of exposure to good things. Commoner! He chastised himself.

"We all start somewhere, Dezzie," said Cassandra, seeming to understand, and he realized that it was the first time that he could remember her ever speaking to him directly, by way of calling his name. He also realized that, in spite of her twang and the "foreignness" that she tried to achieve, her accent was not one from abroad but was familiar, in a vague sense, like the way the people from Western Jamaica spoke, with distended syllables. It was something he had missed before but now, so close to her and actually in conversation, he realized it.

He always found it ticklish, for example, the way that people from St. Elizabeth would say "mawma" for ma'am and "mawsa" for mister, and "aye" for yes. And then, he began to put together

her very light complexion, grayish-blue eyes and maroon hair.

"Yuh from somewhere down St. Elizabeth side?" he asked, more comfortable now.

She said that she wasn't. "From Seaford." They were slowly climbing the stairs, and he had deliberately allowed her to go ahead of him.

"Seaford? Never hear of it."

"Westmoreland. Way up in the bush." She chuckled. "Haven't you ever heard them talk about the German people up in Seaford?"

He hadn't. Cassandra Stockhausen was, of course, referring to her ancestors, a batch of just a couple hundred German indentured workers who had come to Jamaica in the years following the abolition of slavery, to stem the subsequent labour shortage. Most died from malaria, yellow fever and lack of adaptability towards the local tropical climate. They remained staunchly separatist in their thinking, interbred and kept to themselves in the hills of Westmoreland, until relatively recently, so that the three hundred or so remaining residents still resembled very much their German forebears, some with blue eyes, blonde hair, and freckled white skin. Though only a fragment of the language remained, such as "auf wiedersehen" and "guten tag", in the older folk, they still claimed direct German lineage and had only slowly begun to come out of their seclusion and integrate with the rest of the population. Well, Dezzie had no idea of this and ordinarily, it would not have been something he cared much about. But since this was Cassandra, he pried deeper and discovered that her family had come to Kingston after a stint in St. Elizabeth, her widowed mother seeking a better life for the family. The only girl of five children, and the only one of the family to graduate high school, Cassandra was her mother's hope.

Dezzie could definitely see why a mother would pin her hopes on a girl such as Cassandra. She had what it took to churn misfortune into fortune. He certainly understood. His own sisters had left the island with his mother's most eager blessings, and he knew she had tied her hopes to them, that they would somehow marry into some money, or otherwise step up in life, taking her with them. This had not happened and Bam hardly spoke about the fact that her daughters had let her down, had taken up with "foreign dregs", as she called it, who could offer them no better than the local ones. They never returned to Jamaica, and their mother assumed this was out of shame.

Up close, Dezzie found Cassandra to be more approachable. He had always only viewed her from the mirror as she sat scornfully in the back of his taxi, afraid to smudge her suit. Or, he had gazed longingly as she wheeled past after being dropped off at some big shot party or other. Cassandra seemed not so much impressed by the house itself, as by the fact that Dezzie owned it, a detail which he was very proud to repeat for emphasis whenever he felt it warranted. Yes, she had been in many such rooms, seen many such things, often. Yet, she held on to Dezzie's hand as he led her from room to room, as if to indicate: go ahead, show me more. He obliged.

"So all this is yours, huh?" she would say; reflectively, not gasping. And he would again confirm. "I always think one day I'll live in a house like this. For sure."

"Oh, you definitely deserve a house like this!" exclaimed Dezzie. "Well, not to say we don't all deserve some luxury, but you have the front appearance."

Cassandra blushed. "Front appearance. Hmm." She stroked his arm. "I guess one day my dream will come true, and I'll find a nice man with a house like this, who is willing to marry me."

"You won't have any problem getting a rich man to marry yuh, none at all!"

"Hmm. You would think."

"Dacres glad-bag must buss to know him have a girl like you."

"Maybe so. But everyone knows he's not my man. Not my own man, anyway. Not the woman he goes home to, and takes to real functions." She appeared to sigh.

Some moments passed, as they made their way across the redwood floor into the theatre, which required a short, careful descent. "Imagine your face on the big screen. Wow!" said Dezzie. He had instinctively turned on his charm but he still wasn't absolutely sure how to proceed, or if he should. There were odds, and there were consequences. The timing, perhaps, was not ideal. Neither was the setting. Her man was downstairs. His woman was downstairs. His children were watching television in their rooms. But what the heck. He put his arm coyly around her waist, felt tremendous relief when she didn't object, and tremendous pressure within his loins as she pressed her body closer to his. He made to kiss her but she eased back a little, took his hand instead and guided it towards the warm inner part of her thigh, up towards the place where he would find out once and for all that a girl like Cassandra had no time for panties. He nearly screamed in delight, as he massaged her in gentle strokes until his fingers were smooth with dew. He cupped her breasts with fervor, tried to kiss her again, and again she dodged, giggling, and ran off a few paces. She was certainly playful tonight.

"Let's get back then, in case they start wondering," she said, giggling girlishly and leading the way down the corridor.

Dezzie did not understand. Did she want to tease him first? But why the games? He didn't like games, but with Cassandra he would play any game. And he wasn't afraid of Dacres, either. Having a sweet girl like that dangling? Dacres was some fool!

It was truly beginning to seem as if no-one else would come. The oldies but goodies had started but only two couples were there. For any other pair to team up would have raised suspicions, of the kind no-one was mellow enough to risk. Dezzie danced with Precious and Mr. Dacres danced with Cassandra. For variety, they switched partners for two or three songs, then Mr. Dacres announced with half-tipsy fervor that Dezzie was moving in a bit too close, and everybody laughed. Bam gave it a try with the D.J. but after one song, called it quits on account of her painful corns and went back to sit by the pool. "Tell har the boot was too damn small," Dezzie whispered to Precious, and they giggled at Bam's expense. Everyone was in fairly good spirits but it wasn't the bashment that Dezzie had anticipated, and his heart was kind of sinking, except when he remembered the privileges that Cassandra had allowed him upstairs, and then his mind raced and he wondered what else she would allow. How far would she let him go? Was she just a cruel tease? Some girls were like that, and you would get nowhere else with them. When again would he get the opportunity to test her waters, so to speak? Should he be his usual bold self and make a move, or should he wait? He would not be planning another party any time soon, he was sure of that. Let the stuck-up Norbrook bastards stay to themselves. He didn't need them. Let them stay.

What if Casssandra had been drunk, and would not remember anything in the coming days? She would surely shun him, if that was the case, and probably accuse him of harassment to Dacres, who had been so helpful, if it turned out she wasn't up to it.

"Hear what, Dez. Let's go for a little drive out up the hills, just us and the boys," said Mr. Dacres. "Maybe by time we get back, things will be in swing." But everyone knew the party had crashed.

Precious retreated inside and left Bam to entertain Cassandra by the pool, which pretty much meant that the two women sat staring at the ripples and occasionally looked up as the D.J. fumbled at packing away his equipment.

Mr. Dacres led the way uphill with Dezzie in the passenger seat, while the other three men rode in one car behind. Dezzie never imagined that there was so much more to Norbrook. They seemed to be heading towards the Blue Mountains, for all he knew! The road was terrifyingly steep and meandered upward, so that every time there was a brief pause to change gear, he expected with certainty that they would tumble backwards to their death. There were precipices and apparently bottomless gorges. Had it been daytime, he would have consoled himself by the lush jade beauty of the hillsides, the feathery palm trees and bamboos that towered, the soft green acres of grass that spilled over the mountainside. But all this was little consolation at night.

"People really live up here? Lawd!" he shrieked. "Jehovah

Jireh!"

"But why not? It's close enough to town, but far enough away to have fresh clean air. The steepness is a little deterrent for the crooks. A little deterrent. This is where I come when I want to get away from it all. Quite a few friends living up this side. Might sell the house in Hellshire one day, or rent it out, and get something up here." He was maneuvering as he spoke, trying not to make it seem as hard as it was. "You still have to be careful though, you know. People up here don't take time at all. They speed up and down in big fast vehicles that they sometimes can't manage!" he chuckled.

At the top of every ascent, Dezzie felt sure that they must have reached – only to discover that they were going even higher. "Soon reach, man. Soon reach," Mr. Dacres assured him. "Big taximan like you, 'fraid of a little driving?"

"Is not so much the driving, but the hills," Dezzie tried to explain.

Even in the darkness, Dezzie could make out the enormous houses that they were passing. They seemed to grow bigger as they ascended to places where Dezzie was sure Norbrook must have ended long ago and they were certainly in Portland by now. Before he owned one, Dezzie used to question the sanity of living in a mansion. Mark you, he had wanted to live in one, but since he didn't, he felt it pertinent to point out that this was pure madness. A ridiculous notion, for a family of four or five, trekking from room to room like blinking idiots, can't find anyone or anything, too many damn places for them to be. How could someone enjoy a really big house? For entertainment purposes, yes, but what when the friends have left, and the children have grown; the houses become hollow, a place for echoes and eerie shadows and emotional emptiness. That had been his reasoning, before he owned a mansion. But some of these put even his own to shame. His mansion could hold in any one of the bathrooms of some of these ones, with space to walk around. It was as if the owners were possessed by some feverish craze to build build build, add add add, for as far as ground space would allow, and then an upward invasion of the sky till the heavens shrieked.

Mr. Dacres glanced back occasionally to check that the others were still following. They had all been up this far before, but only in the daytime.

"Hey," he said with his usual chuckle that Dezzie could never make head or tail of (you couldn't tell if he was with you or against you with that chuckle!). "I saw you gripping my girl back there. Watch yuhself, Dezzie!"

"Who, me?" asked Dezzie, feigning innocence. "What I do?"

"Relax, man. All I saying, she well outta yuh league, brother. Well outta yuh league. Cass is my girl, yuh know dat, Dezzie. That's the girl I plan to marry."

Dezzie looked across at the M.P. as if he were crazy. "Yuh forgetting yuh done cross dat bridge already, Bossman?" he couldn't help laughing. "What yuh planning, divorce?"

Mr. Dacres chuckled again. It was becoming annoying. "Yuh doan think I'll do it?"

"Not saying yuh wouldn't...but still. Yuh done have har pon lock-down, yuh know weh mi ah seh?"

"Yuh let me worry 'bout dat, Dezzie. Anyway, if yuh want, I can set yuh up wid another girl, light skin same way. Yuh know light skin girls guh crazy for dark skin man, and vice versa! Worse like how yuh have few dollars right now..."

"I guh crazy for all girls!" laughed Dezzie.

They finally cleared a vee curve, the bottom of which Dezzie was sure was the final resting place of many souls, made one last climb and leveled onto a sparse clearing, a small plateau. From here, you could see the entire Corporate Area of Kingston and urban St. Andrew, the Liguanea Plains and parts of Long Mountain, behind which was nestled a small lagoon that Dezzie never knew existed in Kingston. He later found out that this was the Mona dam. Over to the East rose the foothills of the Blue Mountains and towards the West, stretched the adjoining St. Jago plains onward to Spanish Town and Portmore. You could see just about everything from here. The city lights, from this high, dazzled below in a sea of diamonds, rubies, sapphires and emeralds, set amidst pitch black. And further out, the Caribbean Sea, also black at this hour, but still fluid, and hurling several cool gusts of wind towards the five men who stood at the edge of the precipice, looking down. There were two large properties on the land; both owners were abroad, and friends of Mr. Dacres. It was his little hide-out, he explained, to which he had full access as he chose. Dogs barked heftily in the distance but apart from that, pure silence.

All the men were armed, except for Dezzie. He had always known that Mr. Dacres carried his piece on him. Dezzie had often tried to guess where exactly it was kept. One time he and the other taximen had taken a kind of bet, not that they could prove each other wrong or right, but it was everyman's guess. Some said, must be in his waist, others said, could be nowhere else but in the crevice of his back, still others had maintained, strapped to his shin and covered by his pants. Dezzie figured, maybe all of the above. Mr. Dacres was a sensible man. Maybe he varied the location. Maybe, he had more than one pieces. It was something that went with the territory; something understood, even if not asked about.

Now, he could sense that every man had a peculiar bulge and he became obsessed to the point of paranoia. He suddenly felt fearful, realizing for the first time that here he was on top of this back-bush place that probably wasn't officially a part of Jamaica, with four armed men about and German shepherds barking in the distance, and countless precipices in which to toss his body, the scent of which could never be traced from so deep. And then he remembered that he had not even bothered to tell Precious where he was going. Heck, he himself had not known where he was going. He felt vulnerable and terrified and stupid. He backed away from the edge. The other three men were leaning against huge mango trees, planted eons ago.

Mr. Dacres reached into his waistband and removed his gun, held it up into the light so Dezzie could see it. Dezzie jumped back, trembling, but said nothing.

"Just checking," said Mr. Dacres, absently, focusing more on the gun than on the frightened man. "Just making sure it's loaded and ready. It's generally pretty safe up here but yuh never know. People can trail yuh, and it's very bushy. Cyaan let down yuh guard." Satisfied, he replaced the weapon. Dezzie slowly started breathing again but he never really regained his composure for the rest of the night.

"Whe....whe.....where I can get one of that?" he asked timidly.

"One of this? You mean the gun?" asked Mr. Dacres. He chuckled. "But stop! Yuh move quick, my brother! Yuh ready for one of these already? But yuh is real big shot, man! Yuh eva fire one?" Dezzie shook his head. "Yuh eva hol' one?" Dezzie was embarrassed. "Here. Tek a spin." He removed the gun again and handed it to Dezzie, who reluctantly held it in the palm of one hand and touched it with the other. "Fully loaded, Sah. Careful. But what yuh want wid gun though, Dezzie? Man, yuh have to tek lessons and thing like dat. I could hook yuh up wid a instructor, yes, and help yuh get a piece when yuh ready."

Dezzie handed the gun back to him. It felt heavier than he had always imagined, and cold. A bit too cold.

"Yuh know, they do background check and fingerprint and everything, interview yuh family and all that," explained Mr. Dacres, enjoying the moment.

"What? Why all dat?' exclaimed Dezzie.

"What? Yuh have something to hide? Yuh have a criminal record? Any links to hard drugs? Look like yuh have skeletons in the closet, Dezzie?" Seeing that he had withdrawn, Mr. Dacres became sober once more. "Just let mi know when yuh ready, Mr. Big Shot, now dat yuh have things to protect. But anyway, let's go over to the other fellas now and talk some business. Some investments."

Garnet Scott, Leyland Hanes and Oliver Berry had devised a business plan. They wanted to open a same-day loan operation, catering mainly to self-employed, maybe even unemployed, people who were considered high-risk by the banks and had trouble getting loans from the mainstream financing companies.

Since it was determined (by whom, Dezzie wasn't sure) that the majority of these persons were honest, hard-working individuals who would honor their obligations and only needed someone to have faith and extend a helping hand in times of crises, the risk was worth taking. The delinquents would be offset by the accumulative non-refundable processing fees that each applicant would have to make, which varied according to how urgently the loan was needed. Who wouldn't pay four thousand dollars upfront to be considered for a loan of thirty thousand dollars cash, on spot, especially if the banks have rejected and you needed the money badly? The trick was, most people would still be turned down. We have to have standards, still. It's a business, not a non-profit. The clincher: they needed investors, at least to get started. It was a sure thing. This kind of business never loses.

"How many investors, so far?' asked Dezzie.

Well, none – yet. But, one investor with the right capital may even be enough. Who to tell if we could locate such a man?

"Yuh have to think growth, Dezzie. Yuh have to expand yuh money, or it will shrink you," advised Mr. Dacres. "How long yuh think yuh millions going last? Buying a house, yes, but yuh still have bills, and a woman, and children going to school. These things take a toll, over time. Would be a shame if yuh have to sell back the house, to pay yuh bills dem! Yuh have to think investment."

"Let mi run it over wid Precious," said Dezzie. He wasn't having a good gut feeling about it. Invest, yes, but he knew nothing about this type of business, what the risks were. He may not be educated but he had plenty common sense. This was not something to jump into.

"Nobody rushing yuh, man. Tek yuh time. Just a proposal, from one friend to the next," said Mr. Dacres assuredly. The other three men seemed a bit more anxious, as if they had been guaranteed a deal and were wondering what was up. They strolled away for some time and then Mr. Dacres announced that they should be heading back down to Norbrook Proper, and they hopped in. The drive down was even more terrifying. It had gotten darker and Dezzie was even more acutely aware that he was unarmed, a fry among sharks, in a part of the ocean that few divers ventured.

He didn't even mind the chastisement from Precious, who wanted to know why he had taken so long with Cassandra earlier.

"Look, ah tell yuh, ah doan guh fa that type. Dem red-skin girl cyan manage mi. Ah would bruck dem dung within minutes. Strong-body Black woman, mi seh," was all he muttered, and was just happy to fall asleep.

Chapter Fourteen

The landed gentry of the rolling estates in England, the colonial mother, were expected to have, at the very least, a country house and a sprawling estate. With this came wonderful prestige and political leverage, which throughout history, throughout the world, has been attached to the ownership of land.

Land, my friend. Land.

Owning land was once a prerequisite for suffrage – the right to say, of potential candidates who present themselves as possible stewards of your nation: I want this one, as opposed to that one. Not everybody in the nation had that right. The ownership of land, among other things, secured for you that right.

Albeit the lesser nobility – distinctly below the aristocracy and considered commoners to the peerages – members of the landed gentry were upper class landlords who still had high birth and rank, good social standing and wealth. Baronets, knights, squires, gentlemen; some titles hereditary, some conferred. The nouveau riche would immediately sever ties with the tainted trading class from which some had emerged. This landed gentry was, historically, a British social class of land owners who, through shrewdness or otherwise, had arrived at the point where they could now live entirely from the rental income milked from their estates. Though they were often much richer than the aristocracy, the landed gentry were still considered socially below them. The much more populated middle class consisted of the tenants who paid rent on the estates, or were engaged in trade.

Wherever jolly ol' England went, she took her customs and her legacies, her snobs and her airs.

In Jamaica, rich white landowners set up their estates and great houses, in keeping with tradition – with a few peculiar appendages: the rolling sugar plantations, the squalid slave quarters, the gruesome dungeons used to exact punishment.

In later years, many of these estates became what were called "pens". In Kingston and St. Andrew parishes, later to be merged as the Kingston and St. Andrew Corporation, the wealthy residents began buying the old pens and turning them into farms for livestock. Many of these areas still have the word "pen" attached to their names. When the term became derogatory due to partisan politics, some dropped the term "pen" and opted for "gardens".

The affluent community of Norbrook, where Dezzie now lived and where many persons who have come into new wealth aspire to be, was once owned by Jamaican national hero and politician, George William Gordon, who was born in Mavis Bank in the parish. The Cherry Gardens Great House, once owned by Gordon, was a sugar estate which he had bought along with the adjoining lots. Gordon lived here until he was hanged in 1865, for his alleged role in the Morant Bay Rebellion. The second of eight children and the product of a mixed union, Gordon had taught himself to read and write and moved up the ranks of the gentry.

The first black millionaire in Jamaica was George Stiebel, who had acquired much wealth in Venezuela and, upon his return to Jamaica, was appointed Custos – an official who represented the Governor General in the parish. St. Andrew was and still is the most populated parish. He built Devon House in 1881, which still stands as a hallmark along the great Liguanea Plains of St.

Andrew.

So on this side of the island, Norbrook was and still is the place to be, the domicile that declares your arrival among the cream of high society. Of course, the Eighteenth Century English Genteel would snub their noses at these, at best, relegating them to the petit bourgeois from which they would haply chose a butler or a even governess, never a spouse. Which only goes to show, hierarchy is a dynamic element that is very time and space specific. The nobility in one setting is the bourgeois of another. The untouchables here are the touchables there. The clear demarcations of class and skin tone in the West Indian islands, for example, are far more subtle and sometimes nonexistent elsewhere, in a wider society, which is predominantly white; forcing many West Indians who grew up thinking and being told that they were white or near-white, to reconsider, upon confrontation with the same racism that they had meted out to their own people of a darker shade.

Hierarchy is not one of the human constructs. Hierarchy is definitely nature's way. The human factor seems to be the vast disparity between the tiers, and the very limited scope for escaping the ranks born into.

Chapter Fifteen

It's a chance you take when you place seeds into the earth, hoping for something to come of it. But you take a greater chance by putting nothing into the earth. This must have been one of the first lessons man learned, wherever on the planet he found himself. He observed. By accident, he may have noticed something sprout from where a seed once lay and was over time, buried. As with most things, accident became trial, trial became habit, habit became instinct, instinct became a way of life.

When a man has a got himself some land, and that man is a forward-thinking man, this is good. There are things that can be done with land, even bad land, if you are a forward-thinking man. The land will work with you, if you work with it. Sometimes, you have to give it time. Nature doesn't work on man's schedule. This was the first thing to remember.

In his mind, and then several times on paper till he was satisfied with the outline, Ras Negus had divided the land into little compartments, for this and that. A section for vegetables, a section for compost, a section for flowers, a section for the catchment drums and irrigation sprinklers, which a man had come to help him set up. A section for the children to play, though there was ample roaming space down in what they called the gully. A section for Naph-T to do her washing and to hang clothes on two long metal wires stretched across the yard, where the clothes would get plenty of sun. There were at least five moringa trees about the place. The elders had said, this was the most nutritious tree known to man. What luck! Two proud neem trees were laden with ripe berries, where you could reach up and pick. Another highly favoured tree, bitter but full of nutriment.

To the back of the property, a barrage of fruit trees had already colonized about three acres, perhaps for generations now. Who was to tell how long they had been there, or whether they were planted by nature's hand or by man's accidental toss, or by intent. These trees knew a thing or two, had eavesdropped on many an evening conversation of grown folk of yore, had seen many children run and fall and get back up, and run, the way children do. Perhaps had bodies buried under them, from the time when concrete graves and tombstones were rare. Almost certainly had navel strings planted somewhere near; a gesture of hope. These trees were well established, grew high and broad, and those that were in season bore profusely. The children would have much fruit to eat, year round. This was very good.

The wooden house that had come with the property was towards the front and side, a few more fruits trees cradling it and providing shade for the verandah and front yard. It was a big enough house. Rooms for everyone. They could even add more. A pit latrine a little way down from the house. An outside kitchen in the other direction. The decision to keep using these or to add new ones had not been made; did not need to be made just now. More urgent was the matter of planting the seeds, getting the crops ready to supply the restaurant.

In the wee hours of morning, Ras Negus sat beneath one of the breadfruit trees – the one he intended to climb a little later, before the sun came up. He rolled a spliff on the spot, held a meditation for about an hour, his back braced against the bark of the breadfruit tree as the fumes of ganja hit his head with each puff. This, for him, signaled the release of wisdom, the procession of ancestral council. Or, as some would prefer to say, hallucination. But they were dumb; did not understand. Or they did, but would prefer if you didn't. In any event, this inhalation of the healing herbs was a tradition handed down from his fathers, on good recommendation. They swore by the kali weed, and it worked for him. Kept him grounded, all these years. He swore by it, too.

Mornings should be peaceful. Mornings should begin with peace. Calm. Meditation. He imagined the kali hitting his pineal gland. This was what it was said to do. It certainly felt like that was what it was doing. Ras Negus held the vision in his head, the constant image of his land, his restaurant, his family. This thought would sustain him throughout the day.

Now, he would climb the breadfruit tree and pick the ones that were full, to roast and have with ackee for breakfast; a younger one for boiling later, with yams and bananas and steamed callaloo, for lunch. These breadfruit trees were massive, with heavy foliage. They grew to a good twenty feet. He had no catcher this time of morning, and would never run the risk of bruising the fruit by tossing them down, even upon the rich grass. He had no pole, either; had not gotten round to making one with a knife attached to the end, as Derrick, the farmhand had advised. But as he only needed about three good-sized fruit this morning, Ras Negus thought nothing of making three trips to secure each one and return it safely to the ground. He lapped his feet around the trunk of the tree he had sat under, and scaled up quickly like a koala.

The fruit grew about six feet from the base of each branch, seen even in the dim light of before-dawn. A good stretch and he easily wrung each from the stem, smiled as the sap gushed to the place where he had severed the connection. On the ground, he placed the breadfruit stem-down to drain into the earth, so that the sap would not stain his clothes or anything else.

The roosters had been at it for a few hours, taking turns. Every now and again one would jump to it, as if it had dozed off

Landed Gentry

and was suddenly aware of neglecting a vital duty. A few times Ras Negus had seen the shadows of men, farmers, off to their various plots along the hillside, further up, with their crocus bags strung over their shoulders, their faithful razor-edge machetes in their right hands, perhaps a keg of lemonade or a thermos flask of coffee tea in their left. On one occasion since morning, a mule or donkey was in tow, led by a rope. Someone passed with a katta on their head, cushioning bananas, or something. This may have been a female. These things he could barely make out. He guessed what they were, from being familiar. They left before daybreak to get things started on the yam mounds, or the small sparse fields of corn, or the smoldering kilns of charcoal that could be smelt from here; a peculiar, hilly smell. At lunchtime, the boys would take them their bickle before running off to catch birds with their slingshots, or perhaps the wives would take the bickles, depending on a number of things.

There were many things to do before Ras Negus left the hills for work in the restaurant, in the midst of the city. Now that the sun was coming up and the household was stirring, he started the wood fire to get the breadfruits roasting for breakfast. Then, he walked over to the compost heap, a ten foot by eight foot structure comprised of decaying vegetable matter, grass, various organic scraps and alternating layers of dirt. This would provide natural fertilizer for the crops. He walked around to examine the compost, took a sample of the black soil and held it up to the morning light just clearing the trees. He crumbled the mixture so that it fell back into the heap, checking for texture. This wasn't ready. Too soft. Not flaky enough. Perhaps a week or so more. An intense heat rose from the mound wherever he spiked it with a fork. Good. Things were happening inside it. Some white-orange-green mold had formed to one side of the heap, signifying something good, by his smile. He had seen a few earthworms wriggling wherever the fork had stirred the earth. This was the best sign. Wherever there are worms, something good is happening. The whole heap smelled of fragrant citronella released from the orange peels that had been tossed into it weeks ago. He turned the whole thing over with the heavy fork, plunging deep to get the bottom stuff up, shaking and reversing the layers so everything got a chance to be mixed in and set right. Then, he watered the heap, washed his hands thoroughly, and went to inspect the vegetables.

The tomatoes needed fresh mulching; the old mulch having just about settled into humus. They were fit and plump but not yet brilliant red. The irrigation tubes led to this area, the vegetable patch, where slow drips kept them succulent and free from thirst all day. Where there had been the chance of bugs, for instance among the pumpkins where the green aphids would have been rampant by now, he had interspersed patches of thyme, peppermint and cloves, as repellants.

A green thumb was found to be not a necessary requirement, providing your other four fingers were willing to work, were not afraid of dirt, and knew how to wield a machete without removing their own digits. The younger ones were fleeing the farms in droves, rejecting the little cutlets of land that had been diced exponentially among relatives, to not much more than a square foot. Their excuse (apart from the puny size of their holdings) was the absence of the green thumb gene. A very unfortunate fate of unnatural selection but, such is life. What to do? They shrugged, tied their laces, draped their sagging pants just enough to look sad and respectable before their elders. The pants returned to position beneath their rumps, their underpants exposed, so much so that they could hardly walk a few steps without having to haul them back up each time. They hitched a ride to town and generally stayed there; till they developed the red thumb. The trigger thumb. Then, inevitably, they themselves were planted in the soil, but never grew.

The farmers, meantime, one by one, were growing old and weary, dying off or taking to rum. The young ones who did stay, plundered without mercy. It was at a heavy cost. For our decision to not deprive you of our splendid company in your old age, in your sorry state, we shall relieve you of a certain percent of your crops, your livestock, your hope. Is this not fair?

These were things that Ras Negus considered deeply and he tried at least to strike a balance, the city man within him and the countryman within him, the two had to reconcile. They needed each other. He put in quality time in both places. The restaurant consisted of an enclosed dining area, a covered dining area on a small patio, the kitchen and a herb garden out back, for growing fresh herbs and a few vegetables that were always needed on hand. Under the shade of a bamboo gazebo near the herb garden, were several herbs that had been hung to dry before storing. Moringa, neem, dandelion, comfrey, rosemary, peppermint. Many others. They were left in the shade for a number of days, taking care to avoid the direct rays of the sun, then brought indoors to store in glass containers. These herbs were added to the smoothies and freshly expressed juices at the juice bar, or tossed into salads, soups or sandwiches. People liked the ambiance of the gazebo and the scent of the herbs. It confirmed their feeling that they were getting good quality natural stuff from the restaurant. There was nothing customers enjoyed better than the feeling of authenticity, particularly customers who felt themselves to be a minority uncatered for in the regular course of things. They liked to know that they had found their niche, and that the niche was authentic. Finally, a place that sympathized with their longing for natural, healthy food, fresh, raw juices, made with local produce and by local hands.

Not all the customers were of the Rastafarian faith or even wore locks, for that matter. Some could even be said to be uppity society people, based on their dress and the cars they drove, and the things they spoke about if you happened to overhear them as you ate, or served. Indeed, the natural foods trend had hit the upper class big time. It was no longer a grassroots affair. And these people, many of whom seemed to work in the posh New Kingston and Liguanea areas and environs, appeared to have no qualms about sitting down to a plate of ital stew, served in a calabash or bamboo plate. Health was health, was their present mantra.

And this health was affordable. So it allowed even the small fry to dine among the big shots, if even for the lunch hour. Everyone was contented.

Jamaicans had a saying, food business is the surest business. People always need to eat. They can go without everything else, but push come to shove, they must find money for food. Yet, it was still a business and hence, a risk nonetheless. A food handler's permit did not guarantee that you would be found in favour of customers. A location on Dumfries Road, a stone's throw from the New Kingston metropolis, still had a substantial overhead. Ras Negus had hitched his horse on the wave of health consciousness that had been sweeping the country. The risk was paying off. But not only that, this was where his heart was. This was what he truly wanted to do. It helps to be engaged in something that you really want to do.

He had invested half of the money as start-up for the restaurant, a quarter into the farm and roughly a quarter had been put into savings.

The décor for the restaurant was wooden and bamboo furniture, a few wicker pieces, the predominant theme rustic and laid back. Earth tones throughout, kente cloths draped over things. Curtains sewn from authentic Liberian prints through a sistren who had the links. A few Benin heads and Akoaba statuettes, again through continental links. A huge map of Africa near the entrance. Smaller maps of Ethiopia, a life-sized framed portrait of His Imperial Majesty, Emperor Haile Selassie I, seated beside his family; another of H.I.M. reaching forward to pet a huge lion.

There was a section of shelves of books for sale, another section of second-hand books for perusal. By the juice bar and the salad bar, customers could have their dream smoothies and salads done to order, or choose from the menu of juices that Ras Negus himself had created. There were bottles of roots tonic that he had concocted in his hills, bottled, sealed and labeled, from recipes handed down by the elders. You could get Irish moss, coconut water, nut milk, green smoothies, herbal teas, freshly expressed carrot, cucumber and beetroot juice. You name it.

There were four sets of people who frequented the restaurant: the livity set, the faddists, the desperate set and the curious set. Each had their badges of identification. Ras Negus knew each by heart, could spot them as they entered and point them to their heart's desire. It would start with the greeting, upon entering. This ranged anywhere from a bushy-eyed 'Hello', to a polite 'Good afternoon', to a serene 'Namaste', to a defiant 'Hotep', to a declarative 'Haile Selasie I Jah Rastafari eva living eva faithful eva sure!'.

The livity set could argue, only they really had the right to be there. For them, it was a lifestyle, tied in with religious or political views, or both. Some had been born into it, for generations. They wore anything from regular clothes to dashikis to kente outfits to homemade fashions featuring burlap and khaki, to the Nyabhingi wrapped from head to toe. Some, aware of the presence of the heathen, brought their own plates and cutlery with them, and refused to eat from anything else, and preferred to eat outback, near the gazebo. Most had read huge volumes on holistic health, ayurvedic and naturopathic and homeopathic and other alternative ways of doing things, which were really not the alternatives but the originals, as opposed to the allopathic path of death.

The faddists were easily identifiable. They were almost always in yoga pants, vests, track clothes, gym wear, sneakers or any other apparel that would make you know for sure: "Behold! I am a health freak. Approach me with care. I know everything and nothing simultaneously. This is not an easy feat." If allowed, they would have worn nothing to all, if only to impress upon you the reality of their six packs, eight packs, flat abs and toned calves. They mainly frequented the juice and salad bars. They would browse by the book shelves while they waited on their powerful smoothies, but this was redundant because they had read all the books. They would tell you this, as you tried to dodge them. In addition to the juices that they would gulp down on spot, they would order two more glasses to go, to sip at the gym later, or after yoga. These had usually run the gamut of options and would gladly outline to you their progress from vegetarianism to veganism to raw foodist to fruitarianism, back down to veganism because their bodies started craving greens, back down to vegetarianism for some balance because their bodies started craving carbs, ultimately aiming at breatharianism with a major in aligning the chakras. Some of these often came in asking for supplements. Ras Negus didn't sell supplements. He would point them to the roots tonic but they had very little interest in these.

The curious set were dressed like regular people, which they were in every sense but that they had heard about the lifestyle on a radio talk show or had seen an interview on tv and just happened to be passing and wanted to see what it was about. Even their pastor may have mentioned something. Such was the expanse of the present health movement. They may have read or heard a testimonial of someone beating some chronic illness or licking cancer's butt or regrowing some organ that had been severed, or just regrowing some hair, which was enough for some. They wanted further verification, if not for themselves, perhaps for a relative or friend who was too much of a skeptic to be seen here in person. These hardly bought anything but they always promised to come back.

The desperate group bought everything. They brought money because they had heard, these things cost but death is more expensive. They were on the verge of death. They had been diagnosed and had had second and third opinions. Some had even had radiation, chemotherapy, dialysis, surgery. Prognosis poor. This was their last resort. They barely dragged themselves in, overweight, emaciated, achy, nauseous, disoriented. Some were carried in, wheeled in. They had not wanted to come, did not really believe in this hocus-pocus, had tried just about everything else, including oils and potions and guard rings and spells. They were at their last, on their last. They had claimed their diseases and were now on a first-name basis with the ailments. They knew their symptoms back-to-back.

"But dat's the first ting," Ras Negus would say. "Doan claim di diseae unto yuhself. Doan she my cancer, my diabetes, my dis, my dat. Shun it. Shun it! Rebuke it!" He spoke with authority on these things.

Ras Negus advised them what to take, which herbs, which tonics. They said, it looked and smelled bitter. But they supposed death was more bitter. With meals or before meals, or after? They bought several bottles of everything.

This was not just a restaurant. It was an oasis. The Dumfries Road location was ideal. Neither the rich nor the poor felt too far from home. A five-minute drive from work. An half hour bus ride from almost anywhere in the city. The building was neither intimidating nor repulsive. In fact, it was one of those old wooden buildings that had been there from long before this section of the town came to prominence. Everyone loved an old wooden building. The sign out front just read, in beautiful hand-painted script of red, green and gold: "Ras Negus Ital Eats and Juice Bar". A lion was painted at the side.

There were two employees, other than Naph-T, who worked as chef and Desmond, who doubled as everything else and did odd jobs when he wasn't up at the farm. Ras Negus did a little of everything, as well. He was sometimes in the kitchen, sometimes serving, sometimes working in the herbal garden; almost always talking to customers while he did everything. He really felt contented about life. He never hated being a garbage collector, never thought himself less than a man; but he didn't miss it. He had no problem telling anyone what he used to do. He just felt happy now that he was a man in charge of his affairs. He was doing something that he loved, something that he had control over, something that his family could live off and see a way in. A few months did make a heck of a difference. Ten million dollars made a difference in a man's life. A right-thinking man, at least.

The only real hitch so far had come two weeks after he had first set up. There weren't that many customers then. Things had barely started to pick up from the slump one expects at the start of anything. Near the afternoon, when he was out in the herbal garden, four policemen swooped down upon him, took him so much by surprise that he grabbed a pile of moringa bush and started swiping it at them. Instinct. It was the only thing he could think of. The police had been the last thing on his mind. He was no longer at Mulgrave Lane. He was an honest, legally registered businessman.

What could Babylon possibly want with him, now? Luckily, these ones weren't trigger happy. They could have cited his flourish of moringa as an attack, and justified his killing. Stranger things had happened. He guessed they forgave him the ruption, understanding that a man who was corned out of the blue would grasp at anything. But they did turn the place upside-down, searching for ganja. They sniffed every herb hung up to the dry under the gazebo. They went over the moringa and sniffed again like they weren't sure. They checked the kitchen and the juice bar and in every box and basket. They left after about an hour.

Ras Negus was so shaken that he pulled a ganja spliff from his locks the instant they left, lit it and stood by the gate smoking and staring up the road.

Chapter Sixteen

"Straddle me, like you do dem horses."

She was small and thin, almost fragile. Skinny legs and long, black horse's hair. Real hair that you could tug hard on when the need arose. A man should be able to tug at a woman's hair if need be, without fearing that if would come apart in his hands, and her rage come apart with it. He had just about had it with black women and their wigs. This woman here, had real hair, soft like a newborn baby's. It fell all over her shoulders as she rode him, her hands pressing down into his chest, her moon face showing only the little chin and the dark O of her mouth, her eyes closed. He arched his own back from the bed a little, to thrust himself completely into her. He was always shocked of how much of him she could take. He was massive. She took the full length and breadth of him. Who woulda thought?

Many things had surprised him about Biyu. Her mouth barely opened when she smiled, yet she could talk nonstop for hours, after all his own resources had been spent and he wanted nothing but sleep. She had no qualms about cussing and swearing, in fact, she could out-curse a Seventeenth Century British sailor. She had the primmest sense of manners and etiquette, yet she was not averse to smoking a cigarette or a spliff, in the right company, or to downing several shots of Johnny Walker when the situation called for it. She was demure and uncouth, all at once. Alluring and sweetly repulsive.

Biyu was the most beautiful creature in his eyes, someone he felt damn lucky to have, yet she was always accusing him of having other women. He did have other women, but in his mind he gave her no reason at all to accuse him of such perfidious acts. She remained his most precious flower. Couldn't she tell? She was petite and unassuming, yet she could handle a horse twelve times her own weight, rein him in and make him yield, make him jump or send him cross the finish line whether or not he felt like going. But it seemed, she made him want to do it. She made him want to win, to please her. This power that she wielded over the monstrous animal, filled Dean with awe every single time he watched her, made him want to submit to her as well. He himself was well over six feet tall, strapping and swarthy. A man well into his thirties.

In the shower, she reminded him that she was going to be late for practice at the tracks. This was her way of saying, screw me again, a little longer this time. Least, this was what he always took it to mean. He braced himself behind her and pinned her hands out front against the walls of the shower, below the showerhead, so that the water still tumbled down her back and glistened through her hair. With his other hand, he raised her leg so that it was bent at the knee, and he held it there, hoisted, as he entered her and thrust himself in again and again. She groaned softly with every plunge. Chinese women are tight. He had heard this. It had been one of the chief things he had set out to confirm or deny, when he had set his eyes and aim on her. Turned out, they are indeed extremely tight, on the very first go, but after that, no tighter than the average. on the first day that he had see her, he had whispered to himself, if I slept beside her and woke up alive, I would feel like a king. He had found a way to get his daily fix of seeing her ride, by visiting the tracks more often than he needed to, more often than he used to. Till finally, he had smoothed his way into her arms, woke up beside her countless times, and felt like a king each and every time.

On the bed again, he sprawled her open to survey. Everything was still there. The flawless white-yellow skin, clean tiny feet. Suckable toes. Her prim posture as she half-sat, half-lay, waiting for him, a straight plane from shoulder to rear, no undulations.

Mounted, an erect knightly posture at the start, until the ride forces it into a crouch, torso hoisted, head lowered. At the tracks. Biyu sat astride Libido, a three year old stallion. They both had jet black hair that flowed as she graded the horse from a trot to a canter to a full sprint around the paddock, countless times. Tireless. No caps, blinkers or visors now, only the saddle, Biyu dressed in shorts and a summer blouse. One of only three female jockeys on the island, first one ever to participate in the main events.

There were several hardy female polo riders but horseracing was almost exclusively a male-dominated sport in Jamaica. Polo was physically demanding and so was horseracing. In Biyu's eyes, neither contained any more danger for women than for men, yet in polo both sexes competed on the same terms, which was more than could be said for most sports. It had made the news some time ago that female jockeys on the international scene were being deprived maternity leave, or forbidden to ride past the third trimester. A few women had fallen to their deaths on the track within a relatively short time and this had caused a stir. Many of the oldtimers, mainly men, were adamantly against female riders. Unless her father was a trainer or owner, a girl saw little chance of mounting a thoroughbred in a race of any repute. Women jockeys roll differently when they take a fall, it was said, and this difference accounted for their deaths. The crowds and the punters were more receptive but to break down the barriers and the stigma, would take time and dedication. Dedication such as Biyu had.

Seven years of equestrian training, three years on the national Polo team and a natural love for horses, had positioned Biyu in good stead as a local jockey. She had entered with buzz. On many counts, she was a new thing.

In the jockey's crouch, bare knees bent inwards, her small strong hands firmly on the reins. It's more about finesse than strength, her brother had said. This was true. At thirty-five miles an hour, a one thousand pound horse did not care about human strength. But he cared very much about finesse. He would yield to finesse. This Biyu had. She had a way with the horse. She had never raced this particular one, but she would this year, all going well.

The horse was owned by her brother; the only horse he owned. She had been riding it from it was a colt, in endless canters around the paddock, in mock races around the track, but never in an event. She had named it, Libido. Her brother had frowned upon the name, with his usual prudential air, but hadn't objected. It's the way of women. They like to give things strange names. Names that no-one can measure up to. Yet, this was the horse of which it was said, he does not know how to lose the twelve-furlong race.

Michael had bought the horse from the Stud farm, near to the Caymanas Estate. The horse had cost him a decent amount at the time. It had been almost his life's savings. He had friends who owned several horses. Some owned four or five. Michael Could only afford one, at the moment. He chose a good one to buy, though he hadn't known it at the time. He had simply settled for the most affordable thoroughbred, if there was such a thing. Supreme quality at a discount, if at all possible. Libido proved himself to be quite the upsetter. He had a skilled and thorough trainer in Guthrie, a veteran trainer whose family had been in the business for decades. The two grooms, Donovan and Coyote, were like cooing babysitters. They tended to the horse's every whim. Sammy had become the designated events rider after a year and a half of forging a bond with Libido, an unprecedented fourteen Straight wins.

With my beer belly, and the size of my head alone, the horse would topple, Dean laughed to himself. He leaned against the pickets of the paddock. There were two other jockeys riding in this field, a few others across the meadow. Biyu cantered up. Libido neighed softly, came to a standstill.

"He's really easy today. Always easy, but today, very," she

smiled. Libido allowed Dean to pat him.

"He wants a race," said Dean, pointing.

"Who?"

"That fellow there. Seems to be signaling that he wants a race."

Biyu glanced across at Seymour, waved politely, smiled. "I raced him twice last week. Left him in the dust. What, he wants more proof?" she giggled.

"Beaten by a girl. He can't let you have the last laugh."

She signaled to him, "When yuh ready, then." Her attempts at patois always sounded funny in her ears. She wondered if it sounded this way to others. She was born and grown here. Yet, it seemed she spoke Patois with a Chinese accent. What a thing!

"Five minutes!" shouted Seymour. He was not mounted, his horse nowhere to be seen. More than likely by the stables, which was where he seemed to be headed.

Dezzie was standing at the gate of the stables, cursing because he had stepped in horse dung, a common enough thing in a place like this but when you had stupidly decided to wear your name brand white sneakers to a place two-inches thick in droppings, some amount of drama was required to mask your insanity. He tried to scrape it away with a couple handfuls of hay. The smell, of course, lingered, as well as the yellow-green stain.

"Blasted horse shit!" he was cussing, his face wrenched. His style was about to be cramped.

"Yuh sure tek yuh damn time, man, Seymour. Yuh said yuh was just running over there and come back."

"Boss held me up," said Seymour. "Talking crap, as usual. Telling mi rey-rey dat I already know."

"Suh weh yuh seh? Lay it on."

"Impetus. Oriental Connection. She's A Nuisance. Trifecta."

"Yuh sure?"

"How yuh mean, if man sure?"

"Mi jus waan know if yuh sure. Last time yuh gi mi trifecta, mi lose offa yuh!"

"Easy man. Suh dem ting ya guh sometime. Dis one hundred

percent!"

Dezzie hissed. The info his brother gave him from the horse's mouth was always smeared with the horse's saliva. Never dry. Always double risky. But it was better than nothing.

Two men were at the corner of the stable, busily shoveling horse manure into crocus bags. They wanted the manure from right below the open windows and lattices, that had dried out a bit, not so wet or bulky, or smelly. They had shoveled about four bags to the brim and had three more to fill. The one wearing locks looked up. He squinted. The stable was dimly lit, an overcast sky outside. He stood erect to make sure. It was him. he was looking at the man who had given him ten million dollars.

"Selasie I. Jah, Rastafari," he said, his right palm covering his heart, feigning a bow to Dezzie, who took some time to realize what this was all about.

The man walked over to where the brothers were, where Seymour was untying his horse, Impetus, getting her ready for the mock race with Biyu. The Rastaman swiped his hands two or three times across his trousers and extended the right hand to Dezzie, who frowned. Realizing this might have to do with the chores he had been engaged in, the Rastaman chuckled and withdrew his hand. All this time, Dezzie was saying in his heart, you aint no friend of mine. Shoo! Just cause you stole my money and I let you get away with it, don't mean we're brethren. If Bam had been here, she would have scolded him.

The men gathered their bags and hauled them out, one by one, to a vehicle that was waiting under a tree near the stables. It wasn't the first time Dezzie had seen people come to collect horse manure. Many farmers from about the place used it as fertilizer. To his knowledge, they weren't charged by the stables but he wouldn't put it past the grooms to collect under the table. They found very creative ways to make side-money. But here was this Rastaman, who had stolen his money, collecting shit. Dezzie figured the man had wasted the loot already, and was back down to zero. Figured.

"Have a lickle business fi tek care of," snickered Seymour. "A race down the stretch, wid di Chiney girl. Come watch."

Dezzie had always noticed her. Who wouldn't? she did stand out. The only female jockey on the tracks. Plus, she was pretty. Other-worldly pretty. She almost always rode in shorts for practice. He wondered if her legs didn't chafe. But they always seemed perfect. Maybe there was a way about doing it, a way to prevent chafing. Maybe it wasn't even an issue. Maybe it was just his own mind that had a preoccupation with these things, always wondering about the intricacies of women's bodies, what they had on, what they didn't need to have on. He was obsessed with the unmentioned and fiercely guarded secret details of female maneuverings.

Seymour himself was a very experienced rider. It was perplexing to Dezzie that they had come from the same stock both ways, one of average height and girth, and the other so tiny, almost gnomish. His diminutive stature had ruled out certain tasks for him, at least in his mind, and so he approached them with the kind of lackadaisical shrug that made other people write him off in their minds, too. He stumbled upon his niche one day, on a truant meandering to the tracks with some schoolmates, to watch the horses being groomed, en route to catching fish by the Causeway Bridge. He was hooked there and then.

Seymour saw the small bow-legged men on the huge horses. He saw and heard the creatures submit. The small men had power. There was something about them. They were small men in a dangerous job, which required tremendous skill and strength. They were light and agile and graceful. They were disciplined. They rose at three in the morning and made their way to the tracks, or to the paddock, or to the stud farm, wherever they were needed. They were modest and humble, partaking in the sport of kings. Only here it seemed this sort of transferal was allowed, was routine.

The only thing that really frightened Seymour when he started visiting the Saturday races, was the fact that there was an ambulance always trailing close behind the racers. He saw the sense of this twice, on separate occasions, where there were falls and the jockeys had to be rushed to hospital. A groom explained to him, "Life and death. This is a life and death sport. Don't tek it fi joke."

And another had added, "Only sport in the world where ambulance have to drive behind the competitors. Mus and bound, haffi drive behind dem. Most dangerous sport in di world, next to deep-sea fishing. Ask anybody. Not lie."

He didn't need to ask anybody. He quite believed. Seymour had heard of broken necks, mangled limbs, horrendous accidents that had left men paralyzed, disabled, dead.

But the alluring thing was, it was a man alone on a horse. A man alone on a horse. This was mesmerizing. A lone man, powerful and in charge, in direct control of the outcome of something spectacular. People were waging their salaries, their last dollar on this. Many of his friends in the district had dropped out of school and were up to no good, far as he could see. He was not a man of the nine-to-five, or of doing menial jobs with quick turnover rates because the bosses treated you like shit since they knew there were thousands eager to take your place. Seymour was an open-air sunshine kinda fellow, riding on something he could trust, which trusted him. Mutual respect. Ripped denim, shirt sleeves rolled up to the elbows, knee-deep in respectable muck. This had its appeal. The gruesome stories of falls and permanent debility and death did terrify Seymour but not enough; not enough to cancel the glory of one man on a horse.

He himself had risen from stable boy to groom to apprentice to jockey, with the hope of one day being the top joc. Twenty-four weeks training at the jockey's school, drilled by the local stalwarts in areas of horsemanship, race-riding and the rules of the trade. Even with professional guidance on the touchy issue of formulating a healthy nutritional program so they wouldn't run into problems with eating disorders such as anorexia and bulimia, as they strived to maintain that critical weight. That oh so critical jockey's weight. Too much water and weight goes up. Too little water and the brain doesn't function optimally. Problems with dehydration, poor concentration and exhaustion, even while perched precariously midair moving like a bullet. All this was tough. There was also widespread corruption. Everybody knew. The races weren't always straight. Some of the better jockeys ended up migrating to more golden prospects abroad, in Australia, maybe, or on the British circuit , if they had the luck of being handpicked. Seymour would not mind if this could be his fate. He was nowhere near the top of his league and he saw himself in the local runnings for years to come but, one never knew. A good win could propel you.

The horses too had their sad tales. At two years old, the best ones begin their lives as racehorses. An intense and exhilarating stint, replete with rudiments and practice, broken bones and wounds that perhaps never really heal. By the end of their reign, most are weary. Some spend their old age in mockery of their former glory, as exposition horses, giving rides to children along Hellshire beach for a hundred dollars a go, with plastic bags tied under their butts to save the beach from their foul droppings, like incontinent old men in diapers. Some, their accumulated injuries so malignant and oppressive, are given a coup de grace, a salute to millions earned for trainers and owners.

Biyu had left the paddock and was waiting by the tracks. Dean had positioned himself along the sidelines, near the middle where he could get a good overall view from start to finish. They used the enclosures to get a good feel of the race. The grand start, even for a mock. Libido sensed the enclosure and was already in the mood, though he didn't feel the presence of the usual field of horses. He saw only one horse, Impetus. For Biyu, this was one too many for him to see. The rider need always be aware of the presence of the other riders; the horses, need only be aware of themselves, and the wire up ahead. Their eyes were trained forward, held forward. The two horses neighed, trotted about, settled into their enclosures. Seymour gave a cocky smirk, as if to say, this is the real race now. The other two were only pretend. Biyu snickered.

The signal given, they bolted off, an immediate wide gap between them since there was space. Libido very soon took the lead, maintained acceleration and form. Biyu crouched, led him on with words and a firm grip. Seymour too in his hoisted position, trying to provoke a bolt in Impetus but she, as usual, content to lag. Biyu looked back, amused that Libido was not even being trailed in any sense of competition. The gap so enormously wide, Impetus nowhere on the final stretch. Within two minutes, it was over.

Seymour was clearly peeved, not unlike the first two times. He made a show of not caring, since it was only a mock. Both Dezzie and Dean had been following the progress of the short race along the sidelines, cheering for Biyu – Dean, because she was his woman; Dezzie, because she was a woman and was wearing a very skimpy pair of shorts. Had money been involved, he would have bet on her just for that. But though he had cheered for Biyu all the way and had not been shy about it, he admonished his brother for being beaten by a girl.

"Jah know, Star. Mi lose offa yuh!"

"Hush up, Dezzie. Not like is a real race or anything. Plus ting, di horse tiyad. Been revving har all week."

"Cheups! Bout horse tiyad. Guh learn fi ride!"

A brisk athletic descent, landing upright, all smiles as she handed the reins to one of the grooms, Coyote, and dashed over to receive a hug from Dean.

"I will ride him and we will win! I'm sure we will win. We will make history together!"

The grooms were like babysitters, the handlers of very expensive charges whose owners demanded loyalty and accountability. It was the nature of the industry. They took meticulous care of the horses, some to the point of obsession. For some, it was all they did and all they knew to do, all they thrived on doing. They fed the steeds religiously, at specific hours. They cleaned the mess that they made, with a matter-of-fact diligence, immune to the slop and the stench. They fretted when the horses were ill, and slept beside them on the ground, and bottle-fed them if need be. The grooms were fluent in the language of the neighs. Each meant something special.

His practice done for the day, Libido would be groomed. This was done before and after every workout, once possible, a moment of bonding between the horse and the man who was responsible for her care. A clean coat, well brushed, natural oil propelled upward for a radiant sheen. In the wild, Libido would have achieved this by rolling on the ground or rubbing up against the barks of trees. This now simulated under the care of man. A bargain.

Coyote led her into the stables, removed the saddle and within a minute got straight to checking for external wounds, particularly in places that were touched by the jockey's tack. Making sure to secure Libido so he would not stir or kick, a rope tied above the height of his withers, Coyote checked the horse's hooves for nails, screws, pebbles – anything he may have picked up on the track that could lead to lameness. Standing to the side, never directly behind, he ran his fingers through the horse's mane. With a curry comb, he removed the loose hair from Libido's coat, the harder-bristled dandy brush taking off the raised dirt and hair. Short, straight flicks. Deliberate, firm, from the neck to the tail. All the time talking to the horse, "Good, bwoy. Nice, bwoy. Nice run."

He cleaned the horse's face with a damp sponge, wiped its eyes, cleaned out its nose the way one would a toddler during bathtime. Libido submitted, murmuring pleasure, breathing softly.

Coyote whispered soothing words to Libido. The horse responded in kind. The groom picked up the saddle, held it up for weight, as if for the first time realizing the craftsmanship of it, the intricacy of such a mundane thing. Something made to be sat on. That someone would take the time to make sure a thing was curved this way and not that way. He seemed mesmerized by something not even he could figure. He stooped, the saddle in his lap, and as in a trance sniffed the dip of the saddle where Biyu's crotch had bounced for two hours straight around the paddock, where she had held firm her grip to take the horse across the finish line. He inhaled up and down the concave dip of the absorbent leather, rubbing his fingers to catch some of the scent.

He never realized that he dozed away, and was stirred only by the sound of hefty footsteps, Donovan's, entering.

Chapter Seventeen

"Been there. Done that. Cheups."

This was Dezzie's classic response to things these days. He was lying on his king-sized bed watching a local music video featuring an up-and-coming dancehall artiste and his bevy of video vixens, feeling very irritated at how these newcomers threw their bling round.

"Is like is di first dem a wear gold chain! Bun mi fi dem!" he snickered, stroking the two solid gold chains that dangled from his own neck, and the two heavy gold rings on his fingers. "Been there done that, dude. Yuh jus bus an a gwaan suh! Cheups."

He thought it to be well known that some of these DJ's didn't really have it as much as they would like others to think, and were still living hand-to-mouth, paycheck-to-paycheck, like the majority of the population. Only the precious few who really made it big and sustained themselves with more than a one hit, could do otherwise. What a relief that he, Dezzie, no longer had such worries.

Gone were the days when he pushed his shopping cart up to the cash register with much foreboding, and the shame of having to return some of the goods to the cart even though he had tried his best to estimate the prices in his mind, plus the blasted tax; or worse, having someone in the line behind him offer to make up the balance! Gone were the days when he had to cut his eyes past certain things that he longed to know the taste of, consoling himself that they probably tasted bad anyway. Gone were the days when the he paid for everything with a wad of one hundred dollar notes (the standard taxi fare), as all the taximen did. No matter the cost of the thing. The value of their lives was counted in one hundred dollar bills, it seemed. An item costing three thousand dollars was paid for with thirty notes, it not more, and sometimes after two days of beating the road and hustling, sleeping in the taxis because it was too risky to go home and miss the odd passenger. The taxis would reek of sweat and liquor and fornication and masturbation, the feeble scent of artificial air freshener thrown into the mix to try to mask the atrocities. And yet, after all this, after amassing your wad of hundreds, the cashier would still hold it up to the light for inspection, looking for the government gold line, as if you weren't even entitled to have that much. Like, who had time to fake one hundred dollar bills, in this day and age? He gave the cashiers thousand and five thousand dollar bills now. They still held them up to check if they were counterfeits, and their eyes still followed him around the store, waiting for him to slip, but there seemed to be more dignity in this, somehow. Bigger money. Bigger stores. This made better sense.

    He had been observing his neighbours and had decided, it is a myth that the rich aren't happy. Why did people always make it seem like the rich were miserable, that they tossed and turned in their sleep at night, thinking of all the wrongs they have done to the poor? Nonsense! The only miserable ones, it turned out, were those who felt that they didn't deserve it, that they had somehow broken some divine code of wealth distribution and as such were always living on borrowed time. Guilt, was the downfall of the rich man. The ones who had any kind of guilt, gradually succumbed to it and lost their wealth. The ones who had learnt to master guilt, to shun it, and diligently taught this technique to their children, kept their belongings for generations. The ones who came into money by chance and didn't know what to do with it, lost it. Dezzie did not consider his wealth as having come by chance. To him, buying a ticket, better yet several tickets, religiously every day, month after month, year after year, and finally winning, was not chance. It was strategy, if there ever was such. Strategy, man. The rich who had outrightly stolen their riches, or had slept their way into it, or had bamboozled or usurped or exploited their way into it, were not miserable at all at all at all.

No, rich people were not miserable. They did not pine away thinking about the destitution of the others at the far end of the stretch, who lived in the very ghettos that they had to drive through in their Audis every single day, who were most vociferous with their placards on the evening news but so docile in all other aspects of life. It did not bother them one iota that their much was a result of or contributed to someone else's not-much. In fact, the rich seemed always very interested in getting richer. If anything then, they wanted to be more miserable. They had their arms wide open and were fervently chanting, come, misery, come.

One night, Dezzie dreamt that he was rich. The dream didn't say how he had gotten rich, but it seemed he had been rich for a very short time. He was lying on his bed, as he was just now in real life, and he had emptied three bags of money across the bedspread. This was a bedspread made of red Egyptian cotton, and exquisitely embroidered in places. He specifically remembered this, because he had seen the very one in real life in a store just that day, and had vowed to return for it. From the wads of five thousand dollar notes, he took up an unspecific amount and lined them up so that all the faces were turned upward and were neat. They gave off an overpowering smell, like a brand new car or a freshly painted room, nauseating and delicious. In the dream, Dezzie called his mother into the room and invited her to sit on the bed. She sprawled across the notes in girlish gaiety, spilling some on to the floor, tossing some into the air, swiping her hands and legs like she was doing the dry-land version of the backstroke.

"Eva si suh much cash before inna yuh life, Mama? Here. Hold some inna yuh hand. Crisp new new bills fresh from Bank of Jamaica, look like dem jus print. Touch dem. Feel dem."

Bam clapped her hand and shrieked, "Heh-heeey!" the way country women did, when labrish sweet them.

She took a handful of notes and smiled at them, smiled at her son. She stood and started dancing, an old-fashioned dance that she did when she was a girl, the Dinki Mini. This meant that she was truly happy, and Dezzie felt proud. His mother would have no more worries. The Dinki Mini was a funeral dance, but a very lively, happy one. It meant that you should celebrate, not grieve. His mother was dressed in full white robes and white headwrap, like a Pocomania woman.

Normally when you awaken from such dreams, you are very cross to find that it was indeed a dream, that you didn't have a bed full of money with more in the bank, and you generally wanted to go back to sleep. But for Dezzie, he woke up to the knowledge that he was indeed rich. He hadn't covered his bed with money but he surely could. He made sure to always have money in the house. He withdrew the maximum amount of money allowed at the ATM every day. He no longer felt strange or timid or even braggadocios to walk around with twenty thousand dollars cash in his pocket at any given time, as small change, just in case. He remembered those days when something would come up, some emergency or other, some child got sick or the gas finished on Sunday dinner or a light bulb blew or the car broke down and he needed bus fare. If he couldn't find where Precious had stashed her dough, he would wander around the house feeling lost and frustrated, like a vagabond. He remembered those days all too well. He made sure that there would never be a situation that some unscheduled thing was needed and there was no money to go get it, just like that. Those days were gone.

The music videos were still streaming and he was feeling slightly drowsy. He was watching the bling and the hype on the screen and, unconsciously, he was stroking his own bling. He was having a mild erection. This was as much due to the euphoria he was in about his wealth, as well as the fact that Cassandra had agreed to let him take her out tonight. He wasn't sure where she wanted to go. They had decided on a halfway place to meet, that was all. He knew Cassandra had taste. She was accustomed to fine things. She was accustomed to men sparing no expense on her.

The tryst with Cassandra was five hours away. It was just three on a Friday afternoon. Dezzie had come back from picking up the children at their school and had thrown himself down on the bed to watch some tv. He didn't know where Precious was but he was expecting her to barge in any minute now and chastise him about being on the bed in his "outside clothes", as she called them. Hauling germs into the house and plopping himself down on the bed that they slept on. It was a thing she carried over from his taxi days, when she was right by saying that all manner of passengers entered the car with all manner of filth, and that he should put on "house clothes" and wash up before lying on the bed. This just didn't seem necessary now. He wore relatively clean clothes all the time and drove around in his brand new car, which was spanking clean, for your information, and he only sat in clean places these days, with clean people. He could lie on his king-sized bed in his outside clothes, if he wanted. He tried to explain this to Precious but she was stuck in her ways, always accusing him of dragging dirt and bad habits and STI's into the house. You step up in life, and still! People accusing you of skullduggery.

He needed to kill some time. He could walk the dogs. The dogs were something of a controversy in the household. Dezzie had bought three pitbulls. Most people found one pitbull enough of a challenge, and enough of a risk, even for the householders. "You had to go overdo it, as usual, Missa Dezzie," Precious said.

She did not trust the pitbulls, particularly with children about the yard, and so they spent most of their days firmly chained in a kennel and growling viciously with a heavy threatening rasp that made Precious jump every single time. Dezzie refused to admit that he himself was afraid of them. He couldn't explain why he had gotten them, except to say that the household obviously needed protection – but why pitbulls, of all dogs? What about German Shepherds, or Dobbermen, or Alsatians? Those were traditional rich-people dogs. What about those ones? No. He had to go and get pitbulls, dogs who seemed to be in no mood to sign any kind of contract with any human regarding the safety of anyone, not even the so-called master.

The neighbours would watch from behind their blinds or their tinted car windows as he struggled with the leashes, the pitbulls tugging him along. They were in no mood to negotiate anything. Their savage demeanor and ravenous growls made him want to drop the leashes and run. But that would probably spell more trouble than seeing his commitment to the end. When they approached other dogs, the general consensus among the three of them seemed to be, "Let's snap these little buggers' necks! On the count of three!" This sent the other dogs scampering, whining, into their yards, dogs who on their own merit were normally regarded with much respect in the world of guard dogs. Luckily, this was not the place of pedestrians. The precious few people found walking on these streets would cross over to the other side forthwith and stand still as if trying to blend in with the environment. They refused to budge until the dogs dragged Dezzie down the road and they felt the coast was clear.

He didn't feel like walking the dogs. Too much drama.

He could ride his big bike up or down the hill. It didn't matter which direction, people still looked at him the same way, as if they had never seen a man like him on a bike like that before. Why was it that when he did normal rich things that other rich men did, people looked at him funny? In his mind, he was acting like a normal man who could afford a high-powered bike. He was not a dare-devil. He was not being unnecessarily boisterous – though he did rev the bike and try a wheelie or two on occasion. He may not have had much experience with it. He almost got thrown off it a couple times. So what of it? Bikes threw people off. It was a thing bikes did. Why the stares and snickers? His bike didn't make any more noise than other bikes, so why look at him as if he were being a nuisance to society? Like it was a vulgar, unrich thing to do.

Dezzie had ridden up the hill several times to fatten his eyes, to take in the nice scenery, not as far up as the men had taken him but a good way, till it became a challenge not so much for the bike but for his skills. He was still an apprentice. A bike was a powerful piece of machinery. Small as it was, it had been the downfall of many, most of whom had prided themselves on their dexterity and balance. Precious could not understand the allure. She had seen many men die or bedridden from messing with bikes. A virtually unarmored two-wheeler whizzing among metal monsters that weighed tons; this was asking for trouble and with too loud a voice. Why was Dezzie taking up all these things that he couldn't manage? And the sour point was, he rarely asked for her opinion and when she gave it anyway, he ignored it. It was as if she didn't count because she hadn't bought the winning lottery ticket.

He didn't feel like riding his bike. Too much drama.

Dezzie wasn't in the mood for an argument with Precious about anything, either. You'd think a man could have some peace in his own house. He decided to go see what Sherene and Carla were up to. They were the maids that Bam and Precious had hired. They gossiped all day with each other, and about each other with anyone else who had time to listen. They were best friends, from the same community Downtown. They both alerted Dezzie to the fact that they each were going home with grocery from the cupboards, snuck away in their bags every evening, something which Dezzie found very funny because none suspected the other of treason. He didn't tell Precious because she would surely make a big deal out of it, surely fire them or even call the police. She was scandalous like that when she was ready.

He found the two women likable and they did do their work, sometimes just in the nick of time after lounging all day and watching soap operas, like all the maids in the soap operas did; but still. They were jovial and brought life to the house, and so far didn't seem like the type who would spice his food with anything from the obeahman if he did anything to make them pissed, like hold back on their wages. He wouldn't vouch for them one hundred percent, but they didn't seem the type. The family had clean clothes, well ironed, sumptuous meals and dust-free furniture.

"One ting wid ghetto people, dem clean good!" was Bam's usual seal of approval every day when she gave the house the look-over. "Dem poor but dem keep dem place clean."

For Dezzie, he was not going to pretend like he didn't want to screw them both. They were voluptuous women, in their late twenties, strong-bodied and hearty. They were not particularly modest in their dress. Their movements were slow and suggestive, by force of habit, and they were not shy to break out in the latest dance moves in the middle of dusting or mopping or cooking. They never tried their hand at any civilities, or pretended to know anything but Patois. And why should they? They were among their own, at least in this house. Dezzie could hear them now laughing away as he approached the living room, but then he made a u-turn and decided to forego the encounter. Too much drama. He wasn't up to it today.

Fact of the matter, he was anxious. Anxious about Cassandra. His first date with Cassandra. He was too anxious to do anything or be anywhere with anyone else. He could only think of Cassandra, and the nice time they would have later. Maybe, she would let him kiss her, maybe even go all the way tonight tonight. A man's luck was like that. Sometimes it trickled, sometimes it gushed. Sometimes none at all. Sometimes everything all at once. You just had to set your container under the spring, and wait. Wait. That was the tricky part. The waiting.

He had bought her the dress she said she wanted. He hadn't seen it but she had told him the cost and he had given her the money to get it, along with shoes to match, and the gold earrings that she said went so nicely with it.

"I want to look good for you, Dez," in her sultry voice with the Westmoreland accent.

Period pains had Precious coiled up in bed that night. He didn't need to sneak out. She didn't notice him leaving. He only shouted to his mother when he was almost in the car, "Soon come back." And he wasn't sure if she heard.

Learn this: the scent of a woman is different from the scent of a woman's perfume. The scent of a woman is different from the scent of woman's shampoo or body lotion or hair gel or whatever. Very different. A woman's scent came from inside out. It overpowered a man before he knew what was what. It could strangle him before he could say, who dat? Dezzie did not know why smell was such an important component to him, or if it was the same for other men, but it sure was and had always been for him. The scent of the girls he fondled as a school boy would linger on his fingers and refused to be washed off, even with carbolic soap. He would sniff his fingers for hours. It was a heady lingering intoxicating thing. And there were other powerful smells. The smell of money. The smell of new things. The smell of stepping up in life. The smell of a woman who had no underwear on.

It could be said of Cassandra that she was pretentious. Dezzie would disagree, of course, but it could be said. He was not a man of chivalry and he forgot to open the car door for her, forgot to open the door of The Nebulla restaurant, forgot to pull out her chair and wait for her to be seated. To say that one forgot implies that one first knew. So he actually didn't forget. He fumbled whenever they walked even for a short while along the corridors. He somehow sensed that she should be on the inside and he towards the street, but gravity or some stupid force kept moving him to the wrong side, which made her disoriented though she tried to maintain her poise in the skin-fit black dress . The seven-inch heels didn't help the maneuverings, nor did his shorter stature compared to hers, as he bobbed in and out of embarrassment. But finally they were both seated, appetizers ordered, and dinner was off to a start. A bumpy start, but a start. It was better than nothing. Better than just a few months ago, when a girl like Cassandra was off limits, off season. Just off. So progress was being made on all fronts.

Chapter Eighteen

You have three uniforms lined up across the bed, all hemmed so that they are mid-thigh when you put them on. It tickles you that no self-respecting uniform would ever be so short. It really tickles you. You cover your mouth and giggle. The uniform you are wearing is actually your old uniform, hemmed to just below your butt so that your underwear would be clearly seen, if you had been wearing any. The other uniforms, you have sewn according to his specification. Very short, and tight. Your hair is parted midway and the two sections have been tied with blue ribbons, so that your horse hair dangles over your shoulders. You are wearing school socks, no shoes. You contort yourself into various positions, all the while giggling. You press click and upload.

You double-check that the door is locked. You press your ear against the door to listen. You spread your legs wide. You use your left hand to separate your labia. You hold the phone with your right hand and, using your right thumb, you press the button and wait for the flash, wait for the click. You use your right hand to upload the pics and press "send". You wash both hands.

He texts back after five hours, saying that he wants more – this time topless, in the shower, with lots of soap and also without soap. Mix them up. Keep in the ribbons. You cover your mouth and giggle.

Li is smiling. Li is always so happy these days.

Waipo Mingzhu liked to arrange her porcelain dolls. They were her treasures. They reminded her of her past, present and future, all in one. Grandfather Fa was not allowed to go near them. He wasn't clumsy but he was not all that sentimental, and she couldn't risk anyone going round her dolls who didn't have the right sentiment.

For the first time in our lives we do not know where Li is. This is odd. Jingjing thinks it's a crisis of remarkable proportion. This is unlike Li. But then, she's never been seventeen before. People do unlikely things at seventeen – girls and boys. And besides, she was not taken. She left. There were signs. She could be with friends. A party, maybe. You know you never let her go anywhere, Jingjing, even when her parents consent. A young girl needs to socialize. Look what you went and made her have to do. Waipo Mingzhu remembered when she too tied sheets into knots, and scaled windows. But it was Sunday. Did people scale windows on a Sunday?

"Rae Town, wi deh ya!" shouted Mongrel. "Tings aggo nice! Tings aggo sweet!"

Chinno was in the passenger's seat. Four men were huddled in the back. She was scared but tried not to look it. They had passed the Kingston Harbour in the denseness of the night, broke four consecutive stoplights along Harbor Street, for no reason. This part of the town was dead. Rae Town was the place to be on a Sunday night. all this, she gathered from the sparse conversation between the men, which was so interlaced with shrieks and expletives that it was difficult to follow. But as the excitement intensified and they pulled off the main road, the blaring music and shouts from the crowd, she knew they had arrived.

Chinno stayed close to Mongrel. He was the only one she really knew, and only for a month or so. Come to think of it, all she knew was his name, and that could not have been his proper name. which mother would name their child off a stray bastard dog? She had two pics of him in her phone, fully clothed and decent. He had dozens of her, some nude, some in uniforms, some dressed in soap bubbles. She wasn't sure if that had been a fair exchange. Oh well.

And he insisted on calling her Chinno. He had a hard time pronouncing the other name, he said. Liling. Chinno. Two syllables each. But still.

The poverty of Downtown Kingston was striking, even in the night. Liling was used to driving past the garbage-filled streets, the stench that pervaded through the fastened tinted windows of the Hiace van. You were nose-blind during the days but in the mornings it hit the inside of your forehead like caustic soda. Pungent. The harassing fumes from the public latrines in the parks combined with the stale urinate sprayed upon trees, walls, sidewalks, garbage bins, wherever a man could stand or a woman could squat without reproach, it seemed. Or even with reproach, because to some it didn't matter. A leak was a leak, and needed to be done. It wasn't their fault their bladders were full of soda and bag juice and rum and manish wata and uric acid. Renking-tail rumhead dem. They could not hold their water, men nor women.

The vendors sold their wares, their cooked breakfasts, lunches, dinners, their fruits, their dried herbs and roots, sprawled amidst the grime. The shoppers stooped to inspect the merchandise, stooped amidst the grime. One of the dirtiest Caribbean towns, on certain streets. In the prime business district, nearer to the waterfront, a little cleaner. A little more pride. Presentable to foreign investors.

In Rae Town, as in other parts of ghetto Kingston, the most visible structures from the road were the ragged zinc fences, rusty and grey-brown with tetanus, in some places eight or ten feet high, shielding the interior like galvanized fortresses. These were compartmentalized into narrow lanes to make for a difficult chase, but an easy escape for those who knew the windings inside-out. The narrowness of the lanes gave an eerie claustrophobic terror to the entrance for the rookie, winding into dead-end nooks of tenements from whence you always sensed that someone would pounce and undo you; a relief to the exit as the road once again appeared.

Chinno, a rookie in these parts. Luckily, the session was being held in an open area close to the main road, the harbor in full view. She clung to Mongrel, holding his hand – a thing he would never have allowed with anyone else; no other woman had tried it; certainly not! With Chinno it seemed, he could slacken the rules. Other women eyed him but stepped aside when they saw the Chinese girl on his arm.

"Is which Chiney ting dat Mongrel a par wid?" they asked of each other. They dared not ask him. He was the don. You did not ask the don anything. You observed, and what you did not understand on your own within a reasonable time, you asked someone else. Someone who wouldn't shoot you.

Area don at twenty-five years old. How does one achieve this status? You start at age nine, by being raped by your mother's boyfriend, the fifth boyfriend of that particular year and the third to beat her in front of you, and the third that you raised your voice at because that was your mother he was hitting and you weren't going to stand for it. But he was the first to sodomize you and toss you into the streets and slice the side of your neck while he rained down blows on you with his giant prison-labour fists, while you waited for your mother to run to your defense but she never did. So next thing you knew you were in the hospital, Ward Two, and people were saying, how, how this child possibly survive? You fell in and out of consciousness but you were always very, very aware that the nurses were miserable and the food was disgusting and the man in the bed beside you was annoying as hell, and they were looking about some sort of papers to ship you off to a place called "juvenile" because you were now something called a "ward of the state". And your butt hurt. And sometimes it would bleed when you went to defecate. But you didn't tell anyone. You kept things to yourself.

You go to the juvenile place and decide on the first day that you don't like it, and that not even Fawda-God could make you stay. You end up staying for little over two weeks and you make friends and one day they took thirty-five of you to Hope Gardens and returned with thirty-two. You and your friends became "street children". That's what they called you on the news. You and your friends came on the news one time and the people were saying, "Street children are a major problem in society." You saw the news one lunch time when you were in the patty shop in Half Way Tree, begging money to buy patty. You ran to call your friends, and you all watched and swallowed chunks of patty, and giggled. You were on tv. It felt sweet.

You killed your first man at age eleven. He asked for it. Give me the damn watch. What's hard in that to understand? The watch was more important than his life. Oh well. You had gotten the gun from Jookie. This was the second time you were firing it. The first had been when Jookie was teaching you how to use it and you pressed the trigger and nearly shot off his toes. And he ran and you ran, and then you both came back and he slapped you across the back of your head and asked if you were a damn blasted idiot or what. You were not, of course. He saw something in you or he wouldn't have taken you on like a little 'prentice. This second bullet went straight through a man's heart. Jookie sold the watch and gave you one thousand dollars. You didn't have to beg for a week.

By this time, you had been sodomized six times, and raped once by a woman. She was about thirty. She did it on a gyow, a dare, made by some rumhead men in a bar on Luke Lane, who thought you looked like you needed to be broken it. She did this for fun. As far as you know, no cash was exchanged. You were broken in, alright. You decided to return the favour, to others. You didn't need a dare, though. A mini skirt or a normal dress or a budding pair of breasts on a thirteen year old girl were enough of a dare, for you.

You shot five more men and three died. This pleased Jookie a lot and he started taking you to more places. You became the main shotman, shooting straighter than even him, and less fidgety afterwards. You kept a steady head and a steady hand, steadier than his. He started to not like this so much. When you were fifteen, news broke that the great Jookie was dead. You knew something about it.

Long and short, no-one came anywhere near East without you knowing, and especially, no-one left without you giving the go-ahead. Those who came and went without knowing this, did not need to know this. That didn't stop it from being so.

So this Chinese girl who was parring with Mongrel, if you wanted to know, you waited.

She was not the only stranger here. Many bigshots were hanging about, their topnotch vehicles parked right next to the old jalopies and handcarts selling jellies and canes, right next to the mannish wata vendors and the jerk chicken men. On a Sunday night in Rae Town, people seemed to have no grouses or qualms. They came from all walks of life, to the midst of one-a-day country, to dance to Dancehall music and some good old hits. "Dem love wi riddim an wi lyrics an wi dancing an ting but dem nuh love we!" someone had said once, right in this very place. And some people had agreed.

Mark you, the bigger heads who were there had their pieces on or near them. It wasn't as if they were taking any chances, just so we clear that up right now.

There were outright white people at the session, who would be called white people if you hoisted them from Rae Town and dropped them anywhere else in the world. There were light-skinned black people whom nature had seen fit to dip into the melting pot and twirl a couple times, whom in Jamaica were called white people but whom, if hoisted and dropped anywhere else outside of the Caribbean, would have to come to sharp terms with their blackness once and for all. A rapid adjustment of priorities would have to occur. There were outright blacks who could make no legal or logical claim to any other colour, but who felt that class and social mobility somewhat distinguished them from the other melanated Jamaicans. Chinno was on this night the only representative of the Chinese race, a race of which it was commonly and disparagingly said, they all look alike, but on this night in this place she stood out, in more ways than one.

The upper class men had beer bellies and were casually dressed, jeans and a nice polo shirt made from quality cotton, or a dress shirt with short sleeves that said style but not style overdone. They nursed their liquor while they stood beside their cars, their gold chains only barely visible under the slightly opened necks of their shirts. A little hair on the chests, for sexiness. Some were into waxing and had none at all. Equally sexy. Their women wore shorts and sleeveless blouses, or short dresses, moderately seductive but with something left to the imagination. They gyrated, yes, but amongst each other. The upper class men rarely danced. Very rarely. They came to enjoy the music, but upright and alert. They did not dance with their women. This was a no-no. this was not carnival, for God's sake. They were more into the one-man-skank thing.

The lower class men, from the environs, danced amongst one another but were much more expressive. They had choreographed routines that they clearly had been practicing every chance they got. Groups of seven or eight of them would congregate in places and have mini competitions. These men were dressed like thugs and would be very offended if you did not think so. They wore their trousers precariously under their butts, sagging, held up merely by the friction of the butt against the waist of the pants and hence, had to constantly adjust them when they walked or danced. This took a great deal of dedication. The pants sagged anyways but they did not care that some people said this was reminiscent of prisoners who had no belt to hold up their pants; hence, not a desirable image. In any event, not the best situation for walking or dancing.

Their heads were shaven into classic styles, or dyed, or were in cornrows or dreadlocks. Who had bling, wore bling. Who was in the mood for hats or shades, wore hats or shades. Most had some form of tattoo on somewhere visible. Of what social good was an invisible tattoo? Really now. All that pain for nothing? They held cigarettes or ganja spliffs neatly between the middle and index fingers of whichever hand didn't have the bottle of beer.

You had to admit that these men had rhythm and grace, much as you sometimes wanted to look away. Their bleached chrome faces and necks were at odds with the rest of their bodies. In this stone-washed vampire-pale countenance they took great pride. The bleaching creams they would wear boldly slathered across their faces all the live-long day, shielded by a handkerchief or towel or rag draped around the head and neck to keep off the sun, which would undo things if left to its own devices. Direct sunlight would burn and irritate the already chemically irritated skin, and would reverse the effects, if not worsen it. Can't have that. For them, it was worth every dollar, every agony, every stare. A step or two up the complexion ladder. A smooth look, well sought after among their clique, well promoted by many of the dancehall artistes who themselves were heavy bleachers.

What made a man not like what he saw when he looked into the mirror at what his own mother and father had created? What made him want it to be permanently, painfully, radically different? The dark lips and ears remained, as well as some stubborn brown patches that for some reason refused to budge. For those who had the means to venture further than the neck and face, the full-body process would often leave knuckles, kneecaps and elbows looking like blotches of black paint smeared onto an off-white canvas.

But the grace, the rhythm. Undeniable technique. Poise. In this, at least, they moved together, showed that it could be done. It was hard to look away. It really was. They kept their form, these young men, some breaking brand new styles that they would name and claim, like flags rammed into the hard ground of desperation. A declaration of ownership, a rare privilege here. Some were content to execute the tried and trusted moves of the old regime. They were lean. Sleek. Underfed and oversmoked and heavily boozed out.

"But look weh dancehall come to tho ehh? Man nuh dance wid homan again. Man dance wid man. Homan dance wid homan. But a weh dis?"

"A true fi true."

"'Low di yout dem. A new time dis. Mek dem dance how dem waan dance. A fi dem time, not fi wi time."

The lower class women – ghetto gyal, matey, skettel, magglah, hotniss, hot-gyal, good-body-gyal, nice-clean-healty-body-gyal, tight-pussy-gyal – they would answer to any of these, with varying degrees of pride; they were the main event. They too were bleached, but not only that. On top of the ghostly chrome, they were then plastered in layers of cosmetic mess. Almost all wore hair extensions of some kind, hair taken from horses or human women of other races, who were happy to part with it for cash since it grew back. What about yours? Couldn't you grow your own? The only race of women to wear other women's hair with such revulsion for their own. The itching, the bugs, the heat, could not deter them. The receding hairlines and scant undergrowth was a concern, but not enough of a concern, apparently.

Their outfits, or costumes, depending on whom you asked, were primarily nothing more than bikini suits subjected to varying degrees of assault. Nips, cuts, splices, in a quest to be creative and original, to stand out. The shoes, the bling, the hair, the nails, the bags – all this was scrutinized and judged as proof as to whether or not their men spent money on them, and how much, and how often. And since they typically had more than one men, who were unstable and unreliable, this system of accounting was complex. You also had to factor in whether the babies left at home with grandma or siblings were being cared for financially, or if the funds had been diverted towards said attire and paraphernalia. You had to be in the know to determine these things. It was a complex system of checks and balances, and carry-news and suss.

There was a steady spotlight over by where these women

were. They competed among themselves, to see who could split widest, balance on the heads the longest, and dry hump in the most outrageous way – in trees, on tabletops, on fences, on rails, on the hoods of cars. And they had their proponents, in high society, who argued that these were authentic African moves, geared towards the physical and psychological health of the female human form. Well, ok, not authentic African moves. Corrupted but still traceable, and since the corruption was clearly understood by all who would just open a history book, why bring down chastisement on the poor people? They were making do with what they had. We were at that moment witnessing the reclaiming of that which had been stolen, even if not done in the finest taste. Were we not? Give them a break, huh. This, from the proponents, sitting comfy in high places with remote operated shutters and security cameras, and foreign visas. The women, on their part, could not care less about cultural linkages or deductions. They danced because, it felt good to be watched.

This was a first for Chinno, a first of many things. She had surrendered her maiden within five minutes of entering Mongrel's house that evening. It had happened without pageantry, and had ended so fast. It was not what she had expected, certainly not what she had read about, not even what Biyu had mentioned in passing on rainy nights when her two little sisters asked for stories; not fairy tales, grown-up stories. He never checked if she was wet. She wasn't raped but she wasn't made love to. He had bent her over the front of the bed as soon as they went in, the other men still boisterous in the yard, the door just drawn up, not locked. Bad man nuh lock door, he always said. Not even night time door nuh lock. Panties pulled back just enough to enter, himself fully clothed except that his pants were dropped to his shoes. He had tossed the gun on the bed. She saw it every time she opened her eyes from cringing.

She twinged as her hymen gave way and he seemed more annoyed than pleased that he had been her first. He liked the idea but, come on now. It seemed cumbersome that she was so tense, so unsure of what would come next, clueless about how to move and how to take him. He wanted to say, "Move lickle nuh gyal pickney. Back it up." He didn't bother. Didn't felt like he should have to. Ghetto girls are born knowing these things. Other girls had to be taught, it seemed. He had no time to teach, no patience to guide. He liked that she was slender and supple, that her skin was clean with not a blotch in sight; made him want to send her home with all manner of vampire bites, to give her people heart attack. He chuckled to himself. He liked that her hair fell all over the place and that he could grab hold of it, and brush it from her face and sweep it behind her ears, like they did in shows. This fascinated him. But he preferred her in the pics, still-life.

It did not seem to be the wad of pride that Waipo had said it would – it should. She didn't scream but it hurt. And after about half an hour he slapped her thigh, withdrew and said, "Clean up yuhself."

Tonight was the first that Chinno witnessed a live dance session. She had glimpsed it on television, at friends' houses on occasion, never at her own home. She had seen pictures of it, all over the place. Never up so close. The noise was deafening, no matter how far you were from the sound system. She could only imagine what was happening in the heads of those who insisted on standing right next to the barrage of juke boxes stacked on top of each other, and lined side to side. Maybe nine in all. Why so many? The voice of the selectors were annoying as they would never let a song play to any reasonable length without interjecting some irrelevant braggadocios babble. This was a sore point, if you were new, which she was. Brand new.

If she says nothing happened, nothing happened. She's seventeen. She was with friends. Li, next time, don't scale windows. Just ask.

Jingjing had not consciously declared, at any point, I will be a spur in my sisters' sides. It had just happened. He assumed it was a big-brother thing. He was, more than anyone else in the household, balanced between the two worlds. He understood both Mandarin and English very well, and patois, too. He was immersed in all three, daily. He had some street smarts but he also gave right of way to his father and grandfather at home. He helped with homework when the girls were coming up. He prompted them and reminded them to stay focused, and to maintain this all the way through to university, until they had established themselves, married and settled into life. This was the family dream, the family goal, and he was as the eldest the self-appointed steward.

Was he being too harsh, too watchful, paranoid, maybe? He knew what boys could get up to. He wanted to see his sisters safely married, without illegitimate children. But then he remembered that he wasn't married, either, and what a crisis that was for his parents, especially his father, to bear.

As a teenager, a brilliant young man who was Deputy Head Boy at his school and involved in all manner of clubs and what-not, Michael had asked his father, "Do you believe we all have a purpose in life, a role we are destined to play?"

And his father had said, "Yes. And for some people, that role is leech, parasite, street sweeper, gutter cleaner, beggar for handouts. It has nothing to do with race, and everything to do with character."

"Nothing to do with race? Everything has something to do with race. Doesn't it?"

"People think so, and if they think so, you work with that, cause you have to work with them, till you get home to your family. Then, only integrity matters."

"Our nation matters. It mattered to the Chairman."

This, of course, made the older man lean in and smile. To think that his son would bear the Chairman in mind. Fa himself read his little red book daily, even now, the pages still crisp in spite of wear. From the days when he, as a youth, among millions of youth, had been dispatched into the hinterlands of the provinces to play his role in the mighty leap. They had read every page, memorized every word, reminded each other in eloquent Mandarin as they balanced their sole possessions on the weary backs of horses. Uplifting the women, modernizing the farms, education and health and longer life for everyone. The Chairman had orchestrated this. The widespread famine that followed, in which Fa had lost several kin and had been displaced, was a stumble toward a greater leap – he felt then, and still felt now. There were men who disagreed, of course. They were entitled to do so.

"You remember, Jingjing, our people invented the art of silk making. This was a fine craft, a fiercely guarded secret, for centuries. You remember I told you? Fireworks, that came for us. Our people have had much to celebrate. Porcelain. That, too. We built a wall to keep out the Mongols. A long, massive wall. Remember, Jingjing. They couldn't climb it, all they tried. Remember that."

Fa, the patriarch. It was imperative that his people be reminded of their heritage, here in this island where they faced the same racism that they were accused of, as far as he could see, suffered similar prejudices. His name so important to him, yet he and every other Chinese he knew of, male and female, wantonly referred to as "Chin". This so peeved him, and them. Missa Chin. Miss Chin. Chineyman. Chineyhooman. Regardless. Dog-eaters. Called this, by cow-eaters. They took no time to ask. They assumed, all Chinese were the same. Fa had come painstakingly to accept, his people were migrants in an alien land – an island, at that, marooned from their culture and forbidden from participating in this one, for the most part. So of course, we stick together. How can you blame us for sticking together? We shop in droves, travel in droves, count our money in droves. Wouldn't you? Don't you, when you find yourself marooned? Doesn't everyone?

His people had established many shops, imported things, a vibrant entrepreneurial spirit, employing many minimum-wage level natives. Many many. And what thanks did they get? Just accusations. Criticized for sticking together. He knew of fellow

Chinese who were targeted, tied up in their own homes as hostages and ransom demanded. How not to stick together, then? what more security had they? But some had left and were leaving the island in droves – off to Canada, America, England, somewhere where they wouldn't stand out so. Maybe one day too, he Fa would pack his family and leave, to where his enterprise was appreciated.

Fa? Fa? How could you? You are not a clumsy man. What happened here? Fa?

He did not know anything about it. So porcelain dolls break themselves now? Beautiful willow patterns destroy themselves! They were fine this morning. Now, look!

It was Napoleon, Mingzhu. He said it: China is a sleeping giant. Let her sleep, for when she wakes she will move the world. It was napoleon who said it. I remember now.

Chapter Nineteen

Equus. The horse.

Without the horse, man would not have had much of a history. This regal creature has been exploited for the sake of humanity's progress through time and space, noted for its speed, its stamina, its graciousness and its heart – that human quality projected upon and into those deep big eyes.

The first brave soul who made the commitment and hopped on to the back of a wild horse, who knows how many millennia ago, certainly changed the course of history, in an unfathomable way. A decisive and momentous occasion. After thousands of years of carrying man around, of reducing time and distance to accomplishable feats, what has the horse to show for it?

On the vast plains of Mongolia roam the last truly wild horse on Earth. Here, the horse is revered. But there was a time when wild horses roamed freely across the mountains of Montana, the Kenyan savannahs, the Mongolian Steppes and several other regions of the planet. The animal weighing in excess of a thousand pounds was mounted, broken, subdued and manipulated by a creature whose average weight dallies around one-sixth of the horse's. And once broken, and after centuries of breeding, His

Majesty was subjected to all manner of exploits. Sports, pulling ploughs, competitions of all sorts. In mythology, he became the unicorn, the centaur, the Pegasus. He and he alone was selected to pull the chariot of kings, the chariots of the gods. The American Indians, the cowboys rounding up cattle on the South American Pampas, the Arabian knights, the Knights Templar, the Knights Errant, the jousters, the Crusaders, Napoleon on his conquest of empires, all would have come to nought without the horse. Over a million horses fought in world War One, a third of which died, and much of the rest eaten as valuable meat during perilous times. So massive and strong and yet, for some reason, he submits to being tamed. Within half an hour, with the right treatment, the wildest one can be eating from your hand, if he feels like it. And if he doesn't, never. You cannot ride a horse that doesn't want to be ridden.

She will let you know. A very loud neigh or whinny, head high, looking for you; friend. A quiet nicker, a step towards you; hello. A great blow through the nose with mouth shut; curious. Who are you? Why have you come? Have we met? A snort, a deep exhale through the nostrils with mouth shut, a vibrating sound, with head up; checking for danger. You're up to something, aren't you? A squeal or scream; no. Do not do what you are doing. Stop, while it is still safe for you.

The Spanish horse, gorgeous and athletic, the first horse introduced on the island of Jamaica, a terror to the Tainos, who felt that man and horse was one fearsome creature.

When you are six years old and your father and brother both lift you and place you gently into the saddle of a pony, and say, "Biyu, today you learn how to ride." And they also say, "Hold on to these. These are the reins. These will help you." And they also say, "And here, feel how soft she is. Look how beautiful." You fall in love with horses. You grow up thinking that horses are godly creatures, if not gods. You beg to ride every chance you get. You cry when they say, no money for lessons this Summer. You smile and jump when they say, Ok maybe we can see what happens. Maybe.

The equestrian life in Jamaica is associated with the aristocracy. To say that you have been horseback riding, is just the same as saying, I have just returned from breakfast in Paris and lunch in London and hope to have dinner in New York tonight. The jetsetters.

Then you grew older and started playing polo, a game not many Jamaicans played. You felt set apart. The beau monde. The beautiful, fashionable people. High society.

Then, you got much older and your brother says, "Today we bought a horse. A race horse. A thoroughbred. Come look, Biyu. You can name him. And that was it. True love.

Libido was a black horse with a white central patch of soft hair from his forehead to the top of his muzzle, and white socks – solid white markings extending from the top of the hoof to the ankles, on all four hooves. He was now three years old, a maiden, as Biyu was, neither having won a race, hoping to break that maiden and earn their diploma this December at the stakes, and graduate. Being one of only few female jockeys on the island was no easy feat – as if just being a jockey wasn't danger enough.

In the sport of kings, a mere handful of queens. A sport of balance, not leaning too far to the left or right, to the back or front, or risk a fall. A dynamic play with fate, your body hoisted in the air in the jockey's perch, your toes squeezed into the saddle; tempting death. You could be sent hurling over the head of the very horse who just moments before had signed a pact of trust with you. Airborne at forty miles per hour is not the worst part of it. Landing into the fence, or trampled by hooves that crunch into the ground with three thousand pounds of horse power – that, is the worst part. Or, if jockey and horse remain tied and take the fall together as one unit, the smaller, weaker portion of the unit might suffer shattered bones, perhaps death. A broken neck was not uncommon. Even while in the saddle and apparently safe, you might meet your demise when a spooked horse smashes himself into the rails. Anything could happen, when a one hundred pound critter tries to have his way with a one thousand pound beast.

The daily life of the jockey was grueling, usually starting in the wee hours of morning, doing chores and morning works – exercise routines with the horse. And there were other things, less talked about, known but unknown. Quietly kept between them. A jockey must be light, with an extremely thin margin of error. This is non-negotiable. Five pounds above standard weight is asking for trouble. And so, anorexia and bulimia are not uncommon. You must be light enough to be allowed to race. In the trade, the scale is known as the "Oracle", signifying the power it wields over the minds of these men and women. Some feel forced to embark on a near starvation diet of six hundred calories a day, often developing eating disorders.

For a young woman, this can become a whole new realm, women as it were, already obsessed with weight. Biyu had never been fat. Ever. From toddler through to adolescence, she maintained a paper-thin frame, a feather weight. Yet, she worried about becoming fat, becoming too heavy for the saddle. She avoided drinking too much fluids, always conscious of the effect this could have. She would look in the mirror and see fat where others saw skeleton. Diuretics were always nearby, to squeeze out any extra fluid weight she felt she had gained. Running in heavy rubber suits, a last resort, if anything. There were methods. These were things she had gleaned from the stables, from overhearing the men as they went about their rounds. But no one would dare say outright, or chastise a colleague for doing what he himself was prepared to do, push come to shove.

A jockey's daily life was grueling; a horse's even more so. During the stresses and strains of the morning works, anything could happen that would potentially ruin his racing career or, worse, cause him or her to be put to sleep. A horrible leg injury that, despite the best treatment from top vets, had the potential to result in toxemia – poisoning due to the absorption of bacteria formed at the local site of infection. A too rigorous work could result in palpitations of the heart, exhaustion to the lungs, muscles that atrophied over time, counter to intent. Emphysema. A host of inflammatory bone and joint disorders – arthritis, tendinitis, bursitis. An animal that has the potential to live well into its twenties, cut down and reduced to what would be, in the human condition, dementia, senility, depression, despair. When conditions deteriorate to the point that the human can no longer look at the horse with the awe of former years, he turns away, confines the creature to the back stables or quarantine. If the horse is lucky, he is taken out of his misery with one bullet to the head; a coup de grace.

Even in his glory years – the two or three years that he is at his prime as a race horse, and well in demand – Equus cannot help but wonder: where is the herd? Where are the plains? Where is the boss of the pack, our grand mare, grazing by herself, loaded with life lessons? Where are our foals, frisk and strong within the hour of birth; within a few days, walking? Where are the nomadic stallions come to stake their claim at our prize mares? Where is the stud pile that our alpha stallion will sniff, alerting himself to the challenge of another? Where is the hind butting, leg stomping duel of confrontation? We have been looking. We have not seen these things. All we remember is the lasso, the horrendous chase, the herding and the breaking, and the corral. Then this.

The reins and bridles upon us limit our movement. The saddle makes us always feel like a predator is upon us, trying to take us down. That is the way of the lion and the leopard. Their great paws would feel to us like a saddle in the back. We respond by kicking and screaming, to get the predator off. It is our way. The bits in our mouth gives us a choice: submit and comply to the demands of man, or endure the pain of reprimand for the disobedience. And what choice is that, for an animal born to be free?

Libido was from a reputable stud farm but as a yearling he was quite a rogue. It took them some time to break him, coax and teach him to become accustomed to the feel of a bridle and saddle, to carry a rider and yield to his command. He fell many a rider in that first year, particularly the ones who came back down into his saddle with a thud and made him groan. Libido didn't like it. He seemed to always be saying, get offa me, you jerk! Did you ask first? There is nothing like manners, and gratitude. Ask first.

Biyu learnt to always ask, and he submitted with equine grace. During their early morning work, she would mount, always from the left, take him from a trot to a canter to a gallop along a predetermined distance. Libido had come into his own style. A pacesetter, he loved to drive like a bullet to the front and stay there. He tried to stay there. But then he was often winded. Over short distances, maybe. The vet said that was his concern. Lungs needed work. She would take him out more. She would become even more in tuned with his rhythm. They were both novices now but he would be ready by December. He would graduate.

It was an unspoken mandate that Biyu accepted: you will win for us, for the family name. The one horse, which cost a pretty shilling and a half, though they rarely mentioned the sacrifice, only the hope. Jingjing had hired a trainer of very little repute, the only trainer he could afford. It was often said around the dinner table that Libido, with a better trainer, would be unbeatable. He had the constitution of a winner, had been bred from winners. With a year to go in his racing life, this was the time to shine.

The jockey's life had put Biyu face to face with a dilemma. She loved the creature. She often felt as if she was hurting the creature, demanding too much of him, making him do what he did not naturally want to do. His big eyes spoke of pain. She consoled herself with the justification of the trade: look at this massive creature here. Do you for once think that your flimsy weight could be more to him than the weight of a butterfly upon your own back? Do you think he cares about a small metal bit upon his teeth, a saddle upon his back, a firm tug of a rein by way of guidance? What arrogance, to think that anything you did could affect such a mammoth? Justification of the trade, a way of sleeping at night.

Biyu got comfort mainly in the late mornings, after the work, after the cooling down, when Libido was once again calm and his breath had been restored. The horse would look at her and nicker and blow softly, allowing her to nuzzle up and stroke the side of his face.

Chapter Twenty

"Doan show dem nothing if dem nuh ask fi it. Nuh tell dem nothing weh dem nuh ask bout! Jus ansah weh dem ask yuh, straight."

The woman clutched her bag firmly under her arm. It contained all her most valuable worldly possessions: passport, land title, national ID, house title, birth certificate, bank statement, two letters of reference (one from pastor, one from Member of Parliament), photos signed by Justice of the Peace, application form, letter of invitation from relative abroad, receipt as proof of payment for interview, three last utility bills as proof of residence, various other papers that might come in handy. And of course, her Bible and hymnal. She had prayed solemnly last night and this morning, on her knees. She had fasted for five days prior, only drinking tea and some juice until evening each day. Plus, she had asked the prayer warriors at church to intervene on her behalf. She had everything she needed in the bag under her arms, and the Man Upstairs was always in her heart. His will be done. She was ready.

But she kept remembering the warnings she had been given from relatives and friends who had made countless trips to the Embassy of the United States and had gleaned much wisdom and tactics. They could write manuals. They spoke with authority. Only a handful of them had visas.

"Ongle gi dem weh dem ask fa. Nuh push nothin extra tru di winda gi dem. Keep calm an smile."

She was nowhere near late. She had made sure to rise early, put on a nice yellow blouse and skirt suit that she wore to church on special occasions, her spike heels and a touch of nice-smelling perfume. She had her pen. Can't forget that. In fact, she had two, in case the ink ran out in one. Everybody had said, "If dem tell yuh fi come back in the afternoon, yuh know is a done deal. Straight a Farin yuh gone, gyal."

She walked through Mandela Park and crossed over to the route taxi stand, boarded a taxi headed in the direction of the embassy. The driver wanted two more passengers before he would even think of moving.

"Listen to mi, young man. Ah going somewhere. Yuh tink people have all day fi siddung an wait in Half Way Tree? Why yuh tink ah leave ma house if ah dint have somewhere to reach?" she demanded, vexed.

"Lady, if yuh cyaan wait, tek sumting else. I not moving till ah full. Some passenja tink as dem come in driver must lef. Annuh suh it guh!"

She fidgeted with the bag, peeved. This was just one of the reasons that she wanted the visa, to get away from these unruly, unconscionable savages. No order. No respect for people's time. No discipline. Cho! Blasted hooligan. Uncivilized wretch.

She flung the door open, stepped out with much vigor and nearly bounced over a peddler, without as much as a hush. Mumbling to herself and clutching her prized bag, she settled down into another taxi and fumed as the first one drove off, now full with his quota, and this one needing three more.

"Ongle in Jamaica!" she mumbled. "Ongle in dis God-forsaken place!"

There was a queue outside the embassy. She had gotten an eight o'clock appointment. It was good to get an early appointment, that way they might tell you to come back later in the day, which meant yuh gone clear. That's what everybody had said. It was February, not peak time. The wiser heads had advised her, get a date further up in the year, that way you're more likely to get the visa. In Summer, too many applicants clogged the system and made the quota fill up in no time, and much less likely to get a visa. Yes, there was a quota. Doan mek nobody fool yuh. There was a number and after that number, no more. So they said. These people had studied the system inside-out. So time and season were on her side, in spite of the blasted taximen trying to make her spirit cross on this very important day.

The security officer was asking for proof of appointment. She had hers. She handed in her documents. The man standing in front of her also handed in his documents. This was Dezzie. He too had come to try his luck, again. This was his fifth time, and the second since striking it big in the Lot-a-Luck and so he felt justified to give it another run, since he and luck had become friends. He had not waited the recommended year since the last attempt. He too had consulted with the veterans, and had versed himself on the this and that, the do's and don'ts.

Some ladies, capitalizing on the fact that no cellular phones or certain other items were allowed into the embassy, were offering a unique service: they sat on chairs across the road and had transparent bags in which you could place your cellular phones and other valuables, at a cost of three hundred dollars. This was a risk but the uninitiated really had no choice. They had arrived at the embassy with all manner of accoutrement and strictly prohibited items and were denied access, and had to take advantage of the services offered by the lovely ladies. The women seemed to keep their word because several applicants had left their valuables and came back to retrieve them later, with no complaints, far as could be seen. Vehicles zipped by the busy Old Hope Road, people glancing over to see if they recognized any faces among the wannabe expats. When the embassy was at the old location, on Trafalgar Road, the lines were longer and people waited a mighty long time in the broiling sun, and everyone could look and mark your face as one who was desirous of deserting

Jamrock for the Land of Opportunity. Things had improved in this respect. Now the ones who knew were mostly the ones just like you. A hopeful, just like you.

An Indian lady with her three daughters, all in their beautiful saris and bangles. Businessmen in suits looking like they were coming from or going to an important meeting, had dressed for it, and had just swung by the embassy to renew their visas. You could see that their passports were worn from travel and jam-packed with all kinds of important stamps. They might very well hope to be flying off to Chicago this very night for a business convention, from the look of things. They hated having to queue with the commoners but, what to do? What to do?

A lady in a wheelchair needed some kind of surgery for some kind of cancer. She was telling the lady behind her, this surgery is extremely expensive, and radical. And urgent. Visa today, gone tomorrow. Only the US doctors will do it. Only they can. Her head was completely bald and she wore huge dangling earrings. Chemo? The other lady was asking. Yes. Three rounds of chemo but to no avail.

People can chat dem business tho sah! Dezzie was staring at the group of about ten youngsters, accompanied by two adults. He guessed they were athletes of some sort, with their coaches, off to compete somewhere and bring back the gold. He saw an old musician he recognized and he chuckled, realizing that even famous people had to join the lines, too. It had never occurred to him. He reasoned it didn't occur to most.

Finally, a concerted heave at the colossal door, which was marked "door is heavy" as a warning to anyone who overestimated their own strength, underestimated a door belonging to the United States of America. Don't you dare. There was no sign anywhere that said "bullet-proof", but then. Some things went without saying.

The applicants filed in with bright, hopeful faces. Only a few were too lost in their thoughts of escape to spare a pleasant howdy-do. The children were mostly in school uniforms, this in itself supposedly as proof that they were actively enrolled and had something to come back to. Just a holiday trip for the kids, is what we're asking. To be able to come and go. To do a little shopping when we're ready. The parents had begged some time away from work for the big day, but those who could, avoided anyone knowing who did not need to know, lest their name be taken to Obeahman and their chances blighted.

And then a quiet, obedient Indian file into a screening area where they were searched and any forbidden items confiscated and the individual removed from the line, which meant that the applicant would have to return outdoors and leave the items with someone, and start the process fresh in the queue. Luckily, those ladies with the transparent plastic bags were there. Those in the know, like these two here, had travelled light with only the essentials.

Numbers, lines, more screening areas, more lines, waiting. Sit on those chairs in that area there, listen for your number. Make sure to listen. We don't tolerate skylarking around here. We go by numbers. Pay attention.

A few minors accompanied by their adult. People from all walks of life, from all races, with all manner of reasons and excuses why they should be given leave of the Jamaican melting-pot. They who waited on their turns heard everything being asked, everything being given by way of reply, the stuttered attempts at explaining away discrepancies, the pride in the declaration of assets, the stifled suspicion at having to submit to fingerprinting, the stifled annoyance at having to be measured, the shock when the assets were discovered to not have been enough, the despair of yet another wasted day at the embassy, and then remembering that the fees were nonrefundable. But some left with hefty smiles. Triumph. The ones who would come back later for pick-up.

They would have liked if the applicants had been assorted according to class. They generally didn't like to mingle, and even when they did, there was a clear distinction who was who. Here, there didn't seem to be and it bothered them. The lower classes were fleeing poverty, full stop. The middle class were fleeing poverty of a more sober face, but with similar nasty tendencies. They had dug themselves knee-deep into debt of all kinds, taking out exorbitant loans, living outside their means to keep up with their neighbours, dressing to impress, fake it till you make it but this habit you can't break it. They were guilty of all the clichés but the plea was: guilty, with explanation. They felt there should always be a clean and clear distinction between them and the ones who were not them, the ones whose faces crammed the television screen at evening time, begging for justice. They felt this distinction should be maintained, as one maintains a lawn or a fountain or a vehicle; but lately it was not. The appointed leaders had not been seeing to it. The middle class did not feel the poverty line creeping up towards them, so much as they felt themselves slipping down to it. it was not a nice feeling.

The upper class felt themselves living on borrowed time. Their trip to the embassy was not usually as fresh applicants, but to renew or, better yet, to see about getting a permanent stay. The majority of this set used loans to pay for loans, spent exorbitant amounts that they did not really have. They knew how to manipulate figures and balance books precariously over the edge. Their wealth was on paper, in cyber space, in their minds. Declaration of bankruptcy was a pocket card they walked around with all the time, just in case.

The woman in the yellow suit was up, now a subdued version of her earlier self. Very meek, standing at the glass divide. I'm ready. Shoot. She forgot all about the warnings and submitted the entire pouch of documents under the bar, as if to say, I have everything you could possibly want; please, just take what you need from these. The preliminary greetings, in which she over-accentuated some of her aitches and completely ignored the others, smiled more than necessary, almost curtsied at one point. The man without hesitation gently pushed the pouch back to her, asked her for three specific documents, asked her three questions which she found to be very unrelated to the documents she had procured, and then she was told, sorry, not at this time. The United States of America cannot accommodate you at this time.

Please try again within a year or so. All this in a few minutes, when she had expected at least an half an hour interrogation, which she was well prepared for. The quickness of it all left her winded, disoriented, and on top of it all, she wanted her damn money back. But she only whispered, "Thank you, Sir" and stood for a few seconds before stepping away from the divide, tears welding up in her eyes.

"Look like my lady-deh nuh get tru at all at all," Dezzie sighed to himself, and then he was up.

He swallowed hard but approached the glass with gusto. Remember, we mean business here. No dilly-dallying. The white man smiled, said good morning, did not wait for a response before asking for a few standard items. He did not want the whole bunch of papers that Dezzie had brought. Four or five questions, and Dezzie was trying to gauge the look on the man's face. These people are trained to zoom in on things, Dezzie thought to himself. They are trained to know point blank if you're gonna run off, or if you're gonna come back. No matter what you try to tell them. He was nervous. From his experience with these interviewers, and the decisive way the man was shuffling the papers as if he had seen enough, Dezzie thought that things were looking dismal.

"Have you any immediate relatives in the United States, Mr. Grant?"

Dezzie hadn't planned to tell any lies this time around but a wave of desperation swept over him and he told the man that yes, his father lived in New York and was in fact a citizen, employed with the US Postal Service. He got a bit carried away. He even made up an address on the spot, bits and pieces of those he had concocted over the years, and he prided himself in this skill even though things looked so bleak.

The man appeared to reevaluate the situation in light of the new data, and then he made one final regrouping of the papers, patted the file on the desk for effect and handed them back to Dezzie. "You may ask your father to file for you, Mr. Grant." The man said, and ushered him off. He pushed a button for the next number.

Dezzie walked slowly out of the interview office. He stopped in the courtyard where a new batch of applicants had come in from the screening room and were waiting now in a kind of outdoor holding area, under a gazebo. He wanted to warn them, tell them to run, don't waste their time. Seven out of ten of them would be sent home, he figured, a rough estimate of what he had seen transpire inside. Seven out of ten of them had wasted their hard-earned cash; non-refundable.

The United States embassy, if they could read his mind, would have had him know that up to sixty-five percent of Jamaican applicants for non-immigrant visas into the US were approved. They would also have him know that there was no quota, and that all an applicant for non-immigrant visa needed to do was to prove that he or she intended to return to Jamaica after the visit. Dezzie would hiss his teeth at this. He hissed his teeth now, just thinking of the time he had wasted today.

Everybody seemed to be here represented, everybody trying to get away, to flee. To flee from what? Hard times. They would say, in chorus and in earnest: crime, corrupt politicians, high road deaths, missing children, stagnant economy, unemployment, high cost of living, no opportunity, blah blah blah. Fleeing to the Land of Opportunity. Who can blame us?

"America not like it was in the Eighties," a brethren of his had said, just the other day. A returning resident who had come back to set up shop after twenty years of disillusionment, working three jobs back-to-back, for what? "In the Eighties, even Nineties, yuh could come to America and if yuh mek up yuh min' fi work, yuh could work three four jobs and really mek it. But not now. Tings ruff in America now. Annuh like one time gone. People live ere wish dem coulda come back and cyaan come back, too shame fi admit seh tings nuh well wid dem. Life hard all ova, nuh care how yuh tek it. Nuh weh nuh betta dan yaad, my yout'. America aint no bed of roses."

But all these people seated here beneath the gazebo holding area, and on the inside being scrutinized, and on the front being searched for weapons, seemed to be saying, "Well, mek wi guh fin' out fi wiself. Seven bredda, seven different min'. Puss an' dog nuh have di same luck. All wi want is one lickle chance."

Dezzie kicked the dust. He hissed. He slumped. His mind had been set for travel. He couldn't understand why he had been turned down. He should have explained to the fella that he was the one who had won it big the other day. He had of course planned to wheel in all of this, but the time ran off so quickly. It took him off guard. There was no time to explain anything. The man didn't seem to care. But what was this? Nothing made sense.

Dezzie wanted to know what the inside of a plane looked like, simple as it sounded. He wanted to climb to the top of the stairs and look back, not necessarily to wave, but just to look back. He wanted to be up in the air and looking down at houses and cars and trees, and people like ants moving about. He wanted to feel nauseous like people said he would. He wanted to look out through the window and see white above and below and to the side, flying through a cloud, and feeling the bumpy roller coaster turbulence, like they said. He wanted to land in a new place and know that he had the option to return, time and time again, like rich people should.

And so it was; he made the resolve. He would buy the visa. He knew someone who knew someone. Well, Mr. Dacres knew someone who knew someone. There was racketeering at the embassy and a few officials were involved in issuing non-immigrant visas, at a cost. One had been caught just last year and dealt with. But there were always others. Always someone willing to shuffle a few papers around and sign what needed to be signed, for extra money. He was going to buy the visa. Tried it your way. Doing it my way.

Chapter Twenty-One

The blaze itself lasted for six days. The smoke took an unprecedented seventeen days to abate. The Riverton City Disposal Site was the scene of pandemonium.

The noxious fumes and heavy clouds, nimbostratus in appearance and reach, a cocktail of hazardous waste and decomposition, hovered over the city centre and spread to environs. Debilitating. Scores of children and seniors were rushed to hospitals. Businesses and schools closed for days. Even the Port of Kingston was closed at a certain point, and the accountants grabbed their calculators and typed in numbers and held their heads. They were not pleased.

Aerial footage taken revealed the ghastly span of the smoke, like the eruption of a giant volcano with vengeance at its core. The overseas media declared the event a catastrophe. The carcinogenic benzene was said to have been circulating in the air over Kingston at three times the amount considered to be standard, according to the air quality guidelines established by the WHO. The local media was up in arms, on both sides. The government said, it could not have been avoided. We have been plagued by hindrances. A fire at a dump is not an entirely preventable occurrence. Stranger things have happened. The people said, shut the fuck up. Children are dying. We can't breathe. Tell us something better than that.

Twelve reported fires at the national dumpsite in ten years; this one the most massive and costly. Sixty million spent, yet not enough done to prevent or extinguish the blaze, people argued. But why do we even bother to elect these big-belly men, anyway? Of what good are they, if they can't put out a fire? Well, you people started it!

We started it?

Yes, you! Those of you who live near the dump. You started it. It wasn't us Big Shots. We don't mess round with garbage. That much should be known.

"We have no reason to start fire at the dump," the Riverton scavengers argued. "We live off the dump. Why we go light it? No hustler would start a fire. For what? Cheups."

Some said, the scavengers lit it to cause strife, and to benefit from work to help put out the blaze, and clean up afterwards. People in general are cunning. Scavengers in particular are said to be extremely cunning. Observe any vulture. Hyena. The infamous Jamaican John crow. Some said, it started itself but the government did not do enough to stop it.

After the blaze simmered, the cloud receded, the emergency room casualties tallied and the loss to the economy assessed, the scavengers returned to pick through the rubble. There were men, women and children, all ages. Most lived within the vicinity but some came from as far away as the countryside in the West and North. In the country, they just say, "Fling it over bush. Dash it dung a gully! Mek nature eat it till nuttin nuh lef back." In the city, there is enough garbage to sort through and earn a living, if you are resourceful and if you are not shy. It was as shameful task, one they preferred their fellow church members and schoolmates not know about. Of this indignity they wanted to be spared. But if it did come to light, this they could bear. They were tough. Their backs ached from the constant bending. They had a host of complaints which resulted in anything from general weakness to a strong constitution. From one end of the extreme to the other. Some made it, some fell away. No-one knew the formula. A persistent, raspy cough and respiratory symptoms from inhaling dust and fumes. Skin infections that ranged from ring worm to scabies to the unidentifiable. Sometimes, diarrhea. Sometimes, depression.

Seven dollars per pound for plastic bottles. They collected scrap metal to sell to the makers of Dutch pots. They hoisted bug-infested mattresses and couches and sold then for whatever the buyer had to give. One time, one of them found a solid gold diamond ring at the dump site and sold it to the cash-for-gold people for five thousand dollars. He made a profit of five thousand dollars. Not bad. The cash-for-gold people sold it for eighty thousand dollars.

When you are of a certain kind of poor, the junk of the rich can sustain you for some time. You can furnish your home with collectibles, furniture and appliances, and no-one be made the wiser. The scavengers had developed an eye, a sixth sense, to zoom in on certain things, as well as to keep certain things in their peripheral vision. There was junk, there was junk-junk, and there was not-so-junk. There was their-junk-but-not-my-junk. There was my-junk-but-I-can-sell-it-to-that-fella-junk. It was a feeling like opening Christmas presents. You just never knew. It was a thing of surprises. You might find the rotting carcass of a dog or cat, road kill that made its way to the dump. The smell of the site was so pervasive that you became nose-blind to it, and it was sometimes hard to know that you were standing right over a carcass – till you dug or tore or stepped splat into it. Took days to wash off that smell. Others noticed it more than you did. You might find bricks, dirt, knives. Rusty metal beams. Soiled diapers. You hoped never to find a corpse but some of the old-timers said that it had happened, or they had heard of it happening.

Where there is man, there is garbage. No other living organism generates garbage. Everybody else's leftovers return to nature for recycling. Biodegradable. Modern man has become so advanced in his civilization that his garbage needs special care before it can return – for the ones that can return. Some, are a permanent dilemma. Medical and electronic and technical waste are among the most problematic, the most lethal. Archeologists sift through ancient middens, delicate layers of human refuse; we return to our junk, sniffing for evidence of something. Anthropologists try to make sense of it all.

Our garbage has always been important. We are important. We must study the mess we have made. Our garbage makes its way to the depths of the ocean, choking things, poisoning things, suffocating things, annihilating things. Garbage left to pile on the surface clogs the drains, pollutes the waterways and underground drainage systems. The stench rises and strangles. It is unbearable. What is this thing of man, so inexplicably tied to him? And now we hear, our garbage has made its way into outer space. When it accumulates and gravity hauls it back down towards the Earth, people could die. And people are important.

And there is a macrocosm to it. On the city scale, cleansing is needed as the body cleanses. Waste generated must be removed. As in the body systems, so in the city systems.

And so a week after the fire, the garbage men declared a strike.

"Let them rot in their own filth. They don't appreciate our work. Let them pick up after themselves. We are tired of it."

What's their problem now? The country just put out a goddamn fire. Calm yourselves down. Sanitation workers are a little too uppity, for their own good.

What's our problem? We'll tell you.

But first, don't refer to us as sanitation workers. We are garbage men. Show us some respect. "Nuh sweet it up. Wi name rubbishman."

Second, we need better working conditions, more pay, better equipment to work with. This is one of the most dangerous jobs, ever. When we just start the job, we vomit and the oldtimers laugh us to scorn. There is a reason why we vomit. We are working in filth. Other people's shit. What nobody else wants to touch. There is a reason why the old mates laugh at us. They know that in time we will get used to it, like they did, that we will step on hundreds of maggots like other people step on ants – without much thought to it. They laugh because they know that, like them, we can't do any better. This is where we have found ourselves, and this is where we must stay.

The poorly bagged garbage spills once we lift it, it gives way, it splashes all over us. People do not care to bag them properly; they're not the ones taking it away. Sometimes, we step on nails and broken glass. We have no way of knowing, no way of avoiding all of them. We are skilled men, careful men, but one or two get through to us. Sometimes, we get run over by the very garbage trucks, crushed under the wheels.

You people have no education. Why should we pay you more? Can you even read and write? Do you even understand that Jamaican people don't want to pay their property taxes, and so we can't pay you? Do you even get that, sanitation workers? Huh?

The men sought refuge on their trucks. They sat and smoked, and talked. A big powerful truck with a chute that can crush and devour things. They liked their truck. A garbage truck is expertly made for what it was meant to do. A very peculiar, identifiable shape.

The men were on a cigarette break. They sat on or around the garbage trucks, which were parked at their usual spot. No trucks had gone out all morning.

"Same ole same ole," said Ras Negus. "When dem going to start pay workers weh dem due? People want rubbish fi pick up, but no trucks!"

He had come, in solidarity.

"When dem start fi undastan weh exackly wi duh," answered another man. "When di rubbish start pile up pon dem blouse and skirt! When dem start smell the stinkness. Den dem wi know."

"Fiyah wi, dat dem go duh. Fiyah wi and hiyah new man, like what dem always duh."

Usually uneducated, the men were seen by some at the policy-making level as being very replaceable, and very annoying. It seemed logical that people who were replaceable should not annoy. There was a high turn-over rate among the garbage men.

The strike lasted for a week. There was local and international coverage. Some said that it was the garbage men who had started the fire at the Riverton Dump all along, as a prelude to their evil plans. The little rascals! Here's what we'll do. We'll give them till Monday morning. If they don't learn to behave, then we'll hire a new batch. How's that?

Tons of garbage was left putrefying for a week, in the garrison areas, along the streets of the city and the suburbs of Portmore. In the sweltering sun, the stench rose to higher heights, day by day. Vermin soon got wind of the matter, and promptly set in. Flies hovered and maggots crawled in and around the heaps. Dogs and cats ripped the bags, spewing the putrefactive contents of human civilization.

By Monday morning, the trucks were back out.

Chapter Twenty-Two

It seemed these men were always taking Dezzie to places that he wouldn't be sure how to escape from, and for some reason, he always ended up feeling like he needed to escape.

They wanted fifty million, up front, as investment. They tried to come across as if they weren't forcing the issue. They were forcing the issue. Dacres in particular.

They weren't playing good cop bad cop. They were playing "bad cop but we won't leave any trace of the torture". We'll just invite you up here into the vast high hills with us, to shoot birds, with guns protruding from our waists, up here in the wilderness where only we know how to get you back home. Fifty million. So what you say, Dezzie? Deal?

"Dat's a whole heap, man," complained Dezzie.

"Naw, sah!" exclaimed Mr. Dacres. "Whole heap to small fry. Pocket change to 'ristocrat."

"Look like yuh need fi get couple 'ristocrat fi invest, den," said Dezzie awkwardly, trembling, forced bravado.

Everybody laughed, including Dezzie.

"More people soon come on board. Just wait till dem see the progress an di profit," professed Mr. Dacres.

"Suh yuh really tink it go tek off?" asked Dezzie.

"Tek off? Nuttn cyaan stop dis when dis lif. Just need a good-size start-up," Mr. Dacres stared off into the sky with his hand at his eyes, shielding the early morning sun. "Anyhow, wi come to shoot bird, right? So off we go."

The other three men were always awfully quiet, as if Dacres had been the designated talker. They tended to walk a few paces behind Dezzie and Dacres, doing very little talking among themselves. They did not seem stuck up at all, just momentarily reserved, as if in fear of saying the wrong thing and blowing the delicate plan. Perhaps Dezzie was being paranoid. In the right light, they did all look like fairly decent fellas. Maybe just a wee bit standoffish, but that was to be expected, given their positions in life, compared to his. Ordinarily, a man like him would not be in their midst, certainly not in recreation. And yet here he was. That spoke for something. He knew that two of them were medical doctors, the other a successful businessman. Dacres was Member of Parliament. So what did they want with him? Still, the attention and interest were flattering. Doctors generally showed very little interest in him, no matter how pressing he tried to explain that his symptoms were. They usually referred him to the nurse, after a perfunctory scan.

Dr. Garnet Scott had a completely bald torpedo head and a clean shaven face. He was stout, with no hair anywhere in sight to indicate whether he was graying or not, except for his eyebrows which didn't give away much. He probably dyed his eyebrows. You never knew what men of this age got up to, in the throes of a mid-life crisis. It was a thing with some men when they were getting up there in age. They seemed to believe that any presence of hair will conspire and reveal that they were getting to be old-foots. And so every single strand was plucked or shaved or dyed or waxed away.

Dr. Leyland Haynes was tall and slim, had very long slender fingers and spoke as if his tongue was attached to the inside of his cheeks. He wore a small goatee. He had hair on his head but a bald patch was beginning to exert itself out front, top and centre. It was perhaps then just a matter of time before he did as his colleague did and sheared the whole thing once and for all. You want bald? Well, here's bald!

Both doctors had their own practice and operated pharmacies, and both put in time at public hospitals in the Corporate Area. Dr. Haynes had also recently opened a small laboratory, offering a limited number of imaging and diagnostic procedures. Both were still in the process of repaying student loans. This had slipped out and had been whispered but Dezzie was sharp and his ears let nothing slide. Plus, he had convinced himself that he was among vipers, though they were charming and sometimes disarming.

Oliver Berry was the most talkative and extroverted of the three, he being the businessman. He seemed always on the verge of giving away crucial information, the strict secrecy of which had been unanimously agreed upon. Berry had found his niche market by, in his very own words, selling what everybody else must use but nobody thinks about, so that they buy it without even contemplating the cost. And that was another catch – the cost. Extremely cheap. So they thought nothing of paying for it, especially since it was a necessity. His commodities included items such as receipt books, ledgers, attendance registers and so on. Things people overlooked but needed. He printed them and sold in bulk or retail. He also employed sales reps. Business was hard enough in Jamaica and most struggled just to break even. One had to find a niche and exploit it. This was a middle-aged man who looked and acted his age, seemed as if he had developed a loving relationship with his beer belly, till death would they part. He occasionally erupted into raucous laughter and had to be shooed by the others, as if to say, take it easy, man, we not sure if he's one of us yet. Just chill, bro.

Dacres, Dezzie already knew, was full-time politician and businessman. When his duties as M.P. gave him any leverage, he dipped a few fingers into the two other pots bubbling on the back burners. Truth be told, he pretty much left the management of the businesses in the capable hands of men whom he had hand-picked for the jobs. One business, a small motel on the backstrip near Port Henderson, a strip known in those parts as "Back Road". A place notorious for ladies of the night and shady happenings but he could attest to the fact that several legitimate business were being operated and did thrive along the strip. There were losses, of course, and moments when the money only trickled in. But then, as with everything else, moments of flow when the profits were maximized and it felt thrilling to be in business. Not even the fact that the employees stole the food and went home with their bags full of soap, toilet paper and shampoo from the rooms, could deter him at those times. The workers, in the sentiment of so many in similar positions across the island, felt they were entitled to such because of, as they claimed, the low wages. But how much did a man or woman expect to be well paid, doing that type of work? Let's be reasonable. Anyhow, all the packets of special sauce, ketchup, the straws, hand towels, plastic plates and cups that were stolen were somehow retracted from their salaries. A shrewd manager finds a way, which was why he loved those guys.

The second business, a variety store in the one of the shopping centres in Portmore. A host of knicks-knacks. The bread-and-butter items kept near the cashier to lure people in as well as to entice them to spend the last shillings they would have gotten back as change. The consumer was an entity to be manipulated. If you did not manipulate the consumer, he wouldn't know what to do with himself. He literally begged to be tricked and swindled, made to buy things he did not need with money he did not have.

So that was Dezzie's company. From all appearances, good company. They had driven up into the hills of rural St. Andrew, past Red Hills and Coopers Hill, parked and secured their vehicle near a clearing and hiked for miles up into the wilderness. All were regulars at this, except for the man who kept asking if they were sure they hadn't crossed over into Cuba by now. He was only joking one of the four times that he'd asked.

Ok ground rules, for the purpose of Dezzie here: treat every shotgun as though it were loaded. Make sure nothing is obstructing the barrels. Aim and be sure of your target before pulling the trigger. Don't climb anywhere or over anything or at anyone with your loaded firearm. No playing around. Alright, men? Let's go!

It was near the end of August, a cool Saturday morning with clear skies and the promise of sunny weather all day. Two weeks into bird season, roughly four more to go. In the distance, the Jamaican Rufus-throated Solitaire whistled a dirge. A few birds had been spotted flitting here and there during the ascent - the Crested Quail Dove, the Orangequit, the Jamaican Tody, the Ring-tailed pigeon. Dezzie wasn't familiar with these particular ones but the other men seemed quite versed.

"Munro and Wolmers old boys. Been in the gun clubs for years," they explained, which Dezzie took to mean that was where they had developed their rifling skills and impressive knowledge of birds; whereas his school days had been spent in truancy swimming in the brackish pools at the Two Sister's Caves.

Anyhow, he recognized the unmistakable racket of the woodpeckers and the songs of the warblers, both of which were plentiful throughout.

The ammunition had been kept in locked containers for the whole journey up. Hunting licenses on hand. Check. A first aid kit, just in case. Check. These guys may have been arch villains set on exploitation but when it came to bird shooting, they surely abided by the rules. Dezzie was flabbergasted, sometimes peeved, the way they rehearsed the regulations among themselves and carefully outlined them to him, explaining the necessity of each, as if he very much cared. Only designated game birds may be shot – bald pates, long-tailed pea doves, pea doves, white winged dove – and of these, only twenty birds may be harvested by each man per season; no more than fifteen can be bald pates. You would think they were back at medical school, swatting for final exams.

What the hell? How the devil will anyone know if you have shot more than twenty? Because, Dezzie, we take the heads in for inspection by the game wardens. Who wants to run the risk of paying over a hundred thousand dollars in fines, or imprisoned?

Again, who the whats-it-not going to know, if you don't tell them?

A true hunting man just doesn't look at things that way. Rules are rules, Dezzie.

He was beginning to relax, convinced that none of these coons could embezzle anything out of anybody, with their stupid selves. Who ever heard of taking in birds' heads to be counted? Rubbish! He just might lend them the fifty mil after all, see if they could buy some sense. Damn wimps!

So as we were saying: we are well within the approved hunting season. We will only shoot at the designated game birds. We must leave all the feathers on one wing of each bird.

They showed Dezzie photos of such. He already knew many of them. He had shot down many of these, and others, with his friends in the Hellshire bush. Didn't bring any heads to show to anyone to count, like he was stupid or something.

They seeded the area with corn and rice and waited for about half an hour, crouched in the bushes like marines waiting on the enemy convoy to pass, to launch the ambush.

"A great opportunity," said Dacres.

"Yeah. True." Dezzie figured he meant, laywaiting the birds.

"A wonderful chance to invest your money and let it work for you, Dezzie," Dacres continued, his eyes still trained on the open sky, as well as the nearby bushes. "A once in a lifetime opportunity, Dez, just like winning the Lot-a-Luck. Won't come around again. Here is a chance to launch yourself as a businessman, in a sure and lucrative business, with people who already understand business as your partners, and you the main shareholder. People always desperate for loans, Dez. Desperation comes with lots of interest and other charges. Interest comes with ton loads of profit. You would be the major investor, therefore, the major reaper of rewards, my dear man! Take it from me, a great opportunity."

He caught the rake. "Hmm," was all he said, hesitantly.

He had run the matter by Precious, but just hypothetically. They hadn't sat down to discuss it as a legitimate offer that was on the table. He hadn't gone into any details or called any names. He had just asked, what if? And she had said, "Well, dat would sound good. Wi have to invest di money, at least some of it, suh it can turn over. Cyaan just keep spending spending spending."

His mother had said something similar, again, generally speaking, not going on any specifics. He wasn't sure why he was feeling the need to hold back, even with advice from the two women to whom he had always gone naturally to seek advice. Maybe, he needed new input, a fresh voice. He was itching to ask Cassandra what she thought. She would probably know more about big money than Precious and Bam, combined, having been in the position to see it change hands among the rich men she'd dated. She was the type of woman who would naturally be in the know, forever bracing on the arms of big shots. She would have heard things, seen things, gathered little tips and hints as men's tongues ran loose with liquor; tricks of the trade of money-making. More importantly, money-keeping.

His application for a firearm having been denied, Dezzie was content to watch and act as bird boy, running to fetch the downed ailing feathered creatures, removing the entrails as instructed. The still warm bodies of the birds were not piled en masse but stored in clean plastic bags on ice and out of the sun. The work got messy, especially for an amateur such as he, and especially as he was having no fun with all the pesky rules, and with Dacres breathing down the back of his neck.

At one point he was sent down into a small ravine to collect two bald pates that had been shot. He stopped just short of realizing that he was on the edge of a sink hole, probably bottomless. He eased away clumsily from the rift as he felt his feet start to skid all the while becoming entangled in the overgrowth. Any bird that had fallen here could stay, for all he cared. He just wanted to cut this place and go back home. He was exhausted and it was not yet noon, with all the fancy paperwork involved in aristocratic bird shooting. He held on to some vines and branches and worked his way out of the deathtrap, the sinkhole dark and silent below him, as if it knew secrets untold. How many bodies may have been dumped here? Only God he knows!

After ten minutes of strenuous climbing, Dezzie got back to the small clearing where the group of them had hidden earlier, but there was no-one else around. He called Dacres' name several times, no response. He was breaking into a sweat from the steep climb back up. In his mad dash downhill to fetch the stupid birds, he hadn't realized how far he had plunged into the precipice. Had it been a trap, a deliberate decision to do away with him because he was being obstinate and not complying with their request? There was no trace of the men or the equipment they had lugged up to the spot – the ammunition crate, the small ice box, the rags and what-not. Absolutely nothing. In such a short time, all had vanished. Not even the entrails. Not even the blood, the smell, the flies. Had the vultures claimed and devoured them so soon? Or maybe he had climbed back up to the wrong clearing. He had not been smart enough to use any position markers. Rookie.

He looked around the forest in a mad spin, dizzy with exhaustion. He was probably in Cuba, for all he knew. Castro's men had more than likely heard him shouting and had already dispatched a team to track and capture him. He would rot in prison and no-one close to him knew where he was. That was if they didn't shoot him on spot. He didn't really know much about Cuba, except that it was very close to Jamaica and that the army could track and capture people mighty well. Dezzie's head started to hurt. He thought of calling Dacres again but decided against it.

He maintained himself enough to start searching along the ground for a path. There was no real path to speak of, but the footprints had made something of a pattern that he could distinguish from the untrampled brush. He followed it but it took him one mile further up into the mountain before he realized his error and turned back, bewildered. John crows circled up ahead. he remembered hearing them say that Red Hills was about ten miles uphill from Half Way Tree. From Red Hills, they may now be about five miles further up into the mountain. He made a desperate decision to abandon all care and just charge downhill with all his might, maybe even with his eyes closed. With this plan, he must clear the mountain and return to civilization, at some point. He did just that, a wild rush as fast as he could go, his feet landing wherever they found a solid spot, or a spot that seemed solid but almost gave way but he kept right on. Just under an hour later, he heard voices and could finally make out a relatively large clearing. He discerned four figures, three standing, one crouched on the ground doing something. There was a vehicle nearby. It was the one they had come in. It was the men. The buggers.

Dezzie stopped short, trying to cling to a branch. Should he run right into them, when they had left him for dead? Wouldn't they just finish off the job, realizing that the sinkhole hadn't done him in?

But it was too late to stop. He had gathered so much momentum that he could not hold back and there was nothing to break his fall. He plunged right into the three standing men, almost knocking them over. They grabbed him, roaring in laughter, patting him on the back while clutching his shirt to hold him steady.

"Yuh finally reach, man. Tek yuh long, tho!" Dacres shouted, bent over in laughter. "When they do it to me, tek mi less than half hour to find my way back down. Heh heh heh."

"What a man can run!" burst out Oliver, exploding into laughter.

Dezzie was pissed and relieved and disoriented. He wasn't sure he wanted to come bird hunting with these men again. It was probably safer for the birds than for him.

Chapter Twenty-Three

Such a haphazard place. And with a hurricane coming. Portmore was a pain in the fanny sometimes. Sigh.

Some months ago, the weather boys had declared that the island would be hit by a massive hurricane, and the nation immersed itself in the usual flurry of panic. The hurricane watch quickly became a warning. Within twenty-four hours the island was expected to receive a direct hit, right smack dab. No lick-and-promise business. They prayed for protection. They battened down. They called their relatives abroad and had pity-parties. The relatives sent money so the natives could stock up on non-perishable items, candles, matches, water, hair extensions, name-brand sneakers, bleaching creams and such the like. And, the most exciting part, they thronged the aisles of the supermarkets and stripped the shelves bare. They knocked shopping carts into each other and dashed for the last remaining harddough bread and fidgeted in the long lines and made quite a to-do. There were no direct fist fights but harsh words were thrown as they stood in two-hour lines, their trolleys in the throes of late-term pregnancy.

News was coming in that this mighty storm was expected to throw quite a punch, as it had done in the small islands to the South-East along its track. Moreover, it was now over the warm high seas and was gaining strength. All mass gatherings were ordered postponed. All fishermen were advised to find safe harbor. Some flights were cancelled. Things didn't look pretty. Everyone was on high alert and the emergency people were told to be ready to move in. So when the storm made a last-minute swerve to the South-West, people didn't take the news well. They had sat up waiting, with their transistor radios and batteries on hand, fully expecting to be battered and bruised and to hear of widespread death and destruction. No such luck. Not even a drop of rain. Save for an overcast sky and a few gusty winds, no sign of a hurricane. Then the sun came out, bright as ever, and the weather boys were in for it.

"Mi seh, next time dem seh storm a come, a beach mi gone!"

First of all, the weather boys were accused of being in cahoots with the supermarket chains, who were obviously in cahoots with the fellas higher up, who all made a killing every time this happened, at the expense of the commonality. And it happened almost every year, for many years. And John Public fell for it almost every year. And complained every year.

"What if we had said nothing? What if we had watched and watched, and then the hurricane came straight and hit us, and caused catastrophe because no-one was prepared? What would you all say then?" the weather boys chanted, backed by the Parish Council reps. "We have done our job. We cannot tell a storm what to do. We can only guess what the storm will do, and guide people along the worst case scenario, and hope for the best. Lucky for us, grace was in our favour. It is our job to take precaution. We would so the same thing again next time."

And they did the same thing next time. Which was this time. Hurricane Sandy was fast approaching across the Atlantic and was expected to make landfall along the Eastern coast by Wednesday afternoon. This was Tuesday morning. Mr. Dacres was edgy. He had a mammoth task at hand. This one was a category one but massive in terms of its spread. Another direct hit was forecast. People were perturbed. Portmore was comprised of many communities, some of which were low-lying and flood prone. And haphazard. Several Members of Parliament and Councilors were faced with having to weigh the possibility of evacuation in their various divisions and constituencies. Local schools, churches and other public facilities were made available to be used as shelters. The National Arena in Kingston was one of the places made allocated for this.

It was a tough call. A delicate call. Tough and delicate. A servant of the people had these calls he had to make, these life-and-death, make-or-break, win-or-lose calls that he dreaded. And he had to decide soon. If he waited too long, thousands of people might be stuck on any of the two exits out of Portmore into Kingston – the Mandela Highway or the Causeway bridge – in the midst of a monster storm. If he made the call too early, he might be criticized for being an incompetent trigger-happy coon, or at the very least, a jerk who cared nought for the safety of his constituents.

He made the call at seven next morning, when the latest satellites confirmed his worst fears, and the bulletins issued by the weather boys called for swift and decisive action. And now the real headache started. Many residents decided to remain at home and take their chances with Sandy. This was a mighty chance. Early city planning in the municipality of Portmore seemed to have been reckless. The development exceeded the original size anticipated, by far. Communities blossomed and spread and people streamed into them in droves from all over the island, and the infrastructure was not up to the task.

The municipality was only just trying to bring some kind of order to the new developments, to bring the old ones under compliance with regulations – even to demolish some landmark structures that breeched the building codes. An amnesty had been issued, with the hope of getting everyone on board. Mr. Dacres spent many of his days at the City Planning Office, daunted by the sheer volume of applications for building permits, and the equally huge pile of breeches. They did not have enough personnel to go around and check. They sometimes lacked the drive to enforce. Portmore's sheer population size would overwhelm anybody, even those who approached the situation with initial fervour. The problem became even more glaring in moments like these, when the structures would be put to the ultimate test, and lives were at stake. Evacuation was the best call. Mr. Dacres felt confident in making the call. He issued the decree.

The process was sluggish. No-one really wants to leave their home to go huddle in some public place with hundreds of others, perfect strangers albeit in a similar rut, sleeping on cots on the floor, unsure of what the toilet arrangements will be like, children miserable, can't move around as they like, you miserable, having to hold your pee in the middle of the night cause too many people around and you just not used to it. You want to give your cramped legs a good stretch and yawn a good yawn, and you can't even fart the way you would like. Too many strangers huddled, their massive body heat oppressing the place. Even if your next best is to remain and watch as waters rise and slowly engulf your house, slowly ruin fridge, bed, carpet, puss, dog, every striking thing. You tend to want to tarry till the very last minute to make sure you really have to go.

Mr. Dacres went from pillow to post rounding up the civilians who were to be displaced, him wearing his municipality T-shirt and cap for clear identification, so he not be confused with the refugees, as well as because T-shirts and caps foster a sense of camaraderie with the common man. He would not be camping at the National Arena, of course. His mansion was quite safe in the hills of Hellshire, where wise men built their houses. Mrs. Dacres, as first lady of the constituency, was also out in T-shirt and cap, leading the charge of volunteers who were to make sure that everybody and everything was properly labeled and traceable, that the buses were promptly loaded and dispatched. Two government buses made two trips each. A Municipality car with megaphones screeched through the communities making last calls, as the first drizzle started and the clouds grew ominous.

High up in the hills of Norbrook and environs, the big shots had returned from battening down their stores in the business district and making sure their assets were tamper-proof. Looting was a big deal during hurricane time. All these people wanted was an excuse. A hurricane was a grand excuse to delve into things that you are naturally inclined to delve into. The big shots had sent home their workers half day, giving them leave to go join in the national frenzy. The big shots really had nothing major to do but to drop their metal awnings and secure the dogs in their kennels. In the posh communities of Beverly Hills, Coopers Hill, Jacks Hill and Norbrook, they had learnt a few lessons from the days of Hurricane Gilbert, when their huge satellite dishes had been decimated and tossed into gullies, and had made them the laughing stock of the island. A few songs had even been written in honor of this. But the cumbersome satellite dishes were a thing of the past. Their main worries now were their business places being looted, their stocks taking a dive, and the yachts in the marina being hurled out to open sea.

The big shots did not need to scamper here and there doing any last-minute anything. Their pantries were already stocked, year round, full to the brim with delicacies from weekend trips overseas. Long lines in supermarkets rubbing shoulders with the hoi polloi and behaving like food was going out of style? That won't be necessary.

Jamaica was the first island in Sandy's path, the island's first direct hit by the eye of a hurricane since Gilbert, twenty-four years before. Though just a category one hurricane, winds left three quarters of the island without electricity, blew off roofs and killed one man – crushed by boulders in a landslide as he dashed for his house. Trees and power lines snapped. One hundred fishermen were stranded in the Pedro cays off the South coast. Over one thousand people had to seek refuge in shelters. Most schools were closed for a week. The damage was widespread. It was more a matter of wind than rain with this big guy. No less than a hundred million United States dollars would settle the bill.

In neighbouring Haiti, fifty-four dead. Two hundred thousand homeless. In other islands, phenomenal devastation. Entire plantations flattened. Roads impassable for weeks. No light. No water. No familiar comforts of modern life, for some time. The second costliest hurricane in United States history, and the most destructive storm of the Atlantic hurricane season that year.

Mr. Dacres was listening to the news about the devastation and calculating in his head how much of the municipal funds would have to be diverted to disaster relief. He knew he would need to check in with the refugees at the shelters, those in Portmore and those who had been bused into Kingston. He would gladly exchange places with anyone who felt they were up to the task. The logistics of transporting his people back to base, he would have liked to surrender to more willing hands. More capable hands, even. At least, there could be no uproar now about crying wolf. The wolf had certainly come, this time. In fact, the whole island reeked of wolf. The weather boys felt vindicated. They knew their stuff, after all.

Dacres had surveyed his own quarters and found nothing much to be amiss. I mean, it was a storm, for God's sake. You would expect that a few trees be blown down, a light post here and there, some rubble dislodged and thrown about, water settled in places where it hadn't been the day before. Along the beach at Hellshire, the sea had not yet regained its composure; it was still swollen, still fuming, the reeds clinging to the rocks like a million shipwrecked sailors. All this was to be expected. You wouldn't hear him complain about it. The house was intact, the family members were safe. Distant relatives had been telephoned and accounted for. Everyone had stories, which was quite a relief since dead men had no stories. But Dacres had no time for chit-chat. The job now was to attend to his constituents. The task was daunting.

The poor are most vulnerable to disasters – natural and man-made. The poor, the uneducated, are easy to round up and shove into places, under real or false pretenses, for justified or unjustified reasons. A hurricane is both religious and political. Both justified and unjustified.

Huddled on makeshift cots in the National Arena, there was

not one rich man — except the ones touring the facility to access the damage to property and pride; the elected officials. The people's representatives. People had come from Portmore, as well as from flood-prone areas of Kingston — Port Royal, Harbour View, Bull Bay, along the edge of the Kingston Harbor and Windward Road, even from as far away as Yallahs. Because they knew what would happen, they fled before it did. They knew that storms had a thing for zinc roofs; storms liked to make a lesson out of them. The illegal connections of power lines that zigzagged through the shanties would become so entangled and hazardous that nowhere would be safe to walk. Along the water's edge, monstrous waves would thrash themselves against the retaining walls and dykes in ten foot towers of rage, taking with them anything they very well pleased. The people had seen this happen. They needed no more convincing, no more urging. They were poor and they had learnt that disasters hated the poor more so than anyone else.

The plebeians had abandoned their wooden houses and zinc roofs when the megaphones sounded through the communities, urging evacuation. They left the dogs and cats and rats and cockroaches to fend for themselves. These could not be provided for at the shelters. There were strict regulations, due to shortage of supplies. Besides, the poor don't have pets. They have stragglers that they might feed and be kind to in the normal course of things, but when disaster struck, the poor had only the poor. It was every creature for himself.

Those who had neglected to bathe before heading out carried a scent about them which was aggravated by the cramped conditions. Families huddled on the floor, on cots, their essential belongings stuffed into plastic bags and school bags and boxes. Whatever they had by way of identification, was tied in transparent plastic and kept close to them at all times. Money, if they had it, received the same treatment, secured to an inside garment with safety pin or tucked into bosoms.

The shelter manager and Red Cross volunteers made regular rounds during and after the storm, issuing food packages, feminine hygiene products, sheets and blankets, water, maybe some pain and fever medication for an ailing child. Those who would need tarpaulins later on could get. The old, the infirm, the desolate, the dependent, made up the bulk of those displaced.

The Rastaman went around handing out packaged meals.

"What dat?" asked an old woman, a cancer patient who had come with her sister, both in their seventies.

"Greens," answered Ras Negus. "Gi yuh back some iron. Buil' up back yuh structure."

"Doan like callaloo," the woman scoffed, but she took it anyway and, after picking about in scrutiny, dived in with relish. Her gums couldn't manage the yams. She sucked on the sweet potatoes and pumpkin.

A man in a wheelchair, one leg amputated at the knee, the other missing three toes, was sipping ginger tea that the Ras had handed him. He had exactly five teeth – the two eye teeth and three round the back, which all showed whenever he held back his head and laughed at some joke the Ras was cracking. Hard times, but wi still haffi laugh. True? True true. Fi real.

Naph-T and another worker were helping to share and distribute the food. The restaurant had suffered minor damage, nothing to cry about. Back home, a few fruit trees were down, countless fruits on the ground to be gathered and sorted later. No damage to any structure. Nothing irreparable. They still found what they needed to prepare a meal that served seventy persons. Not everyone could get, but at least the older folks and the children were served first.

A news team had arrived and the crew was going about getting footage and conducting interviews. Some of the people shied away and some flatly refused to be filmed. We are poor but not frightened. Fame no longer appeals to us.

The younger ones, mainly, gathered round, curious and excited to see the cameras. Mr. Dacres was in his element. He was beaming. He had seized the photo op and had scuttled over to where Ras Negus was handing out the food packages.

"Take one of me feeding Miss Mae," he hinted at the

cameraman, a massive smile, poking a spoonful of callaloo into the mouth of a lady whose name was certainly not Mae – though it could have been.

"Take another of me chatting to these little ones," he instructed, patting a small boy on his head and pretending to ask something that showed much care and concern.

"OK Let's go over there by that guy in the wheelchair," he said again, and the media entourage followed him as he heeled off in the direction of the diabetic five-toother.

Dezzie had his newspaper folded on the table and was about to search for the Sports section, the only section worth reading, to check if the hurricane had in any way hampered the races. He hoped not. But a photo on the front of the main section caught his eye and he grabbed the paper and held it up.

"But nuh Dacres dis?!" he exclaimed. "Rahtid hole!"

And then he zoomed in closer. But who was that in the background? Wasn't it that Blasted Rastaman who seemed to be popping up everywhere? "Eva present eva faithful eva sure!" mocked Dezzie. "But watch di lickle wretch. Weh him up to now? Probably done off di money and have fi seek shelter at Arena. Homeless already." He chuckled.

Chapter Twenty-Four

At the centre of the commotion was a woman and three men. The woman was probably in her early thirties, short and plump; the men in their mid-twenties, ignorant and uncouth. Children of the great unwashed, sucklings of neglect.

They were in a club near the pier. The woman had recently entered and almost immediately, the three men had made various attempts to mount her, while standing. They stayed from a distance and leapt in her direction, sometimes landing on her back before sliding off, sometimes missing her altogether and trying again. She was giggling in mock resistance, unsure if she should be terrified or just embarrassed. They did not seem to be strangers. There were signs of commonality among them. The crowd took turns cheering and rebuking the savage display. The DJ was admonishing them to stay within the video light so that the to-do could be duly videotaped and posted on social media.

The woman wore a thin summer dress. She had very possibly left home feeling dandy, feeling like somebody. She had put on a thin floral dress. This was hauled from her body, hoisted above her head as she resisted and giggled. She was left in her underwear, revealing a sorry state of being obese and unpresentable. She protested, to no avail. The men continuously tried to mount her back, then her front, all while standing. They tugged at the dress, which sometimes covered her head in their attempt to get it off, all the while shouting to each other, "Hol' har! Hol' har! Nuh mek shi get weh tonight! Hey gyal, weh yaw guh?"

They stayed from some distance and jumped right on to her, several times, them fully clothed, she exposed but for her panties and bra. They grabbed her wig from her head, revealing an unkempt tuft of humiliation. Then, they proceeded to place a white keg over her head, knocking it when it was in place, as one would beat a drum. The men were horribly bleached out, their faces three tones lighter than the rest of their bodies. Their voices and words were coarse and crass. They proceeded to dry hump the woman, one from the front, another from behind, while the other continued to beat the keg on top of her head. She protested in vain, and the audience watched, some in raucous laughter. Nobody said, this is someone's daughter, more than likely also someone's mother; above all, this someone! This is deathly wrong. Stop it!

It was unclear whether they intended to rape the woman in front of the crowd, or if it was some act of vengeful public humiliation for some private wrong she had done, or if it was some crude initiation ritual into some unfathomable thing. It was anyone's guess. No one was explaining anything. The newcomer could not for the life of him follow the proceedings.

The dancehall had become a place of debasement and grotesqueness. The oldtimers, coming back, would shriek in disapproval. Not that it was ever a place of refinement, but things had deteriorated. Almost any crude fad quickly took root and spread with cancerous metastasis. They were known to set their own private parts on fire with kerosene, jump on to each other from trees, hang from branches and posts. Almost anything went. It was a matter of seeing who could outdo the other in debasement and debauchery.

The men finally released the woman. Someone returned her dress to her. She faked anger and then giggled awkwardly, storming off to go dress on the fringe of the video lights. She could no longer hold their interest. She was no longer in immediate danger. Something else took centre stage. The real show had begun. Ten thirty on a Saturday night.

This was what everyone had travelled to Montego Bay for. They had come from all over the island, and the world, to see the crowning of the International Ruling Monarch of the Dancehall. There had been smaller Ruling Monarch shows throughout the year in various locations islandwide but this one was the main event, the one where contestants came from several other countries. Every year, a queen was selected. The prize: one million dollars, a trophy and the right to the title, for a year, till someone ousted you the following year or, if you may, the option to defend your honor.

For this reason, Mongrel had endured his cronies yapping in his ears for the entire four hours drive from Kingston, all so he could watch Chinno on stage. He knew she had what it took. He had been grooming her for this, taking her to all the shows so she could see how it was done. And she was enthralled by the whole thing. Shy at first, but eager and willing to learn, and very excited about the competition. The chance to win a million dollars after one night of dancing. She couldn't think of any competition that her of her friends at school had heard of, academic-wise, with a one million dollar prize attached. Not to mention the fame. Although, the fame would bring for her some reckoning with her family. That was for another time, which she pushed as far into the future as logistically possible.

The most dancing Chinno had done before meeting Mongrel was ballet. She had studied ballet from age four. Her parents and brother had seen to it that all the girls went to ballet lessons, violin lessons, piano lessons in classical music. They were versed in Beethoven and Bach, Mozart and Chopin. They could play the Blue Danube and several symphonies, with their eyes closed. They could recite the famous English sonnets like they were written in their native tongue, the tongue of their fathers. They could cabriole and chasse and pirouette and plie, on very cute little tippy toes. Chinno had not forgotten these though she hadn't practiced ballet for some time. It was a part of her, as much a part of her as the Mandarin that was enforced at the dinner table and the lectures of Waipo Minghzu about the fiercely guarded art of silk making, and the readings from the little red book, by grandpa Fa, when they were younger and still attracted to laps.

Dancehall called for more than tippy toes. It called for everything. Rhythm. Poise. Balance. Flexibility. A sense of timing. Originality. Most of all, it seemed, it called for the complete absence of shame. You could not be shy. Chinno had been not so much shy as sneaking. She had danced with Biyu and Fenfang countless times in front of the mirror, the way sisters do, in their room, mimicking the styles they had seen on the television, or that their friends tried out at school.

No one knew where Chinno was. This was the first time she would be away from home for a full night. How could she explain that she would be in Montego Bay contesting to be Dancehall Monarch? This was just not something one could explain. And it was not her first trip to Montego Bay with Mongrel, either. The other day, they had made an early trip down and spent three hours loafing around Barnett Street and the lanes leading off, while Mongrel "collected", as he called it. she didn't ask what he was collecting, one for fear of knowing too much of the gory stuff and two, for fear that he might become peeved and shout at her. He shouted at people. She suspected there were things she should not know, for her own good. She assumed he would tell her what she needed to know, when she needed to know it. Mongrel was an irritable man, a little gentler towards her than most but one should never push it.

He obviously frequented Montego Bay, probably made four or five trips down each month. And the region around Barnett Street was his HQ, even though the police station was along this street and the rookies were always on beat.

There was some entertainment on stage which went on for about two hours before the main event started at midnight, to whip the spectators into the necessary frenzy. Many things were being passed around – liquor, spliffs, knives, guns, cameras, STI's.

A vibe was being built, they would say. You had to build up to the main event, like sending a woman up to her climax. The build-up, the suspense, were important. The woman and three men who had had the altercation, or whatever it had been, earlier had retreated into the background, their savage ritual having set the stage for the theme of the night.

One by one, the dancers were being called out on stage, to show what they got, to prove that they were the Ruling Monarch. Forty contestants from all over the world, every continent but Antarctica represented. Of these, eleven Jamaicans, including Chinno, vying for the one million dollar prize. South Africa, Spain, Japan, Slovakia, Poland, Sweden, the United States, the Caribbean, all represented. Every country declaring, my women too can dance.

Some had landed in the island weeks before, to get a feel of the place, to vibe and merge with the local dance scene, try out their moves and get a sense of how they fared. Some kept a low profile, not wanting to jinx their chances. Others, bolder, seduced the limelight from the get-go, making friends, establishing their fan base for exploitation later. The competition was stiff and the organizers were serious about giving the people what they wanted, and expanding their reach with every year of the staging. There was nothing lacking by way of promotion leading up or coverage at the actual event.

The participants took things to a level of seriousness that defied gravity. Chinno had practiced her routine. She had watched videos, kept her eyes trained on the dancers at clubs and parties, and practiced while she bathed and walked and slept.

During the quarter finals, one contestant set her vagina on fire. As counter-intuitive and counter-productive as this would seem to most, the spectators were more shocked about the fact that the fire was allowed to burn for so long, than that it was lit in the first place. They had grown numb to outrageous acts of self-inflicted violence. It was just now a matter of extent. She kept dancing with her shorts ablaze for umpteen seconds, either in too much of a revelry to realize that Rome was burning, or too zoned out to care. By the time she did realize and did care, and started hopping up and down and patting her pubis to out the flames, she had suffered some very bad burns to her labia and inner thighs. The spectators roared in shock and amusement, a few dashing on stage to assist, slapping her hard in the groin with whatever they could find, as the fire raged with gathered strength. She was dragged offstage and the fire put out. She and the fire both, disqualified.

It came down to the top eight, then the top three. Chinno was a prime contender. The cultural bandits, as they were called by some, were very strong in the competition. Chinno was among the main contenders.

"Mek foreigna come lick unnuh outta unnuh owna ting!" some shouted. "Pure foreign gyal up deh, an foreign gyal cyaan even dance, cyaan even wine! But how dat fi fair, tho?"

"Dem judge ya blind or wha?" demanded others.

"Unnuh lef di gyal dem. Open competition. Anybody can enta. Grudge unnuh grudge dem choo dem white an pretty," some chimed in.

The women balanced on their heads with their feet wide open in the air, gyrating, kicking. Skin-out, as they called it. They had mock sex with the air. They did acrobatic maneuverings, splits, somersaults, everything to prove that each was more flexible, more skillful, more resourceful than all the others. They brought props on stage – mannequins, dolls, pom poms, whatever it took to stand out. Chinno had dyed her hair in two places so that she had a purple streak and an orange streak, one on either side, and these caught up in ponytails. She wore white bobbysocks and eight-inch black heels, a black leather mini skirt and orange tube tops.

Mongrel watched from the sidelines. He felt a sense of pride that he was responsible for Chinno. That's what he felt – he was responsible for her. He had broken her. He had trained her. He had entered her. She was his. From that first day they spoke in the wholesale Downtown, just after he had killed his close friend and had stepped away like it was nothing, hiding out in the store till the coast was clear. He had claimed her from that day. And he had done what it took to wheel her in. It felt even sweeter to wheel in this Chinese girl. Not everyone could do it. He smiled when he thought how skillful he was. He told her what she wanted to hear. Cheups. Every man did that, sure. But there was something more to him, he suspected. She had done his bidding, to the very last dot. The more she complied, the more excited he became, the more pics he wanted her to send, the more obscene the poses, the more risky the whole thing became – for her. Life had ceased to be a risk for him. Life was life, at the end of which death awaited. So what of it. For some, like him and his kind, death came much earlier, that was all.

His bosom friends had all been shot or were rotting away in jail, or were anxiously waiting for one of the above. He had played an instrumental part in some of this. So what of it. They would have done him in first, given half the chance. It was all about the first draw – the speed and the dexterity. It was all about the movement of eyes in tune to the movement of hands, in tune to the movement of hearts. Allegiances were fickle. It was all about seizing the opportunity. It was all about taking a girl who learned fast, very fast, and putting her on the stage and saying, dance.

The crowd was delirious. They cheered and raised their hands in a frenzy of patterns that only they understood – the code of the underbelly. They raised their bottles of liquor. They raised their lighters. They raised their ganja spliffs as if in defiance of Babylon, who was certainly lurking in the midst. They raised their raucous, frantic voices. They were ecstatic, extremely happy with the selection. Chinno had won. Only a handful were displeased, and quarreled among themselves about what they would have done had they been made judges – which was why they had not been made judges.

As protocol, Chinno did the honour of one more dance before claiming her trophy and million dollar check.

"Nice. Nice," was all he said on the drive back, the others sprawled out on the back seat from overdose and general exhaustion. "Wi go lodge the check to the bank when time come.

It go look suspicious in your account. Meantime, dat odder lickle ting."

He dealt with these matters, always. He had dealt with the fake identification. She was not yet eighteen years old, the minimum age for entry in the competition. He had dealt with getting her into everywhere she needed to get into. He had dealt with the fake friends who spoke to Waipo Mingzhu and Jingjing on the phone, claiming that Chinno was with them at the mall, at the theatre, at Devon House, at a number of other places that a normal seventeen year old girl was entitled to be at. He had dealt with the United States visa for her to carry out that other little thing, which they had discussed in detail and which she had agreed to do.

"Dem naw suspeck you. Yuh mad? Sweet lickle Chiney girl."

Li is missing, again. It seems serious this time. Biyu doesn't know. Fenfang doesn't know. Jingjing has gone looking. He'll find Li and bring Li back. Big brothers are capable beings.

Chapter Twenty-Five

There's something called 'new money' and there's a way you walk when you just come into it.

If you're a man, you glide and dip, hands gently swinging behind you, head erect, eyes slightly tilted down, working on your condescension. Three glides to every one dip. If you're a woman, your hand is permanently bent at the left elbow and left wrist, cradling your purse, permanently straight on the right, smoothing your linen skirt over your thighs. Males, black full-grain shoes polished to a sparkle, to match belt. Females, six inch stiletto heels or name-brand wedges, to match purse.

If you're old money, you recognize new money at first glance. If you're new money, you don't realize just how conspicuous you are, till it's too late.

Bam had been eying the real estate agency for weeks. She nearly poked her head through the window every chance she got to drive by the mall on Constant Spring Road, whether she was with Dezzie or Precious being shuttled to some place or the other. Today, she asked Precious to park just for a minute so she could pop in somewhere and get something. She didn't say where or to get what. Precious parked in the shopping mall and pursed her lips and hissed her teeth as her mother-in-law wheeled away. The two had become at odds for some time. They tolerated each other, but sometimes things came to a head and words were thrown, and words were caught and thrown back. Not nice words, please note.

Bam strolled into the agency, her purse tucked under her arm. Immediately, a sales girl came to her aid. The speed with which she drew attention reminded Bam very much of the times when she entered the posh furniture stores in Liguanea, when they were decorating the house. The sales people would dash to ask her what she wanted. It seemed very much that they meant, "What exactly do you want in here, Miss? We don't cater to the likes of you. Can't you see the price tags? Our couches and beds and dining room sets are imported from Europe. No local artisan could create these. Our proprietor travelled all the way to France and Germany to select these pieces herself, and ship them with the utmost care. Very tasteful and elegant. Can't you see the price? These vases and rugs were handpicked from the Middle East. Why don't you try the stores further down the road? Do yourself a favour, huh, lady?"

And they would trail her with their eyes and shadow her every movement till she exited the store. She made a deliberate point of fondling the price tags and asking, "So these already have the tax included?" or, "Jamaican or US dollars?" just to piss them off, to see them roll their eyes at her simplicity and their terrible fate for encountering this wishy washy woman on such a fine day like today. But she would return later, after she had decided on her purchase, and she watched as their faces morphed from disdain into shock into the most courteous accommodation.

So now the receptionist felt that the woman's presence in this office was so out of sync with things that should happen in the world, that there was a need for her to meet Bam half way down the lobby and enquire what her business was; just in case this lowly creature had dragged some ungodly thing into their sacred space and ought be thwarted before the entire office needed to be quarantined.

"I'd like to buy an apartment," Bam said.

The receptionist scoffed, pursed her lips and stood immobile for a minute.

"An apartment? You said, buy?"

"Buy. I said, buy."

"Oh." She wanted to add: that will be all then, thanks for the laughs, and usher the woman through the door. But Bam continued,

"And I'd like to buy it cash. In the Norbrook area, preferably."

"Cash?"

"That's right. Cash."

"Well. We normally go by appointment. I'm not sure if Mr. Gangley can accommodate you. If you'll just have a seat, Ma'am. May I have your name, please?"

"Evadne Tucker."

The receptionist pretended to scribble something on her file clip, gave Bam another once-over, and wheeled off down the corridor. She knocked on the door at the far end and stood waiting for a response.

Roger Gangley sat at his desk, frustrated. He had sold absolutely nothing this month. Only two houses the month before. The houses that he took people to show around could just as well had been haunted. One actually was. A politician had shot his wife and her lover, and then turned the gun on himself, four years ago. A very ghastly scene it had been. He had come home to find the two lovebirds on his king-sized bed, doing you-know-what. It had been too much for his poor heart, already weakened by the decadent lifestyle, the booze and the high society parties and the frequent overseas trips to attend unnecessary meetings, paid for by the rabble. Anyhow, the apartment was still on the market. Gangley swore that his clients could see the apparitions hovering about the place. Why else would they shun the apartment so, and be so hesitant to see it, so quick to leave? Superstitious. Jamaicans were very superstitious. The asking price of the apartment had been reduced several times and was now at half the original price, to no avail. The family was now offering it for twenty million, negotiable.

The local real estate market was experiencing a boom, in fact, was on a major rebound given certain favourable circumstances that year. For one, the "brand Jamaica" had been promoted big time at the Olympics in London that Summer, in addition to the fact that the island was celebrating its fiftieth year of independence. The marketing people had put their backs into this one, gone all out encouraging returning residents to come back and recapture their little slice of the homeland. There were record low rates for mortgage being offered from financial institutions. Additionally, there had been record remittances the previous year, people sending back money for their relatives to build and buy stuff, get things moving in the little island that wasn't so young anymore. National pride had been restored. People were regaining a confidence that had been long on the decline. All around him business was booming. So why was Roger Gangley in such a slump? Somebody explain.

It wasn't as if he didn't know his market, didn't know his stuff. Thirteen years at this shit. Framed certificates on the walls to prove it. An office in an established section of town. He knew whom to target and with what. The young cocky professionals, hit them with the townhouses and apartments in Kingston, a few chains from the city centre where they had good access to the throbbing nightlife; one or two bedrooms would do them fine. The more mature, settled family type tended to want to live out in the suburbs, in bungalows or two-storey houses. The seniors who still had access to some money, hated the townhouses because, who wants to climb stairs several times daily just to use the bathroom? And then, everybody could hear you flushing the toilet! Seniors would have none of that nonsense. For them, somewhere quiet, self-contained, where grandchildren could safely visit and play for a while but would easily feel too confined and ask to be taken home. He knew who wanted what, and who could afford what.

The houses Gangley sold were high-end. He catered to the elite. No shame in that. It was big money that came less often, as opposed to little money that came fast. You choose your battles.

He had been doing well for himself so far but, this past year, dunno. He somehow didn't have the drive, couldn't find the energy to hit that sale home. Midlife sluggishness, he guessed. Unless someone specifically wanted a particular house and came with the intention to buy it, he just couldn't sell it.

Gangley was reclining in his chair, his feet up on the desk, his arms bracing the back of his head, thinking about how far away his next vacation was. The last one had been three weeks ago. He had gone resort-hopping on the North coast, him and the girls. Two weeks of unbridled pleasure, with two best friends who didn't mind sharing him in the interest of a jolly good time. Liberated women. His kinda girls. The sweetness was still in his system, lingering. Next time, he would take them to Negril. His people owned some seaside cottages and estates out that side.

He heard the knock on the door. He really wasn't in the mood to pitch anything to anyone who hadn't already made up their mind to buy something. There were seven dossiers stacked on his desk, of properties for sale, which had been there forever. The owners had been ringing his ears off, impatient for good word. Who the hell did they think he was?

"Come in."

"Good morning again, Mr. Gangley. There's a lady here who says she's interested in seeing some apartments." Her whole tone and demeanor added, *but I'm not too sure about this one, Sir*. She almost winked in conspiratorial heads-up.

He exhaled deeply, adjusted his position, tried to put on his "buy it now if you know what's good for you" face. It wasn't working. He himself wasn't buying it.

"Sure. Send her in."

Bam entered, realized at once that she was not welcome, and sat down primly without being offered a seat. She told the man what she wanted. He repeated her words, to double-check. She confirmed. She wanted an apartment in the Norbrook area.

"Why specifically, Norbrook?"

"My son lives there with his family. I live with him but I would like somewhere of my own, close enough." She was using her best English, and managing well.

"I see. Your son lives in Norbrook." He really wanted to ask, what is your son's profession? But there were subtle ways of finding that out. He handed her a form. "A preliminary form, background information that we need, to get things going." She started filling it out, stopping occasionally to ask him something, to make sure she was interpreting certain questions right. It took her a good fifteen minutes.

"How much did you have in mind to spend? What range?" he was still only half interested. In spite of the fact that he had distanced himself from the multitude and had declared his niche by way of location, some still got through and tried to waste his time.

"I'll just hear the prices, and decide," she said.

"Will you pay through an institution, by way of mortgage?"

"Oh, no. Strictly cash."

"Cash?"

"Oh, yes. My son won the Lot-a-Luck the other day, you know. Desmond Grant. You heard of him? I can pay cash."

"I see." This changes things, somewhat.

He actually stood. Moved closer to her.

"I do have some apartments I could show you, right now, if you like. One apartment in particular, I know you will just love. You should be able to afford it, given your position."

"Right now? Oh, well." It was just matter of telling Precious that she would catch up with her later, though her daughter-in-law would be peeved for having waited so long already, and having the children to pick up from school.

The apartment was located on Helena Drive, in a cul de sac cradled by the hillside. Inside was musty. Gangly quickly got to opening the huge windows, to air out the place.

"The view is just superb," he said. She nodded. "Cool breeze coming down from the hills. Peace and quiet, all to yourself."

"It's kinda scary for a little old lady, all by myself."

"Oh, not to worry. The neighbours are close by, and very friendly. Quite approachable."

He showed her the rooms: two bedrooms and two bathrooms upstairs, guestroom and bath downstairs, kitchen and living/dining room. A small washroom out back.

"These damn stairs, though. I'll break a hip going up these."

"No, no, you won't," was all he could say, adding a nervous chuckle. "You won't."

They did not stay more than a minute in the master bedroom, where the ghosts hung out. He wasn't chancing it. And this one looked like she could not only see ghosts, but would spare a minute to rebuke them in the name of Jesus. She looked the type, and he wasn't having it.

"This apartment would suit you very well, Mrs. Tucker."

"Miss."

"Oh, my. You look like a nice married lady. Some women just have that 'married' look about them. Respectable, you know."

She blushed. They discussed cost. He told her he would make a concession for her, being a single woman – not something he usually did but, she was so amiable and respectable. Instead of the sixty million being demanded by the owners, he was going to give it to her for fifty-five million. Yes, they were going to give him hell when they found out but, not to worry, Miss Tucker, he could handle the likes of them. Just leave everything up to him. closing cost, legal fees, everything included. He would handle all the paperwork. Sometimes, Miss Tucker, a businessman's discretion is called upon to offer a discount. This was a part of business. A little loss here and there; can't always be gain gain gain.

"You said there were other apartments?"

"Well, there are, Miss Tucker, but you know what? I'm not even going to bother to show them to you. That's how positive I am that this is the one for you. And besides, I do not see where I could offer this great discount on those other apartments. Those owners are more sticklers, you know what I mean?" he winked. "They're hard on the money."

She frowned. "Well, I guess you've been in this a long time. You know the ropes." She swung round, looking again at the rooms, the fixtures, the space. "It nice. It really nice fi true." The

English relapsing.

"let's go back to the office and start the paperwork. You said your son will be the one signing off?"

"Oh, no. I have authority to sign. I have power on the account." Whatever that meant, sounded like reasonable grounds to step on the gas through the afternoon Kingston traffic and get the wheels a-turning.

It had become something of a torture – a self-inflicted one – being anywhere near her children's school. Precious regretted with all her might the decision to have them enrolled in this school. Good school, yes, academic-wise, but lord the things she had overlooked, the things she just never knew before now! Snobbish teachers, snobbish staff, super snobbish parents. And the students? They took snobbish to a level where a professional mountaineer would be giddy. It wasn't so much that her two children started asking for new stuff, brand name stuff, really expensive and decadent and, some would say, really unnecessary stuff. She personally liked the idea of buying her children nice things. Not that she wanted to spoil them but she wanted them to have what she considered to be a good life. She didn't mind spending on them. What she didn't like was the way her children were made to feel that they didn't belong, that they were less than worthy and that they had to do so much more just to fit in. it was as if they were morphing into creatures that they were not, just to gain acceptance. And this was what bothered Precious.

The hoity-toity looks and the half-hearted patronizing responses from the other parents whenever she tried to be sociable, that she could withstand. Precious was no softy. She was a girl of the streets and she could deal. She merely learned to distance herself from them when she could, to avoid meetings and to stay in the car when time came for pickups. But her children, she did not want to expose them to the drama, the rending of their self-worth, the daily challenge to their right to be among the crème de la crème. Before they knew what upper class even meant, before they knew that they had come from the lower class and had been deposited in the middle of alienation, they were happy, carefree children, romping among their peers. Now, they were very conscious of not having this and needing that, and when are we going to get such-and-such, and how come we haven't travelled abroad, and did you know that Samantha and her entire family spent the entire Easter holidays at a luxury resort in Montego Bay? The entire family!

Some people were born into a privileged life. Some people were not. Some work their way on to the A-List. Some con their way. Some sleep their way. Some win the Lot-a-Luck and drop, bim bam buff, with no manual or chart or map, and have to feel their way through it. And their children have to feel their way through it. And their wife. Make that, their pissed long-term girlfriend. Make that, their pissed common-law baby mother who no longer saw the benefit of this blasted Lot-a-Luck foolishness. Money, yes, but money running out. Money trickling out of all kinds of places. Dezzie seemed to have no interest in investing anything; just spend spend spend. He mentioned an investment the other day but that was it, just a mention, no follow-up. And he didn't entertain her questions these days. Made her feel as if she was bothering him, or prying, like an annoying child. Like she was a loafer in his house, with no rights. A freeloader, relying on his goodwill.

Dezzie had his mother's name on his account. Bam could draw money as she pleased, without any stops, it seemed. Precious couldn't. Precious had to go to him for everything she wanted. In fact, everything she needed. His mother could draw money; Precious had to beg him every single time she had an expense to cover. Yet, Dezzie didn't want her to work. She had given up her business Downtown, only to come now depending on a man, something she had promised herself never to do. He gave her the money, yes. But why did she have to ask for it? Why not give her an account, open it in her name or make it so that she could draw from his, as Bam could? The whole thing wasn't right. Whose purse did he raid back in the day when he was struggling, hers or his mother's?

Dezzie had another woman. Precious knew it. She wasn't

asking anybody. Which fool doesn't know when her man has someone else? They had sex, yes, but he did it with an attitude like: if you don't wanna give me, that's fine. I'm good.

Let's face it: Dezzie was never Mr. Romance. He was never Mr. Loverboy. But he had his moments when he would at least try his hand at some petting, getting her in the mood, doing little things to please her and not just thinking of himself. Not now. They had starfish sex because he never saw to it that she was really in the mood and ready to take him. so she just let him have his way, the few times he wanted. But then, she too started to lose interest because, she was scared of him giving her something. She didn't know who he was melling with, or how many of them, or whether or not they were clean women. There was no telling what he was bringing home, when he came home. He had given her genital warts before, and Chlamydia, then turned around and accused her, when he knew he had been the one running the town red.

And then he would come home and throw himself on the bed – that bed that their children sometimes sat on. She didn't know where his hands or his mouth or his genitals were coming from. There was no trust in the relationship.

One night, Precious found herself screaming, "Nuh touch mi, Dezzie, nuh touch mi, man!" because she smelled another woman's perfume on him. She felt another woman's presence on him. She couldn't explain it. Couldn't prove it. And when he tried to hold her hand, to calm her down as not to scandalize the household, she just heard herself screaming at the top of her lungs, "One day, Dezzie, yuh gwine sorry! Hear mi? Yuh gwine lose every striking cent. Mark my word, hear?"

Bam had been lying in her room and heard the confrontation. She shook her head. Bam knew about Cassandra. She liked Cassandra. Nice pretty long-hair girl. High colour and everything. Walk nice. Dress nice. Very speaky-spokey. When Cassandra came to visit, Bam cooked for her, entertained her by the pool, chatted up to her – all this while Precious was elsewhere. Bam saw the pout on Precious' mouth when things were awry in the house, when an argument had started and would not finish and people were vexed and trying to hold it in. Bam saw all this. She also saw when Precious tried to make things right, to make things work, to try some lovey-dovey stuff on Dezzie, just for old time's sake. Things that lovers did. If she wanted to burst a pimple on his forehead, the way she always did back when, Dezzie would push her away. If she wanted to cuddle up in the sofa during newstime, Dezzie would complain that he was hot and needed to breeze out – with the air condition unit running.

And as for Miss Mother-in-Law, she strutted about the house like a peahen, ordering the maids about, deliberately telling them to do or undo things that Precious had decreed the opposite of. And when the tongues clashed, they did clash.

"Is my son ring yuh want? My son done know who gwine get him ring, Missus!"

"Look like is you want yuh son ring!"

"Well, me more likely fi get it dan you!"

"Yuh talk it like joke!"

"Hurry up an gwaan back a Portmore, suh mi son can get fi married who him want fi married. Him nuh want yuh."

"Well, who want yuh?"

"Nuff man want mi! Excuse mi!"

"Excuse you!"

And so on and so forth.

Bam had a taste for young flesh. She had been getting some, which was why she felt so desirable. The pool man and the gardener, both. The fear of God had been effectively banged out of her, it seemed. Maybe, she subconsciously associated wealth with having one's way, regardless of consequences. Or, maybe wealth simply meant there were no consequences. In the movies, the soap operas, the reality shows, rich women did as they very well pleased, no matter their age. In fact, it seemed, the older the bolder, and the more sexually liberated. Yes, that's it. She was trying her hand at sexual liberation, a thing much repressed from where she was coming. Old ladies cared for their grandbabies and "locked shop", resigned themselves to going to church and preparing for the final day of reckoning. Old ladies thought nothing more than being acceptable when time came to meet their maker. Sex? If partaken in, certainly not talked about. Certainly not with twenty-odd year old men, hired to keep the pool free from debris and the lawn free from weeds. There were poor old ladies and rich old ladies.

The journey into this bourgeois thing – this sexual liberation – was at first daunting, intimidating. Bam stood naked in front of the mirror and held her sagging breasts in both hands, then released them and watched them tumble over her chest without the least turgidity. She sighed. Nothing near like the stiff, perky mounds of years gone by. She had two chins. Two bellies – a big one that flapped over her groin and a little one just below her breasts, to keep the first one company. A scar where two babies had been delivered by Caesarean Section, surrounded by stretch marks. Wrinkles beginning to form all over. Little warts popping up on the sides of her face, under her armpits, her neck. Age spots on her arms and feet, lighter than the rest of her complexion. Her skin, no longer supple but thin and sagging. This body of a sixty-something year old woman, worn with living and loving, giving birth to life, suckling life, tired. This, she presented to two men at a stage in their lives when they were easily comparable to bulls, stallions, studs, anything virile and sturdy.

Surprisingly, they both took her with reckless abandonment. If they found her body repulsive, they didn't show it. If they had to imagine being with a firmer, more attractive chick in order to get off, they did so with her none the wiser. They laughed while she rediscovered things she had forgotten about her body. Her days of pleasing and being pleased, returned. How long it had been since she felt the power of a man – a young man, at that – plunging through her at top speed, full force. That feeling was incredible. She wasn't sure if they knew about each other. She didn't very much care. Remember we said, sexual liberation. So in fact, it tickled her that they might know, that Precious might know, that everybody on the block and down the hill and across the island might know. It thrilled her.

Chapter Twenty-Six

"The two suitcase dem exactly the same, Chinno. Doan the gyal send the picture of her own? Stop behave like yuh nuh have nuh sense. Everyting gwine guh smooth smooth smooth."

"Is har first time, dawg. Das why."

"Mi know, dawg, but shi jus fidgety suh star! Cool nuh, young girl."

He pressed 'end call' on his cell phone and hissed.

His first time at the Norman Manley International airport. His first time on a plane. Dezzie looked around in awe. He tried not to ask too many questions, tried to read the signs and follow the crowd, get a general sense of where to go and what to do. He kept checking to make sure that he had all his documents; he felt certain he had left something, but he couldn't tell what. He checked again. Everything seemed to be there. Fifteen minutes later, he got a serious premonition and checked again.

He cleared customs, waited in the departure lounge for three hours because he was extra early. They had said, make sure to get there early because it's Christmas time and many people will be travelling. But he had overdone the early thing. Well, better early than holding up the plane, or worse, missing the flight. He bought a sandwich and washed that down with a beer.

He looked out the window at the planes taking off and landing. He listened to the announcements being repeated with half hour regularity, till he was cloyed. Yes, we get it. Do not leave your luggage unattended. Anything found unattended will be confiscated and destroyed. We get it, lady. We get it.

Bam had seen to it that he was fully loaded with the usual going-away bickles, for it was written in the great books that one could never leave Jamaica for Foreign without taking little samples of island life to the homesick expats. It was unthinkable. Fried snapper and parrot fish. Roasted breadfruit, sliced and fried. Ackee and saltfish, well seasoned and peppered. Bammy. Festival. Cornmeal pudding. Dezzie was a walking culinary delight.

His flight was called. He boarded. He climbed the stairs he had always wanted to climb, but forgot to turn back and look around, the way he had imagined. Too many people were coming up fast behind him and then by the time he remembered the ritual, he had already found his seat and couldn't take the hassle to go back. The snobbish looks on the faces of the people in first class made him feel so unwelcomed, made him want to shuffle quickly past and get to the economy cabin, with the other underprivileged ones. What was the big deal up there in first class, anyway? Did they feed them on champagne and whatchamacallit? Caviar? Did they give them gold and diamond in little goodie bags as they disembarked? Maybe that section of the plane wouldn't burst into flames if there was a crash. Dezzie made a mental note that next time it would be first class for him, no less. He couldn't imagine how he hadn't thought of that before. Wasn't that like the very first thing you made up your mind to do when you got rich, to fly first class?

Desmond Grant, after years of yearning for this dream to come true, was off to New York City. They had said, keep your coat near cause when you come off the plane, it will be seriously cold. We don't mean Jamaica cold. We mean freezer cold, frost coming from your mouth cold, urine freezing in your bladder cold. And don't bother to think that we only mean one jacket. We actually mean three. And you need to change into some decent winter shoes soon as you land. And when you get there, remember, the key thing is layers. Layers layers layers. Don't forget. You can't survive a New York winter without layers. What yuh mean, layers? Man, just do what wi seh, huh? Yuh want to learn the ropes or what?

Layers of vests and undershirts and tights to insulate from the terrible drifts of cold air coming down from the Arctic and hitting the Americas without mercy. Socks. Can't forget those. Scarves to preserve your neck. No one – we mean no one – should see your neck during a New York winter.

Dezzie called to tell Cassandra that they were about to take off – just waiting for three more passengers, blasted late-comers, always holding up other people's progress. He hoped the plane would leave them. Serve them right. Cassandra didn't pick up, after three trials. So he texted her and waited but after twenty minutes he had to turn off the cellular phone. He just hoped she had gotten the text, expressing his undying love, and how much he would miss her. He was never this mushy with anyone before but, maybe it was age.

They wheeled down the runway and then they were off. Desmond Grant was in the air, looking down at trees, people, mountains and cars, and then, the sea. The wide Caribbean sea. Nothing but sea for miles. And then, nothing but clouds. Then the Atlantic Ocean. More clouds. Then it kept switching from ocean to clouds to ocean to clouds. Then he fell asleep.

Exiting the terminal was like stepping into a deep freezer. And then, you were required to remain in the freezer until you got a cab, which dilly-dallied throughout the streets with aimless deliberation so as to run the meter and break your pocket, cause he knew you didn't know the place. Damn taxi drivers! Then you remembered that you used to be one.

Dezzie's aunt lived in Harlem. He hadn't seen her since he was a young boy and, true to tradition, she looked him over from head to toe and chirped about how he had grown. For God's sake, it's been twenty-odd years, of course I've grown, Aunty Enid. You have grown, too, I might add. A lot.

She lived alone and would enjoy his company for the month that he would be there. Her husband had died. A white man, succumbed to cancer of the colon. The couple had endured much, an inter-racial marriage, Harlem being particularly tough for this type of thing. She had pictures of him framed around the house, pictures of them both, their wedding day, special occasions. The marriage had produced no children. Mule, Dezzie had heard his relatives say of his aunt while growing up. Mule, cyaan have nuh pickney. It was the first and last thing people always said about a childless marriage, that somehow the woman was at fault, never even pausing to consider that there might have been something wrong on the man's side. When he was young, before he understood the term 'mule', Dezzie always wondered why everyone was calling his aunt a jackass, when he knew her to be a very nice, sensible lady.

Dezzie had specifically chosen to go during winter because he wanted to see snow; simple as it sounded. He wanted to experience snow. A wonderland of whiteness, as it was shown on television and in the children's books when he was a boy. The soft powdery flakes that drifted on to your face, beautiful snowdrops, each of which it was said was completely different from the other. Two days into his first snow storm and he didn't want to have anything further to do with snow, thank you very much. If it were declared that there would be no more snow in the world ever again, Desmond Grant would not mind, would not care in the least. In fact, would endorse it.

It was a white Christmas. Tinselly and spectacular but bitterly cold. Everyone was so wrapped you couldn't see their pretty clothes underneath, until you were well inside, and then you had to put on twenty pounds of armory to go back out again. It was in the end not worth all the hassle. There were some sunny days in December. Sunny, not warm. In New York, there's a difference. Big difference. There were days when the sun was full in the sky but if you dared step out without a coat, you were history, my man! You would catch a head cold so fast it would take you out of operation for a week. It happened to Dezzie so he could testify. His aunt had warned him, always make sure to have your head covered. But no, he was Mr. But-the-Sun-is-Bright-Outside Grant. That would teach him. Six days in bed with snot dripping from his nose and a wicked cough and sore throat, and his aunt worried sick that he had pneumonia cause he was roasting with fever and could barely eat. Six days confined to a small apartment in New York with an aging aunt who wanted to hear everything that had happened in the past twenty years, though you were on the verge of death and she herself said so. No fun at all.

The snow cleared for a short while but heavy snowfall was predicted for the coming week. Weeks. It would be downhill from here till the end of February. Who wanted to catch their last dose of the great outdoors, do it now or forever hold your peace. And that's when Aunty Enid decided, let's go visit Uncle Lewis in Chicago.

"I know he would glad to see yuh, Dez," she said.

And so it was. They set off by train and crossed the hinterland of the North-East, zipping across the Northern tips of five states, from New York to Illinois. It was during this trip that Dezzie realized, this is Jamaica except with brick buildings, wider streets and snow. It aint all that. When he had visited the malls, he had hissed. Jamaican malls could certainly compare; some might even exceed. Now, looking at the commercial district as the train choo-chooed by, the bland grey exteriors, no rich Caribbean flair, no exciting colours, he exhaled, "Suh, this is the America everybody crazy 'bout? This is it? This is America? Cheups!"

They left the city and passed the rolling meadows and farmlands of the countryside. Rivers. Lakeside houses with acres of lawns, cornfields, factories. Woodland cottages that called to mind fairytales of children off on adventures. Endless miles of green and blue with the white snow still wedged in places, melting but taking its own sweet time. Beautiful, yes. Beautiful, but not home. Not Jamaica. Not Yawd.

During the eighteen hour journey, the train stopped four times under several pretenses but Dezzie realized, these were cigarette breaks. At each of these stops, huge sluggish men and huge frowsy women and skinny dudes with tattoos and skinny chicks with nose rings would disembark and stand on the platform to smoke. They got a good half hour to explore the mesmerizing depths of tobacco. They dragged themselves back in reluctantly at the final whistle, and settled back for another long haul through the great expanse.

And the eighteen hour train ride turned into twenty-nine hours of hell. The train broke down in two places, in the middle of the night, deep in the hinterland, and had to be repaired. Dezzie didn't know where in the great United States he was and he didn't care, because from all indications he was not in Chicago. Some backwater town along the lakes. Some passengers cut their losses and found other means of getting to where they were going. Dezzie and Aunt Enid had to stay put. They had depleted the food they had carried. All the water. They were hungry and thirsty and needed good sleep. Their legs were cramped from coiling up in the seats to sleep, having opted out of the expensive sleeping cars, never expecting this caliber of delay. Never again will I take a train in America. Never again.

On Chicago's South Side, new rules. This time, stay low. Low as you can go while still maintaining regular everyday functions, like walking and talking. His uncle lived on the South Side. Here, it was said, if you wanted to be shot, this was the place to come. This could be by stray bullet or by one that had your name on it. South Side was the place of options. This gang or that. Die now or later. You choose. Sometimes not.

But people were living a lie, though. Jamaicans in New York and South side were living a lie. Dezzie couldn't speak for any others but he saw these ones at work, lying their tails off. They weren't doing all that well at all. Not as well as the letters and telephone calls would have their relatives back home believe. Many many were living hand-to-mouth, taking jobs they would never have accepted back home. They coiled their tails between their legs and stepped right up into Uncle Sam's public buses, whereas back home they only drove in cars and scoffed at public transportation. They were good boys and girls, waiting patiently at us stops in the snow.

Some lived out of their cars. Some huddled in people's basements, splitting an already meager rent with umpteen other individuals, or crammed into apartments sleeping on blow-up beds on the floor, dodging the landlord and avoiding eye-to-eye contact with their children's school officials. They were at the mercy of so many things, of so many people. Spouses who had arranged business marriages and later demanded terms that were not originally agreed upon, but since you were stuck in a sticky situation, facing deportation or compliance with unthinkable, disgusting things. Bosses who knew the situation all too well and would not hesitate to have you deported unless. Unless. Unless. Even Dezzie shuddered. Even Dezzie.

Yes, he brought back many nice things. Even in the snow storms that followed, there had been some shopping. Aunt Enid had her own batch of people to send things to, and Dezzie of course had his. He had brought everybody's measurements and he knew who wanted what, and who would just love what, and who would look so nice in what. He bought several lingerie sets for Cassandra, perfume, designer shoes, four leather handbags, several expensive outfits and a big white soft teddy bear with a red satin heart. He was lugging four large suitcases, and braced himself for the extra charges at customs.

The girl stood out because she was so skimpily clad and was traveling from New York, where there was a mighty snow storm still in effect. It was a wonder the flight had not been cancelled. Don't talk too soon. A yellow tube top and a brown leather batty rider shorts. Well, she was headed to Jamaica, so. Skimpy it was, then.

Chinno was easily recognizable as the reigning Monarch of the Dancehall. She drew attention now wherever she went in the island and many places overseas. She lugged her one grey suitcase towards a group of girls, seemingly returning from school for the holidays. They greeted each other. The girls were abuzz with excitement. Their old classmate, a celebrity. But she looked so different. So grown. Maybe we should have opted for the video life too, huh, instead of wiling away our days at college. And for what? A degree that guaranteed nothing? They weren't sure whether to call her Chinno or Liling. Would she take offence? To which one?

"I figured we'd run into each other based on what you said, Liling, but we still weren't sure," said Stephanie, embracing her former classmate. "So good to meet up on social media after a whole year, huh? And now here we are, going back home on the same flight. This is great."

Liling smiled.

They chatted for a while. "Tell you what, we'll catch up after we land, heh, girls?" Chinno said, and she wheeled away with the grey suitcase, checked in and went into the bathroom.

She was feeling queasy. She had swallowed forty-two pellets, the way he had shown her how. She had practiced with whole globe grapes for width, flame grapes for length, to prime her gullet. Forty-two pellets, her first go. Some pros couldn't take that many, after a lifetime of go's. Girl, yuh cut out for this shit. She smiled.

Chinno stared at her reflection in the mirror. The hair dyed blonde this time. Green streak. This had become expected of her. She almost felt like she would disappoint without the pomp. The drama. And who wanted to disappoint anyone, least of all, fans? Very very least of all, Mongrel. He was depending on her. He had made this clear. People were expecting this shipment, bad. She stared into her eyes, her pupils somewhat dilated, for no reason. Well, maybe reason being, she was terrified. Strung. Hadn't slept. Could barely walk upright for the cramps in her belly. And in clothes so revealing. An indiscretion. She knew her suitcase was alright. She checked it in without so much as a fidget.

Back in Jamaica. Long lines stretching to forever. Many flights had been held up due to the snowstorms in places, and now there was a backlog of people who were glad to be back in the sun. But man these people move slow.

Someone was being eased out of the line, taken aside. Immigration personnel and police officers were slowly swooping down, touching their walkie talkies, on high alert.

"What is your name, Miss?"

"Stephanie Johnson."

"Did you pack this suitcase yourself?"

"Yes, Miss. I did."

"Please, come with me."

Dezzie stood behind the girl. He was keen to see that something was happening. Something out of the ordinary. In the news, later, maybe, they would hear more, if anything. She was flustered. She had no idea what was happening, but she complied, calmly, intelligently. College girl.

In the car, Chinno coiled over in excruciating pain. Her belly cramping, burning, feeling like she would burst. She had read, these things could rupture. You could die. It would not be long if one did rupture, and this a four hour flight.

"Nuh vomit in here, young girl. Brand new carpet," was all Mongrel said. He was pissed, as pissed as could be. Yes, Chinno got away with the forty-two pellets, but the damn suitcase got snatched. The boys in New York knew their stuff. They knew how to pack a suitcase. And Chinno had made sure to buy the exact same type that she knew the girl would have. It should not have gone wrong. Everything had been planned. It should only have been a matter of switching back the suitcases afterwards, when it was safe. Five kilos of cocaine, gone. Well, good thing they had taken the precaution of switching the suitcases, or Madam Queen would be going to the iron gates. Now, to get Chinno home and flush out the pellets before she ruined his carpet.

Chapter Twenty-Seven

A beautiful woman is almost guaranteed to experience beautiful things. She will know in her lifetime what it feels like to be desired, to be kissed from head to toe, to be devoured alive, squirming and moaning. Soft, clean skin commands that you kiss it. Sweet-smelling hair makes a man's mouth want to linger at her neck and stay there for hours, days, years. An ugly woman might never know these things. Unless she is extremely lucky, an ugly woman might always have to wonder.

So a lady must attend to her hygiene, to her grooming. She must be impeccable, always presentable. She must have a regiment: facial masks, soaking feet, pampering. This may take hours each day. It is well worth it. This, as taught to Cassandra, by her mother. Codes of seduction.

It was an investment. A business, if you may. What's wrong with a business? You invest. You hope to make a profit. The more you put in, the more you get out. The more you place yourself at a premium, the more you may demand.

My girl, you come from a people called, "the Red People". We are from German stock. Light skinned. Some local stock mixed in, yes, but not much. You have to drop the "aye', the "mawma", the "mawsa" and all the other drawn out syllables. Drop them. Speak properly. You have to climb up. You got the looks. Your mama saw to it you got the looks. Now, use those looks.

Country is not for you. You can come from a place and decide you are no longer a part of that place. Nothing wrong. You don't have to feel tied to that place. Your future is not in Westmoreland backbush. Your future is in mansions, in Kingston and St. Andrew. Help your people, yes, but maintain your distance. Don't let your navelstring pull you back down and tie you down. Rise.

Gold digger? Why would you say such a thing? What a horrible combination of two very beautiful words.

So they were on their honeymoon. The choice had all been up to her and she had chosen for them to spend it at a resort in Oracabessa. A small private wedding, a scant, hurried reception. Very few guests. Very few pictures taken. Bam was beaming. No one gave Cassandra away. None of that traditional stuff. Bam was disappointed about this but eventually she said she understood. Some modern girls had very new and specific notions about marriage.

Mrs. Cassandra Grant lay in bed with her husband, watching him sleep. She despised him.

"Take your pills. Make sure," her mother had said.

Her mother never had to say. She would never think to bear that man's child. Are you crazy? First thing every morning, a pill and some water, before a prayer and a sigh.

Dezzie stirred. He looked across at his wife. He smiled. She smiled back. He pursed his lips. Kissy kissy. She frowned, bent forward so he could kiss her on the cheek. "Breakfast. Love too much kiss," she teased.

"God, I love your hair," he said, trailing her as she strolled off into the bathroom to shower. "Women like you doan need no wig. Just natural nice nice hair. Doan know why black woman have to always have in wig! Cheups!"

He stood, collected the two used condoms and wrapped them in newspaper, threw it in the bin. It had been a small point of contention, why he, a married man, still needed to wear condoms. "I just like it that way," she had said with an air of finality. "For the time being." With some concession, followed by the smile that always won him over.

"I just feel calm wid yuh, Cassy," he said, poking his head through the bathroom door. She drew the shower curtain with a snap. "Yuh just mek mi feel calm."

He had not been sure of marriage. Definite as could be, he was madly in love with Cassandra. But he was not a marriage-minded man. Luckily, Cassandra took the matter into full control and set him down the straight and narrow. She was such a smart, level-headed girl. And so bold. That was the thing. Her level of confidence. Women of her complexion had a level of confidence. He had noticed it. They held the world by the collar and shook it, till the world complied with what they wanted. They made the world want to comply. Confidence. It was what dark-skinned girls lacked. It made him not want to marry them. Cassandra selected her ring, showed it to him, and he approved the purchase. It cost a fortune but, so what? That girl knew what she wanted in life. She would take him far.

After Bam moved out and into her own apartment, Precious caught the rake and made her move before she was asked to do so. No one had to explain to her what was what. She was many things but no fool. She took her children and moved back into her house in Portmore, with nothing more than the clothes on their backs. She cried, of course, for days. No one saw, but she cried. and she thought very long and hard about how she would pick up the pieces of her life again.

Another disruption for the children. Precious had always chastised women who claimed to stay in a relationship because of the children. Now she realized, it wasn't so clear cut. Yes, she left, but it was a tough decision. And it had taken her some time to muster what she needed to muster. Leaving was never an easy feat. Leaving, with children involved, was a mountain of a decision. Yet, for their father, it seemed not so much. He could always hide behind the excuse that, their mother took them. She must know.

"Kiss mi neck!" he exclaimed. And his wife asked what it was.

"Dis Rastaman here, bwoy. Look like dem set him pon mi. Cyaan guh nuhweh and nuh si him, to rahtid!"

She had lost interest. Turned the tap back on.

On the television screen, Ras Negus was on stage with his entire family, collecting some award or the other. This minute he's homeless; next minute collecting award. Dezzie sat at the edge of the bed, with the remote in his hand and his mouth agape. Maybe if he listened further, he would understand.

The "Outstanding New Entrepreneur of the Year" award for Kingston parish goes to Emmanuel Stewart, otherwise known to us as Ras Negus. Entrepreneur? What's that? Dezzie asked Cassandra. She didn't know, either. And she was getting peeved at him for interrupting her bath.

"What the hell kind of award is that, tho?" asked Dezzie to himself. He was absolutely clueless.

Chapter Twenty-Eight

The baby's name was Mosiah. Ras Negus had caught his head as he plopped into the world. His father was a businessman, his mother a homemaker. As good a deal as any child could get.

The restaurant was flourishing and Ras Negus had hung his award on a wall near the entrance: Outstanding New Entrepreneur of the Year!

This meant a lot to him. The innovation and community service had been so rooted in him, he had not seen it as a separate effort towards winning any prize. He had not known the prize existed. He was informed he had been nominated, by whom he did not know, but when his name had been called and he was declared winner, he was very appreciative. For a business to flourish in this stifling economy said something of the individuals behind it. He shared the prize with his wife because he knew he was indebted to her, and though her name was not on the plaque with his, through no fault of his own, he acknowledged her in his few words he gave in acceptance. And they both would have a say in how they would use the five hundred thousand dollars award that went with it, of course. Sticking to their prudent original plan, some was to be saved, some invested.

A new word now in his vocabulary: entrepreneur. He was one. He hadn't realized. He was surely one. It sounded nice, too. Sounded fancy. Ras Negus wasn't sure if he had a knack for business so much as he had a drive to succeed, which worked just as well. Plus, he was contributing to the health of his people, and building a small empire for his children. A small one, but one more nonetheless. They would have something to carry on, to retain and build on after he was gone. A family business. He liked the sound of that! He would teach his children to be frugal, to take calculated risks, and to give back. Their main investment for now would be towards their education.

Naph-T, content now that the business had established itself, decided to concentrate her efforts on running the home and the farm in the hills. They had hired two other workers at the restaurant and one other at the farm. Housewife and farmer, this made her happy. That she was there to see her children off to school in the mornings, standing at the gate and watching as they climbed the little track to the primary school, and that she was there at home when her children returned from school, a meal ready and waiting for them, was all the world to her. She was nurturer, stabilizer. She provided a clean, safe home. She was affectionate towards their father. She helped them with homework. She was content in this.

Naph-T lay on the bed in the noonday, watching her son tug at her titties, first the left, then the right. He sucked voraciously, as his father would say, gulping down every drop of the goodness. The child was looking up at her and reaching his tiny hand to play with her face. She pretended to nibble his fingers. Every once in a while, as she smiled, he smiled. Then the suckling became less and less forceful, his breathing became slower and softer, and he was off to sleep, his two pegs biting down gently on her nipple. She let him stay like this for a while. Sometimes, he would fall asleep on the breast and every jerk would stir him back to resume his suckling.

The afternoon was bliss. Naph-T thought back of Mulgrave Lane, where she had been terrified to open the doors or even the windows in the heat of the day, scared of being invaded by thugs or, worse, Babylon. Now, a cool breeze coming in from the hills, Miss Inez dozing on the verandah waiting for the stomping footsteps of her grandchildren to be heard chasing each other down the path. She had picked mangoes to hand to them. She always had some fruit for when her grandchildren returned home in the afternoons.

Yes, bliss. The hills were bliss.

Chapter Twenty-Nine

"Suh, how much fi one a dem things ya?" Dezzie asked, knocking on the hull of the yacht. This forty-five foot boat was named "There She Rides".

The men looked from one to the other and then burst out laughing.

"Yuh planning to buy yacht, Dezzie?" asked Dacres.

"Just asking." Dezzie held on to the rails and looked overboard, timidly.

He was terrified of being at sea. He was definitely a land creature. It was his first time going out this far. Apart from little jet ski rides that had skimmed the surface off the coast at Dunn's River Falls, and little half-mile joyrides at the pity of the fishermen at Hellshire when he was a boy, that was it.

He could see about four or five life jackets and tubes attached to chains and he figured he had the option of putting one on, but since none of the other men were wearing life jackets, he didn't want to look like the one and only wimp. Even if it meant he would have been the only one floating after the wreck, being cool was preferable to being afloat. Dezzie remembered when he had looked down from the plane and seen tiny specks of brown on the sea — boats! Those men were crazy! Trusting yourself to that great big water in nothing but a piece of wood? Preposterous! But here he was, and surrounded by sharks.

He had a little street smarts. He always knew at least to check for guns. First instinct, look for suspicious bulges. But then, that's where the street smarts ended. Cause after you confirmed that all six men had guns, then what? You were still out in the middle of the sea with them, and you had nothing. Not even a pocket knife. Which boiled down to trusting your life to men you hardly knew, and whose good intentions you couldn't vouch for. Which was no smarts. Pathetic. Dezzie wasn't sure why he had come. Why he kept letting Dacres talk him into going to these places. Was he so desperate for acceptance? He didn't even like these men. And him now married to Dacres' one-time side chick. But what of it? It's not like Dacres had planned to marry Cassandra. He had his chance. A man came in and did what a man should do. Made a wife out of a beautiful girl. Wife material. Dacres couldn't hold him up for that. They were still man and man. Women shouldn't come between men.

These weren't the three investors. Another batch this time. Dacres had many friends in high places. Perks of being a politician. You got around. You met people. You took numbers. Contacts. It was all about maintaining contacts. Scratch my back. That sorta thing. Favours came in handy on the rebound. These ones seemed even more well off, and much more reticent. Even when they laughed, they did so grudgingly, as if the laugh was costing them money. They were generally somber. Cautious. It was as if mistrust came with the territory. They were naturally suspicious of those who huddled too near.

"This is how serious men fish," said Dacres, always the most talkative in these settings.

When they had gotten to a certain point, the men unloaded equipment and started setting up for the catch. Sturdy lines and hooks, quality stuff. Top of the line equipment. Dezzie could see. Fishing had never really been his thing but the exposure should be good. So this was how the big guys did their thing. Far far away from the shore, far out into a good clean seawater, far from the small fry and the pollution of the harbor, and out to where the big fish would surely bite. So this was how.

These guys were powerful, toned, all wearing shorts and muscle shirts so that their huge calves and biceps protruded and their six packs were clearly defined beneath. They worked out, all of them. Two hours at the gym per day, at the very least. They wore jewellery. Gold chains, bracelets and waterproof quartz watches, and wedding bands. All had rings from their respective alma maters, showing allegiance to their old boys' clubs. One even had an earring in his left ear and a silver ring on his left pinky finger. They wore designer shades, for style as well as practicality. Sun tan lotion, upon the insistence of their wives. They were wealthy men. It showed. Dezzie didn't know exactly who this yacht belonged to. Could have been anyone of them, from the look of things. He wasn't told and he didn't ask.

The waters off the coast of Jamaica's Southside teem with fish. They got to where there was not a piece of land in sight, steadied the boat and dropped their lines. They were aiming for blue marlin, tuna, mahi mahi, sailfish, barracuda, kingfish, any one of those big guys, maybe even some lobster or a shark. Yes, they had caught shark before. These amateur anglers knew their stuff.

Oddly enough, it was after the boat stopped that Dezzie developed motion sickness. He never did get his sea legs and had spent the entire trip clinging to the rails, even while the others hopped about doing this and that. Now, everything came to a head and he was nauseous. He had tried to keep his cool but his belly wanted to erupt. The men were eying him, all the while reeling in their catch. They pouted at him and signaled to each other, as if to say, look at that idiot over there; the one trying hard not to vomit into the sea. Take that back. The one vomiting into the sea. One of the men held him as he gripped the rails. They led him into the interior, handed him a towel and made him sit on the floor. And then it happened.

Dezzie sat, stupefied. His head was spinning from the seasickness, his mouth bitter from the vomiting. He was in a sorry state. So at first he wasn't sure if he was dreaming or if someone had actually whacked him across the side of his face with the handle of a gun. Yep. Someone had done just that. No dream.

Two men held his hands spread-eagled and kept them firmly to the side. He had no use of them. When he came to from being gun butted, and tried to ask, "Wha? Wha?" that was when Dacres rained down a series of punches into his face and chest. Dezzie was bleeding profusely from his lips and from a gushing wound across his forehead.

"Next time, yuh find yuh owna bloodclaat hooman! Yuh dutty dog, yuh!" was all Dacres kept saying. The two strong men holding Dezzie down were silent. The others, perhaps, still fishing, making sure the coast was clear. "Lef my raas hooman!" Dacres repeated, firing more punches. Dezzie moaned and pleaded.

"Put him faceway over di couch," Dacres instructed. Dezzie was made to stand. He could barely hold himself up. They draped him over the side of the couch like a crimpled, bleeding piece of calico, dyed red.

Forty minutes went by. The men had caught some snapper, several pounds of mahi mahi and had hauled in a king-sized barracuda. This was their triumph. They were celebrating with shots of Johnny Walker, all round. They were taking turns to hold up the barracuda and snapping pics for the wives, and to show off on social media.

Dacres emerged from the interior, straightening his shorts, peeved in the daylight to discover that there were a few smudges of blood near the pockets. He sat down, exhausted from the exchange. After a few minutes, and still breathless, he motioned to one of the men, "Tell him to come here."

Someone went back for Dezzie, and he limped up to the deck, his head throbbing, his muscles sore and tender from where he had been penetrated. He kept adjusting his shorts. They somehow just didn't feel right on him, and would never feel right again, he suspected.

"The divorce papers. Everything goes to Cass," Dacres huffed, his anger not yet spent. He had a good mind to give Dezzie another whack. He had been holding back for so long, biding his time, waiting for this special moment. "Sign them," he demanded. He handed Dezzie some documents. "My lawyers draw them up." One of the men nodded nonchalantly. Dezzie figured he had been the draftsman here mentioned.

"How a mus sign this, Star?" Dezzie tried to protest.

"Look here. Tink is nothing fi just bus two shot inna yuh blouse and skirt and fling yuh ova deh suh? Tink is nothing?" Dacres pointed at the wide open sea, furious with waves and harbouring how many sharks.

"But how a mus duh dat, Boss Man?"

"Boss man? Yuh fuck mi hooman and tun roun' call mi Boss Man? Look here, sign this shit before mi get mad."

Dezzie signed his signature in all the places indicated by the lawyer. He looked around at the other men. They were unconcerned, packing away their equipment, getting ready to go back onshore, congratulating each other on a superb catch.

Going in, Dezzie stood against the rail, clinging, feeling nauseous again but no vomit would ever be brave enough to come. Not now. Dezzie was quiet for the rest of the journey. He did not say a word, to anyone or to himself. His mind was blank. His face had a downward tilt, his eyes counting the ripples that hit against the side of the yacht, like they never learned: some things you just don't hit against.

Chapter Thirty

It was an active twelve months. Jamaica's year of golden jubilee – five decades with no umbilicus. It was a yearlong celebration that took epic proportions and at times raised eyebrows about the chunks of money being designated to mark the occasion. It was a year of unbridled spending. After all, one does not turn fifty every day.

And what a coincidence! In the capital city of the very colonial power from whose severance she was emphatically celebrating, the thirtieth Olympiad was underway and the Jamaicans were "jaminating". Twelve medals in all. First, second and third place in the men's 200m sprint. A gold for the women in the 100m. The "Lightning Bolt" was declared fastest sprinter in history.

In Half Way Tree square, where the events were being televised blow-by-blow and larger than life via huge, well positioned monitors, there was full scale pandemonium among the rabble. And in the homes, pot covers and pans and anything that could clash and made a thunderous sound, were being clashed. It was the time of the common man reclaiming his significance by hitching his wagon to national stars, who were for the purpose outfitted in the colours of the land, carrying the flag high or wrapped around their shoulders. For the peasants, who knew little of the sacrifices made by the athletes or the tedious hours of training, a sense of significance again after a four-year hiatus. They held their champions to strict account, and a slip could mean sudden death with them. People who couldn't walk an inch without aching, demanding a record sprint each and every time.

An active year. It was the year that Glason Dacres took up office as Mayor of the municipality of Portmore, after a rigorous campaign that almost left him in hospital due to the surge of energy expended over such a brief time. Portmore's mayor was the only one directly elected by the people, and Dacres had seen to it that the people knew what he was about. The political rallies across the umpteen communities, the speeches till he was hoarse with laryngitis, his wife behind him pee-pee-cluck-cluck with the bottle of cranberry water. The door-to-door visits shaking hands and smiling till his teeth were permanently fixed like a Cheshire Cat and his head kept nodding on autopilot. But he was alright. He sought the endorsement of pastors, educators and all lovable and respectable people.

There were magnanimous billboard pics of him in suit and tie with arms folded across his chest and a stern look upon his face, the way people do when they mean business. These were mounted at the three strategic entrances into the municipality, with the caption: "Welcome to Portmore. Vote Glason Dacres for Mayor".

And then there was Hurricane Sandy, and the bussing and the headache and the floods. But he was alright. Then there was the matter with a certain Mr. Desmond Grant, a matter in which his hand got a little dirty and drastic measures had to be taken but all in all, he was alright.

This was the year of the great Riverton Dump fire, the smoke seen around the world, it seemed. Everybody coughing up reasons, excuses, suggestions. But the smoke did clear.

It was the year of the fire at the Pearnel Charles Arcade, across from the St. William Grant Park, where Precious once kept her shop. Some stores and stalls had been damaged. When precious had heard the news, she couldn't help but feel the pain of the shop owners, from little stall to big store – business people them all. Some had started with two pairs of shoes in their hands, peddling. Then, they upgraded to a traveling bag into which was stuffed all the wares that they had bought or taken out on credit, and from which they would earn a meager profit. Those meagre profits reinvested, and so on, and so forth, till they could afford a stall, their clothes hung from racks along the side of the arcade. And after many many years – ten or so – finally, a small cubicle; a store. And it was nothing short of heart-rending for this to go up in flames.

These men and women had mouths to feed. The men had umpteen baby mothers to support, the women had their children to care for – many of whom had been deserted by their fathers. These were businessmen. Businesswomen. In their own right. They knew their trade back-to-back, front and side. They knew how to bargain and negotiate a sale, how to read a face; a buyer's face, a miser's face, a gullible face, a time-waster's face.

Precious could not decide if she had been lucky or not. Had she still been at the arcade, would hers have been one of those gutted in the fire? Would she have perished in the fire? There was no telling what would have been. She decided that she had been lucky.

Dacres was happy that at least now, Cassandra lived where he could see her more conveniently, and securely. And he was happy for her, being a woman who deserved all good things. The house was just the right size for the family she would one day bear him, in his mind. In Cassandra's mind, perhaps a different scenario. There were hills. There were mountains. A brief pause at the top of one knoll did not mean you were done with climbing. And what hindered ascent more than the annoying complaints of children?

It was the year that Desmond Grant received in the mail a statement of overdraft, which he could not explain but then, after some thought, he could explain. He now collected mail at his mother's apartment, where he lived. He had come almost full circle and things were gradually drifting back to the way they were, almost, like it never even happened. He did not feel like a rich man. Had he ever really felt like a rich man? And now he was contemplating buying a second-hand Toyota and running taxi again. He hadn't fully decided yet.

And here was this apartment, a gorgeous exterior but the inside was crumbling. Termites had gutted much of the furniture that had come with the house, as well as the mahogany paneling and skirting. The house was a pretty girl with no morals. Voluptuous and bubbly but air-headed. The red cherry cupboards and chests of drawers were falling apart at the hinges. And the private space that his mother had wanted to accommodate her trysts with the virile young lovers now had to be compromised, and she didn't appreciate it one bit. Bam was fuming at the mouth regarding the situation with Cassandra. She had outgrown her infatuation for the mythical creature and was now able to call her what Bam now knew she was, which was a name that would so ruin the integrity of the paper it was written on that it shall be here written as, unmentionable.

Bam wanted Dezzie to get a lawyer and fight this shit, forthwith. Gonna let her cruise in and rob everything from under yuh behind? Dat lickle red-tail puss-yeye wretch! Push come to shove, Obeah wi seh! Put har name pon parchment paper an' is Portland fi har backside!

Dezzie could not tell his mother all the intricate details of the situation. He only said, "Mek it rest, Mama. Jus mek it rest."

The apartment was Bam's, yes, but bills still needed to be paid, the property needed upkeep, people still needed food. These things were concerning.

This was the year when Cassandra felt the most accomplished in her life. She was not done with climbing but she could rest a little, take off her shoes, put her feet up. She had fired the maids and had hired one of her choosing, through an employment agency, and she had been very specific about whom she wanted. No one too young, no one too voluptuous, no one too ambitious. Her mother had said, a woman's lot in life is tied to the men she refuses and the maids she chooses.

For Waipo Mingzhu, this was the year of remembering the Yellow River and the way the young men risked their lives to get close enough to her window, so they could whisper her name, when she was a flower. Well, they certainly felt like they were risking their lives. And the three porcelain dolls, all broken. They were smooth like a baby's bottom, and so beautiful. Who would do such a thing?

Li, so quiet. Li, not laughing, not even smiling. Dancing? Ha! Li won't dance again, ever. Come, brush Waipo's hair, Li. No? But how? Come, stir some lo mein and chop sui in the wok, toss in some pork cutlings. Your favourite. No?

Li won't eat. Won't talk. Don't hold the child like that, Jingjing! She can walk by herself. Don't haul her into the room. And who is that? Dr. who? Why is he here? What does he want with Li? Don't break my doll!

And Biyu getting ready for a big race. The family's first really big race. This would be the year.

It was the year that Jingjing decided to take a wife, a Chinese girl from Mandeville, good family, sweet girl. Homely and unplucked. They would be married at the end of the year. Not the end of their year. The end of our year. This was our "Year of the Dragon". And the next, the "Year of the Snake".

A respectable Chinese girl, a doctor, Grandpa Fa beaming with pride. Finally, grandchildren will be mentioned. A humble, dutiful wife, modern, yes, but traditional. Not a headache in sight. Not even one.

So why then, Jingjing, are you here with this woman, wrapped under a sheet, and the sheet moving, and the bed making all manner of strange noises? Explain.

Michael leaned against the bedhead. He liked to smoke after he had shot his load. They were in a motel around the Back Road. Cherry was on her lunch break. He would take her back within the hour. They had locked the Lot-a-Luck outlet for the occasion. This happened every Wednesday at two o'clock. He didn't call her by her name. Now that he thought of it, he could not remember one time calling her by her name; maybe on that first day, when he hired her, but not since then. It was always just a matter of motioning with his hands or pursing his lips or making some sound to indicate what he wanted, needed her to do. Or just the fact that they were alone together so he was clearly talking to her. Never by name. And as for Cherry, she called him, Sir, when the need arose. It hardly arose. They understood each other. Knew their roles. Knew their places.

For Cherry, she knew exactly what to do, what not to do. Her main task was to listen. Not too much talking. What need would she have to yap to this Chineyman, about things he could never understand? He understood that he needed to help her out with her bills, some grocery, a miscellaneous item of clothing here and there – nothing fancy, nothing dramatic. She understood that he needed someone to listen. Not someone to talk to; someone to listen. There is a major difference. She understood that he needed her to do certain things that he would not dream of asking certain other girls to do. That was enough understanding between them.

Michael dabbed the butt into the ashtray and released it, eased back on to the bed and lay on his stomach. Cherry took the cue and started to massage him, from his shoulders down. A little jojoba oil, a drop of tea tree oil. She had spent some time as a masseuse in a spa. She had spent some time doing many odd things. A little hair dressing. A little cosmetology. Nothing stable. He was beginning to relax, his muscles loosening their tense grip on the realities of life. She knew he was at the point of greatest ease when his legs spread slightly and his toes started to coil and twitch. This was the moment she usually reminded him of some promise he had made, maybe a telephone bill that was due, or a pedicure course she had wanted to sign up for. She was timing him for the perfect moment. His body was sinking deeper into the sheets. He was loving what she was doing. Sometimes, her long fingernails slipped and dug themselves into his flesh and he cringed. Then she quickly patted the area, in mock apology. Hush. He loved it. The spot would swell red on his white-yellow skin. She kissed it. Sucked on it.

A little more to the right? Sure, babes. No prob.

He eased up his head a bit. He felt a confession coming. Here we go now.

"You know, I paid them to whack that asshole," he said, proudly, calmly. She didn't ask which asshole. He would tell her, in time.

"That shithouse on the news last night. What they call him? Mongrel? That ratbat shit!"

This alarmed her, but she kept her composure, continued the massage.

They had found the head twenty miles away from the body. Severed, with something not very sharp. A deliberate choice of equipment. A hit. They were going for anguish. Torture before death. The body badly beaten – kicked, punched, stabbed fifteen times. The head, gagged at the mouth, a bullet through the left temple. An overkill. A message: he was your don, not mine.

The great Mongrel, dead. A host of speculations. Rival factions. Police. A drug deal gone bad. Ousted by a beloved compatriot bent on power. It was any man's guess. The masses, as usual, their faces up in the camera, we want justice! We want justice! Really now? The women with setters in their hair, slips barely holding up their breasts, flip-flops being dragged through the streets as they rushed towards the news crew. The Poochie-Lou type. Threatening reprisal, demanding justice or else. By next week, murals of his face along the walls of the shanties, painted by up-and-coming community talent that never got the opportunity to develop into something. Him decked in his bling, holding a beer. Only a vague likeness. This is how we want to remember him, our community hero. You newspeople are biased. No one tells about the children he sent to school, the women he gave powdered milk for their babies, the Christmas treats he funded with bounce-about and rides and ice cream and everything. Everybody wants to talk about the young girls he selected for himself as their mothers watched from the windows, hands on cheeks; the drugs he distributed; the dozens of men he killed. Everybody wants to talk about that. Yes, man. Only the bad they always want to talk about.

A funeral thronged by the followers, their allegiance dwindling with every ashes to ashes, dust to dust. Fickle. A street dance afterwards in commemoration, everybody dressed to the teeth, new clothes bought, hair done up, sexiness galore. A new dance move just unleashed. By the week after that, a new don would emerge, staking his claim.

Cherry did not ask him, why? Why would you do such a thing? He would tell her, in time.

Michael rolled over. Enough of the silly back rubbing. He wanted some head. This was not spoken. It was understood. She got to it. That he would return the favour was completely out of the question.

"My little sister. He got my baby sister pregnant. You think I would allow that bastard child to come into the world, bring shame on my family? I let the doctor scrape it out. Scrape it out." He arched his back. He was nearing that moment. She always took him there. Always. Damn this girl, man. She knew her stuff.

"And you know who else? Know who else I'm after?" He was panting now, somewhat spent. Might need another cigarette, maybe a cold beer. Later, a quick shower before going. "Know who else? That damn taximan who win the Lot-a-Luck. His brother rides at the track. I have a plan for him. Big plan for him."

Dezzie? Cherry hadn't seen Dezzie in a while. She had heard rumours about him. But you know, people always spread rumours on you when they see you stepping up leave them. They had pointed out to her a young girl who it was said had carried his child. A very young girl, dropped out of school. She didn't know how true it was. She had glimpsed the girl a couple times, the toddler toeing her heels, holding her hands, being dragged and cursed for not keeping up. Jingjing

A big plan for Dezzie? The man may have been a jerk but he won the Lot-a-Luck, fair and square. Wasn't that the deal? You wager your whole life, maybe – maybe – a million chance to one, you win? What was there to plan for him for? Just for spite? He hadn't held up the Lottery company at gunpoint and demanded the heap of millions. Dezzie was a pain in the rumpus, she could testify, but for all the money he had pumped into the system, he deserved his winnings. Hundreds of thousands of others could live vicariously through him. They knew they would never hit it so big. They were content with the few sporadic winnings, at least to break even every now and then, to offset their bets. What was his grouse with poor Dezzie? So what, a man shouldn't win a game of chance, after he bought his rightful shot at it?

She said nothing. He took her back to the shop. A line had already formed outside, the people murmuring, as usual. She pouted, opened the shutter and started collecting the bets.

And Michael drove back to his office in town, where he could relax a bit without interruption. A man needed an office that no one else had access to, especially when he had things on his mind.

This office. It was conservative. He didn't mind it. He was not a flashy man. He had planned for success and he had gone into a successful venture. To him, a business as respectable and legitimate as any other. To the vociferous religious people, not so much. Of course, he himself didn't gamble. He cautioned his friends and kin against gambling. He and his, they invested. Both were risky ventures and the participant stood to lose – but how much, and how often? Michael invested his money and made sure to diversify the investments so that the potential loss was minimized. He consulted his expert risk management team. They talked every week. They were young like him and knew their stuff. He had stocks and shares and bonds all over the place – well, in specific places. Strategic places. Returns were guaranteed. At the very least, to break even. And the returns from these investments were banked, or reinvested further, for posterity. The wholesale Downtown well-stocked. Perhaps, another wholesale established on another street, in time.

The average gambler never breaks even, unless he wins the big one. The consecutive losses are enough to negate all winnings, so few and far between.

But if a man voluntarily said, "here, take my money", he'd

take it. Michael set up a business to collect the disposable incomes of people who had the least incomes to dispose – the poor, the elderly pensioner, the uneducated, the superstitious – hoping to win against insurmountable odds. But this was exciting for them. This was what the high-riders and the holier-than-thou's failed to understand. This was exciting to the common man, the mere prospect, the anticipation of winning was for some almost as exciting as winning – which never happened – but the expectation to win, the plans of what they would do with it, that was real, indeed, and worth every penny. It was more likely for them to be struck by a bolt of lightning on a clear summer's day, than to win the big one. Michael knew this. He tried to justify this within himself.

But he had witnessed the few winners over the years and he knew that the winnings generally didn't last. The government took a chunk and his company took a chunk. The luxury cars that were immediately bought were pricey to begin with and required registration and licensing fees, ongoing costs associated with maintaining a new car, such as higher insurance coverage and expensive hard-to-get parts that often required specialty installation. The insurance coverage for one year could buy a decent car, plus change. The coverage for five years without accident could buy another car. The houses procured in high-end areas of the city came with hidden costs, not just property tax but upkeep and utility costs at much higher rates.

All this was learnt the hard way, while he watched. But what was he morally-bound to do, tell a man how to spend his money? No such thing. So giddy with new winnings, most people didn't know these things upfront or even cared, or even think it would apply to them. They wouldn't listen to sound advice, anyway. Winning the lottery sent them into "outlier shock" and they now felt themselves immune and exempt from all things that affected other people.

Michael had found a way to rationalize his possible role in anyone's downfall. He was no more a factor in their rise than their downfall. He merely provided a service, an opportunity. What they made of it was up to them. How much they wagered was up to them. They came of their own free will. This particular winner, though, peeved him. The man was obnoxious and crude. So undeserving.

And there were other things on his mind. That a savage uneducated thug would make a murderer out of him, a whore out of his baby sister. That the once fresh and vibrant Liling had receded into herself like a tributary of the Yangtze, retreating from mother's call to the sea, no longer exuberant, no longer flowing. Some rain, he hoped, would revive her in time. She was young. Some time away, abroad, to resume her studies. Perhaps, never to return. He would see to it. He thought about this a lot.

Michael Chang – Jingjing – felt the weight of the world on his, the smallest of shoulders. That people had been feeling the need to question lately, what exactly are the Chinese up to? They've been dispatching their people to the far corners of the Earth, like reconnaissance aircraft. Their students flock to the best Western universities, lapping up our knowledge, scanning our secrets with their photographic memory, establishing little China Towns all over the place. And then, they flood our markets with their barrage of stuff, just because they know how consumerist and undisciplined we are. It's not fair. Their investors have been globetrotting, buying up land in the most unlikely places, making deals and forging alliances. What exactly are the Chinese up to? Think we're not on to you, huh? Huh? Think we're blind? This was the talk on the lips of the political pundits, the economic analysts, the soothsayers.

A Jamaican told him once: the Asians are unfinished. They have not been properly made. They have no backs, hardly any eyes to speak of. Have they ever won any race, ever? Ever? Have they ever won any kind of contest? Ever? Only thing we can say, is plenty of them. Plenty plenty.

A giant shifts and people run for cover. This is to be expected. A giant scratches his back, they think he's reaching for his sword. This is to be expected. Even if it is a giant composed of the smallest men. But it's one billion small men. That's an awful lot of small men.

Grandpa Fa would say that the Chairman would say: in our quest for dominance, let us stick to the ancient ways. Let us send forth our people, to gather and come back, to learn and come back, to see the world and come back.

But has it not been said, whereas the Caucasian is often overt, the Asian is insidious to the very end?

Chapter Thirty-One

The white Toyota motorcar was parked in a small clearing beside the fire department in Waterford. It had been parked there for three days, on and off, drawing the suspicion of the police officers from the station nearby. For brief periods during the days, Dezzie would pull out and do a few trips along the route to Naggo Head and back, to hustle some lunch money and buy something to eat for dinner. At night, he slept in the car, the windows down, sometimes his feet stuck through the half-open door. He had not had a bath in three days, since he left Bam's apartment. The passengers made vociferous note of this.

There is just so much a man can take, hearing his mother being banged by men who were young enough to be her sons, young enough to be his baby brothers. They were raging bulls and knew nothing called restraint. And Bam, in the midst of her sexual liberation, knew everything of abandonment. Three to four nights a week, sometimes even during the days. And his mother's voice whispering to them, "Tek time! Tek time! Dezzie in di next room! Lawks. Whoa."

His mother had never been much of a whisperer. Not that he wanted to dictate her life, or deprive her of anything, but it didn't feel right to him. Dezzie hadn't declared that he was leaving, or why. He had just left.

And he went to Greater Portmore to try and get Precious to take him back, in the night hours. She got mad, went into the refrigerator for the coldest bottle of water, and poured it over him through the window, and told him to remove himself from her yard before she called the police. He slept right there coiled up under the window, sobbing like a child whose toy had been shattered by a bully. He didn't want back the toy. He didn't want to fight the bully. He was just perturbed that the whole thing had happened. He didn't care who saw him sleeping beneath the window. He didn't care who pointed. He didn't care about the ants crawling all over him or the mosquitoes biting, or the stray dogs looking at him suspiciously. He slept, knowing that Precious was on the other side. Then he left in the wee hours of morning. He was giving her time to come around. He hoped she hadn't moved on and replaced him with someone sensible.

Some good could come from a man spending three nights in a second-hand Toyota parked outside a fire station and within range of a cesspool treatment facility. He comes to accept some tough facts of life. Ok. Cassandra didn't love him. She had never loved him. She would never love him, not for all the money and cars and houses in the world. He wasn't her type. He wasn't her type. He wasn't her type. He got it now. Attention could be bought. Time could be bought. Love could never be bought.

Next. He didn't love Cassandra. He was obsessed with Cassandra. He was in lust with Cassandra. He had been jealous of Dacres' access to Cassandra. He had worshipped the handkerchief that Cassandra blew her nose in. He would have given anything in the world, just to sleep next to her and wake up knowing she was in the shower washing off the grime of their coitus. He didn't love her.

The woman that he loved was in Greater Portmore, strung up for what he had done to her, just waiting for the chance to pour some more cold water on top of his head and hear him shriek. And he would deserve it. He wanted her to forgive him this one last time. He wanted to be the best that he could be for Precious and the children, to work from the ground up. He wanted to help her set up her stall Downtown. And no more gambling for him. No more.

Now from where he was parked the stench from the sewage works was bearing down on him. He always wondered how the people in the vicinity of the sewage works could stomach to live so near. The stench was at times overwhelming. But it seemed they had grown noseblind to it. They went about their daily activities, none the worse, it seemed. Although, it was said that the women in the area were so fat and rosy because of the polluted air that they inhaled, day in day out. He didn't know how true it was. But they were indeed fat and rosy. A matter the authorities could look into.

Dezzie shifted position in the car. It was about five in the morning. A few people were already on the road heading out for work and school, hoping to beat the crowd and the maddening traffic. He thought about walking across the road to get some creamy hominy corn porridge from one of the street vendors. He would make sure to tell them to put lots of condensed milk and sugar. Dezzie dug into his pockets and came out nil. Some of what he had eaten for dinner must still be in his stomach, and would serve till he could hustle something. He consoled himself with this, though he knew it wasn't true.

Dezzie held up his arms one by one, sniffed them, pouted his mouth and nose in disgust, make a sound of repulsion, scratched his left arm and lay back down into the back seat of the car. He heard a knocking sound. Someone was tapping on the top of the car, or on the bonnet. He wondered if it was one of the firemen, come to warn him again to leave the premises. Damn blasted sissies. Wasn't there a fire somewhere to be put out? That's why people's houses were always being burnt to the ground. It seemed that government personnel only harassed people that they were being paid to protect and assist.

But it wasn't the firemen. It was his brother, Seymour.

"Hey. Hey," Seymour said, bending and peering in through the open window. "Dezzie. Dezzie."

"Mi nuh deaf, Star!"

"Dezzie!"

"Yow. Cool dung di noise, Star!"

He still had matter in his eyes. His brother reminded him of what he already knew: he needed a bath. A good long one, with lots of soap. Dezzie just didn't feel like it. Life had taken such a turn for the worse. His house and cars gone, albeit into the capable hands of Cassandra. His accounts overdrawn. He had cut off all ties with her, as ordered by Dacres. Naturally, he had also cut off all ties with Dacres. He feared the man. It used to be that Dezzie respected him, maybe revered him, then it got to where he started not being so much awed but felt on par with the man. Now, Dezzie feared Dacres. He saw that Dacres was capable of bad things. Dacres and his fearsome henchmen.

Seymour advised his brother, as a point of public service, to come with him to the track and use the showers by the backside, the living quarters. Dezzie saw this as something feasible to do. In fact, he had meant to swing by the track today. He wanted to have a word with that cranky horse, Impetus.

"I have a fresh change of clothes that you could use," Seymour said, "and some breakfast. Yuh lose weight, Dez. Yuh lose weight bad bad."

Dezzie hobbled out of the car, his legs cramped. He stretched, yawned, kicked his feet out for circulation. Sniffed himself again. Force of habit. The track wasn't far away, almost literally behind where they now were.

Unlike most others, Seymour made it a point not to question Dezzie regarding his fortune or the loss of it. Their father had come and gone back to the country, raging mad from getting nothing, even though he had deserved just that. Being forever the more humble and, if you may, docile, of the two brothers, Seymour tended to take life in strides. He was quiet and unassuming, mild-mannered, extremely short and tiny, which suited his profession very well but made the general public sum him up as being a pushover. Bow-legged, in the custom of jockeys, like he never did straighten from out of the jockey's crouch since the very first day he had settled into it. Seymour only knew that his brother was now broke, no longer the high-flying, big-talking guy who came to the stables in name-brand shoes and outfits, then complained about the mud. That Dezzie had won so many millions to begin with, had been a shock, too good to be true. That it was now no longer true, seemed more in keeping with reality, in Seymour's mind, and he found it less questionable and more acceptable than the first outcome had been.

What would his brother do now? It was anybody's guess. Seymour only knew he had a brotherly duty to keep Dezzie clean and inoffensive to the public. He had offered to put him up in the small quad where he lived with his family, but Dezzie had refused. Apparently, the man had other plans. Knowing Dezzie, he would be soon to arrange to shack up with some woman, more than likely one of shady character.

"Yuh check on di children?" Seymour asked, like a barrister making sure his client's bases were covered.

"Yep," was all Dezzie said.

Then Seymour left. He had a very busy day ahead. This was not a race day, but would be a day of trials to size up the horses and make predictions. It was very early in the morning, yes, but the grooms and the walkers were already busy taking the horses on their morning work, their denims rolled up at the elbows and the ankles. Today meant business. Later, the fillies and colts would be taken through the paces to gear them up for the big day, in two weeks. The Derby. The stables and tracks were abuzz with activity. The smell of horse dung, the musty equine smell of sweat and estrus and spunk all mixed into one heady assault on the nostrils.

The trainers and owners were out, making their rounds and eying the competition. Such and such is a horse to watch, they would note. Such and such has lost form. Such and such seems to be easily winded. All this would be duly noted, good news and bad news. A sore point among them was the fact that the Derby had been moved from June to December this year, on Boxing Day, which had taken them out of whack in a number of ways expressed and unexpressed. A sour bunch of rich spoiled brats, these men were generally felt to be. There was no pleasing them, so nobody tried to.

The trainers and owners complained about everything. But the stakes were high so it was understood that these men would be grumpy about seemingly trifling things. An ordinary jockey riding an extraordinary horse could be catapulted to superstardom after one race. And then, great expectations and the lure of rich pickings would keep him there. The purse was great. The purse pretty much belonged to the owners and trainers – the said grumpy ones – the jockeys being self- employed athletes and for the most part ununionized, had to have skills of negotiation in addition to riding, but a champion jockey could take home a solid pocketful of change.

The stakes being so high, both jockey and horse were pushed to their absolute limit. Injury was inevitable, for both, at some point. This may have been a dying sport but the men at the helm would milk it dry before it succumbed.

There was some complaint that the superior horses were allowed to run against the inferior horses, severely limiting the sense of competiveness with no real chance of the less experienced horses winning. Trainers were said to be well aware of this. But on a small island with so few horses, what to do?

The retired five year olds would typically be highly strung, a pain to handle. Many would be slaughtered, considered too much of a hassle to keep in the paddocks for the rest of their days. For the studs, a life of celebrity awaited. But for the vast majority, they were forced to settle into the squalor of disenchantment, after their glory days were done. One or two might end up on the beach at Hellshire, giving rides to children for a hundred dollars a stroll down the beach and back.

Dezzie took up his usual position, sitting on the ground beside the horse. He had something of a confession to make to the horse. He did not know why he felt so guilty about this, when he should in fact be feeling proud. He had outsmarted them. Well, at least, they hadn't beaten him to everything. He had held a little back.

He whispered to Impetus, almost scared that someone else might hear. The horse perked her ears.

"Listen up," he started, looking around. "Dem tink mi bruk, but mi nuh bruk bruk bruk to dat." He grinned, proud of himself. "Mi still have one mil, stash in anodda account." He grinned again, insanely, a bit too pleased with himself, enjoying the moment immensely. "Listen, a want fi bet everything pon you, in the big one. Tell mi straight. Bet it or not?"

The horse whinnied, turned to look at Dezzie as if she understood. She whinnied again.

You have your last million dollars in your name and you want to wager it all on me? That's deep, bro. That's some heavy shit.

"Yes or no?" asked Dezzie. A horse with so much damn attitude should at least have learnt to say a simple yes or no by now. "Help mi out this one last time. I will never gamble again."

Impetus stepped on spot a few times, fanned her tail and turned her head away, as if to say, let me think about it. These things have to be thought through. Meantime, don't do anything hasty.

"You a mi last hope," Dezzie said, not laughing now, almost pleading. "Dem tek everyting, except this one last mil. Help mi multiply it back, nuh."

He had no intention of telling anybody about the last million dollars he had to his name. Only the horse. This was between him and the horse. He would wager every striking thing. Every red cent. Lucky thing he had stashed that million aside in another account, in another bank, with nobody's name in it but his. He was still fidgety because Dacres had the kinds of connections that made him seem ubiquitous, like he could be everywhere at all times and have access to all manner of classified information, including people's personal banking files. Dacres was an extremely dangerous man, and the funny thing about it was, he didn't really look it. He looked like your regular lying, conniving, money-swindling politician – nothing more. Whatever Dezzie was doing, he had to be quick about it, before Dacres got wind.

So it was imperative that this horse make up her mind once and for all to win something, one single deggeh deggeh race, in all her life. Don't know why he believed in this horse so much. Impetus did not have any drive, though it was clear to everyone that she had the latent skill, the raw talent to carry a thing through. She didn't seem to see it in herself, nor care that others saw it in her. Maybe he should split the money and wager on one or two other races, try for the quinella or trifecta in several races. There would be nine races on the big day. But no, Desmond Grant was an all or nothing kinda guy. A big fool or no damn fool at all.

"Tell yuh what. Lata," he said to the horse. She neighed.

The stable hands were edging about, untying the horses, leading them out for more works. There would be an afternoon trial, to see who was ready and who was not.

There were ten runners in the field. The gorgeous black colt, Libido. The chestnut mare, Impetus. These were the two horses that most eyes would be on. Like Dezzie, many were waiting for Impetus to drop the attitude and get with the program. She was the type of horse who, if told to jump, would ask, why? Why should I jump? How will jumping benefit me? She would never do well on the steeplechase. Never do well in polo. She was a warrior horse. A racehorse. She just didn't know it yet.

Impetus had become somewhat of a stall walker, fidgety and fretful, constantly on the move around the stall without resting. No one knew what was on her mind. She was very ill-tempered whenever the set was being exercised together. During her schooling, when the set was being familiarized with the starting gate and racing practices, she shied and screamed as if to say, I want no part of this. I don't see where this benefits me in the long run. She roared, a deep whistling sound, and stood obstinately like her muscles were tying up, as if she was paralyzed. She was often left in the paddock on many morning conditioners when the exercise riders were working with the set, preferring to do her own thing with Seymour. She was definitely short and in need of much work to get her into winning form. So washed out she was at times. A nervous wreck in the barn, sweating profusely under no duress. Time was running out but Dezzie was adamant. He saw something in that mare from day one. Not that he had the special eye for anything, but still for all.

A horse who was accustomed to steeplechases, jumping over a series of obstacles on a course which was often a gentle incline, or one who had been predominantly a polo horse and used to a more stop-and-go play at a more leisurely gait, would require a lot of adjustment for the flat races, as this. Both Libido and Impetus had been reared as racehorses from day one. From her conformation – her bodily proportions – and her general gait during a race, you could see that Impetus was made out to be what the jockeys referred to as a router or stayer, a horse that does well over long distances. Even her trotting stride was magnificent, her girth expansive and a sure indictor of superb muscular development and lung capacity. A contender if there ever was one. She just wasn't up to it. Built for it, but not up to it. That was her problem.

So these preliminary races were to serve as a tightener, a trial to get the true sense of how the field would perform on the stretch under real pressure, as opposed to the more lax conditions of the morning workouts. The trip of every horse in the trials was significant because now was the time to correct any issues. They would watch to see the level of difficulty, and make adjustments. To pick out the morning glories – those horses who performed extremely well in morning exercises but did not reproduce that same form during trials. It was a chance to fine-tune, to perfect. The stakes were mighty high. Mighty high.

A simulation of the seriousness that would be the Derby. The horses were rated on their past performance – racing records, earnings, bloodlines, composite form, any major issues that it has had for good or bad – but always a sharp eye was kept for something outstanding, something new. Each horse's trip would be scrutinized by jockey, trainer, owner, as well as the die-hard stragglers who turned up for even the trials and lined the areas near the fence to watch and make their very best guess. Some spent their every breathing moment at the tracks. It was a wonder how they found money to make so many bets. Yet, they were always in the red of things, hopping about making predictions. For some, this was their way of earning. This was their bread. Making and selling predictions, claiming knowledge if not outright expert knowledge, at least, accumulated amateur knowledge. Worth a dime. They bought the papers and watched the news for one purpose and for one purpose only, to see the races – the forecasts, the announcements, the commentaries, the pros, the cons. Horseracing was their life.

The valets took great pride in keeping the riding gear and equipment clean and shipshape. The nylon bridles fitted on to their heads, with reins and bits attached. The reins – long leather straps connected to the bit and used by the jockey to guide the horse, better yet, to control him, show him who's boss. The saddle hoisted and thrown so as not to hit the horse but to land snugly into the concave indentation of its back. This took practice. There was a finesse to it. A thoroughbred racing saddle is the lightest of all saddles. Beneath the saddle, a saddle pad, a piece of felt or sheepskin as a base for the saddle. On this, the horse's name and program number, perhaps a special colour for identification. Below that, saddlecloth for absorbing the sweat of the creature during the intense activity of the work or the race, as well as to provide a cushion to the aching muscles below. Man does have a bit of conscience. He does. A wee bit.

Earmuffs over the ear to keep out all distracting sounds, to dispel all rumours that he might not win. Vizors over the eyes for focus. Blinker cups to restrict his vision so that he wouldn't swerve from objects that were on the track or in his mind. Strips of cloth to tie the tongue and keep it stable, so the horse will not choke in his own excitement, his own terror. Muzzle put in place over the mouth to prevent the horse from biting itself or someone else. For the riders, lightweight fiberglass helmets to protect the head from injury, in case of a throw or a fall, a very likely situation.

And they were off!

Starting at a breeze from the backside – past the stable areas, the sleeping quarters, the kitchen. A moderate speed throughout the field, except for the two pacesetters – Libido and Oriental Connection. Biyu tried to ease back a little so as to allow Libido to conserve its strength for the homestretch. But the roguish horse would have none of this. He needed no breather, he always told himself. Not yet. Later in the race, he might regret this. Impetus, as was her style, dead last, trailing the field. She loved the back, then she would try to make her bolt and extend herself to the end. But half-heartedly. This strategy had not worked so far but she was sticking to it. It was her way.

A total of five runs, with the homebred Oriental Connection taking four wins, the final by eight lengths, which had her trainer and owner in quite a whizz. Phenomenal Phloe took the other win, a rare white filly reminiscent of the Camarillo, but with a few brown spots and a lone mustard stripe down its face, its white mane clipped into tiny bows for showmanship. She was ridden by Tahir Purai, the nephew of her owner. She had been told by her trainer, go and deal with the matter. She had dealt with the mater, maintaining her gallop along the straight and not budging. She was one to watch. But she only took one race. Impetus didn't place and didn't care. Libido took two second places, one third. He was winded. We will work on that, promised Biyu. We will work on that. She was determined for them both to break their maiden, not only to place, but to win – to begin their winning streak.

The hotwalkers came out, their time now to take the heated fillies and colts on their cooling down exercises. The race had sent them all into a frenzy, a thing not very good for the heart if sustained. The hotwalkers had an important job, to restore the horse's body to normal temperatures after the race. This they did by easy walking; slow steady trotting around the paddock. Some soothing words, perhaps. There there, girl. Easy now, boy. You did good. You did good. Afterwards, a gentle massage. Some cool water. A lunch of soft moist mash, a hot or cold mixture of grain or other feed, to replenish their energy. We know we sent you to gallop down the track for no apparent reason, but here's proof that we do care. Eat this.

And in the isolation barn, those who were felt to be in need of medical care – maybe a fracture sustained, or a lung condition that had come to the surface during the trials, or arthritis that had flared up and needed ointment or bandage. Give him three days rest; him, a week. This one, light activity until we give the word. Perhaps, to be drenched with anthelmintics, to deworm. Parasites of all kinds were known to severely hinder a race, and sway the results.

"That blasted horse! After the long talk dis morning!" shouted Dezzie to himself. He had been following the races from the sidelines. He saw where Seymour had tried his best but Dezzie knew, this horse will only move when she wants to move. "Gonna need to sit her down again. No Mr. Nice Guy dis time. Damn stubborn horse!" he hissed.

He waited until they had cooled her down, fed her and now she was all alone in her section of the stable, in her usual frisk. It was as if she was waiting for him. She rolled her big eyes. And before he could even speak, her eyes said, did I promise you anything? Did I, Mr. Dezzie?

Michael – or Jingjing, whichever you prefer – walked over to the groom. He handed him a wad of money, a small leather pouch, and patted him on his back. "Remember what we said. Remember what we agreed," he said. The young man nodded. "Yes, Boss. Everything done organize. Everything copasetic."

And this was to be Dezzie's coup de grace, the final blow to put him out of his misery and return him to his rightful ranks.

Chapter Thirty-Two

It was said that the Derby was very much a jockey's race, that the outcome was heavily reliant on the strategic technique of the rider, on his judgment and sound execution from start to finish. It was said that the jockey must be keenly in tuned with the pace of the race, making all the adjustments where necessary, keeping his horse fresh for the homestretch. A race is a race. A race is quick. This was a profession more of skill than strength. The jockey must be quick, must make split-second decisions in the few minutes he has to go get that money. The whip is not to punish, but to guide. The horse should go where you send it, how you send it, when you send it. And why do you send it? for the money, of course! The key was for the horse to finish, if not first place, at least in the money, and by as wide a margin as possible – not by a nose or a neck or a head or even a length; but by many lengths. An unquestionable margin, with no stewards or photofinish to determine the champ.

It all stems from man's obsession with winning things. It is a distinctly human trait. No other animal wants to win anything, per se. To win a mate, perhaps, but not for the sheer glory of winning, just to say, I have won and that is all. The ones who do, have been trained to do so by man. Other animals chase for food, for play, for escape to live another day. Man is the only one who burns his heart, lungs and muscles out when he doesn't have to, expending next to all the energy that he has gained from eating, and challenges his fellow men to come along with him in this insane quest. Man loves to win and what he cannot outright win on his own, he trains someone else to go get it for him. Someone bigger, stronger, faster, less likely to question the sanity of this exploit. And he says, go get that money! The horse, majestic, fast and strong, was singled out as the animal of choice for this task. In exchange for fodder and a bowl of water, go run twelve furlongs in the space of a few minutes. It is no wonder that even the raw capacity of man's equipments are measured in horsepower.

Madam Cheetah is the swiftest of the land mammals, blazing at sixty miles per hour, but within less than a minute she is winded, exhausted, cannot go on, gives up the chase. Madam Horse in a flash accelerates from a trot to a gallop of over forty miles per hour and sustains that for a number of miles. One stride, one breath. One stride, one breath. Conserving her energy through efficient use of her lungs and her massive spleen, Madam horse can run for longer than any other mammal her size. She will take you where you want to go, much further and in far less time that you could ever imagine going on your own.

And if some people had some money that you wanted, you might say to them: listen. Here's what we'll do. All of you, put your money in this purse here. I won't even touch it till the appointed time agreed by us all. I have some horses, all very fast. Some faster than the rest. You choose the fastest, based on what you have seen, or just on your gut, or on a dream; it doesn't really matter. Pick which ones will win. I dare you. Let's see how good you are. When the race is done, and the dividends are posted, we'll split the proceeds. I'll take the horse's share, since they are my horses. You'll take the ass's share, since you're an ass.

The Derby was about to begin. In the enclosure, the parade of horses. This particular batch, a field of ten horses. All sophomores, three year olds in their second year of racing. The favourite, Oriental Connection. Libido a solid horse, a sure contender. Impetus, no one knew what she would do. The jockeys in their silks – jackets and caps – awaited the time for their mount. The paddock judges were on cue, to make sure that the conditions were met – condition of the horses; condition of the track. Everything was being scrutinized. The horses were saddled and paraded in ritualistic fashion. No one here thought that this was absolutely necessary, but it was absolutely done. They could not remember why. Perhaps, an appetizer. A pony, trimmed and prettied up, led the parade of the field from the paddock to the starting gate in ceremonial slowness, past the stands where the spectators might see their favourites, the ones on whom their dinners and their rents and indeed their present lives had been hitched.

At the post, the gate crew led the horses into their stalls – small mechanical partitions – into which they were confined until the starter was ready to release the stall shutters. The Derby, of course a simulcast event, was being transmitted to other tracks, offtrack betting offices and other outlets for the purpose of wagering. Those who had placed their wagers and were unable to make it to the track, were at home crouched beside their radios or within two feet of their television sets, reluctant to miss a thing. The touts ran from pillow to post, professing to have advanced information on the race. There was still time to change your mind, they said. Listen to us. We know. The horse told us, in no uncertain terms. And all we ask for are a few dollars and you too will be in the know.

The races were officially declared open, by men who had never sat atop a horse in their fat lives. The minor races were run, some light entertainment followed. A few horses were scratched from certain races, the reasons to be later disclosed. Then the event of the day. The final race, at three o'clock in the afternoon. The classic. The jockeys mounted from near side, took their post positions, their tack in place, their feet securely wedged within the stirrups. A few horses were on the bit and eager to run, ready to fire. Neighing; anxious. Libido one such.

And they're off!

The fillies up against the colts. The pacesetters immediately claimed the front, leading the field by an instantaneous length and a half, the gap widening by the second. Both Libido and Oriental Connection fired with a burst of acceleration, fully extended and maintaining top speed. The track hard. Dry. Relatively even. Six horses bundled in between, shut off and unable to improve their position much, some claiming the rail, some on the outside, others in the middle looking for a clearing and trying not to brush against each other. Impetus, contented to trail the field, but at steady gait. She had held up the start by a good three minutes, the rest of the field becoming agitated. Impetus, in her usual nonchalant way, had dwelt and refused orders, and was extremely late in breaking the gate, so she now trailed by three lengths.

Seymour was driving her, urging her strongly along, to no avail. She had become so distanced from the field of runners that Seymour feared she would never regain a position of contention. The horse sulked and refused to extend herself. He tried whipping her, which seemed to only make her cross. Dezzie watched from the stands, his heart in his hands. Impetus hadn't really promised, but she hadn't said no, either. It would be hit-or-miss.

Seymour kept reminding himself that Impetus was a stretchrunner, that she would double-up and go all-out near the end of the race, just in time. She had never done this. It seemed to be her philosophy but she had never executed it to the end. But if you watched her, as he had done time and time again, you could see that this was how she had worked things out in her head. She liked to watch the field extend themselves and become winded. This seemed to amuse her. Just that she never followed her plan through to the end, almost as if she got bored. Never enough time to make up for all the distance lost skylarking in the first three-quarters of the race. They had been kidding themselves with this lazy, good-for-nothing horse, was Seymour's take on things. He had a good mind to abandon the race, heave her to the side and dismount, while he still had some pride. Bad enough Impetus did this in the trials. But to come to the Derby with this madness. He would never ride this stubborn horse again.

If he was going to risk his life for something, it would be for a horse who valued his time and need to earn a living. Here he was, perched on top an animal, his butt in the air, his knees bent forward like he was some sort of acrobat, and for what? He was going all-out; the horse wasn't. He was almost standing now, poised with his toes agonizingly pinched into the stirrups, the rest of his body hovering over the horse. All the other jockeys were doing the same, given, but at least they were being taken somewhere, on some kind of mission, with some purpose. Their crouch meant for something.

It was a common thing for people to say: if the horse could talk, this. If the horse could talk, that. If the horse could talk, the other. If they only knew. If Impetus could talk, she would have said: I saw the look on the face of that bum. After some thought, I decided to help him out, to take pity on him. This one time. I decided to win, for him. A promise in exchange for a promise. And me just one more year before I am put out to pasture; my dream. I decided to endure. But look. Did you not see that I was drenched with poison? Did you not see them take me to the side and administer the dose? And did you not see that Libido was hopped? Do you not now see that I am aching, that my insides burn like wildfire? I am trying, but it is hard.

The gap between the frontrunners was widening. Libido, for some reason, spit the bit and easing down on her aggression, Biyu concerned that she was no longer feeling the pull that she had been feeling from the eager frontrunner. But what was up? Jingjing had said that the horse would be given something, a little booster. Biyu hadn't liked it, but then she figured, big brother knew best; if it will help the horse through. And Jingjing had assured her, it would not be detected when they went to the spitbox. No need to worry. Just a little something extra to help him through. But the dosage seemed to be affecting his heart and lungs adversely. No longer moving handily in a form of contention, he was faltering. Biyu pressed harder, trying to drive him.

Past the halfway mark, Oriental Connection now claimed the lead, a clear monopoly for two lengths. Phenomenal Phloe with steady action, driven by the bat. The stragglers all out and trying desperately to break from the bundle. The jockeys all set down and assumed a lower crouch in the saddle, driving the horses with everything they had in them. The crowd, the agents, the racing pundits mad with excitement, looking for their favourite, listening keenly to the race caller and awaiting the stretch turn and the position call at the final furlong.

At the head of the stretch, with the cheers at fever pitch, Libido suddenly bolted and veered to the outside, heading for the rail. The rank horse headstrong and refusing his rider's commands, continued his mad course and slammed into the fence, throwing Biyu before himself tumbling. The ambulance that had been trailing the field rushed to the site of the tumble, the horse writhing, Biyu motionless. The rest of the field, oblivious in their frenzy, a headlong full gallop towards the wire.

Excruciating cramps in her abdomen and legs, Impetus had trailed for the entire race up to the turn of the stretch. Then suddenly, as if all the pleas from the wayward man had conglomerated into one firm resolve in her, she gathered her focus and went into her strategy. The homestretch. This was her turf. This was where she unleashed everything that had been pent up.

Seymour, confused and amazed, tried to equal the horse's new gust of force with a few hits from his stick, but soon found that he had no need to. She was running on her own, building momentum with her own resolve. He only held firmly to her reins, no tug on the bit, just holding her, riding her. With speed only comparable to lightning, Impetus cleared five horses, then six. Two horses up front led by a length. Within seconds, they were behind her. The crowd was whipped to a frenzy. The race caller had gone mad. The trainer, delirious with worry, kept shouting, "Seymour, you blasted fool! You'll kill the horse! Ease up, you idiot! Don't pressure her so much! You're killing the damn horse!"

Seymour couldn't hear what the trainer was saying, but he knew what he must be thinking – what anyone in his sound mind would think- what Seymour himself was thinking: any minute now, this horse is going to collapse from exhaustion. No natural horse could make up for that length within that time. He wanted to tell them all, it isn't me. She's driving herself. She's doing this on her own. All by herself she had pulled away from the field, and with her innards in a riot. It isn't me.

Impetus was now clearly in the lead, the gap opening at mad pace. Fifteen lengths. Twenty lengths. Twenty-nine lengths. This horse has gone mad! Thirty-one lengths through the wire!

Everyone in the stands was standing. Nobody could sit through such a thing. Hats were thrown. Race cards and books tossed in the air. The placing judges beside themselves in disbelief. The bookies wet with sweat and urine. The broadcasters in awe. "Now that is a record that might stand forever!" one declared.

Those who had not witnessed the feat and had only heard, were busy asking, "Impetus won? But how? Impetus? By a neck? By a nod? What? Thirty-one lengths? Stop playing around now! Expect me to believe that?"

And then, "Stewards enquiry! Hold your tickets! Hold your tickets!"

The results were not yet posted. A protest rose up among the stewards. The horses were led to the spit box for post-race testing; their saliva, urine and blood samples drawn. Two horses had been doped; one for the better, the other for the worse. Yet there it was, by five o'clock the next afternoon, Impetus with garlands strung around her neck, posing for photos, flanked by the smiling faces of her connections. Seymour, holding her reins and stroking her, whispering apologies about ever doubting her. She would be fine.

Michael Chang had been waiting at the end near the wire.

He had not seen Biyu take the fall but news came to him quickly. He was flustered, disoriented. He could not fathom what had happened. At first, when he heard of the fall, he had assumed that it had been Impetus. That had been the plan, after all. He also fully expecting to see Libido break the stretch on her drive for home. He had been certain to give the groom the dosage specified by the vet he had consulted. The correct dosage to Impetus. The correct dosage to Libido. He had been assured that this had been done. So what now? His sister rushed to hospital, seriously wounded, but coming around. Libido facing possible disqualification, and with broken bones to boot. Impetus winning at thirty-one lengths. Thirty-one lengths. And now a steward's enquiry. This was outrageous. He had been assured that the potion was untraceable, but even so, things had not gone as planned. Not at all at all.

And worst of all the worsts, that hooligan, Dezzie whatever his name was, jumping the rail like a bloody lunatic, screaming his lungs off and behaving like a mad man. What was the world coming to?

The taximan sat beside the horse, and he didn't care that the horse was making a sore point of ignoring him. He knew she was only pretending. He knew she was listening. Dezzzie massaged the full girth of her. She liked it but she didn't say. She didn't want him thinking that she would put up with this kind of mush all the time.

"Tanks. Tanks," Dezzie said. "Tanks."

She neighed, as if to say, remember your promise, Mr. Dezzie.

He would go to Precious and plead with her again. And again. She would take him back if he changed his dirty ways. She was a good woman. He knew this.

And then his mind suddenly fixed upon the Rastaman. Dezzie didn't remember his name. He wondered what the man was doing. How he had fared. He wondered if the ten million had been as much of a curse upon his knotty head as it had been upon his, Dezzie's, bald head. He chuckled. Knotty head. Bald head.

Horse head.

He glanced back at the horse. So it had come back to man and the horse. The horse and man.

Kamau Mahakoe

Landed Gentry

ABOUT THE AUTHOR

Multi-award winning Author/Private Tutor, Kamau Mahakoe is one of the most prolific and passionate writers in the Caribbean today! Kamau is the 2014 recipient of the UNIA Marcus Garvey Centennial Award (Jamaica Chapter) for contribution to the field of Education. Kamau is a 2014 recipient of the prestigious "Outstanding Educator" award from the University of Chicago. She is a two-time Adult Champion in the Jamaica Library Service National Reading Competition. Kamau gives voice to an authentic Caribbean experience while exploring themes that are universal and complex. Kamau has been a homeschool teacher/private tutor for nearly two decades. She lives and works in Portmore, Jamaica.